A GOD OF DARK AND SORROW

BEASLEY NESTER

A GOD OF DARK AND SORROW

BEASLEY NESTER

BEE PUBLISHING

A God of Dark and Sorrow

Published by Bee Publishing

First Edition published June 2023

Cover Illustration © by Alice Maria Power
www.alicemariapower.com
Cover Design by Whimsy Book Cover Graphics
Interior Formatting by Whimsy Book Cover Graphics
www.whimsybookcovergraphics.com
Character Illustrations © Vincent Li
www.vincentliart.com

Trigger Warning: Please know that while reading, this book depicts abuse, anxiety, depression, trauma, and war.

For Aurora, Madness, Alfonso, and Luna.

For finding me in the darkest of times, and guiding me toward the light.

Juvia's Castle
Seventh Realm
Dark Manor
Wastes of the Third Realm
Wandering Plains
Mulga Woods
Dandfol
Secret Valley
Second Realm
Fourth Realm
Caris
Sanston
Last Hope

Realms of Nelabac

First Realm

Sixth Realm

Fifth Realm

A Brief History of Nelabac

Nelabac was once ruled by demons, Ancient Magicals, and the realm of men. Countless centuries of unruly battle and slaughter led to divine intervention. To the creation of gods.

Over five thousand years, they appeared: the God of Earth; the God of Air; the God of Lightning; the Goddess of Water; and the God of Fire. Together they became known as the Elemental Gods. High off their new-found immortality and power, the Elemental Gods turned on one another. War sprung across the Realm.

Over two millennia of war, immortals dragged countless mortal souls into their ranks. The majority did not survive the fighting. Balance did not exist between the Five Elemental Gods. Just as the world was about to crumble, two sisters were chosen to create peace: the Goddess of Light and the Goddess of Dark. The Sisters of Balance created harmony among the gods and the Realm. Together, they separated the lands into individual realms for each god to rule, and for five hundred years, Nelabac held peace—but that changed when the Goddess of Light turned on the Seven Realms of Nelabac.

With the might of her forces, the Goddess of Light sapped the life from her realm, killing all that once dwelled on its grassy, light plains. Not an ember of light shined through the clouds and shadows that were left in the wake of her destruction.

Horrified by her sister's actions, the Goddess of Dark took action. In order to save the remaining six realms of Nelabac, she had to seal her sister away, but that kind of magic required sacrifice. After long disagreements and arguments, the Goddess of Dark and the Elemental Gods agreed to seal the Goddess of Light with all her power and followers so their ideals could harm no other realms. But something went amiss in the spell, a mistake that forever changed the course of Nelabac.

A century after, the Goddess of Dark awakens from a time-forgotten slumber to a ruined war-torn world and is forced to walk an unlikely path to save everyone.

Gods of Nelabac

Lust, God of Air and Ruler of the First Realm

Possesses the power of winds and sky

Advisor: Aster

Aurora, Goddess of Dark and Ruler of the Second Realm

Possesses the power of darkness, shadows, and ice

Advisor: Mako (deceased)

Luna, Goddess of Light and Former Ruler of the Third Realm

Possesses the power of light, crystal, and snow

Advisor: Sabelle

(The Third Realm was destroyed by the God of Light during her reign one hundred years prior)

Blesk, God of Lightning and Ruler of the Fourth Realm

Possesses the power of storms and electricity

Advisor: Bolt

Oberon, God of Fire and Ruler of the Fifth Realm

Possesses the power of fire and heat

Advisor: Draken

Terra, God of Earth and Ruler of the Sixth Realm

Possesses the power of earth and nature

Advisor: Eden

Juvia, Goddess of Water and Ruler of the Seventh Realm

Possesses the power of water and control

Advisor: Katerina

Saintly Order

Saints are immortal beings created by gods to serve them and their realm. In exchange for immortality and unique abilities, saints serve under their god until the end of days or until their death. Saints have the mark of their god on one of their palms.

Missioners

Perform smaller jobs around a god's home, grounds, or in the surrounding towns.

Guards

These warriors train to protect their realm and its citizens. Often stationed in various towns and outposts throughout their realm.

Agents

Spies and ambassadors that often gone for extended periods of time. They are very skilled in their elements and have good relations with saints from other realms.

Unique Saints

Advisors

Are chosen by divine forces. They offer advice to their god, care for the other saints, and act as a liaison between the realms. Possess the strongest connection to their powers and are often their god's most trusted companion. Advisors are always part of a god's Inner Circle.

Inner Circle

Chosen by a divine force, members of the Inner Circle are their god's closest companions. Their god often seeks their counsel and friendship. Often have a strong connection to their powers gifted to them by their god, but not always.

"IS THERE ANYTHING WORTH MORE THAN PEACE AND LOVE ON THE PLANET EARTH?"

– Peridot and Steven, *Steven Universe*

"STOP FEELING SORRY FOR YOURSELF. AS LONG AS YOU DO . . . YOUR LIFE WILL BE AN UNENDING NIGHTMARE."

– Osamu Dazai, *Bungo Stray Dogs*

Part I

The Girl

Prologue

I woke to the smell of charred skin.

How long had it been? Days? Months? Years?

My bones and ligaments cracked and popped as they reformed. I screamed as my body broke and healed over and over again.

Once the pain subsided, I sat up. Decay consumed the landscape. Bodies of mortals swung from houses and shops. Others were tied to posts in the center of town. Some had frozen to death, their skin coated in blue and purple frost. Blood smeared and stained whatever this town had been.

My hands clenched at the festering heat in my chest. Fear. This feeling—this long-forgotten feeling was fear. It was not for the horror before me but because I knew who had killed these people, and somehow, she had managed to do so from the magical cage I had trapped her in.

I fought to stand and find survivors, but there was nothing left. I had given away my powers, my Dark Saints, and the love of my life to wake up in a Nelabac where evil had not won.

And I failed.

"How does it feel, sister?"

I felt her before I saw her. The person I loved so dearly. The one I had destroyed the world for seemed cold. She seemed cruel. I dared to look where she stood, glistening in her destruction.

Luna appeared the same as she always had: strong, proud, and beautiful. Her long, near-white hair almost grazed the ground and blew in the wind with her long crystal-lined dress. She adorned herself in diamonds and opals, A beautiful sunstone dangled in the center of the crown above her forehead.

It was only when I met my sister's eyes did she truly feel different. She was hollow, empty of all of what used to make Luna, Luna. This was my sister's body, but it was not her. Nothing about this person, this ruined landscape and people, or this war, was my sister.

"Luna, what happened?" I reached for her again. "What happened to you? How can I help you?"

"Everything I've ever done, Aurora, was to protect you." Her tone sharpened, her eyes budding with tears. "Everything was always to protect you."

I did not realize how badly I trembled until Luna's soul touched mine. It was dark, more along the lines of my power, but something tainted it, but deep within the light's rays, I felt her.

"We can still change this," I begged, tugging the edges of her dress. "We can still save the Seven Realms and the people of Nelabac—"

"It's much too late for that!" Luna pulled away with a snowdrift surrounding her, and she levitated into the sky like a fallen angel. "You shouldn't have sealed all the gods away. You shouldn't have locked me away. Your sister!"

"I wanted to stop you, Luna! I thought it was the right thing to do." I tried to find my feet. So much sacrifice and loss, all for nothing. "I know the sister I've always loved is still inside that shell of snow and crystals and shallow light that you've encased your soul in."

My sister paused, and for a moment, I thought I'd found her. I'd brought her out of the dark she had clawed into. But when Luna's white eyes met mine, a hollow, empty voice found me. "What's been set in motion cannot be undone, Goddess of Dar. Not even you can stop me."

Gut-wrenching fear returned as a bouquet of seven white roses, dipped in blood lay before me. I had doomed Nelabac from the start, and Luna would not stop.

No—this was only the beginning, and the gods and realms of Nelabac were next.

GODDESS OF DARK

Chapter 1

The Goddess of Light had won. Despite Aurora and the Elemental Gods' best efforts to prevent it, the crumbling of Nelabac had come to pass.

How? The Light Saints should have gone with Luna. What did we do wrong? What did I do wrong?

Shadows crept from her palms. Darkness had always lived within Aurora. From the day she became the Goddess of Dark, she had to learn how to control emotions. It was done by giving away pieces of her soul, creating followers known as saints, but she had sacrificed them, the Dark Saints, to save Luna. And now, with the Dark Saints dead, all the pieces of her soul had returned. Aurora controlled nothing now, let alone her own darkness.

She felt their whispers.

Fail, fail, fail, they sang. *You have failed! All your fault*

"Stop."

She begged her mind to calm, to find solace. To grasp anything salvageable in the grief.

Her fingers rubbed against the lace of her white dress.

Oh, Elaina. She worked so hard on this dress. She searched for months to find my favorite lace.

The Dark Saints were gone. Their years together protecting the Second Realm had amounted to nothing. At that, the remaining power of darkness twirling around Aurora faded. For they no longer possessed strength. Like their master, they no longer willed to carry on.

Her fingers pressed into the dirt. Aurora had nowhere to go and no one to seek, but she had to escape the desolation. To escape a place her sister's armies had destroyed in the name of spite, hate, and vengeance.

I was once the strongest of the Seven Gods in Nelabac, able to keep all of them at bay with just a snap of my fingers. Now I'm as powerless as a moral.

Day turned to night. Aurora trailed along the grass and dirt long enough to reach a town. Well, what resembled a town. The buildings did their best to stay standing. The residents walked in rags and broken-down armor.

I don't know if I trust them, but I need them.

Aurora stumbled down the hill. Each step felt like an eternity. A wrong step would lead to a fall. At the bottom, Aurora collapsed. The agony and weakness of her mind and body had caught up.

"Help. Please, help."

Someone scooped her up. Aurora turned up, trying to catch a glimpse of the mortal.

Mako?

For a moment, this person resembled her lost companion. The one she trusted more than any other.

A warm, familiar soul.

The morning chime outside Aurora's window did not help the pounding of her head.

Aurora woke in a small bedroom, a red chair her only company. The wooden floors sloped upward from rain and the passing of time. The walls were patched with either cloths or rags to keep as much of the draft out as possible.

Someone had removed her white dress and clothed her in tan slacks and a white tunic. Her hair fell free of its usual two long braids.

There was no way of knowing if someone was home without using her soulception. This power allowed a god to search souls and learn their intentions. Using it would give Aurora a much-needed advantage, but the other Gods of Nelabac would learn her location, and Aurora was in no state to fight or deal with the Elementals or her sister.

She sat up, cautious of her weakened body. Aurora ran her fingers down her ribcage and legs, feeling every notch along her skin.

I've turned to skin and bone . . . something I did not know was possible.

Each step felt like the first. The action reminded Aurora of the babies that mothers and orphanages brought from across the Second Realm to Dark Manor for blessings. For them to be touched by a god. Their legs wobbled, but they still found a way to keep going.

I never thought I'd take inspiration from a mortal baby.

Aurora reached for the hand mirror sitting in the red chair and stared back at the ghostly figure. Her cheeks clung to one another, hollowing out like a cave. The bags under her eyes had always existed, but something in them had changed, too. Her long, black hair nearly touched her rear. It was frizzy and in desperate need of a good brush and a wash. It was also coarse and unnourished. Aurora had never been vain, but she nearly broke at the state of her eyes.

They were gray, Not the endless pits of onyx she had loved since she was a child. Since she became a god. Their dark, murky coloring reminded Aurora of who she was, and now they were the color of a weak and defenseless field mouse.

The bedroom opened to a small living space and an empty kitchen. It held a few cabinets for food and a burning kettle, as well as a dining table, chairs, and a brown rug. Beyond was a small living space with blankets and a family sketch framed on the mantel.

The glass was gone, but the wooden frame kept the sketch from fraying. It captured a family of three. A muscular man wrapped one arm over the shoulder of a large-set woman who held a small child. They looked happy, but Aurora noted a more profound emotion that loomed in the woman's eyes. A look that peered into Aurora's soul through the sketch.

This is her home.

"Oh, good, you're up!"

Aurora flattened to the ground, partially from her atrophied muscles but mainly from the unexpected voice.

"Gods." She rubbed her spine.

She peeped up at the window to see the very boy from the photo.

"Sorry about that." He crawled through and helped Aurora into a chair. "Momma's not gonna be happy about you getting out of bed on your own. She's really busy running the town. I'm Brooks, by the way. What's your name? Where are you from? We found you—"

"Brooks, give the girl a break. She's just woken up, and the last thing she wants is to be pestered."

The man and woman from the sketch walked through the door. Both wore poorly-made armor and carried rusted weapons at their hips.

Neither held magic, but Aurora sensed a depth to the woman. The sheer weight of her soul overpowered the room.

"We are glad to see you up, girl." The woman made her way around to the couch. "Though, I wish I could offer you better medical care. The healers I know are in another realm at the moment."

Despite their kindness, Aurora did not know if she had woken at a time when her existence would be met with acceptance or resentment. If she was forgotten entirely. On top of it, mortals could not see her, a god, in such a pathetic state. What would they think of her then?

"You've met my son, Brooks. That's my husband, Gabe," the woman said. "And I'm Manda. I run this village."

"Where am I, exactly?" Aurora asked.

"You're in Last Hope, the town just below Sanston."

Sanston, that's near the southern tip of the Second Realm.

She was in the Second Realm, in her homeland, and surrounded by her people, but they hadn't the slightest clue that she was their god.

"Manda and I found you a few days back." Gabe sat down.

"What?" Aurora did not fathom that she'd been in the hands of these mortals for so long and slept through it all.

"You've been in and out," Brooks explained. "We thought you were a goner."

"Not possible." Aurora almost laughed at the idea—

"Trust me," Brooks scoffed, "you were a near goner."

"*Brooks.*" Manda sharpened her tone, and her son complied.

"He's not wrong," Gabe's eyes darted to his wife. "We saved her life."

"We are glad to see you better." Manda gave her husband a look that meant a scolding later. "Now that you're up, can I ask where you came from? It looked like you were leaving Sanston."

Damn.

Aurora gave a slight nod to confirm. Glares sent around the room told an ominous tale. Aurora realized the town she had seen destroyed was Sanston.

"We are so sorry for your loss, dear." Manda's eyes softened. "Do you know if you were the only one to make it out alive?"

That had been real and not just the darkness playing tricks on me.

Darkness rose at the edge of her fingers, but Aurora pulled her hands back to her chest, concealing it.

"The Light Knights," Brooks said, fear coating his tone. "They're moving closer and closer to us every day."

"It was about time they reached us." Gabe rubbed his temples. "How many towns are left in the Second Realm now? Two? Us and Dandfol?"

"Enough," Manda commanded the room. "The last thing she wants to hear is about her destroyed village."

Gabe and Brooks pursed their lips but obeyed. The hatred in their eyes was toward the Light Saints—Light Knights, as it seemed they were called in this age. It further confirmed that Luna's power had remained in Nelabac, and her saints had battled the mortals in her absence.

Her bones weighed Aurora deeper into the chair. The mortals mumbled among themselves about sending scouts to look for Light Knights. Aurora only sat, thinking of how to rid herself of the budding emotions. By standard, it was performed by giving away pieces of the soul and creating saints, but there were no dying mortals by Aurora's side now, and by God's Code, she refused to take the life of a healthy and able.

So down she shoved them to the pits of her soul.

"You're going to need to rest for the next week, girl," Manda said. "So don't go rushing off, understood?"

Aurora knew the reality of her body. She expected to walk by tomorrow and gain full mobility within the week, but she kept that information to herself.

"Why don't we bring you outside for some fresh air?" Gabe suggested. "That will do ya some good."

"Aye." Manda rose from her chair to the door. "Gabe, carry her."

The village looked as Aurora remembered: rundown and more like a passing outpost. People stood in line for sour-smelling soup. Others observed from their homes or practiced their weaponry. Everyone held hunger and eagerness in their eyes for something other than a typical, terror-filled day.

A few children played, swatting small sticks for swords. Women rocked infants in chairs, and the men sat with empty eyes. Everyone in the village wielded a weapon or wore armor of some kind. Even the children with sticks for swords possessed poorly forged daggers at their sides.

At the end of the row of homes and storefronts sat a chapel. Above, the dark symbol of the waxing crescent moon remained. No longer made of black diamonds carved from the mountains in the Seventh Realm, but someone had taken the time to paint it outside the building.

These people, or at least some, still believed in the gods. Aurora held back the swelling of tears, begging them to recede.

Gabe leaned against the porch, rustling his pocket. He pulled out tobacco and a match. "How did you do it anyway?"

The last thing Aurora wanted was to answer to a mortal. "Luck, I guess."

"It must be hard for you, losing everyone you know and love."

She had lost all those she loved. Never another conversation or laugh. Her closest friends, her Inner Circle, were obliviated with everyone else.

A day meant for celebration and community among Aurora and the Dark Saints was the day everything collapsed. They were to gather in the valley at Dark Manor and dance until morn at the Summer Festival, but when Aurora's advisor and dearest friend brought news of the Goddess of Light's declaration of war, everything changed.

The Dark Saints had agreed to their sacrifice. They would have done anything Aurora asked, but they had always meant more than simple subjects to her. They were her family. Those she spent five hundred years getting to know were dead, had moved on to the Land of the Deserving—

But were they there? Is it even possible for saints to join those ranks in the afterlife?

"It was for nothing." She closed her eyes and ran through the spell over and over, searching for just what had happened for everything to go so poorly. But there was nothing.

"It was simply for nothing!"

Gabe turned from his son. "Girl, you okay?"

"I mean," her voice shook, "they can't truly be gone, can they? Can those we fight so hard for really just disappear?"

Gabe put down his bowl. "I think you need some more rest."

"I don't need to sleep!" She pushed to her feet. "I've been sleeping for what feels like years. *Years*!"

Manda rushed outside at the noise and looked at her husband.

"She's having a breakdown," Gabe said.

"I see that."

"Do something," Gabe said. "You're better at all this than I am."

Ice spewed from Aurora's feet. "Don't talk like I'm not standing right here!"

Manda and Gabe gawked at the ice. More and more of the villagers took notice of Aurora's outburst, but she paid them no mind. Aurora did not understand what was happening to her or how to take control.

The darkness taunted, *Let it out! Let it out!*

"You're exhausted and in shock from everything that has happened." Gabe moved closer to her cautiously. "Please, just let us take you inside—"

"Don't touch me!" Aurora pulled at her clothes. "The dress, my white dress!"

They were not *her* clothes.

Aurora felt herself sinking. Aurora could o never stop the fall on her own. Only Elaina and Mako held power to do so, but they were dead.

There's nothing left for me.

Manda scooped Aurora up and carried her to the bedroom. Manda took Aurora's hands.

"Look at me, girl," she ordered.

Aurora refused.

"I said, look at me, *Goddess of Dark*."

Shadows, darkness, and ice spewed from Aurora's skin, consuming the small bedroom in a capsule of despair. She existed in the world she ruined and was cursed to walk through it alone.

No longer a pillar of strength but a pillar of the past.

"My grandmother told me stories of the gods and saints," Manda took a seat at the foot of the bed, not a hint of fear in her tone. "She spoke of the Dark Saints that visited the towns and the cities to make sure we were safe, well-fed, and above all, happy in your realm. She spoke of their kindness and of the good they did for the Second Realm."

Aurora curled into her ribs, pushing the bone-rattling pain.

Empathy, I feel empathy.

"She always believed a girl with long black hair and eyes of onyx. My grandmother said you held the power of all things dark yet had the kindness and grace of all things good. She said you would come back and save us from the growing dark within the light. I believed her, so I prayed. I prayed for the day you and the other gods would hear the plea of the people you left behind and fix the mess you created."

The gods leaving. The Dark Saints' sacrifice. The world falling to war after five hundred years of peace. The Goddess of Light betraying Nelabac . . . it was my fault.

"It was not an easy decision." Aurora concealed her guilt. "The Dark Saints chose to leave knowing their sacrifice meant saving the realms."

"Did they *truly* have a choice?" Manda asked, enraged. "And, if so, would they be satisfied to see what came of that sacrifice? That their deaths meant nothing?"

"I would watch it if I were you, *human*." The shadows sharpened. "You forget you speak to a being far greater than you could ever hope to be."

"I know whom I speak to, *Aurora, Goddess of Dark and Ruler of the Second Realm*, but you're in a mortal's back bedroom, collapsed from your own fear and grief." Manda's eyes and words were as sharp as knives. "Despite the stories and what you grew accustomed to then, you are not special to me of the people of this age, Goddess of Dark, and I don't plan to treat you that way."

Dark ice sparked across the floor, spiraling to the crease of Manda's neck. Aurora did not like being tested, especially by a human.

"You won't kill me," Manda smirked. "You wouldn't dare to hurt me."

"What makes you so confident?" Aurora forced the ice to break Manda's skin, the blood dripping ever so slightly.

"Your godly instincts are too strong, plus you're too much like me. You feel your morals pressing right against that holy soul of yours." Manda easily snapped the ice, showcasing just how weak Aurora truly was. "With your Dark Saints gone, your entire being has returned. You have the emotions of a human again. A *mortal.* The only difference between us is that your powers still reside inside you, and you have immortality. But that alone can't possibly defeat the armies of Light Knights—well, to you, Light Saints—their commanders, and their god."

Every word the mortal spoke was the truth.

"It wasn't supposed to be this way." Aurora sat up. "Luna and her forces were supposed to disappear with us."

"She may have left this world when you and the other gods did, but her powers, saints, and armies remained." Manda wiped the blood off her neck. "With you back, I can only assume the Five Elemental Gods and your sister, the Goddess of Light, have as well."

Aurora had nothing left. No saints. No strength. No support. She doubted many mortals still believed in the gods, and if they did, they chose to acknowledge the gods as nothing more than a childhood bedtime story to give hope of a new world.

"How do I begin to rebuild?" Aurora had no council, no one to trust with her true identity. "How do I stop her?"

"You need to end this how you should have one hundred years ago."

Aurora flinched at learning she had been gone for one hundred years, but there was no more room for weakness. "*That* was and never will be an option."

"You must choose, Aurora." Manda grabbed Aurora's shirt. "The Realms of Nelabac or your sister!"

"I never wanted this!" The darkness inside begged to pull her down again. "I never wanted this war. To lose my sister. To be a god."

"None of that matters, Aurora. You were chosen for this, so you must end it."

Like the other mortals and Magicals of this world, Manda did not know the *true* reason for the war and Luna's fear: the Soul Keepers. The forbidden magical tools were forged to seal a god for eternity. To cast them into an infinite void of nothingness. Luna had feared the Soul Keepers more than the other gods since their discovery and wanted to end the humans and Magicals for their creations, but the other gods disagreed. It went against everything in God's Code. Together, the Elemental Gods and Aurora opted for the spell to seal Luna and her powers away, which had resulted in catastrophe anyway.

But the war, now, would end if Aurora could find the Soul Keepers and destroy them. There would be no need to kill Luna. She could repent, and Nelabac could walk toward a new age.

But how? How do I begin such a journey?

Before the sealing and the spell, Aurora had resources. The other gods and their saints had trusted her. She had an abundance of power at the tips of her fingers.

"Manda?" Then, one question dominated her consciousness over ones with much greater importance. "Where's my white dress?"

"In the dresser draw, but Aurora, you need to leave the Old Age behind." Manda did not bother looking at Aurora. "Or else you'll never save the new one."

Chapter 2

The sun rose high that morning, but Dark Manor did not need it to feel warm. Dark Saints danced about the manor, readying for the coming festivities. Guards returned from their missions, agents went from place to place until Aurora ordered them to stay put, and missioners carried baskets of food, crafts, and decor over the entire manor.

The Goddess of Dark peered at them from her kitchen window. For the first time in a year, the pieces of Aurora collected in one place again. The Dark Saints never dreamed of skipping out on the Summer Festival. Not because they would miss the fun but because they knew Aurora would freeze them into the next Summer Festival they so dared.

The Dark Saints came and went for months on end, only popping by Dark Manor for a day or two before venturing back into the Second Realm or other realms as ambassadors of peace. The Summer Festival put duties aside and gave the Dark Saints time to enjoy one another and remember their second chance at life. To embrace their immortality.

Missioners and guards moved back and forth from the main houses to Flower Meadows on the other side of the lake. The decorated handcrafted tables Aurora was gifted from the Earth Saints of the Sixth Realm. Their

legs were made of vines and roots. Flower blossoms and moss filled in the crevasses. Aurora used permafrost to keep them in an eternal bloom.

Her soul soared in the skies for the events to come, but when Aurora thought of the dreaded task at hand, her soul fell back to Nelabac.

Baking was not her specialty, but she had lost a bet to Tempton, one of the Dark Saints of her Inner Circle, and she was now charged with the task of preparing dessert for the Summer Festival. This year, the Dark Saints chose a bundt cake.

This will teach me to challenge a swordsperson to a duel ever again.

She moved about the kitchen cleaning while she still had sunlight to spare. Flour, sugar, dough, and flavoring covered the counter, sink, floor, and by some chance, the couch far on the far end of the living room.

"Gods," she sighed.

Usually, Aurora would clean immediately, as a dirty kitchen always proved a bad start to a new day, but that early evening Aurora kept her eyes on the setting sun. Feesr air rushed through the window. Aurora sensed a storm brewing, one prepared by the God of Lightning on the horizon.

Blesk is out of his mind if he thinks he's going to send a storm my way.

The apron stopped at her knees and tapped at her movements. Aurora felt silly shuffling across the floors, but she did not want to ruin her newly sewn dress. The pure white fabric with lace embroidering would easily stain. One of her eldest saints, Elaina, had sewn the dress for her to wear at the Summer Festival. Too excited to wait, Aurora went ahead and showed it off.

Strands of hair danced with the wind. It had grown well past her hips. Aurora preferred her hair braided in two, but that day Aurora left her wild and madly tangled. That day was more special to her heart than the Summer Festival. Strands of hair took to the fading light and danced until a steady knock echoed on the door.

She scrambled to remove the apron. "Come in!"

"Aurora!"

The door flew open. Her brow pinched. Squinting, Aurora spotted a man. His figure, dark yet familiar, was fading. She called after him, begging him to stay, but the figure disappeared like dust in the wind.

Outside, the sky was blood red. The flowers wilted and the lake ran dry. The wind picked up and shook her home, tearing it away piece by piece. The walls stripped away and Aurora sank in a pitch-black vacuum.

The screams of her Dark Saints echoed all around. Aurora called out, begging for any one of them to respond, but the dead did not call from beyond the grave.

The screams intensified the further she fell, and horror filled her being with the realization that there was no way out.

"Stop . . . Stop—"

Aurora snapped awake, heart pounding and sweat dripping. The memories of that last day were as clear and vivid as if she had lived it over. Wrapping her arms around her body, Aurora reminded herself it was all a dream.

But not entirely. There was screaming all around.

Somewhat unsteady, Aurora found her feet. She dug through the dresser and found her lace dress. She tore off the bottom hem and tied it to her wrist.

I won't leave them behind. Not yet.

Aurora forced open the door to smoke and fire. Her legs wouldn't respond, so Aurora crawled across the floor.

Ice, weak and fragile, spewed from her hands and feet to stop the burning and ash that met her skin. She was dizzy at the sight of it all. She eyed the window, the one Brooks had climbed through the day prior, and made her way to it. Pulling with all her strength, Aurora looked out it and saw the commotion.

The people of Last Hope were either dead or dying. Men and women were impaled by crystals of white snow and light and strung across the porches of the homes like seasonal decor. Light Saints—Light *Knights*—dressed in white and golden uniforms and robes filled Last Hope with carnage. Some covered their faces with masks resembling animals.

Her innocent people ran, screamed, and prayed as they were stripped bare of clothing, dignity, and breath, and all Aurora could be was watch.

Aurora tried to spew some small ounce of ice or darkness, but there was nothing. There, in the face of the enemy when she was needed as a god more than ever, Aurora was nothing.

Just how Luna wants it.

The front door busted open. Aurora held her hands up against the unknown intruder.

"Rory!"

It was Brooks, accompanied by Manda. The child appeared fine, but Manda was in brutal shape. The woman had done what she could to free her child of the chaos and bring him to the Goddess of Dark.

The child collapsed, sobbing into Aurora.

"Why have they attacked?" Aurora asserted herself. Behind, more children spewed into the room. Two looked under the age of twelve, while the other was in her teens.

The sword at Manda's side was drawn and bloody. She had fought her way through but had been unsuccessful in avoiding injury. "Aurora, they are going to kill us all."

"I can do something." Aurora pressed to her feet. "Let me go out there and try—"

"How can one who can hardly stand face an army of over a thousand?"

"I'm stronger than I look!"

"You are *weak*, Goddess of Dark!"

Aurora felt her soul stir in a way she had not felt since Mako had revealed that Luna was slaughtering mortals and preparing for war.

"Aurora, you must take Brooks and the surviving children and flee to the Fourth Realm." Manda fell to her knees.

"Why the Fourth Realm?"

"It is as safe as a place can be for those caught in the storm that is the Second Realm." Manda pressed her abdomen. "Take the children. It is the only way to keep them alive."

"Come with us." Aurora tried for some solution to save the one person in the world who still believed in her. "Please, Manda. You are someone I can trust. Someone who *knows* me."

Manda revealed the true depths of her injuries. A stab to the stomach so deep not even Aurora's powers would save Manda.

"Mommy?" Brooks' hands wrapped around her torso. "Mommy, I don't want to go with Rory."

"You must." Manda ran her fingers through her son's hair. "She will get you somewhere safe. Will get you to the others. From there, they can get you to Dandfol."

"Mommy, I don't want to go to Dandfol without you!" The child grasped his mother tighter, realizing that moment was his final with his mother, in their town and in their home.

Aurora let her soul search the deepest parts of Manda's wounded body to find some fragment of hope to save her, but there was none. The multiple gashes to her stomach had caused too much damage.

"Goddess of Dark." Manda grabbed Aurora's arm with a grip of a warrior.

"Yes," Aurora confirmed. "I am here, Manda. It's me."

"Aurora, please." Manda was so very weak. "Please, save this world. And please save those children. They have so much to look forward to with you back now.

"My husband"—she slowed—"is gone. I cannot fight for my child any longer. There is nothing left of me to fight for, dear girl. War grips hold of everyone, leaving no innocents in its wake nor end." Manda's soft brown eyes peered deep into Aurora's soul. Her hands stroked gently along Aurora's cheek, wiping away icy tears. "Aurora, it is time for this generation to lead with you by their side. For this cycle of war to end. For the Dark to save the Light.

"I was wrong, Aurora. You cannot defeat the Goddess of Light alone." Manda took her hand and placed it on Aurora's cheek. "No one can do anything alone—you need them. All of you survived for a reason."

The mortals and Aurora sat around Manda's body for what felt like an age. Manda died with faith and hope that she had left the world in the hands of the Goddess of Dark she had grown up hearing stories about and furiously believed in her whole life.

The mortals now knew who and what Aurora was, but that did not matter. All they had left was one another and the drive to destroy their enemies and redeem all they had lost. From her own experiences of war, Aurora knew if there was any hope of saving the few people in that room, they had to move.

She had done this. To Manda. The people of Last Hope. The Second Realm. Those affected by the war in the Seven Realms of Nelabac suffered from her mistake.

The Dark Saints had sacrificed their lives to fuel power strong enough for Aurora to seal her sister. The Elemental Gods had left Nelabac to a time and space unknown to seal her sister. All of it was for her sister.

It truly was for nothing.

Glistening shadows poured from Aurora's soul as she broke. She had doomed Nelabac when she only wanted to save her sister.

The children and Brooks cried.

"It's all right," Aurora reassured them her power would not hurt them. "I'm going to make the bad guys go away."

Aurora cast out the shadows to the Light Saints beyond the confines of the home.

The power raging before them was the essence of darkness itself. It was the last drop of true darkness that dwelled in her Altered Realm. The Altered Realm was where a god's true power lay in waiting, hoping for moments of release.

In using this power, the other gods would learn Aurora's location, but that meant nothing to her. What her sister had done to the people of Last Hope and those of Second Realm was unforgivable, and Aurora wanted her sister's Light Saints to suffer as similar fate as possible.

Maybe it was the darkness or the assistance of the Altered Realm, but Aurora found her feet with solid legs. Aurora's eyes glowed like obsidian flames, ready to engulf all in its path.

"Grab onto me and shield your eyes, children," Aurora ordered, and they obeyed.

True horror filled Last Hope. The welcome sign hung in two pieces. Gabe was strung between it by a cord. Both his eyes had been gorged and tied to his hands.

Each step through the village brought more agony and more pain. Mercy was shown to no man, woman, or child. Some hung from the tops of buildings, torched and exposed. Those had their mouths sewn shut.

Aurora looked at the chapel. Smeared in blood, a sun covered the symbol of the moon. Luna craved for her sister to know she was alive, for Aurora to know *she* was all-powerful, and *she* would accomplish her goals in ending mortal and Magical life. To end the lives of those who dared oppose her.

Light Saints rushed. Their bodies moved in sharp, quick movements from under their robes. Their heads tilted back and forth, their expressions concealed by masks.

Aurora clenched her hands and let the darkness take the light. She felt them, the Light Saints. Their sad and hollow lives were blown into the debris of the night. They felt much like her sister, empty and longing. As if they were devoid of a heart and a soul.

"This what happens to saints who are pawns to a soulless god."

Her sister had fallen so far, so deep into despair, and Aurora never saw it.

The sun rose over the distance, but no one in Last Hope would rise with it. A tug pulled on her pants. It was Brooks. His eyes and cheeks were stained red. Behind, the other children gathered near.

Aurora released her powers, and the Altered Realm disappeared. Aurora offered a slight smile. Her body begged to give out. Any power or strength she had built up over the night or stored away during her time away was gone, but the children who had only known defeat could not watch their protector fall.

"Come." Aurora placed one hand on Brooks' head and extended the other.

The eldest gripped Aurora's hand. Blood coated her hair and linens, but she braved the invisible barrier between her and Aurora. All those children had ever known from immortals was destruction, war, and blood. They had never experienced the kindness of the gods and saints.

Mortals should not be caught in the crossfire of our battles.

The other children gathered behind Aurora, and together they staggered out of Last Hope for the last time. Vultures and other scavengers circled above to feast on what remained, but Aurora wouldn't allow it. At the top of the hill, Aurora ignited her soul for what she knew to be the last of a long time. The children's souls targeted her every move.

Black ice stained the ground and stretched toward Last Hope. It coated the bodies of the dead, sinking deep into their skin and piercing their bones. Buildings became sheets of black ice and shadows. And once everything and everyone Aurora touched became one with her soul, she set them free.

Black crystals caught shape in the soft light of dawn. The winds would carry the dead to the Lands of the Deserving. A place where those of good spent eternity, deserving of a life of peace.

"Where do we go now, Rory?" Brooks looked up with broken eyes.

"Where do most refugees go?" Aurora asked. "Manda mentioned there were others?"

"Caris," he said. "They're in Caris."

"Then that is where we go. We head for Caris."

Chapter 3

Aurora never mentioned the dangers lurking along their path to the Fourth Realm. Caris, the city capital of the Fourth Realm, was home to Blesk, the God of Lightning and Ruler of the Fourth Realm. Blesk had always been a prickly and stubborn older man, and he had loathed Aurora's plan to use the Elemental Gods' powers to seal Luna away. What fate would bring her when she reached the refugee camp outside the city, Aurora did not know, but she had to hope it found her after the children arrived in safer hands.

The children were quick on their feet and decent foragers and hunters. The youngest among them was Brooks, at just seven, yet he was the best hunter.

Aurora found herself struck, saddened by their skills. The skills were those Aurora used as a child, surviving and fighting to stay alive during the Second Gods War. The days she fought to leave behind had somehow weaved back into the now.

In the late evenings, when the night was her highest, Aurora heard the children choke on nightmares. What they had lived through came hunting in the night. Aurora lay beside them and whispered stories of when spring and summer were full, and grasses and flowers covered the Second Realm.

"There were festivals with food and endless celebrations of good," Aurora explained. "Humans, Magicals, and saints joined one another for games and laughter. It was a beautiful time."

The stories comforted not only the children but also herself.

Aurora's nights were haunted like children. Her dreams began the same each time, with her standing in her kitchen covered in flour, waiting for the Summer Festival to begin when a familiar presence knocked at the door and ended with the cabin in a pit of despair.

Despite how weak she felt, Aurora woke that fourth morning together before the children to a stronger body. The sun peered down, warming the chill stuck in her bones. That was a testament itself to how weak she had become. Aurora thanked the gods she no longer wobbled like a toddler and instead staggered like an intoxicated.

She pulled her hair in two braids, sporting it as she always had. She used the lace from the hem of her old dress to tie the ends off. Manda had told her to leave the dress and the past, but she refused. Not yet, anyway.

Once the children were up, they moved quickly. The children were exhausted, but their eagerness kept them moving steadily. After four days of traveling, they neared the border between realms.

"I think we will be there by noon," Aurora said.

"But you're old," Brooks said. "How do you know how long it takes to get there?"

"*Because* I'm old, that's why!" Aurora ruffled his hair.

He laughed, and Aurora smiled.

"I can't wait to see them again." Brooks often stayed by her side, helping her keep up on the journey. "All of them are awesome and really fun."

Aurora huffed. "You keep mentioning *them*, yet you never say who *they* are?"

"You're just going to have to wait and find out."

"Fine," Aurora said. "How long have refugees from the Second Realm traveled to the border of the Fourth Realm for safety?"

"You ask too many questions, Aurora." Brooks rolled his eyes. "It's like you're from another time or something."

"Brooks, I *am* from another time, remember?"

"Oh, yeah!"

The children accepted Aurora as the Goddess of Dark and Ruler of the Second Realm. Brooks was the only one familiar with the title and the weight it bared, thanks to his mother. The only real questions the children asked were if Aurora could make shadow animals or ice sculptures. The former, she answered, *I've never tried*, and to the latter, she told them, *not at the moment.*

Little of her powers had returned. Thankfully Light Saints nor gods had come after them in the days following the devastation in Last Hope. Aurora felt the gods were planning her demise. The children had skills but not ones to keep them alive from immortal attacks. No mortal possessed such talent or magic.

When Aurora was mortal, healers, weapon wielders, wizards, beasts, thinks, and many other Magicals were rare but not unheard of. The oldest and original magic users, Ancient Magicals—the shifters, elves, dwarves, and faeries—were believed extinct. In today's age, Aurora was sure that magic altogether, aside from the gods' power, was gone.

In the First Gods War, life fought as one army to protect their world from the demons of the Grounds Below. Ancient Magicals gifted some of their magic to select humans and animals alike for the entirety of Nelabac to stand a greater chance against the threat. That magic was carried on through bloodlines but, over time, was diluted, forgotten, or snuffed out completely.

Aurora hoped one of the mortal children had buried their magic deep in their souls, but Aurora felt nothing among them. No power of rarity or spectacle, only true, mortal humans.

All the more vulnerable and powerless. All the more reason for me to protect them.

Aurora felt electricity. She almost stopped, but the eldest child, Daria, spoke up. "It's the electric fence I told you about."

The children explained that the Fourth Realm had formed a pact with the Light Knights of the Third Realm to keep the peace at their shared border. The agreement allowed Light Knights to hunt Second Realm citizens as long as those of the Fourth Realm were kept safe. The Fourth Realm had built extensive electrical walls surrounding its cities and towns to ensure their safety.

Initially, Aurora was shocked, but they explained the Fourth Realm was not the only realm with such precautions and protections. The Water Saints of the Seventh Realm had refused to work with the Light knights, so they forged the miles-high wall of water to protect their borders. Mortal and immortal alike, the Water Wall was wide and deep enough to keep anyone in or out of the realm.

"What of the Fifth Realm?" Aurora grew frustrated by the saints' collective lack of sympathy shown to her people. "Do refugees not go there?"

"Yes, but only if the refugees survive traveling through the Fourth Realm," Daria explained. "With the Light Knights roaming the realm, it is near impossible. The other option is to go through the Wastes of the Third Realm, which is just as dangerous."

Luna's once-protected Third Realm had become a land of rot and ruin. The citizens of the Third Realm were killed before the spell, but the land remained. The Light Saints—Light *Knights*—used their former realm as their home base. Located in the center of Nelabac, there was no better base of operation. Light Knights had drained the rivers, destroyed the forests, and sapped the life out of the very soil. Over the last one hundred years, the Third Realm had become a dark, despairing, wasteful land where no light shone and probably never would again.

The forest paths merged with a dirt road, and the electric-charged wall sparked nearby. Its lines of blue and yellow currents traveled down the Second and Fourth Realm border, connected by spacious iron columns. Beyond lay the iron walls of Caris.

The iron walls were high enough to conceal Caris from anyone on the outside. The steel panels were charged with volts of electricity. Lightning

Saints patrolled the top while others marched along the base of the walls. The gate itself resembled the electric border, unseen yet heard.

The Lightning Saints wore long black pants and jackets with leather boots. Guards, saints selected to protect the borders and cities of their realm, wore goggles over their eyes and a glove on their right hand. Aurora noted others with helmets and masks, the agents, the ambassadors and spies. Aurora knew a symbol of crackling lightning scarred their left palms, displaying ownership and service to the God of Lightning and the Fourth Realm. Each Lightning Saint held a rod or spear, a new weapon to Lightning's arsenal. Aurora assumed they helped generate a greater mass of electricity.

Then, she saw people. Her people. Citizens of the Second Realm huddled in groups, shoved tight together, carefully lined against one another without more than a foot out of space between them. Aurora looked up at the trees and saw why. The Light Knights lingered like wraiths.

"Why do they not attack?" Aurora leaned down to Brooks.

"There's a rule," Daria explained. "Light Knights can only attack at night and from a one-mile distance."

The camps were far worse than Last Hope. Despite the suffering, the people had a slighter sense of security.

Though she was once mortal herself, Aurora was above them now, and yet she could not fathom treating them to such savagery. If Aurora crossed paths with Blesk during her time in his realm, he would pay for the crimes of his saints.

Just because these people were not chosen for such a destiny does not mean they deserve such a dreadful fate.

No one took a second glance at Aurora and the children. A woman and four children coming from war-torn lands, seeking shelter was nothing new.

"I still don't understand why no one travels to Dandfol," Aurora said. "It seems like the safest bet."

"Since it's home to the Resistance, if you go, you're willingly joining the fight," Daria said. "Not everyone wants or is able to fight."

Dandfol, the eldest city in the Second Realm, now acted as the base for the Resistance, a group of Second Realm citizens doing what they could against the immortals and Light Knights running amock. The city of lights and theater sat on the far west side of the Second Realm, partially occupying the ocean. Patrons had visited not just for its lively entertainment and unpredictable atmosphere but for the beautiful structures, layouts, and people. Dandfol was built as a last stand.

"Daria, how are we going to find them?" The youngest girl, Kelsa, asked. She clutched her stuffed animal tightly. Aurora thought it was a bear, but it was so old and torn to bits Aurora was unsure. "How are we going to find Alfonso and Madness?"

Aurora thought the latter name peculiar and not very fitting of a mortal. It was something ancient and dark, something of such nature that had died out from Nelabac a long time ago.

"We'll look high and low!" Brooks scanned the crowd. "Tobias and Cerene might be here if they're not delivering goods from Dandfol."

Aurora wished to peer inside the children's souls to get an image of what the mortals they sought looked like, but that would draw power from the Altered Realm and, in turn, would only draw unwanted attention.

Suddenly, Brooks halted. His little legs hopped up and down as he pointed to a young woman. She had tight, brown, coiled hair that halted just below her shoulders. Her bright yellow tunic and pants complimented her brown skin and yellow eyes but also made quite the statement. The leather straps across her thighs held daggers and other weapons. Black boots traveled up to her knees, giving length to her petite figure.

"Cerene!" Brooks called out. When she looked up, Cerene was the most devastatingly beautiful woman Aurora had ever seen.

"Brooks?" Cerene dropped the clothes in hand and ran to the child, pulling him into a swinging embrace. "What in God's Realm are you doing here?" Cerene looked behind him, at the other children, and then at

Aurora. Then, like a flame igniting, she understood. She lowered Brooks and turned toward Aurora. "No."

Aurora gave a nod, confirming her fear. Cerene pulled Brooks in close, and the child let out a sob. Aurora noted that Cerene held back her grief for the child's sake.

So much care.

"Come." Cerene took his hand and gestured for them to follow. "Our camp is just up here."

Aurora let the four others go ahead as she took up the rear. They walked another few hundred feet to a tent with sleeping bags. The campfire was lit with a pot of stew boiling. The children sat around the fire, and Cerene poured each of them a big ladle of the stew.

"Would you like some?" She extended a bowl to Aurora.

"Thank you." Aurora took a seat by Cerene. "I'm glad we made it to you."

Cerene looked at the children, who were lost in their soup and conversation with one another. "How many days ago?"

"Four," Aurora said. "I had come from Sanston a few days prior. I assumed the Light Knights waited for the right moment to strike."

Cerene tapped at the cup in her hands, eyes on a distant time or place. "I was planning to head that way tomorrow with my companions. We had some leftover bags of food from the Resistance to take."

Aurora took a last bite of her soup, the only thing she could bare to do.

"Me too."

A mortal was giving her sympathy and grief. A mortal felt sorry for her when this was entirely her fault.

"I'm Aurora," she said, "but you can call me Rory."

"Cerene Misrinda." Cerene smiled and shook Aurora's hand. "Thank you for saving the children."

Aurora changed the subject. "So, Dandfol, are you part of it? The Resistance?"

"Aren't we all?" Cerene laughed, propping herself up. "No—I mean, yes, I am—but not as active as I'd like to be. I want to go to the fronts, but my parents refuse."

"And with good reason." A new voice called over from the fire. "A war zone is no place for a child."

"Twenty-two is hardly a child, and a war zone is all the more reason for an archer as good as myself to go, *Tobias.*" Cerene stuck out her tongue. "We can't all be two-hundred-some years old like you."

A man stepped through. His skin was dark, with silver markings covering his hands and feet. His eyes were orbs of silver.

"Tobias, this is Rory." Cerene gestured to the newcomer. "She brought Brooks and the others here from Last Hope. Rory, this is Tobias Evergreen."

With animal-like stillness, he stopped. Aurora sensed a warrior in the man, one of ancient times, though he looked just slightly older than her.

Magic?

"Two hundred and eighteen, to be exact." Tobias took a seat.

Magic.

"I'm sorry for all the trouble that has fallen on you and the children," Tobias squatted beside her. "Times in the Second Realm are not what they once were."

"Once were?" Aurora cocked her head. "What do you mean?"

He grinned. "Wouldn't you know?"

Aurora felt her jaw nearly drop. "I don't know what you mean."

"I believe you do, Rory." Tobias countered, but not with malice or hate but in acknowledgment.

"Well, this got weird." Cerene clapped her hands and let out an awkward laugh. "I'm sure Rory and the kids are tired. I'll get them settled in the tent, and then we can wait for the others to come home."

Aurora did recall Brooks mentioning two other names.

Cerene went over to the kids and gathered them up while she stayed out with Tobias. His eyes shifted from Cerene and the kids to Aurora.

When they were gone, Tobias lowered his head in a bow. "We've long awaited your return, Goddess of Dark."

LUNA
GODDESS OF LIGHT

Chapter 4

Much like in the days when she was a new god, Aurora found herself struck still as stone. But she remained calm, steady.

"I fought in a legion for you one hundred years ago," Tobias said. "When the Gods of Nelabac disappeared."

Her stomach churned. "A legion? For the Second Realm?"

Tobias nodded. "I will tell the full story later, as my companions will be joining us shortly, but please know, Aurora, I am beyond glad of your return. Those alive from the Old Age have done our best to remember you, your kindness, and your strength."

It hit Aurora that the mortal before her was a Shifter, an Ancient Magicals capable of shifting into a dormant animal form. It explained his eyes, markings, and age. Questions formed on the tip of her tongue, but she remained silent as Cerene appeared from the tent.

"They fell asleep the moment their heads hit the pillow." She reached for her bowl. "Rory, Tobias and I are going out to meet some friends of ours for training. You're welcome to join, but I'm sure you're rather tired—"

"I'll come!" The excitement of Tobias' revelation flowed through her veins like shadows caught on the wind, reviving much of her missing strength. "I mean, I need a break from the children. They're wonderful and all, but I'd enjoy some adult company."

"All right then." Cerene smiled and extended a hand. "The more, the merrier."

They walked to a small clearing in the woods past the refugee camp. Two people were already there. Both seemed close to Aurora's mortal age, like Cerene and Tobias. One was near her height, while the other was much taller. Between the two sat a tiny sandy-tabby cat, its eyes the color of honey.

He'd make a great scarf.

The little cat's ears perked up and raced up to Cerene, Tobias, and Aurora. The cat took liberty in rubbing over Aurora's boots.

"Rory, this little dude is Baer." Cerene leaned down and petted the stretching cat. "He's my little companion."

"He loves me more." The shorter man called from the clearing.

Aurora gave the cat a good pet. "Nice to meet you, Baer."

"About time you guys got here!" The shorter one called out again, waving his hand at them.

"This is the first time we've arrived late," Cerene retorted. "So, you can stand to wait a few minutes."

They approached the new mortals. The shorter and louder one's tunic had a few tears and snags, as well as his pants and boots, but his glasses didn't bare a single scratch. Through the glare on the frames, Aurora caught a glimpse of his light-violet eyes.

"My apologize, Miss Cerene Misrinda of Dandfol." He bowed in a teasing manner, then shifted his attention toward Aurora. "And who might this lovely lady be?"

"This is Aurora. Rory for short."

"I'm Alfonso Hunt, but my friends call me Al." He extended his hand. "Why were you so delayed?"

Cerene told both him and the other man of Aurora's tale of Sanston, the destruction of Last Hope, and how Brooks and the other three children were the only survivors. By the end, Alfonso was shaking; the other man pulled out a tobacco roll.

"Is Brooks okay?" Alfonso asked Aurora directly. "Did he-did he watch them die? Manda and Gabe?"

"Yes," she said, her voice strong, "but he was so brave. Through it all, Brooks and the other children walked out stronger."

"Does that really matter? Why does it matter if they're made stronger in this Grounds Below of a world? A world the Gods of Old cursed us with when they left us all behind?"

Aurora recalled the names the children had used to describe two of their friends. She had met Alfonso, so she assumed the other man was Madness. His hair sat neatly on his head like a blanket of snow, matching the paleness of his skin. Aurora noted a bandage wrapped around his left forearm. His clothes were also the same as his brother's but in slightly better condition. He possessed exquisite rose-pink eyes, but something haunted them. Something Aurora could not put her finger on but felt in her soul to stay away from. Felt it was something never to disturb.

"Let's not have *that* conversation again." Cerene walked up and placed her hand on his arm. "We each know where we stand on said subject. What happened to Brooks and the children and those displaced in the war is a tragedy, and we can make a change. Remember that, Madness."

He walked deeper into the clearing.

I see the species of man has not changed. Stubborn and moody as ever.

Tobias joined Madness. Alfonso looked back, offering Aurora an apologetic grin. Aurora took a seat on the grass, her body exhausted.

"Those two have experienced more loss than any I've met." Cerene sat down next to her. "Orphaned at five, they only had each other after losing their village and parents. The two are more brothers than most blood siblings could ever say about one another."

"They're brothers?" Aurora asked.

"They would move sky and earth to keep one another safe."

Sounds like a set of siblings I used to know.

"Tobias and I are much the same," Cerene explained. "I've known him since I was nine. We've been partners since I was old enough to leave Dandfol."

"Partners?" Aurora asked, a little hesitant.

Cerene burst into a fit of laughter. Aurora peeped over at Madness, Alfonso, and Tobias, the three staring, confused.

Cerene wiped away the tear. "Partners as in a fighting team."

"Oh," Aurora blushed. "My apologies."

"Tobias has a preference, and we are not it." Warmth filled Cerene's eyes. "I was twelve when the five of us met. Madness and Alfonso fifteen. Baer was a kitten, and Tobias, well, you know, he's ancient."

"You're lucky to have such close companions."

"Well, in day-to-day life, people become your friends. In war, people become your family."

Aurora had found many of her Dark Saints during the aftermath of the Second Gods War. They became the family she and Luna never had.

"You have a family?" Cerene asked.

"I did, once." Aurora replied. "A long, long time ago."

"Look, I know Rory just got here and all," Alfonso shouted, "but we did not come here to gossip!"

"Maybe we're talking about you?" Cerene called back.

"We came out here to train." Madness threw the tobacco bud in his mouth to the ground. "Can we get to that?"

"The men are *so* cranky today," Cerene said through her teeth.

"I heard that!"

Cerene helped Aurora up, and they joined their companions. They stretched and moved about in the clearing, waking their muscles and joints. Cerene and Tobias stood as a team against Alfonso and Baer. Aurora sat in the grass next to Madness. She noted his eyes were focused on the duel about to take place, but Aurora knew his other senses were honed-in elsewhere.

"Do you not fight?" she asked.

"No," he said. "I heal people."

"A healer?" A magic passed down from the faeries, healers were sought across realms for their knowledge of the body and abilities to fix many of the worst of wounds, both mortal and immortal. "It's nice to help rather than hurt."

Aurora felt a tension with Madness she had not felt with the others. She did not know how long she would be in their presence, either, so she needed their trust, yet some dark and deep worried her. A need for vengeance poured from Madness. A dark presence Aurora knew was not of this world. His lips twitched and fought back something nasty.

But what could it be?

"You all know the drill," Madness called out. "The duel lasts until someone's pinned."

"That someone is normally Alfonso," Tobias called across the clearing.

"And, *go*!"

Alfonso rushed his opponents. The two small rods in both his hands transformed into massive weapons: a gold-plated hammer and a bronze ax. Aurora gasped, for the man was a weapon wielder, a Magical capable of wielding the ancient weapons of dwarves, creatures not seen in thousands of years.

Wielders hardly learned they possessed the ability to handle such magic, let alone the weapons to do so. The Weapons of Ore, as they were called, only took to their true shape for those with the bloodline of those they were originally crafted to serve. Weapons of Ore were magic believed lost with the dwarves and wars of the early days. The weapons gave their wielders immortal-like speed, upped their strength, and improved their accuracy of attack and defense.

Aurora watched the feline next. Baer's body grew and grew as he shifted into a larger form of himself. His honey-crisp eyes darkened and morphed to the color of ripe apples. He was a beast, an animal gifted with Shifter magic.

Remnants of the Ancient Magicals existed in the mortals: Tobias, a Shifter; Alfonso, with the Weapons of Ore from dwarves; Madness, with the healing of the faeries; and Baer, with the blood of shifters. Aurora's eyes stung with tears.

"Hey,"—Madness interrupted her moment—"you're missing the best part."

And he was right. Aurora stood from her spot on the ground as Tobias transformed into his Shifter form: a giant, towering wolf. The silver markings mixed with his midnight fur. Each line formed its own pattern, interlacing and swirling throughout his fur.

"Magnificent," Aurora gleamed. "Is Cerene also?"

"No, she's the only true human among us, but honestly, she's the most gifted."

Cerene moved like a cat in the night. Agile and swift, dodging each blow from Baer and Alfonso with ease. On top of that, her aim was unmatched by the likes of anyone Aurora had seen in her five hundred years.

All of them used their power with the combination of their partners. If Baer defended, Alfonso leaped into action with the Weapons of Ore swaying through the air like extensions of his limbs. Tobias defended as Cerene aimed with her bow and arrow from his back.

"I've never seen anything like this before." Aurora's soul was elated. "They fight together as if they've been doing it for hundreds of years."

"When you're fighting for your life, all you can do is get killed or get better at killing." Madness cocked his head. "You've managed to survive for this long, right? What, like, twenty-some years?"

"You ask questions like you're entitled to their answers." Aurora kept her eyes on the duel.

"Maybe I am."

"Again, who gave you such authority?"

"When a strange girl shows up with children who are basically my little siblings, claiming their parents are dead, and their entire town murdered alongside them, I get a little entitled." His eyes narrowed down at her. "You get that, right?"

The shadows begged to pour from Aurora's hands and wrap around his throat, but that same something told her otherwise. Something said for her to let their conversation end. To Madness, she idled in his space with his brother and their family. She was a stranger who had mysteriously survived numerous attacks from Light Knights without clear answers.

A yelp broke from the duel. Alfonso and Cerene danced in the art of one-on-one combat. Cerene easily dodged the hammer and ax, but besides the bow and arrow, she had no other real way of taking on the offensive. Alfonso used both his ax and hammer as shields or weapons against her swift attacks.

"You give in yet?" Alfonso teased.

"Have I ever prior?" she smirked.

"Then get ready for the speed."

Alfonso redirected his magic to increase his speed, moving at a rate difficult for one to follow with the naked eye. Cerene stood strong, tracking his every movement. Stillness overcame the archer, and just as Aurora thought Alfonso would strike first, Cerene fired. The arrow landed on Alfonso's ax.

"You could have injured me!" Afonso looked at the arrow.

"You know you're the only reason we still need to practice, right?" Cerene snickered. "You need to change your attack patterns."

"Ha-ha, very funny," Alfonso said. "Maybe we can discuss strategy over dinner one night?"

Cerene cocked her hip. "Over a pot of four-day-old stew?"

Tobias trotted over to Cerene, tilting his giant head into her chest. Baer receded into his smaller form, looking rather defeated. The beast slunk across the ground and onto Cerene's feet.

"I'll never understand how you can keep up with my speed." Alfonso collapsed and grabbed Baer, forcing him into a snuggle. "Baer and I just can't figure it out! Can we, bud?"

"Are you sure you're not Magical?" Aurora asked Cerene. "That was rather impressive."

Cerene winked. "I'm just that good."

"Seeing so many Magicals in one place is special." Tobias transformed back. He picked up his robes and dressed. "I have not seen it in a long, long time."

"Since before godless country?" Alfonso asked, teasing.

Tobias darted his eyes to Aurora. "Maybe."

"Well, I'd love to hear about it sometime." Aurora needed a way for Tobias to speak further of the past, the years of war she had missed, and what he had seen. Tobias was her only source of liable information.

"Tonight then!" Cerene shot up, clapping. "When we get the kids fed and back to sleep, Tobias can tell us all about it."

The five of them made their way back to camp. Along the way, Aurora noted just how far out they had traveled.

"Why do you go so far out for training?"

Aurora noted their pause.

"It's just easier." Cerene strode forward. "We like to try new techniques and spread out—Oh, *gods*, I left my bow."

"Do you want me to go back for it?" Tobias turned to her.

"No, I'll go back with Baer. Al, could you take Aurora—"

"I got her." Madness moved to Aurora's side before anyone could protest and placed her on his back. "Alfonso, go with Cerene and Tobias."

"Mad, you know Cerene and Baer are capable of defending themselves," Alfonso said. "I don't need to join them."

"Just go."

Alfonso pursed his lips but took off after Cerene and Baer. They walked rather slowly. Tobias lingered ahead, looking back.

"I've got her, Tobias," Madness called. "Can you run back and check on the kids?"

Tobias seemed hesitant but walked on ahead and out of sight.

"Can you tell me why you've singled me out when we've only just met, Madness?" Aurora shrugged him off. "Or is it, Mad? Can I call you Mad?"

"No, you can't call me that—in fact, don't address me." His rose-pink eyes glared.

Aurora pushed to her feet. "What is your deal? We've *just* met."

"*You're* my deal." He moved in. "I can just tell you're *not* good."

Again, Madness didn't appear as much, but again, that same tingle in her soul twitched. Aurora realized it was his soul pleading for help. She wanted to touch his chest and peer into it, to find what latched onto him so tightly.

"You are connected to the past. I don't know why or how, but you are." Madness stepped closer to her. "Some part of me just knows it. You're connected to the Gods of Old, and I don't want it around my brother or my family for much longer, got it?"

"What's so bad about them? The Gods of Old." She leaned in closer, wanting a rise out of him. "You seem to have it out for them."

"The older generations still believe in that mess. They believe the Gods of Old will come back and save us, but I don't see the point in believing in gods who abandoned their people."

"Even so, who do you think makes the trees grow? Pushes the air to the crops? Waters the fields and heats the world?" Aurora came to her own defense. "Who decides where to spread the light and dark of this world?"

"Maybe it all just exists? Sure, maybe they contributed—if they were real—but they don't work the farms, plant the seeds, or stop people from doing right or wrong." Madness added before walking off, "And I sure as the Grounds Below don't see them ending this war."

Chapter 5

Aurora carried herself back to the camp, straggling behind Madness. She felt ice and darkness prickle inside, both from anger and fatigue. She wanted to show the mortal man just who he was dealing with.

But this is not the place . . . plus, he is a Second Realm citizen.

The children woke up just after sundown, full of energy and empty bellies. Alfonso and Brooks held a long embrace, the two glad to be reunited. Kelsa and Daria gravitated toward Cerene, and Philip lingered near Tobias. Madness kept his distance from them all.

Cerene moved picking up the bowls. Alfonso helped by taking his and Aurora's.

"Enjoyed your food, I see?"

"It was delicious," Aurora said through the last gulp.

"I cooked it."

"You know I cook all the meals around here." Cerene came up from behind and knocked a cloth against his head.

"Ah," Alfonso winked, "that must be the reason we keep you around."

"You boys would be lost without me." Cerene leaned into him. "You and the gods know it."

"We certainly do."

"Speaking of gods," Cerene whirled. "It's almost time for the kids to head back to bed."

There were protests, but eventually, the kids said their goodnights and trucked back inside the tent. The whole scene reminded Aurora of the sleepovers she had with the children from the town closest to Dark Manor.

Aurora loved children, but it was against the Gods' Code to create immortal ones. Being stuck at such a young age for eternity would prove more a burden than a gift, so Aurora and Elainarelieved mothers and orphanages every few months by spending time with the children.

My dearest friend . . .

Cerene exited the tent with five small glasses in one hand and a bottle of brown liquor in the other. Aurora had somehow opened herself to the chance to discover what happened after she left and how the realms crumbled. She tried not to look too eager as the others remained cool and collected, probably having heard this tale many times.

Tobias returned from his Shifter form. Cerene sat to his right, pouring the whiskey. Baer padded into her lap. Alfonso lay on the ground by Aurora while Madness took to spot at his brother's side.

"I was one hundred and eight when the Goddess of Dark and the Dark Saints of the Second Realm disappeared one hundred years ago," Tobias began his tale. "For a time, saints from the remaining five realms of Fire, Water, Earth, Air, and Lightning protected the Second Realm citizens. After the Light Saints—as Light Knights were named then—finished laying waste to their own lands and people, they moved in from the Third Realm to the Second Realm to slaughter as many citizens are they could. This era became known as the First Great Saint War.

"When the carnage was at its highest, the allied saints worried over the fate of their own realms. They had a duty to protect their own lands and their own people first. This led to a division among the saints, as some deemed it their duty to protect the Second Realm—to protect all the people of Nelabac. Majority of the allied forces withdrew, while the few stayed behind and fought for the defenseless."

Saints breaking from their realm—from their *god*—was unheard of, if not impossible. Saints were bound to the will of their god to serve to help *their* lands and to help *their* people prosper. To serve against those orders or that will, gods, Aurora did not know what kind of punishment that entailed.

"This new legion of saints became known as the Soldiers of Night." The name itself sparked a light inside Aurora. Even the faces of the mortals glowed in the campfire light. "The Soldiers of Night swore to protect the forgotten mortals and Magicals who had lost their lands, saints, and beloved god. I found the Soldiers of Night not long after the Light Knights had killed my entire family. I became a messenger on the battlefront. I was among many Magical and Ancient Magicals but was the youngest. Saints who chose to join the Soldiers of Night were seen as traitors and exiled, never allowed to return to their own realms. Over time, the Light Knights' armies grew, and a grand battle between the Light Knights and Soldiers of Night dawned.

"The Soldiers of Night's home base became the Goddess of Dark's home, Dark Manor. It also happened to be the location of the final battle. Magicals such as wielders, beasts, and healers flocked to fight for the cause and fight for their land, and finally, one summer's dawn, Light Knights rose from over the top of the crater and charged into Dark Manor.

"The Soldiers of Night—creatures of mortal and immortal, Magical or not—fought side by side for the first time since the First Gods War five thousand years prior." Tobias grinned, but not at the grandness of the story, but at the memory of it all. At the pride of being part of the union of the races of the realms. "The Light Knights' numbers were near twice that of the Soldiers of Night but fought at half the strength, half the heart. The battle lasted hours. Light Knights and Soldiers of Night slaughtered one another until the commander of the Soldiers of Night called for surrender."

"But why?" Alfonso asked. "If the battle was an even match, why call it off?"

Tobias' tone shifted. "The Light Knights had deceived the Soldiers of Night, for the majority of the Light Knight forces had rushed the surrounding cities and towns, slaughtering all they came in contact with. The commander of the Solider of Night crawled on his hands and knees, pleading with the leader of the Light Knights to take the Soldiers of Night as prisoners and leave the Second Realm at peace." Tobias trembled, lost in his hatred. "That *woman*, known for her ruthlessness and killing abilities, did not listen and instead did what she's best at."

Aurora knew *who* Tobias spoke of with such vial hate: Sabelle, the Goddess of Light's advisor. The advisor enjoyed the calamity of pain she would inflict on others. She had always been that way. Why Luna saved the woman was beyond Aurora's imagination.

"She and the Light Knights killed everyone in the Field of Flowers that day," Tobias explained, hate coating his tongue. "Thankfully, she kept her word and left citizens of the Second Realm at peace . . . for a time."

Cerene rubbed her fingers through Tobias' fur, "Tobias, I know I told you it was 'story time' tonight, but I did not know you would go this deep."

"He must continue." Aurora knew the Shifter did not want to say much more, for his eyes held that of someone who had watched comrades and friends die for the sake of others, but she had to know. Aurora needed everything he had to give. "What happened next? Of those who battled and lost?"

"He mustn't *do* anything." Cerene snapped.

"Cerene, it's okay." Tobias took her hand, and reluctantly, she silenced. "When the battle turned south, my commander told me to run, so I did. I do not know what happened after that. It is hard to recall . . . Even the faces of those I fought beside are forgotten. Their names also slip my mind. From there, many other wars and battles ignited, but none were like the First Great Saint War—the war that sparked the New Age. An age many prayed would spring forth the gods again so that they would save us from their calamities."

The shadows of the night fell, taking the shape of their master. "Thank you, Tobias, for serving when the Second Realm needed you most. I am so sorry the Dark Saints and myself were not there to help you."

It was time for the loyal people of the Second Realm to know of her return.

"What, Dark Saints?" Alfonso spoke up. "*Yourself*? What's going on here?"

Eye darted around the campfire between Alfonso, Cerene, and Madness.

"Rory, what do you mean by *and myself*?" Cerene questioned. "Are you Magical, too? Were you there?"

Aurora looked at Tobias. He sat still, his eyes telling her the next moves were her own to make.

"She's one of them." Madness moved in front of his brother. "She's a *god*."

Cerene pinched her brow, but Alfonso snorted. Tobias growled, that predator and protector taking life.

"Not just any god, Madness," Tobias snarled. "She is Aurora, Goddess of Dark and Ruler of the Second Realm. She is *our* god."

But with their close friend so sure and the other viciously defensive, Alfonso and Cerene took Aurora in. They each held what Aurora thought was a different emotion: confusion, hope, and resentment.

"Do the children know?" Frustration coated Alfonso's voice. "Do they know who you are?"

"We were together when Manda died," Aurora said. "We were together when Last Hope was destroyed. We set them free together."

"You did this!" Madness rushed forward at Aurora and grabbed her. "You did this to the world!"

She watched his rose-pink eyes shift to a blood-curdling red. Every part of her wanted to reach inside and feel just *what* magic he possessed. It was dark and dangerous, so much so, Aurora believed it could end her immortal life.

"Madness"—Alfonso ran to his brother—"stop this—"

"Don't blame me for the fall of Nelabac!" Aurora stood her ground. "This would never have happened—Luna, the gods, and this war—if the mortals hadn't made—"

Revealing the Soul Keepers would put the mortals at risk. If the gods learned of their interactions with Aurora, they would hunt them down for even the smallest amount of information. The mortals before her were powerful Magicals, but they were still mortal, capable of dying by a saint's or god's hand.

"Why did you do it?" Madness threw his arms. "You condemned your people to a century of pain! You sacrificed our protectors! Did you stop for one second about what might happen if your plan didn't work?"

"I did not know it would fail!" Aurora felt the fires of her soul swirling. "The spell, the sealing . . . I did not know it would fail." Before she knew it, she was sharing more than she ever meant to. "I did what I did to save everyone. Maybe-maybe if the spell failed on Luna, then it failed on my saints. Maybe the Dark Saints are imprisoned or trapped—"

"Oh, they're dead, Rory." Madness moved away, ill intent in every word. "If they lived, they sure as the Grounds Below did a crappy job of protecting their people!"

All I wanted was to save the world and my sister. Was that so wrong?

"Madness, this is a shock to everyone. Now, stop it!" Alfonso placed both hands on his brother's chest. "Reel it in, *now*. If she really is this Goddess of Dark, we don't need to unleash anything . . . Got it?"

"We don't want to wake or worry the little ones, either, Madness." Cerene leveled. Her tone was as kind and caring toward him as Alfonso's.

Tobias stood by Madness, but not in a defensive stand for himself or Aurora, but for Cerene, Alfonso, and the rest of the camp. Baer crouched at their feet, not sure of where to leap among the chaos.

Madness was right. Her dishonorable actions had brought on everything that had developed over the last hundred years. Ranging from the destruction of the Second and Third Realm to the decision of the saints to put walls around their borders to keep danger out, Aurora's cowardly way of dealing with her sister had plunged Nelabac into ruin.

"Darkness can be found anywhere." Guilt consumed her. "It seeps its way into a person's heart and soul through the tiniest of cracks and spreads like wildfire. It grips a person and drags them down. The cycle, going on and on and on until they're gone."

It was the reason she had been created: To keep the world from going down a dark and twisted path. Aurora was the bridge to help those lost in the dark find the light. Luna was created to keep light afloat. The sisters had once upheld the utmost important jobs of any mortal, immortal, or creature in Nelabac.

I focused so much on maintaining balance in the natural world that I failed to see when my sister needed me most.

Mortals were not to concern themselves with the issues of the gods, but from the moment Aurora chose to stay in their camp that evening, she had dragged them into the affairs of immortals.

Affairs only I alone can fix.

She was weak. She was whole. She was utterly as close to mortal as she could get. So much was wrong with her, and fixing the world was only the beginning.

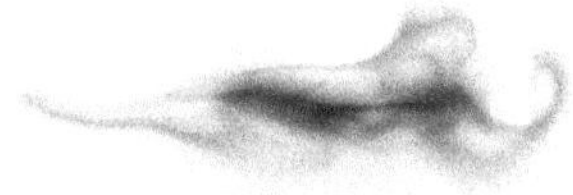

A few nights later, Aurora heard distant screaming. It was the hunting of Second Realm citizens who had stepped outside the one-mile radius. The Light Knights were having fun.

Everyone in the tent seemed asleep except Brooks. His eyes were wide open, struck with fear.

"Don't worry, Brooks." Aurora took his hand. "They can't reach us here."

"You promise?" He seemed hesitant to believe her.

So Aurora swore, "I won't let them come near you."

He soon rolled back over, sound asleep.

The mortals had kept their distance since Aurora's reveal. Aurora hadn't blamed them. If Aurora was back, it meant all the gods had returned, and the world they had grown up in was about to change. The war itself was about to escalate.

Aurora was unable to fall back asleep. She had not observed who was inside the tent, so when she stepped out, it was Madness and Alfonso maintaining the fire. Madness' eyes barreled into Aurora before he stood and walked from camp.

"I only came for some air." Aurora sat on a log across from Alfonso. "Tell your brother he can come back once I'm done."

"Ignore him. His rage comes from his own darkness, ways that he feels he has failed, Alfonso poked the dying embers. "But more than anything, Madness wants this war to be over . . . and to see the Second Realm as home again."

What Madness possessed that was darker than her own . . . the thought angered her. "I'm going to go for a walk."

"No need." Alfonso held up a hand. "I mean, I don't mind keeping you company while you're out here. You don't seem to bite."

She complied, slightly delighted.

They sat in silence. Aurora held her hands over the fire, letting its warmth fill her icy soul. She let the black ice dance across her skin. It did not last long, as her powers were fragile, unable to hold their own against a simple, mortal flame.

"So, you want to tell me your full story?" Alfonso leaned on his arms, the Weapons of Ore dangling at his side.

"I've told you who I am," Aurora said. "What more do you need?"

"I want to get to know you," Alfonso said. "How did you get here? Where did you go? Anything to help me feel I can truly trust you."

Not that the mortal should question her honor, but Aurora found herself wanting to share. Alfonso, compared to the others, had an easy soul. A soul that welcomed those around it and let others feel a sense of comfort in its presence. Cerene's was similar, but she was much more independent and fearsome. Alfonso made someone feel they belonged, no matter the circumstance.

"The gods existed in Nelabac for five thousand years before the fall of the Godly Order." Aurora hopped into the details, hoping Alfonso would share them with the others. "Over three thousand years, the five Elemental Gods took form: earth, air, lightning, water, and fire. They formed in their time of need and by some power even beyond us gods. Soon after the creation of the last Elemental God, the two-thousand-year war, the Second Gods War, began."

"Even the gods have gods?" Alfonso asked.

"Terra, God of Earth; Lust, God of Air; Blesk, God of Lightning; Juvia, Goddess of Water; and Oberon, God of Fire, all went to war. Each Elemental God claimed more rights to power and land than the other since each had the upper hand regarding one another's power. Their power struggle created a war based on more rights for more land and people and controlling Nelabac. Balance no longer existed. At one point during the Second Gods War, two new gods spawned from the clashing of the five elements: the Goddess of Dark and the Goddess of Light. The Sisters of Balance."

"Your sister?" Alfonso asked.

"With our creation, the two thousand years of fighting ended, and the Seven Gods of Nelabac moved the world into a state of harmony. Peace existed for five hundred years, but something . . . "She kept the Soul Keepers to herself. "Something snapped in the Goddess of Light. Over time, she began to see mortals and Magicals as foul creatures that needed eradicating. Originally, the Goddess of Light's intention went for just the mortals, but in the end, it became all beings of Nelabac. All the same, the Goddess of Light took the Light Saints across the Third Realm, slaughtering all life by the masses. She slaughtered everyone." She nearly wretched at the thought.

"Under my plan, the five Elemental Gods and I chose to do something about the Goddess of Light's rampage." Aurora shifted in the grass. "The only way to end the Goddess of Light's presence without killing her was to place her in an enchanted slumber—to send her away for some unknown amount of time. It would sap her power and keep Light Saints from doing further harm."

"Why not kill her?" Alfonso asked.

"Some of us felt the world would fall out of balance if we killed her," Aurora said. "We've never lost a god before, let alone kill one. We don't know what would happen if we ever did. But, above all, she is my sister."

Aurora did not lie. That was much of the reason several of the other gods were motivated not to kill Luna for her crimes. How would Nelabac change if one that was created to balance it, no matter how heinous they were, was gone?

"Magic that powerful required more than just strength. It required sacrifice."

"And you sacrificed the Dark Saints."

"If I wanted to seal Luna's power for good, something of equal value has to be exchanged." Aurora winced. "Saints are beings saved before death, alive through the force of a god's will, might, and magic. The Dark Saints were the strongest part of me. They had to be used to seal Luna and her powers away.

"Killing her would erase the power of light from Nelabac altogether, but sealing it away would prevent Luna from creating further damage—not eradicate the power completely." Aurora continued, "I had convinced the gods to each give up a piece of their power. After some explaining and pleading, the gods agreed to go through with my spell."

"So that's why you have no power?"

"*Little* power—thank you." Annoyance managed in her tone. "After we completed the spell, it went wrong. We all disappeared, and I lost everything except my life. The other gods' saints were left in Nelabac to guard and protect it until our return."

It was all Aurora could offer them as to why the spell did not work on the Goddess of Light the way it was intended. So much was given to end a god and her war without success, and there was no true answer as to how it happened. And despite the horrid truth, the mortal relaxed. Alfonso only shifted back and forth between his hips, eventually settling his gaze on the fire.

"Someone must have tampered with the spell." Aurora rubbed her hands as the twisted cold of black ice lingered across her fingers. "Whatever happened, it's why I'm so . . . so I'm *this*."

Guilt, along with many other emotions, had chipped away with each Dark Saint Aurora had created. Now, without saints to help keep mortal habits at bay, Aurora's stomach and heart churned with emotions.

"You mean," Alfonso said, crouching down next to her, "it's why you're crying?"

Aurora touched her icy fingers to her cheek. She almost laughed.

"We each have wrongs to right. Burdens to bear." A new voice echoed from the tent. Cerene had eavesdropped the entire time. "Some just have bigger issues to atone for.

Aurora did not deserve their grace or their kindness. Mortals had never been so tender-hearted. Aurora remembered their greed and selfish nature. She wondered how else humanity had changed since the gods left.

"You two switched it up," Alfonso said.

Aurora furrowed her brow. "What do you mean?"

"The Goddess of Light—the essence and symbol of good and purity in this world wants to end it." Alfonso shifted his hands. "While the Goddess of Dark—the one who possesses the essence of loneliness and void of hope—wants to save the world."

Darkness had always been associated with evil, but now its destiny was to stop the dimming of the light in Nelabac, and it was as damned as the Grounds Below if it failed.

What a fitting thought for this war-torn narrative.

Chapter 6

The days that followed were slow as Aurora worked to gain the mortals' trust. Every morning Aurora gathered food with Alfonso and then dispersed it to the refugees with Cerene. Madness kept his distance, interacting with her on a need-to basis. Tobias stuck close to her side, the desire to protect his god strong.

I hope the rest of my people will feel as he does one day.

Each morning Aurora's soul grew angrier. Her people were dirty, emaciated, and unbelievably hopeless. Cerene introduced Aurora to them one by one, saying she was joining the cause to change the realms.

"You know the people so well." Aurora complimented Cerene as they paced back to the campsite. Aurora faced her people, sharing food and kind words, but they did not know who she was. "You have a true connection and understanding of them."

"I've been a part of the Resistance my entire life." Cerene's eyes locked onto a memory. "My parents fought for mortals and the Second Realm long before I was born. They organized groups to send to the Fourth Realm and sent others and themselves to the fronts to fight side by side with the Fire Saints. They started it all, and I carry that with me."

"Mortals fighting immortal battles," Aurora lowered. "I outlawed that long ago."

"With the gods gone, their laws went with them," Cerene said. "Most don't come back, but they know that going in. It's more than fighting for the Second Realm and for freedom from the Light Knights and this terrible scenic view. It's about fighting for those seen as lesser to be seen as equals."

"I outlawed it because when I was mortal fighting in a god's war, I had no choice, but you all do it willingly." Aurora faced her. "Why sacrifice your lives when you know there are those more than likely to survive fighting for you?"

"We want to fight beside saints, not behind." Cerene smiled. "If we have the heart and a soul to fight, then why not? Why not let us make the sacrifice?"

Aurora walked on. "Mortals are not as weak-minded as they once were."

"Gods, no. We had to get smarter when you all left."

At camp, the children played with some wooden toys Tobias and Alfonso had found in the city the day before. Caris held one section within the gates where refugees were allowed to enter and stay for several hours, the Merchant's Quarters. There, they could sell what goods they had and make somewhat of a living to buy food, shelter, and clothing. Aurora wanted to visit, but she feared getting too close to Blesk.

She wondered if Blesk or any of the other gods had learned her location and were simply waiting for the right moment to strike or if they were tending to more pressing issues among their realms.

"Breakfast this morning is sunny-side eggs from Mrs. Deloris' chicken coop," Alfonso cracked an egg against the pan.

Brooks sighed, long and hard. "But Mrs. Deloris' chicken eggs taste *bad*—"

"Brooks," Cerene snapped, "Mrs. Deloris doesn't have to share her eggs, but she does."

Brooks looked like he wanted to protest, and by the looks on the other children's faces, it seemed they agreed with him on the taste of Mrs. Deloris' eggs. Aurora grew curious herself of—

"They're not worth trying." Madness approached. "Her eggs are terrible."

"Are you a Think as well as a healer? Is that why you're so moody?" Aurora cocked her head. "You're stuck reading everyone's thoughts?"

Madness snorted and sat down. "I am not a Think, my dear. You are simply too easy to read. Rather simple in general, I might add."

Aurora pursed her lips. "And what am I thinking now?"

"That you are extremely curious as to why I am speaking with you." Madness grabbed a bit of bread.

Aurora unhinged her jaw to protest, but he was, in fact, correct. Ice prickled the air. "You're rather chipper today. Why?"

"I am going to the market, which means I get a full day's break from you."

"Why are you going to the market?" Aurora sat beside him, rather too close as their thighs brushed. "You never leave the camp."

He pulled out tobacco. There were two rolls left. "I don't like someone else to pick out my leaves."

"You know, those are terrible for you. Mortals came to me with their lungs rendered destroyed. Their hearts riddled in disease."

"They keep me calm." He lit one of the two. "Would lose my temper without them."

Aurora held back a laugh. Madness already had the shortest temper of anyone she'd ever met and did not believe tobacco truly kept it at bay. The only other being in Nelabac who had just as short a temper was Oberon of the Fifth Realm.

"Well, only hope those don't kill you in the end."

"They won't." Madness lowered the cig between his hands, and Aurora swore she watched a shifting in his eyes. "I'm bound to be taken by something much more wicked."

"Like what?"

"You're no different from them." Madness stood. "You see mortals as pawns, and you're our queen."

"And you aren't the only one who has suffered at the hands of war," Aurora snapped. "At the hands of the gods. How else do you think I ended up here?"

His rose-pink eyes faded fast, and Aurora saw his struggle to keep the malice under control.

"Trust me." His eyes faded back to pink. "I know all too well about the burdens of war and what can follow a person in the shadows."

"Are you always this rude?"

"And are you always this big of a pain in the ass?"

How one mortal found such a way to rattle her nerves drove the ice through her bones, but Aurora ceased the pointless argument. It would get her nowhere. That mortal, in particular, had so much internal pain. Pain that haunted him over so many years had made itself at home in his soul.

Misery loves company, and Madness has become its dearest friend.

"How sad."

A noise scurried at her feet. Baer displayed his fresh prey. He pawed at the tent, asking her to open it.

"Oh, sorry, Baer."

Inside, Baer approached every one of them as they went over what they needed from the market, sowing off his fresh squirrel.

In their short time together, Aurora had grown rather fond of the mortals. Tobias acted as the group's parent, looking after the others like a doting uncle. Madness played the role of the looming older brother, often interfering in keeping Cerene and Alfonso's bickering to a minimum. Baer sat by their feet, waiting for scratches.

Being with a found family was nice, but Aurora had to part with them. A god working with mortals was unheard of—if not blasphemous. Plus, if they journeyed with her any further that she would focus more on keeping the mortals alive than prioritizing her mission.

Aurora wondered back outside the tent.

Juvia would lose her respect for me if I so much as thought *of entertaining mortals as my companions.*

Juvia, the Goddess of Water and Ruler of the Seventh Realm, was Aurora's closest ally before the sealing of the gods. Aurora knew finding her way to Juvia was her best bet in ending the war. Under Aurora's current circumstances, she could not travel through her shadows and darkness, through the Void, to the Seventh Realm. She was much too weak to use that power. She also knew Blesk would never allow her to use his portal. She had to reach her personal portal back in Dark Manor, but Dark Manor was weeks away from where she was now—

"Rory, we're heading out!" Cerene crawled through the tent, Madness and Tobias behind. The children played by the fire. "Do you mind keeping an eye on the kids while we're gone?"

"Of course not." Aurora wanted to see inside the walls of Caris, but it was too risky.

"Oh, Cerene, let us come!" Kelsa begged. "We want to go!"

"Yes, *please*. We promise to behave." Philip pleaded next. "We won't touch a single thing."

Cerene hands found her hips. "It's not you two or Daria I worry about. It's *him*."

"Me?" Brooks scampered from his seat. "Why me?"

"Because you are too much like someone *else* that I know." Cerene's eyes turned to the last person filing out of the tent."

Alfonso stepped through. "What?"

Brooks waved him off. "Oh, I won't do what he says. I won't even look at him. I'll listen to you, so *please*!"

Daria even batted an eye or two at Cerene, sealing the ultimate guilt trip.

Cerene sighed. "Fine, but *one* thing out of place, and you're back at camp. Got it?"

The kids jumped with hoorays and quickly dressed. Alfonso complained about his apparent questionable behavior to Madness and Tobias, but they only turned in agreeance.

"Aurora, are you sure you won't come?" Tobias asked. "Baer is off hunting again, so you'll be here alone."

Aurora appreciated the kind gesture. "I'll go as far as the gate."

Madness seemed displeased, and Aurora reveled in it.

Refugees filed into the city by the masses in the mornings. Many went to beg for coin or sold their goods, while others went simply to escape the monotony of the passing days. The children bounced around, playing tag before reaching heavier foot traffic.

"Kids," Cerene called them to her side.

Alfonso caught up to Brooks and placed him on his shoulders, ceasing some of the chaos. Aurora watched Cerene's mouth form, *thank you*, and Alfonso winked.

"What is the deal with you two?" Aurora leaned to Cerene.

Cerene jerked her head. "I haven't the *slightest* clue of what you mean, Rory."

"Don't play coy with me." She had always been one weak for gossip.

"There is nothing like keeping a man on his toes, Rory." Cerene trotted along, her coiled hair bouncing with each step.

Aurora cocked her head, a smile spreading. "Why not now?"

"With the unpredictability of each passing day, with the war. . . "Aurora noted the sadness and hope in Cerene's gaze. "I'm sure when the time is right, we'll give it a proper go."

What a romantic gesture.

At the gate, Tobias corralled the children to his waist. Alfonso put down Brooks, and the child ran with his friends to the Shifter. Madness lingered behind them. Aurora noted how he fiddled more with his pack of tobacco than she had seen before. Alfonso moved to his brother and tapped his shoulder.

"Kids, the rules inside the gates are far more serious than outside." Words stuck when they came from Tobias. "You must behave and not stir unwanted attention. Do you understand? It could cause danger to some more than others."

Tobias wore a long-hooded cloak, gloves, and boots to cover his silver markings and silver eyes. Alfonso's belt did not carry his Weapons of Ore. Madness and Cerene, too, had left their weapons behind.

"You know about my ax and hammer?" Alfonso lowered to the kids. "Well, if the Lightning Saints find people like me, or Tobias and Madness, we could be in big danger."

The kids' eyes held understanding. It was not the time to ask about why those with magic feared discovery, but whatever the reason, Aurora knew it went against everything in God's Code.

"I'll take my leave now," Aurora said. "If any kids want to come back, now would be the time to say so."

"I do." Brooks held deep-rooted fear. "I don't want to go."

"I'll find you a toy!" Philip offered. "Do you want a bear or wolf?"

Brooks thumped his chin for a second. "Um, a bear!"

"But *I* have a bear!" Kelsa complained.

"But I want one, too!"

"You can *both* have a bear." Cerene ended the fight. "Let's go."

Aurora and Brooks waved bye and headed back for camp. They skipped and hummed to the rhythm of their feet touching the ground.

It was like when Elaina and I would go and pick flowers in the fields. We would skip and sing, picking the prettiest of flowers along the way.

Brooks suddenly slowed, releasing Aurora's hand. "What's going on?"

"I don't want a bear anymore." His eyes and face scrunched up tight. "I want a wolf—a wolf like Tobias."

"Maybe next time." The others were too far ahead by this point. "Let Philip get your bear, so you and Kelsa—"

"If I run, I can catch up. Before they get through the gate!" And Brooks was out of Aurora's reach before she could even try to grab him.

Panic set in. Aurora's body was still far too frail to run and catch up. She jogged as quickly as her feet could carry her. She called out to Brooks.

"Brooks, stop!" The child refused to slow down. "Remember what Tobias and Alfonso warned against!"

But he kept going, and they were inside the gate before Aurora knew it. Her eyes glanced at the Lightning Saints patrolling at the top. Their eyes peered down at the commotion. Brooks weaved in and out of the crowds, only drawing more attention. Aurora could tell the refugees' souls were anxious, and the Lightning Saints were eager to fight.

This is bad.

To some relief, Aurora heard Brooks call out to the group, and Alfonso responded.

"Brooks, we were wondering where you went." Alfonso remained calm, but the guards kept their eyes on them. Madness lingered not too far from his brother.

But it did not matter, for three Lightning Saints jumped down from the wall and made their way to Alfonso and Brooks. Aurora halted, not daring to take another step. Her discovery would put Alfonso, Brooks, and every other mortal along the gateway in grave danger.

"What's going on here?" A Lightning Saint stepped up to them. His blond hair was pulled in a tight bun.

"Nothing wrong here, guard." Alfonso pulled Brooks closer to him. Alfonso lowered his stance, almost as if offering a bow. Aurora scowled, as saints deserved no such worship. "My brother here changed his mind in wanting to come into the city, is all."

"Your brother?" The guard raised his brow.

"Adoptive," Alfonso stated.

The guard looked down at Brooks. "What did you go back for, boy?"

But Brooks could not speak. Fear rippled out of his soul and into the world at the Lightning Saint. Pain and suffering were what saints had brought Brooks. This Lightning Saint was not different from the Light Knights that slaughtered his family and friends before his very eyes.

"Well?" The saint raised his voice, the electric rod in hand above his head. "Answer!"

"Guard"—Alfonso pushed Brooks back further—"he is new to the camps. He just suffered the loss of his whole family."

"I thought he was your brother?"

"He is my brother *because* of those recent events."

The goofy boy Aurora had become acquainted with became a protector. More guards jumped down from the walls and surrounded the two. One, a woman, stepped up and whispered into the other's ear.

"You need to come with me." The Lightning Saint reached for Alfonso. "There are rumors of the Resistance rising along our borders. We need to take you in for questioning."

He took hold of Alfonso's arm, but out of nowhere, Madness was between them. He fought to break the hold the Lightning Saint had on his brother. An evil crawled, one that pricked the very air.

Tobias grabbed Madness' waist, trying to break his friend's grip.

"We've done nothing wrong to you or to those of Caris!" Madness shrugged off Tobias and marched to the guards surrounding his brother. "What's so wrong with a kid changing his mind?"

"Back off, mortal." The blond guard shoved Madness, nearly knocking him over.

"Mad, go." Alfonso fought back now, but not for his sake. "I'll be back before you know it."

"*No*." A cruel voice poured. "What have *any* of us ever done to them? To *anyone?*"

A guard pulled out a long rod that sparked with electricity. "I need some help here!"

Alfonso fought harder, bucking and punching as Lightning Saints to reach Madness, but he was trapped in a frozen state. The Lightning Saints moved to Tobias, Cerene, and the children. Chaos was unfolding.

But something darker and more sinister than even the cruelest of nights and shadows Aurora could produce loomed in the air. It was magic unlike any Aurora had ever felt, and it terrified her. It was magic pooling from someone in the crowd. Some instinctual part of Aurora knew she had to do everything to keep it from exploding.

Aurora had never thought about the consequences of her actions, really. She did not think when it came to saving Luna or what would happen to the people of the Second Realm when she and the Dark Saints disappeared. She did not think of how the balance of the world would fall when the gods were gone. She did not think at that moment, either.

Shadows burst, spreading like mist through the gate. Aurora felt a power she only felt when needing to protect those she loved. Ice formed sleeves of armor and laced around her fingers like elegant black gloves. Her hair flowed like silk curtains caught in a windstorm. The power of darkness swirled around her, the mortals, and the Lightning Saints. Dusty shadows stilled, and the Lightning Saints lost their interest in the mortals.

"Release them, Lightning filth." The Goddess of Dark was before them, and she was a grander prize for the taking.

She rolled her shoulders and stood tall. Darkness consumed her eyes, filling them like the glistening star-filled sky. As strong as she forced herself to look, every part of Aurora screamed. There was no real power, only a small amount that kept Aurora alive, and it would die if this did not end soon.

It has to hang on until they're safe.

To her pleasure, the Lightning Saint obliged and released the mortals. Aurora sashayed over to the Lightning Saint, the one with the bun who had caused the mess.

"Why do you pick on the weak? Have you forgotten your teachings?" she asked. "Do you forget that you were once mortal? You were once defenseless, weak, and in need of help?"

The Lightning Saints cowered. Even in weakness, Aurora still brought fear to those below her.

But before the Lightning Saints could offer some excuse for his behavior, a crackling sound of a whip struck the ground.

Gods save me.

"Well, well." A familiar voice cooed. "How lucky am I that you stumbled into our borders?"

Bolt, the Advisor to the God of Lightning, hovered behind. Blesk only sent his advisor to do his dirty work.

Aurora faced Bolt and five other Lightning Saints at his back. Each was a member of the Inner Circle and held more power than regular Lightning Saints.

"It seems you've accumulated a new scar." Aurora stepped toward him. "It suits you."

"I got it a few wars back." Bolt traced the scar running from his eye down and across the rest of his face. "How long has it been? I've lost count after so many decades. So many wars were fought since you abandoned Nelabac."

Lightning Saints surrounded Aurora and the mortals, each heavy with bitterness and vengeance. She did not blame Bolt or the Lightning Saints. When Blesk disappeared, the responsibility for the Fourth Realm's safety had fallen on Bolt's shoulders. but Aurora felt no empathy for the advisor. Bolt had done this to her people, put them on the borders, and gave them nothing when they needed a hand.

"You can't imagine the shock Blesk felt when he learned what had happened in the last century." Electricity sparked over his palm. "How he reacted when he found the Fourth Realm in ruins because of your foolish decision."

"It was not only my decision," she threw back. "All the gods—"

"Don't 'all the gods' me!" Static swarmed. The Lighting Saints readied for an attack. Other refugees had already fled the gateway. "I was there, too, or do you forget? I was there when you suggested using a spell instead of slaughtering a tyrant!"

Bodies tensed from both sides, and the sparks on Bolt's fingers spiraled toward Aurora, but she did not break. She threw her right arm up, redirecting the lightning through the shadows and up into the sky. Her bones cracked, but Aurora silenced the pain.

"For one hundred years, I watched this world suffer!" Bolt stalked forward. The other Lightning Saints trailed behind him. "I watched your people flood the Fourth Realm from fear of death and of the wars around them. None of your people wouldn't have suffered if you hadn't played the role of hero!"

Bolt jumped into the air and slammed his hands together. His lightning spiraled right for the mortals. Aurora pushed her hands into the ground. Ice shot forward, shoving the mortals out of the way. Without a second to spare, lacing darkness across her arms, blocking Bolt's attack.

The clash of lightning and shadows sparked the gateway. Aurora screamed, struggling against the tiny fractures breaking up her fingers and arms. Even though the Lightning Advisor could not kill the Goddess of Dark, he locked on with such intent.

"Your saints would still be alive!" Bolt pressed. "Even Mako, your precious *Mako,* would still be alive!"

Her eyes flickered. The Altered Realm begged to take over and end her pain and this pathetic fight. In the place where Aurora and darkness met, she felt nothing other than power, but there was no room for error now.

Aurora's arms had shattered, but she still had her legs. Aurora pushed on Bolt and flipped back and away. Her feet hit the ground, sprouting ice under Bolt's feet. He went flying.

Aurora spun. The mortals were corralled. Lightning Saints pressed them closer together like sheep for the slaughter. Their spears pointed and charged with thousands of volts of electricity.

"Let them go! I'm the enemy here—"

But that had been their plan. Through the electrical currents circulating through the air around them, Bolt traveled and grabbed Aurora by the shoulders.

"I can't kill you, but this is a close second." Electricity buzzed. "Bye, bye."

Her body faded away, yet her consciousness remained. Aurora felt death as her body burned away and reformed in seconds that felt like hours.

Bolt stood above, watching her exposed body make itself again. Aurora's muffled moans consumed her as her lips reformed. The mortals' faces twisted in pain at her own. Bones, organs, and skin regenerated in an agonizing pain Aurora knew never existed.

"How does it feel to die twice, Aurora?" Bolt asked. "It's too bad I'm not Blesk. I would have enjoyed watching you disappear permanently."

Her body fought back, wanting to gain control of the shadows and become one with them, but her powers were out of reach.

The little left inside was not enough to bring her back to sanity, but it was enough to stop the agony in her body, the humiliation of her nakedness, and to keep the Lighting Saints from harming the mortals.

"Enough." Was all she managed. "Bolt—enough."

The Lighting Saints looked to their advisor. Bolt kicked Aurora over to her back.

"Are you embarrassed, Aurora?" Bolt teased. "Embarrassed that what you have to fight by your side are mortals? You're a failure, Aurora. We saints know it, the other gods know it. Even you know it."

"I'll . . . I'll do what you want." Aurora struggled to her knees. She slumped over to cover herself. "Please . . . please just leave them alone."

Bolt held up his hand, and the Lighting Saints stopped. "Will you come with us?"

Aurora's hair had somehow not fried with the rest of her. It hung loosely from the lace ties. "Only if you leave them alone."

"I don't want them coming back for you."

"They are just mortals, *Bolt*." Aurora looked at him and then at the mortals. Their eyes held horror, but not for themselves. "What can they do in the face of immortals?"

"Rory," Cerene cried out.

"Silence!" Aurora let her eyes flicker enough to scare them. "I am the Goddess of Dark! You will obey—"

"You have my word."

Madness' eyes hovered on that line of pink and red, but there was solidarity in his conviction. For once, Aurora was thankful for his coldness.

"Good," Bolt demanded. "Now, Aurora, take us home."

Aurora snorted, knowing what he meant. "Drag me through town—shame or shun me or do your worse, but I will not take you through the shadows. Through the Void. The palace is just there."

"Take only me then." Bolt waved his hand. "The rest will stay with the mortals to ensure they do not follow."

Aurora bit her lip.

"I refuse."

"Have you not been to the palace before?" Bolt pulled at her scalp. Aurora yelped in rage as she was treated like a rag doll.

"I know how that power of yours works. If you've been somewhere before, you can sink into their shadows. Now I'll ask again"—he pulled tighter—"have you been there!"

"Yes!" Everything hurt. "Yes, I have!"

This would certainly kill her.

"Wait."

Madness looked at Aurora and removed his shirt. He did not look away when he tossed it at her or when the Lightning Saints shooed him back. Aurora looked only at his offering because if she looked into those rose-pink eyes to thank him, she would break. The shirt was just long enough to cover the parts of her that mattered.

Bolt grabbed Aurora's scalp, making that his anchor for transport. The other saints held onto his leathers as Aurora steadied herself. Aurora shook, her breath uneven at the probability of her powers completely failing.

"If this kills me, you know what he'll do to you." She spat through her teeth.

Bolt leaned down and said, "Between you and me, Goddess of Dark, nothing would be sweeter."

Aurora did not linger on the comment and what it meant, on what inner conflicts took place in the Fourth Realm over the last century. Aurora lowered her eyes to the mortal's feet. Lighting Saints pointed their electric rods, threatening them if they so much as breathed too deeply, but despite their cruelty, Aurora knew the Lightning Saints would abide by their agreed rules. The mortals would remain safe, and Aurora would gladly suffer again and again if it meant so.

The Void found her then.

The pockets of darkness only existed for Aurora. It was a mode of transportation to places she had seen prior, but it taxed on her body. It was a power she used in times of great need or desperation. Aurora searched for the familiarity of Blesk's throne room and its absurd grandness, and she found it—and her body sprawled on its crystal flooring.

She gasped, reaching for air to hit her lungs. Aurora's skin pulled at gravity from the shadows, calling her home.

But she was distracted.

"Get up." A Lightning Saint pushed Aurora to her feet, settling those senses to fall into the Void. Aurora knew if she used that power again, anytime soon, she would cease to exist. The Void's hold on Aurora was far too strong.

The Lightning Saint practically dragged her through the palace, eventually needing assistance.

Let them drag me to the old coot.

Each step through the large throne room jarred the fractures in her body, but Aurora endured, barely conscious to notice much pain. The Lightning Saints dropped her on a mustard-colored velvet rug.

At the top of the crystal staircase sat a tiny man surrounded by floating pockets of green lightning.

"It's good to see you, Aurora."

Aurora looked up at Blesk, the God of Lightning, eyes blazing.

You will not break me.

Madness Hunt

Part II

The Boy

CHAPTER 7

Madness hated Lightning Saints, but after the last five days, he now loathed them. They not only hovered over his and his family's every move for five days after they dragged Aurora away, demanding not only their whereabouts and conversations but taking what little food they had and bullying their neighbors for information they did not possess.

I'm already a prisoner from within. I don't need further confinement from everywhere around me, as well.

Alfonso and Cerene kept Madness calm, assuring him their circumstances would pass. Much like Madness, Tobias was on edge. He stalked camp anxiously, unable to settle for more than a few minutes at a time. Madness knew it came from his friend's time at war and at the unpredictability of an enemy. They saw what happened to Aurora and how she dissipated and reformed. At the bat of an eye, they, too, could turn to ashes, only they wouldn't be reborn.

"That stupid girl."

No, not girl. She is a god.

When the Lightning Saints had returned them to their camp, Alfonso explained what Aurora had told him about the events one hundred years ago. It made him resent her more.

She was the reason the Second Realm was a war zone. The reason his and Alfonso's families had died. The reason Manda and Last Hope were slaughtered. She was the cause of so much pain. But, even so, the pain Aurora had felt and screamed out into the world when she was burned was a pain Madness wanted Blesk and the Lightning Saints to pay for.

No one should suffer like that, not even her.

The Pull pressed against his chest. Madness' cursed magic had always had a hold on him and on his emotions and every thought. The Pull wanted more power, but Madness struggled every today to silence it. He lit another roll of tobacco to subdue his magic, The Pull.

That raging bitch—with everything that's going on, she's just begging to—

"What you up to?"

Alfonso joined him. The Pull faded, as it always did in his brother's presence. His brother was the only shining light this life. The reason Madness pushed through every single day.

Thinking." Madness said.

"Not too hard, I hope." Alfonso poked at the fire. "You tend to overthink, brother."

"Those saints did a number on me."

"At least they are gone." Alfonso kept poking. "Everything could have ended very differently."

"Yes." Madness hated agreeing. The Pull knew Madness' weaknesses and exploited them at every opportunity.

"I'm glad Rory came to our aid."

"It's Aurora. *Not* Rory." Madness corrected. "She's not our friend, Alfonso. And we were never hers."

"We met her as Rory. She'll always be Rory."

Something else lay on his brother's mind, but Madness signaled for his brother to hold it.

With the Lightning Saints gone, their morning routine returned.

Before the kids and Aurora joined Madness and the others, they regularly visited their neighbors, met up with informants that had traveled from Dandfol about the Resistance, and trained deep in the woods. Kelsa, Philip, and Daria stayed in the tent with Brooks. None of the children wanted to leave the tent. They were too scared of what lay beyond their immediate surroundings.

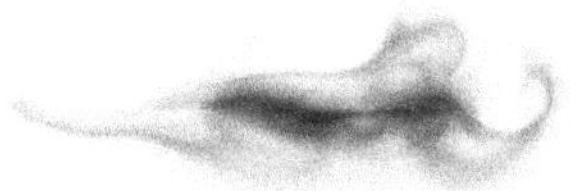

Madness calmed a little with the return of his routine. He visited their most-direct neighbors. He was glad to hear most were doing well and nothing was out of sorts. When day turned to night, Cerene warmed broth. It was enough to warm the children's bellies and send them to bed early.

The kids held sorrowful eyes, Brooks especially. He had lain in the tent the last five days, crying into the stuffed bear Kelsa loaned him. No matter how many times Alfonso and the rest of his companions reassured him the events were not his fault, Brooks never believed them. His cries only stopped when he dozed off.

"Those kids." Cerene stepped out of the tent from tucking them all in. She took a seat beside Tobias and placed her head on his shoulder. "We need to get them to Dandfol. It's not safe for them here anymore."

Staying with the rest of the refugees at the border was dangerous. Tobias and Cerene feared retaliation from the Lightning Saints was not far away and that they would enforce newer, stricter laws with the return of the gods.

"Do you think it's time?" Alfonso asked. "Will your parents *finally* let you join?"

As a group, they had discussed joining the Resistance, but Cerene's parents had refused time and time again. The four of them would never separate, so they did what they could at a distance.

"I feel my parents have no choice in the matter," Cerene said. "The real war is coming."

They sat in silence. Not even a bad joke or two. Cerene gave Baer broth, but the beast did not want it. No one wanted to eat.

"Do you think they're torturing her?" Cerene finally broke. "Torturing Aurora?"

"What? No way." Alfonso put down his bowl. "Even if they did, it's not like they could kill her. You heard what Rory said: only a god can kill a god."

"You saw, same as me, how the lightning split Rory into millions of pieces, and she glued right back together. How she shrank in pain and embarrassment." Cerene stirred the pot further. "Just because she's a goddess doesn't mean the human in her is gone."

"That's exactly what it means, Cerene." Madness slammed the bowl.

"She still feels!" Flames illuminating Cerene against the night. "I mean, you saw how she fought for us—Grounds Below, how she would have *died* for us!"

"As she should. She's the one that put us in this predicament!"

"She's trying to right her wrongs!"

Tobias growled. "Can we please—"

"She is only sorry for herself and that she lost everything!" Madness never raised his voice to Cerene, the kindest person he had ever met, but she was wrong. "She is an immortal being who is only out to protect herself."

"Then she would have let those Lightning Saints kill us."

"Enough!" Tobias rumbled loud enough to be heard across the entire camp. The camps around them did not look their way, but Madness knew they listened. Gossip had spread that the Goddess of Dark had been captured and was being held in the God of Lightning's castle. Madness knew some suspected that person had been their "friend" Rory.

"None of you understand what she is, what she has done, or what she must do!" Tobias rose to his feet. "Aurora is one of the rulers of this world. We do not get to decide if her decisions were mistakes or not. The decisions of a god have no right or wrong."

Tobias had always been devoted to the Gods of Nelabac. He had been a child during the times of the gods, had fought in their wars, and watched countless of his kind, his friends, and his family die for them. Madness understood his friend believing in something more powerful than himself but could not understand, with everything he had suffered, why Tobias still believed in Aurora.

He'll learn when everything he's found is taken from him.

"The real war, one I fear will decide the true fate of this world, is coming." Tobias continued. "I don't want any of you near it."

"What?" Alfonso said. "You're not coming with us?"

"Take the children to Dandfol, and convince your parents to halt their attack."

"Tobias, I don't understand." Cerene faced him. "We promised never to split from one another. The five of us, always!"

"Cerene," Tobias took her hands, "I spoke to one of my informants who came directly from Dandfol. He told me the word is spreading that Aurora and the other gods are back, and with it, the Resistance wants to unite for war."

"Then we can go to Dandfol *together*."

"But the alliance can't happen without Aurora." Madness heard the pain in his dear friend's voice. Cerene was his friend's chosen sister. Leaving her was an impossible choice for Tobias to make. "The Resistance will fight with or without Aurora at their side. You need to save what people of the Second Realm remain so we can enjoy it as we once did when all this is over."

"So, you're leaving us?" Cerene demanded, using the voice they all feared. The one that meant blathering their ears off until she got her way. "You're leaving me? To do what, find help?"

Tobias gave her a look, and Cerene's eyes widened in an unspoken acknowledgment. Madness and Alfonso glanced at each other. They both were clueless as to what secret their two friends had kept from them, but whatever it was, it was enough to tear these two apart.

"I see." Cerene was rarely defeated. "I see you've picked them over us."

"Cerene, it's not like that. I need their help—"

"Oh, but it is, Tobias." Cerene held back tears. "We've been together since I was nine. The two of us have been friends since I was twelve! I need you. Gods, I need all of you!"

Madness could not take the idea of his family being split apart. Tobias was his dearest friend, and Cerene his joyous little sister. Without them by his side, what was the point?

He stormed away from camp for the woods. He needed space, a place where the breeze swept through and took his thoughts with it. The fighting and bickering meant nothing to him. Ensuring they were somewhere safe, *that* meant everything.

Somewhere far from where the mass of this war was to ignite in full at any moment.

But Madness was powerless to that. There was nowhere safe in the world of Nelabac.

If it's not even safe for a god, how can it be safe for the rest of us?

Even if he resented her, Madness knew they needed her for the wars to come. She was the symbol of their realm, and the people would look to her as hope. Aurora Goddess of Dark would turn the tides of the war, but not from that castle where she was being held hostage and tortured.

Madness thought of her final moments before Bolt forced her to sink into those shadows. It was a longing pain, watching her fight for them. To see her exposed—gods, he wanted to crush the Lightning Saints for putting her through that.

"Having a change of heart, Madness?"

It was awake.

"Stop it."

"But, am I wrong? You see, she has value."

"Go away!" His fingers stiffened on the box of tobacco. It was not until Aurora showed up did The Pull speak and controlled his thought so heavily again. Not since childhood, when Madness never knew control over The Pull existed in the first place, had It pulled at his soul so strongly.

Please, he begged silently. *Go away.*

Something rubbed against his shin. Baer's sweet eyes looked up at Madness concerned. Even if the beast did not know their tongue, Madness knew Baer understood.

"We have that in common, don't we, little guy?" Madness scooped Baer in his arms. "Sometimes sharing what's going on inside is not that easy."

"Hey."

Alfonso crouched beside his brother.

"He brought you here?"

"Of course, he did."

"He knows what I need." Madness scratched at Baer's head. "As do you."

Alfonso grinned. "Cerene is going with Tobias."

"She convinced him?"

"More like if Cerene doesn't get her way, then there will be consequences."

"That's Cerene for you."

"No better girl out there." Alfonso smiled. Madness had always noticed the way his brother and Cerene acted. Their nurturing and constant bickering with one another. Madness would let his brother decide what to do with those possible feelings. Madness assumed they were both waiting for the war to end so they could care for one another on a deeper level without fear of losing the other too soon.

"Do you want to go and join the Resistance?" Alfonso asked.

"You know we can't, Al." Madness put a hand on his head, the other shaking the tobacco roll to his mouth. "You know we need to stay secluded, just in case—"

"I know." Alfonso reached for his brother's hand. "I know, but I also know you'll be worried sick if we stay separated from them."

"Yeah." Madness mustered.

Silence filled the air. The brothers sat, looking at each other, the sky, or the dimming campfires.

Alfonso broke first. "They're going to rescue her."

Madness fumbled Baer. "Why? Why are they doing something *so* stupid."

"Because we need her. We need her to win the war." Alfonso moved carefully. "I believe Aurora is the only one who can stop the Goddess of Light."

"There are five other gods to stop her!" Madness shrugged. "Luna is a tyrant, Alfonso. We've been fighting her saints and followers for the last one hundred years, and I'm sick of watching our people die. Let the gods take care of her. Let Aurora clean her own mess!"

"I did leave out one detail the other day." Alfonso's purple gaze looked through the glasses and Madness' soul. "When I told you what Aurora shared."

You know the Goddess of Light is her sister, right?"

The world fell silent.

"The Goddess of Light is Aurora's sister."

Madness' heart skipped.

"It was then I forgave her for the war. For leaving us defenseless for the last one hundred years." Alfonso reached for Baer. "Aurora did for Luna what I would do for you and what I know you would do for me. We know all too well what it's like to be controlled from the shadows."

Madness scowled at the bandage on his forearm. Underneath the wrappings held hideous scars of the past—parts of him that only Alfonso and his friends knew about. Concealed were the parts of Madness he hated the most, yet those were the parts Alfonso and his friends found a way to accept. Even when Madness had done unspeakable acts, Alfonso loved him. Forgave him. And he always would.

Madness almost laughed.

"Come."

Madness marched back to camp, Alfonso and Baer heavy on his heels, and barged into the tent.

"Change of plans," he announced, "for everyone."

"What do you mean?" Cerene asked.

"We're sticking together."

"No, Madness," Tobias argued. "We can't. What I need to do—I can't put you both at risk."

"What?" Madness felt something like joy when he said, "You think we're going to let you two rescue Aurora without us?"

And like that, five mortals agreed the only way to save the darkening of their realm and the rest of the world was to join a war among immortals.

"There's no going back."

CHAPTER 8

With numerous and unknown challenges ahead, they planned swiftly.

"Where do we start?" Alfonso whispered over the fire.

"Getting the refugees out of here and to Dandfol will be our biggest hurdle," Tobias grumbled. "Retaliation from the Fourth Realm is bound to happen, too."

"I'm sure they'll be happy to have us out of their hair, though." Cerene pierced her lips. "I'm sure they're ready to clear out the pets."

"Who will care for the children in Dandfol?" Alfonso asked.

"Both Philip and Daria have family within the Resistance," Cerene assured them. "I'll see to it in the letter that Kelsa and Brooks are also cared for."

"This is great and all," Madness interrupted, "but how are we going to convince the refugees to leave the Fourth Realm? To leave what little protection they have to trek across the Second Realm? Dandfol is well over a month's journey—two with a group this large."

"How can we ensure their safety?" Cerene agreed.

"All we can do is tell them the truth," Tobias spoke honestly. "The truth about Aurora and what's to come and make what decision is best for them."

Cerene furrowed her brow. "There must be more we can do."

"Not everyone survives war, especially the innocent," Tobias stated. "We need to let everyone decide their own route in this war, Cerene. That is the freedom we want. The freedom we are fighting for."

Madness saw the fight in Cerene, but it settled, knowing Tobias was right. Not everyone would want to leave or believe leaving was the safer route, but letting the citizens choose what was best for them was part of what they were fighting for.

"Next task: how are we going to rescue Aurora?" Alfonso leaned back. "We are breaking into a *god's castle*, after all."

"We'll cause a distraction," Tobias said.

"What in God's Name is going to distract saints and a god?" Alfonso chewed his bottom lip. "What, we get into a big brawl outside the castle?"

"This is where we split into two teams," Tobias explained. "Alfonso and I will cause the distraction while Cerene and Madness go with Baer to the palace." The beast gulped at his name. "Baer will pass as any cat catching pest. Once he's in the castle, the protest will begin, which gives you two"—he pointed to Cerene and Madness—"the chance to find Aurora."

"Lightning Saints will have to leave their posts when the distraction starts," Cerene nodded along. "With them distracted, the idea is to rendezvous with Baer, and hopefully Rory, and make it out of the palace grounds and escape into the chaos."

"Exactly."

Hundreds of complications brewed through Madness's mind. They were a band of Magicals and humans. What chance did they stand against a god and saints?

Madness did not like leaving Alfonso unprotected and without him. He knew his brother was capable of defending himself, but Grounds Below, anything could happen with immortals involved.

"Full of doubt, Madness?"

Since they did not go to the Caris five days prior, he was out of tobacco. Madness rubbed his palms together, their friction his needed distraction. He hated when the pull called on him when he was with his friends, and it had only worsened. Almost every day now, it teased, egging him to give in.

Madness eyed Alfonso, hoping he would notice, but his brother remained unaware. His eyes were half shut, just waiting for the okay to sleep. Madness managed a grin, and The Pull left.

"What is this distraction going to consist of?" Alfonso inquired. "I'd like to know what I'm getting myself into."

"You'll know in due time," Tobias said. "After we've successfully rescued Aurora, we'll head out of Caris and to one of our contacts not too far from the border."

"Members of the Resistance?"

"Yes, and good friends of ours," Cerene said. "They'll be glad to take us in."

"Now, everyone, sleep." The steadiness of Tobias' voice offered comfort. Their friend had the most experience in life and in war, and maybe that would lead them to succeed. "Tomorrow, we start spreading the word of the departure. We have lots of ground to cover while doing our best *not* to look suspicious. I'm sure the Lightning Saints remain watching our movements."

With so many people in the tent, Madness felt even more trapped than usual. His head raced, the thoughts never ceased. He made his way outside. The open sky normally calmed him, but he only thought of Aurora.

She believed in her sister, even when the world did not. He resented the Goddess of Dark for betraying her people but admired her for sticking by her sister. The one she loved before any other, much like him and Alfonso.

Madness did not know how, but they would rescue their friend—

God. She is a god.

Madness would keep her at a distance, but deep down, he knew only time would tell if the ice sharpened around his heart for her would remain or melt away.

Over the next three days they spread the word of Aurora, the gods, and of their plan to save the Second Realm and Nelabac. They split into four groups to cover more ground, the children accompanying them. Kelsa tagged along with Madness. He enjoyed her the most of the four children. She was kind and proved rather convincing to those who found him unpleasant.

The five days following, refugees filed out in groups. The Lightning Saints took little or no notice of the dwindling displaced Second Realm citizens. Madness was sure Caris and its citizens were thrilled to see the lands outside their city clearing. With one day remaining before the rescue missions, they were hard at work, helping the last few hundred refugees pack up their belongings for their journey to Dandfol.

So much work for that damned girl.

More refugees wanted change than expected, especially the elders. None of them lived during Aurora's reign, but their parents and grandparents had, and they had kept fate in her return.

Manda had stuffed the belief of the Gods of Nelabac down his throat. But they had destroyed the world; how could anyone place faith in them?

"Because people need something to hold onto in the darkest of times, Madness." The Pull interjected its unsolicited opinion. *"No matter how absurd it seems, people need hope."*

Kelsa was with him, so Madness ignored The Pull, not wanting the child to witness his struggle.

Then, as if she had read his pain, Kelsa took his hand. "Let's head back to camp."

A kind tug back to reality.

"Right." Madness returned the squeeze, his silent thank you.

Kelsa ran to the other children and discussed her day. Madness noticed the improvement in Brooks' mood over the last few days. He had grown less distant and reserved. The shock of losing his parents and the incident with Aurora had traumatized him in ways no child deserved.

It was within Madness's abilities to numb emotional pain, but he never used that power. He only did so when someone's pain was unbearably endless. Madness had learned that feeling pain made the difference in one's strengthening or breaking. He had considered numbing himself to his own despair, but Madness feared what that would do to his friends. To his brother. His power.

If that power was released, they would be doomed.

By the fire, Cerene sat. "How did it go today?"

"Most in the inner sector of the eastern wall has departed," Madness said.

"Any deciding to stay behind?"

"Some, but not nearly as many as I expected," Madness eyed Kelsa. "This one is a convincing speaker."

"Is she now?" Cerene turned to the girl and grinned. Kelsa bit her lip in a sweet smile, knowing what Madness said was true.

Tobias summoned Cerene and Madness from the tent. Baer was curled in Alfonso's lap, and Tobias packed his belongings. Madness took a seat beside his brother. The heaviness of the day drifted away.

"Out of roughly twenty thousand, Second Realm citizens, almost sixteen thousand have left or will be gone by tomorrow," Tobias explained.

"The others believe this is the safest place for them." They saw the hurt in Cerene's eyes. She was a caretaker and giver, and leaving anyone in harm's way brought her great distress.

Tobias took her hand. "There is a greater purpose at hand."

"Tomorrow's the day." Reluctantly, she moved on. "Mrs. Deloris agreed to watch over the children on the way to Dandfol—"

A shiver traveled down Madness' spine. Fall was coming, but the shift in the weather felt like the winters found deep in the northern parts of the Third and Sixth Realms. Where the mountain tops stayed white all year round and the sun never shone. Then, screams erupted.

Outside, snow fell, soft and gentle. The coolness of breath took form in the chilly air.

"I see you."

Madness stiffened. "Did-did one of you say something?"

"No?" Cerene shook her head. "Why? What did you hear?"

Alfonso stepped to his brother. "Was it—"

"No. It wasn't *that.*"

The whispers traveled on a draft, in and out of their ears like a playful melody. As if settling in for a long winter, the chill burrowed deep into their bones. Around, the other refugees were stepping out of their tents to take in the phenomenon.

But Madness and Tobias knew this was not simply snow.

They saw her only when the snow took shape in the harsh gusts of the wind. Snow danced in a fearsome rage. She wanted them to see her as a higher being. A deity not to worship, but one to fear.

Snow covered the entire landscape in a blanket of white. Madness and the others struggled to stay on their feet from the relentless sleet. The cloaked figure lowered. She hovered in a long, beaded white gown. It and her snow-blonde hair remained still in the maddening wind. Diamonds, opals, and a large moonstone draped her head like a crown.

The illusion of the Goddess of Light possessed power Madness had never seen or felt.

If she is this intimidating as an illusion, what's the extent of her true power?

The snowy figure reached out a hand. Gales of wind strong enough to stir mountain tops stripped their lungs frigid. Madness spotted the trees, grasses, and underbrush through the sleet and wind. Show hardened to sheets of ice. Crackling, aching pain echoed through the camp.

Madness knew what was coming.

"Take cover!"

He grabbed Kelsa and fucked as the life around them shattered. Shards of ice sprinkled around the refugees. The Goddess of Light shattered everything in her path, striping her enemies of their safety in the chaos. This was only a taste of what lay in waiting for those daring to oppose.

And as quickly as she had appeared, she was gone.

"Are you all right, Kelsa?" Madness looked the child over.

She nodded *yes*, but she cried. "You're bleeding."

Madness felt open wounds along his back. He looked at his friends, who, too, bore injuries. Cerene's hands were bare, with cuts. Tobias covered a wound over his cheek, and Alfonso's head bled.

Campsites and belongings scattered the barren campground. Other Second Realm citizens cried and pointed at the sky.

Madness rubbed Kelsa's back, comforting the child. "We'll be okay, don't worry."

Madness felt this was a lie because the light had taken every place and every person any of them had ever loved.

And she'll continue like this until her sister is dead and Nelabac is under her command.

This had been a warning: do not meddle. Luna wanted them to flee and never think of Aurora again, but her threats wouldn't work. Somehow, Luna knew they were going after Aurora, but she did not know anything about them. She did not know that the strength of a human soul was ten times that of a saint's or a god's.

Madness stood taller in his decision to rescue Aurora. The destiny of Nelabac lay in the light or dark—and darkness had to win.

Chapter 9

They had walked with the morning sun to the Fourth and Second Realm border. No Light Knights were hanging in the trees or lingering in the bushes. Madness assumed they had departed or they were not allowed to attack such large groups.

Parting with the children hit Madness harder than he anticipated. They each had brought a lightness to their camp and had filled it with laughter.

"We want to go with you."

Brooks pleaded, gripping tight to the stuffed bear. Daria, Philip, and Kelsa stood beside him. Despite Brooks' plea to join them, he and the other three held fear in their eyes. They had witnessed firsthand what happened in war.

But we are going to fight for them. To let them have a childhood before it's too late.

"We talked about this." Alfonso lowered and took Brooks by the hands. "War is no place for children."

"But you're only, like, twenty-something!"

"You're right," Alfonso said, "but I'm a bigger kid who needs to go and do this. And when you're a bigger kid, you can do it too."

"I can be like you?" Brooks asked. "Like Mommy and Daddy?"

Madness knew the loss of Manda and Gabe wounded them each, but it cut Alfonso deepest. Manda and Gabe had treated Madness and Alfonso like their own, but the couple had held a special place for Alfonso because of his friendship with Brooks.

"You can be just like your mom." Brooks collapsed into Alfonso, and he just let him cry.

A tug pulled at Madness' pants. It was Kelsa, looking up with begging eyes.

"You be strong, okay?" He squatted to her level. "And don't let Brooks get out of hand."

Kelsa wrapped her arms around his neck.

His hands hovered in the air. He didn't know what to do. No one hugged him, not even his brother. But slowly, naturally, Madness' arms lowered to return the embrace.

"I know you'll be okay, Madness," she said.

He smirked. "We'll *all* be okay."

Once goodbyes were over, the kids were handed over to Mrs. Deloris. Madness and his friends watched until the kids were nothing but distant shadows.

"You guys ready?" Tobias asked.

"More than ready," Alfonso answered.

Cerene walked toward the gate first. "Let's go get our friend back."

Baer rode on Cerene's shoulder, his tail twitching. Tobias shifted back and forth, uncomfortable in boots. He typically wore only a cloak and undergarments, as they were easy to remove for his transformations, but now he wore gloves and boots to protect his identity.

"*Nervousness is a good thing, Madness.*" The Pull called. "*I would be worried if you were not.*"

The camps were abandoned. Debris and broken tents scattered the landscape. Items were left behind.

"Luna's display persuaded many refugees to leave," Cerene scanned the land. "Most refugees that had refused to leave over the last week plan to over the next couple of days."

"Many are going to need to go into Caris for supply, too," Tobias added. "It will be easy for us to slip in."

"I guess we can thank Luna for *one* thing," Madness said.

The gate was miles back. Madness did not want to mull over the tasks ahead, and he sensed no one else wanted to, either. So, to ease their nerves, he asked, "Fall or spring?"

The polls continued: birds or bats; swords or shields; ale or liquor. And through the many lists, Though, it was pie or cake that created the most debate.

"Cerene," Alfonso argued, "no one prefers a freshly-baked pie when a nice fluffy cake is sitting in front of them."

"Cakes are a dime a dozen, Al," Cerene counted. "But a pie—I mean, a *good* pie in today's age is priceless."

"It's priceless because people are giving away pies for free!"

"I would never have guessed *pastries* to make or break this relationship," Madness rolled his eyes.

"I know." Tobias chuckled. "Everyone knows the right answer is cake."

Madness agreed.

Static filled the air, and Alfonso and Cerene fell silent. The gate was in sight. They stopped and gathered in an abandoned tent. Once inside, Tobias took the lead.

"Entering the gate will go smoothly for the most part," he explained. "We must be on our toes."

"They know the Second Realm citizens are leaving the Fourth Realm, but they know why," Cerene said. "Guards are looking to question anyone for a number of reasons."

"*We*"—Tobias pointed to each of them—"especially need to be careful. Lightning Saints could be on the hunt for us for our relationships with Aurora. Maybe assuming we would go looking for here, despite the warnings."

Tobias added, his voice a stern warning. "No matter what happens, do *not* engage."

"Outside food and animals are not allowed from within the walls," Cerene said. "So—"

"What will that mean for Baer?" Alfonso held the beast to his face. "Do we have to eat him?"

The beast hissed and leapt back to Cerene.

"No," she laughed. "It means we will have to put him in my bag and hope for the best."

Tobias stroked Baer's head. "This is going to be a tricky operation. Not only because we have to hide Baer and my markings, but we also have a healer and a weapon wielder. Four Magicals to one group."

"Not your typical refugees." Alfonso crossed his arm.

"If the Advisor or Lightning Saint that was present when Aurora was taken is at the gate and recognizes us, Madness said, "it's over."

"Let's just hope it doesn't come to that." Tobias gripped his glove. "Remember, if anything happens while we are going through the entrance, ignore it."

"What we need to do is more important than what we want to do." Cerene's face was still, lacking her usual cheer. "I know, for some of us, it might be harder to ignore what's going on around us, but—"

"But, we must keep going," Tobias held Madness' gaze for a moment longer, a subtle warning for his friend.

"Follow the plan." Cerene squeezed each of their arms. "And see you all on the other side."

They adjusted their clothes and secured their weapons. Madness pulled on his bandage for good measure.

"Wow." Alfonso patted the pocket where his Weapons of Ore were stored. "We certainly are fools."

They disbanded and walked forth.

Tobias trekked ahead, followed by Madness and Cerene, looping in each other's arms and Baer in her bag. Alfonso fell to the rear. As Mrs. Deloris had mentioned, refugees packed inside the gates that day, gathering the last supplies they needed for their journey across the realms.

With so many people pushing to pass through the gate to reach the city, Madness lost sight of Tobias and Alfonso to the crowd, their clothing too similar to those around them. Madness glanced at Lightning Saints patrolling the top of the gate. There were more than usual, and the static consumed the air—

"We're maybe four feet inside, and already you're pulling at me." Cerene stroked his arm. "We don't want any unwanted attention, do we?"

Madness resisted her gaze. "No, we don't."

"I want this over, too, Madness." Cerene laid her head on his shoulder and whispered. "All of it."

He returned the gesture. "Soon, we'll have avenged everything they've taken from us."

Madness held Cerene's hand tightly as they shuffled with the crowd. Guards did not say anything as they passed, but Madness looked around.

Where was Al? Did someone take him—

"*Brother*, can you take my other hand?" Cerene intertwined their fingers.

Madness took the offer in an instant. "Sure thing, *sis*."

"We'll be fine." *Always steady. Always so confident and sure.* "We'll *all* be fine."

Lightning sparked a few steps ahead nearer the city entrance. A Lightning Guard stood over a man he had struck with an electric rod. The middle-aged man was ill, visibly drained of color, and suffering from a bad cough.

Not someone to take as a threat. As sure as the gods, not someone to deserve a beating.

Do not engage under any circumstance.

"I want the truth." The Lightning Saint leaned forward, the electric rod raised. "Tell me what you came for."

"Please, I swear." The man sweated profusely. "I have a family waiting nearby. My children are sick, and we are heading out today. I only need medication for the road—"

The Lightning Saint struck the man across the face with his boot, and blood spewed. The Lightning Saint pressed into the man's back.

"He's done nothing wrong, Cerene." Madness pleaded, almost desperate.

"We knew what we might face." Cerene pressed forward, her voice strained. "We mustn't engage."

This was hard for her as it was for him. They had to ignore what they witnessed for the greater cause. If they fought, they could be discovered, or potentially, The Pull could break free.

What would we do then?

"Please," the man bowed. "I beg of you."

"You dare ignore my request? You're a mortal—a human at that." The Lightning Saint pressed his rod against the human's throat. "This is going to go one of two ways, mortal: We can go about like this until your guts smear the ground and I put you on display for the rest of your people to see what happens when they deny a saint, or,"—he raised the rod again—"you can answer my question!"

The crowd gasped, too afraid to watch and too scared to run. This was why Madness never believed in their protectors. Why over the last twenty-seven years Madness had resented the Godly Order. Saints deemed mortals' disposable and forgot that they, too, had once been mortal before a god deemed them worthy. The Lightning Saint's vow to protect the mortals of the world had become a soiled declaration.

Disgusting.

And. felt his eyes shift. The Pull came undone.

Madness gripped the saint's wrist with the might of its equal. Malice and desire for blood that lived in Madness boiled to the surface. Static erupted from the Lightning Saint, though it only bounced along Madness' skin. He felt nothing but bloodlust.

"Who in God's Realm might you be?" The Lightning Saint shook his arm free.

"Brother?" Cerene walked around. "Where did you go?"

Madness said nothing as the anger within grew. Cerene had never been able to help Madness when The Pull was unleashed, but he needed her to try. "Over here."

The old man Madness helped had already scurried off. Madness did not blame him for getting as far away as possible.

"You know I have difficulty getting around without help," Cerene said. "Be a dear and get back over here."

"Your brother is interfering with an interrogation." The Lightning Saint never looked from Madness. "You are guests within the walls of the Fourth Realm."

Oh, how cruel of him. The Pull wanted to play, but Madness pushed it down.

"Oh, but kind saint, please." Cerene batted her beautiful eyes. "I know my brother is a hot-headed *idiot*, but I promise to keep him in check."

Gods, she's going to give me an earful for this later.

Madness stiffened at the thought, knowing Tobias and Alfonso would enjoy every moment of the scolding.

The Lightning Saint looked away as another saint, a woman with long black hair, jumped from the iron walls. She approached the saint before them. He nodded, though he did not appear happy.

"Go on ahead," she ordered, her eyes burrowing into Madness. "But, watch yourself, yes?"

Rather than striking fear through Madness, her remark filled his need to defend. His temper not only slipped mentally, but it boiled over. Madness felt the red hit his eyes.

Madness blinked and took hold of Cerene's arm. The black-haired saint walked away, leaving Madness and Cerene with the one.

"Before you go: What do you know of Goddess Aurora?" The Lightning Saint said. "The world knows she has returned, and Master Blesk seeks information on what lies she may have spread before her capture last week."

Madness furrowed his brow. "What lies?"

"That she has returned to save this world when she is the very one who destroyed it."

Madness looked to Cerene. "Look—"

"We don't have a gods-damned thing to share with you." Cerene beat him to the punch. "Now, good *day*."

Without a look back, they proceeded through the remainder of the gate. Madness had nearly blown their cover. Cerene rambled on, scolding him as they walked, yanking on his arm so tight Madness thought she would pull it out of its socket.

But Madness could feel nothing but The Pull. He saw nothing but Her pressing against his conscious, reaching to take control. He felt hollow, in need of a filling only The Pull provided.

"It's happening." Cerene realized.

"Almost."

"Imagine Al." Cerene set aside her anger. "Remember, we must reach Rory so we can stop what is happening to the Second Realm."

Aurora—the girl they had come all this way for. The girl Madness found himself nearly crumbling to save.

That centered him and pushed the reddening of his eyes away.

Why that damned girl?

Finally, they crossed into the city.

Caris remained prosperous and untouched by war. Rows of market stands filled the streets, buildings stretched as far as the eye could see, and the people moved freely. Kids ran cheerful, women laughed with shopping bags in hand, and men stumbled out of the bars they had slept in the night before. Madness wanted to yell, order them to look past their gardens and see the horrors that lay on the other side of their protective walls.

Madness shook the thoughts. "You see them?"

"See who?" Alfonso patted their shoulders from behind in an instant. Tobias appeared beside him.

Relief flooded Madness. Both his brother and his dearest friend were safe. They had all made it across the gate.

"I was worried." Madness slightly shoved his brother's chest.

"Yeah, I noticed." Alfonso's smile disappeared. "I saw you have a little moment back there."

Madness straightened his clothes. "Yeah, and?"

"Yeah, *and*—are you good?"

"He's fine," Cerene reassured, stepping between them. "Let's get off the streets so we can talk, yes?"

"Lightning Saints might be watching our every move now," Tobias agreed. "No more surprises."

Madness shrugged off his brother and friends and strode into the streets of Caris. He didn't need their chiding, not when so much already went on inside his own head.

Alfonso Hunt

CHAPTER 10

The four weaved their way through masses to the narrow neighbourhoods'. The alleyways of Caris were polished, so clean of outside filth it was as if the ground carried electricity to zap anything away that was not meant to be there.

The people of Caris, citizens of the Fourth Realm, moved with freedom resembling ignorance. They strolled through the streets, pockets full and bellies fat. Off appearance alone, one easily spotted the difference between the citizens of the Fourth and refugees of the Second.

People of the Fourth Realm dressed in fine robes and linens, and crystals and imperial topazes draped across their bodies like tangible bolts of lightning. The humans were no saints but were proud of their realm all the same. The people of the Second Realm wore rags. Even inside the walls, Second Realm citizens moved like animals on high alert, scared to be feasted on.

After today, there would be no need to return to such a place.

They walked to the Merchant's Quarter, where they would find toys, cookware, weapons, and endless rows of trinkets in the dirty streets. Many were abandoned due to most refugees migrating to Dandfol, but some remained to sell their remaining goods. Cerene peeped inside every tent, speaking to those who had remained. Madness knew she cared about the people deeply, maybe even more than Aurora. Her parents worked hard to keep everyone who came to them in Dandfol safe and fed, but that kindness did not reach everyone, and he knew Cerene felt guilty for that.

Alfonso bounced around each tent, too, with the purpose of purchasing *everything*. In an armory, he wanted the blades and knives that decorated the tables, their hilts decorated with lions and ancient dragons. Some had Aurora's symbol—the waning crescent moon—while others bore no design. Regardless, Alfonso picked up each and displayed his skills.

"I've never understood why weapons are allowed to be sold within Caris,"—Alfonso tested a sword—"but we can't bring them in."

"Because the Lightning Saints take a portion of the sales," Madness explained. "A tax, they call it."

"Oh, Mad!" His brother picked up a two-handed sword with the sigil of a lion. "You should get this."

"I'll stick to my small and shabby sword, thank you." Madness patted his bag where his small sword was concealed. It was good for poking holes but not slaying enemies.

Alfonso pointed at his brother. "It's literally as dull as your jokes."

Madness knew Alfonso was attempting to move the stiff air around them. Alfonso did what he could to help his brother, but sometimes Madness' own stubbornness stood to test the thickest of air.

"Sir, if you're going to play around, get out." The merchant stormed from across the tent with a broom in hand and swatted Alfonso out the door. He tripped into the street.

"You deserved that." Madness leaned down to pick up his brother.

"*Not* another word."

Madness felt the weight of their quarrel lift off his shoulders. Madness never liked arguing with his family, especially Alfonso. Never Alfonso.

Tobias walked past them. "It's time."

They gathered away from peering eyes and ears. Once they were sure of their surroundings, Cerene took the helm.

"Madness and I will get Baer to the palace," she said. "You two get to work."

"You got the supplies?" Alfonso asked Tobias.

"We need to go to another part of town for what we need," the Shifter explained. "We'll meet at noon. That gives us about three hours."

"Right." Alfonso extended a hand. "Give over the coin. I'll be in charge of supply."

"Not so fast, Mister Big Bucks." Madness held the coin poach at his side. "Tobias will handle the money."

"What?" Alfonso snapped. "Why him?"

"Where should I begin?" Madness cleared his throat. "You want to buy *everything*."

"You'd spend it all in a soulbeat!" Cerene agreed.

"They're right." Tobias chimed in. "You will."

Alfonso pursed his lips and moved his hands. "*Wanting* to buy and *actually* making the purchase are two *very* different things."

"Yes, they are, however"—Tobias snagged the pouch—"you are someone that thrives on the fine line separating the two."

The group split into two: Alfonso and Tobias went back to the Merchant's Quarters, and Cerene, Madness, and Baer headed toward the palace. Madness worried for Alfonso, but he knew his brother could handle himself, but Madness never shook the fear that filled his soul whenever they were parted. It was like each parting indeed held their last moments together. Madness' stomach churned at the thought.

He and Cerene walked through the city. The palace's rising pillars and turrets came into view. Smoothed steel and other refined metals were used to craft the gaudy structure. It glistened in the sun as a shameful display of power.

There were a few worship halls in this part of the city, similarly designed in a grand fashion. The polished steel and topaz-filled symbol of lightning dangled across the archways and sparks of electricity bustled. Citizens shuffled in and out to chiming bells. Lightning Saints passed by, observing their surroundings and nothing more.

The wealthier citizens of Caris strolled through the city in shoes of velvet. The cobblestone streets were spotless. The Merchant's Quarter had covered his shoes in mud and gods knew what else. The shops' windows reflected the morning sun, the items behind it bathing in its warmth. Women sat outside cafes, sipping tea and eating pastries. Children ran and played in their imagination with dolls and plastic swords.

The palace was a few blocks over, and citizens and refugees mingled in this part of the city. Some spoke and even shared a meal. A crowd gathered and watched performers at a square decorated with spitting fountains. One shared fancy card tricks, and the others guzzled fire.

"We shouldn't linger." Madness wanted to press on for the palace.

"We have time." Cerene's eyes focused on the man and woman gracefully consuming flames. "And I've never seen a fire breather before!"

"I doubt a Fire Saint would be performing circus tricks in the heart of the Fourth Realm."

"Don't be such a downer, Madness," Cerene shooed him away. "While we can, we should enjoy the simplest pleasures of life."

"And those pleasures entail watching fire breathers?"

While Cerene watched, Madness observed. He did not listen to the refugees, for his people would not know the inner workings of the city. That knowledge lay with the nobles, the women and men sitting at tables discussing the economy and politics.

Most talked about the new restaurants or the parties and celebrations in the coming weeks. Some spoke regarding the gods' return, but not a word of Aurora.

Lightning must have kept that knowledge under lock and key.

But there was something more to the secrecy. From what Madness knew from Aurora and Tobias, as well as from rumors and ancient tales, the God of Lightning was a boastful man who took any chance for glory. He would want to show off his prize.

But why—

"I know about a stone."

The voice pressed right against his ear, like the loudest of birds singing in the morning before he was ready to rise. It tickled against his neck, but when Madness turned, there was no one.

"I heard a rumor about a powerful stone."

Again?

A tug came from the hem of his pants. Madness half expected to see a child or even Cerene playing games, but it was not. It was an older man half his height. Glasses protruded off the bridge of his large nose. One would think he was a Dwarf, but the man was lanky and dressed in a brown-pleated suit, though it was in desperate need of a tailor.

He makes Alfonso seem like he's got it all together.

"Can I help you?" Madness furrowed his brow at the peculiar man.

The man turned from the crowd toward the winding alleyways. He lifted a finger, beckoning Madness.

Madness searched for Cerene, but she remained enchanted with the performance.

I'll be back in a soulbeat. Cerene will never know—Madness chased down the man—*That's not true. Cerene* always *knows.*

Even with his tall stature, Madness struggled to keep up with the stout man. He followed him down the streets to a dead end where the man waited at a door. The doors throughout Caris were made of steel, but this door was black, half the size of the rest, and made of raw bark and tree material.

The man peered through the door and looked down both ways of the alley. "I heard a rumor about a powerful stone to seal the darkness."

Madness approached the door, but something stopped him. Something begged him to turn and *run.*

It was not The Pull, but it was his own damned common sense.

"What-what stone are you talking about?" Madness crouched, preparing to squeeze through the door's frame. "What does a stone have to do with—"

"Any of it?" The man entered, leaving the door open behind him. "Only *They* know the answer to that."

"They?" Madness crawled through. "They, as in, the gods?"

"I haven't a say, my boy. Haven't a say."

Madness had never liked riddles. He was not even sure if this *was* a riddle or if the man was simply messing with his head.

"We need to go." The Pull knocked.

Madness snickered. *Ah, so that was you begging to leave before?*

"Don't mock me, Madness. For once, you should listen."

Madness wanted to make it uncomfortable. Make it regret all the years of taunting and transformations. It was his chance to play.

The space squared too small for Madness to truly call it a room. Books lined the walls from floor to ceiling. Two giant barrels sat in the center of the space, holding odd trinkets and ornaments. Under the endless sheets of parchment spread across the floor, a foul smell rose from a purple carpet. Behind the counter and stained oak walls, clocks of all shapes and sizes hung, their hands either spun out of control or not at all.

"*Now, do you see my distress, boy?*" The Pull practically purred at Madness' realization.

I hate sharing a body with you. Madness reluctantly agreed they needed to make a hasty exit.

He turned for the door, but it flew shut and locked. The mottled curtains covered the windows and shrouded the room in darkness.

The man sprang up from the counter. His eyes observed the room as he leaned back in the air, folding his legs as if sitting back in a chair.

"Who in the Grounds Below are you?" Madness reached for his bag, for the hilt of his sword.

But Madness knew what this man was, what kind of ancient magic he possessed.

Wizards forged the magic of the mind and experiments. Like the other Ancient Magicals, their magic was believed a gift from beyond the gods. When the fight against the demons spewed five thousand years ago, they shared their magic with mortals, gifting the bloodline of Thinks, Magicals capable of peeking into someone's mind and learning their deepest thoughts or secrets or their next few moments.

The wizard lowered to the ground and extended an arm, palm closed. A red glow, like one of a controlled fire, escaped the cracks of his fingers. He opened his hand, and resting in it was a firestone. Colors of rust, tangerine, and blood filled the stone. Its smoothed edges were forged by the tools of a jeweller or magic. From the pressure pulsing from the stone, Madness guessed the latter.

"Take it," he said. "The Goddess of Dark will need it."

"What? How-how do you—"

"Don't worry about that part, boy. All will be revealed in due time." He smiled, placing the stone in Madness' hand. "That stone will help along the long path to defeat the Goddess of Light."

"Why would I believe this would help her when you refuse to answer any of my questions?" Madness stuffed the stone in his pocket. "Who are you?"

"You don't trust very easily, do you, Madness Hunt?" He crossed his hands behind his back. "I'm someone who has seen Nelabac through many lenses and experienced many lives, so I know the ways of this twisted world better than even the gods. So, as you prepare to partake in an unprecedented adventure, I offer you some advice: See the beings of this world with a fresh lens."

"Why would I see the world for anything other than what it has given me?" Madness asked. "Nelabac, those who control it, they don't want what is best for it."

"Time can turn a person into someone they never intended to be." He offered a weak smile. "As difficult as it is, do not blame saints for the faults of their gods. They have become cruel and wicked from all that has happened, not by their own thinking."

"What do you mean?"

"The soul of a saint reflects that of their god; they are bound together for eternity. They all are not what they've become—not all the wicked are evil."

Madness fell still. *If that were true, what would that make me?*

"Anyhow," the wizard said, "you have a friend looking for you—"

Cerene. Madness placed the firestone in his tobacco box.

"—And she does not seem very happy about you disappearing on her—"

"Yeah, I don't need you to tell me that."

"Then you better get going!"

With a flick of the wizard's finger, the door flew open and blew Madness out. Before he had a second to gather himself, he heard her.

"Where in god's name have you been!" Cerene used that tone he both loathed and feared.

"Do not forget this either, young Madness." The wizard's voice echoed through Madness' mind. *"Even a boastful sun is penetrable."*

Madness groaned for numerous reasons. He found his feet just in time for Cerene to deliver a hard smack across his arm.

"Cerene, you forget your strength—"

"And you forget *me*!" Her eyes carried a fierceness Madness did not want to detonate. "*I've* been looking everywhere for you. The performance ended, and I thought Lightning Saints had taken you!"

He fumbled with his tobacco box with the firestone inside. "I was just in this store with this strange man—" Madness reached for the door. But it was gone, replaced by the regular stone wall. "It was *just* here."

"We don't have time for this." Cerene dragged him along the alley. Gods, after today, he would never hear the end of it from Cerene. "Baer is getting restless, and we are running out of time. Noon is an hour away."

He knew now was not the time to convince Cerene of what he had witnessed, so instead, Madness followed Cerene through the streets of Caris toward the palace, holding the tobacco box in his hand, careful not to lose it.

CHAPTER 11

The palace's spiral-metal towers stretched beyond the clouds. Guards dressed in rubbers and equipped with electrical rods and spears patrolled the palace walls for any disturbance. Madness assumed with the gods waking, the realms in ruin, and Luna stirring the war, Lightning Saints were prepared for anything to happen.

"We need to walk around and find a place for Baer to sneak in." Cerene led the way.

They walked casually around the palace gates, acting more like refugees who had never been to Caris before. A few guards glanced in their direction, but Cerene flashed a smile and waved, and the guards went about their day.

On the northeast side of the palace walls sat a natural area with underbrush and a few scattered trees. At the base of the wall, a river ran through a small drain wide enough for Baer to squeeze through to enter the palace grounds. Both Madness and Cerene looked around before opening the backpack for Baer.

The beast crawled out and stretched. Rolling in the soft grass, Baer was blissfully unaware of his human companions and that it was time for his big task.

"Baer—Baer look at me." Cerene cupped the beast by his front underarms. His body dangled, and his focus fell on her. "You have to get in and find Aurora. Once she sees you, she'll know we are here for her. More than likely, you'll hear an alarm, and that's when we make our move to meet you and Aurora in the palace. Got it?"

Cerene lowered him to the ground. His honey-colored eyes widened, realizing it was time. He readied his paws, kneading at the grass.

"You're going to do great." Madness gave the little beast a good head pat. "The guards and other Lightning Saints won't notice a cat inside the palace once the commotion starts."

Baer rubbed his back against them both, then took off through the bars of the small drain. Cerene held the collar of her yellow tunic, eyes on where her tiny friend had disappeared. Madness put his hand on her shoulder, giving what small comfort he could.

"You know he'll be fine." He pulled her close.

"I know." She pressed her face into his chest. "But, if I lose anyone else to this war, Madness, I don't know what I'm going to do."

They found a small cafe with a decent view of the palace gate. The tea nearly took the remainder of their coin—not to mention, the cafe owner almost did not take their order, but thankfully Cerene knew how to swoon any man or woman. The two took their time, waiting.

"What are you doing?" Cerene gestured to his pocket.

Madness furrowed his brow. "What are you talking about?"

"In your pocket?" she laughed.

Madness ensured no one watched as he revealed the firestone. "This is what the guy gave me."

"What guy?"

"The one I saw when I wandered off earlier?" Madness said.

"Oh yes." Cerene sat back, crossing her arms. That attitude alluded. "When you ditched me."

"I did not—" *No point. It's Cerene. The woman is always right.*

In hushed tones, Madness explained the bizarre encounter with the wizard, the hole-in-the-wall shop, and the glowing firestone.

"He somehow knew exactly who I was," Madness said, "and our purpose for being in Caris."

"It's pretty." Cerene turned the firestone around and around. "All he said was it would be of use to her?"

"He said in due time it will all make sense—or something like that."

"You did not pay attention?"

"The guy was a wizard, Cerene. The whole scene proved rather distracting."

Cerene slid the stone back over. "Hopefully, Rory will know what to do with it."

If we can get her.

He doubted their plan. Between the Lightning Saints and the vastness of the city . . . the outcomes were endless. Deadly.

"Don't worry, Madness." Cerene's voice was like a general to her troops. "We'll get her back, and everyone will stay safe. I know it."

"Madness turned. "It's not her I'm worried about."

"Yeah, yeah, whatever you say."

The sun peaked. It was time. But as Cerene and Madness sat, waiting, they saw and heard nothing. Had they made it? It was possible Alfonso and Tobias failed and were revealed—

The ground rumbled. Then gasps echoed. And fire shot into the air. Explosions went off across the back walls of Caris, clearing the way for chaos.

Citizens scurried, fearful and unknowing. They listened to the breaking of metal and the walls crumbling. They didn't know the citizens of the Second Realm were about to fight back and change the war.

"Looks like everyone was on time," Cerene smirked.

They pulled out their weapons. The rescue mission was in play.

Several of the Second Realm citizens who learned what Madness and his friends were doing wanted to help, and they were the perfect aids in detonating the bombs. The range of the explosions would only damage and hopefully break the iron walls where they connected.

This *gives the citizens a taste of what it's like to be us.*

As planned, the Lightning Saints guarding the entrance to the palace scurried for orders. One along the top called out commands. Guards flooded out of the gates and dispersed to the streets. Between the running citizens of Caris and the unorganized Lightning Saints, Cerene and Madness made their move.

They sprinted toward the gate, sliding in behind the closing iron bars. Through the empty courtyard, they ran, and in the distance, they heard more shouting and more explosions.

Please be careful, you two.

"Halt!"

Two agents—Madness knew their rank by the thinness of their clothes and smaller, daintier weapons in their hands—ran toward them. Agents worked as spies or ambassadors between the realms and had the most training and drive to keep their god safe. Their weapons raised high, ready for attack.

Do not blame saints for the mistakes of their god. The wizard's warning rang through.

"Rioters have breached the walls!" One said.

"Oh, please,"—Cerene pulled out her bow—"that tacky wall *needed* to come down!"

Cerene moved like second nature in the face of her enemies. Madness hadn't seen her in true combat in so long, he had nearly forgotten just how gods-damned good she was. Cerene nocked her bow and fired at one of the agent's weapons, knocking the weapon from his hand with one shot. Madness drew his own weapon and sliced the other Agent across the abdomen, knocking him out. Cerene knocked out the other, came up from behind, and kicked the other across the face.

"Gods, I did it." Madness caught his breath. "How did we pull that off?"

"Exactly as Tobias said we would." Cerene ran forward, dragging one of the Lightning Saints with her. "With a bit of luck."

They tucked the unconscious Lightning Saints against the wall and peaked inside the palace.

Lightning Saints crowded the center foyer of the palace. Madness and Cerene pressed against the wall, trying to stay hidden. More Lightning Saints rushed and gathered closer to the door.

"I was hoping Baer would have been here by now," Cerene said.

"Maybe Aurora is on the far side of the palace, and they haven't reached us yet?"

"Or maybe the dungeon?"

"Even with the God of Lightning angry enough to take Aurora as a hostage, he wouldn't stick her in a cell." Madness tapped his foot. "Do we dare go in after them?"

"We wouldn't make it two steps before capture," Cerene sighed, "but I do believe we dare."

Lightning Saints continued to rush past. Then, he looked at the two knocked out by his feet.

"Put on their clothes." Madness grabbed the larger one's clothes.

"Their clothes are much too big," Cerene complained.

"Fudging a story dressed as Lighting Saints will be a lot easier than fudging one dressed as ourselves."

Madness felt they were out of tune with the latest trends, as if Lightning had not updated their wardrobe in over a century. Cerene's fit much too long. The collar pressed against her chin, the pants bunching at the top of her boots, and the glove was too large to grip properly. Madness' disguise fit too tight, nearly strangling his every body part. The glove didn't even fit over his hand.

"It's a good thing your clothes are so thin," Cerene giggled. "Or else you'd have to strip right here and now."

"Are you ready?" Madness held his sword. He worried about his tobacco slipping out of his pocket, but he also was worried about losing the Firestone.

"Yes," Cerene jumped, adjusting the clothes. "Let's go."

"Wait." Madness adjusted the goggles over her helmet. "Won't Lightning Saints will sense our mortal souls?"

"We have to hope there is too much chaos for anyone to take note." Cerene walked first. "The sooner we do this, the sooner we can take these ridiculous outfits off."

Madness and Cerene hugged the metal walls, making their way up one of the double staircases. The crystal floors refracted light from the stained-glass windows, filling the room with vibrant, colorful hues. Electricity bounced off the large metal chandelier.

Madness eyed the center floor. Behind the many bodies and boots of the Lightning Saints, he noticed the mural of crackling lighting, the Lightning symbol, embedded across the floor.

"Hide your right hand!" He threw his own and slapped Cerene's down. "They'll notice we are missing the Lighting symbol—"

"You two!"

Madness and Cerene tensed as a Lightning Saint marched in their direction. Her face pinched tighter as she approached, and an electric rod stood ready.

"What are you two doing?" Her arm extended toward the space below. "The Inner Circle ordered all agents to gather the rebels destroying our city."

"Are they really?" Cerene questioned.

"Excuse me?"

Madness elbowed her gut—*hard.*

"Ignore this one. She forgets her place." Madness snapped, instilling some confidence, reaching for any truth the Lightning Saint might believe.

"Where are you two headed?" The Lightning Saints moved closer.

Madness took a step back. "We were sent to guard the Goddess of Dark."

Cerene seemed to pick up what Madness was doing and followed his lead. "Orders from the top."

The Lighting Guard pinched her brow and stopped. "Who sent this order?"

"Bolt, of course. Rumors of an escape are floating around." Cerene backed away." He said it was top secret, only those of the Circle to know."

Madness knew they were caught. The Lightning Saint was sure to sense their souls—

But she was distracted—her attention of drawn to the main door.

"A crowd!" A Lightning Saints rushed in. "A crowd is growing!"

"Go!" The Lightning Saint's nose twitched slightly as she turned and hurried down the staircase. "They have come for her!"

Cerene and Madness took the opening and sprinted down the hall.

"You almost ruined everything!" Madness hollered as they ran. "What were you thinking?"

"I was thinking they were wrong." Cerene sighed. "We may be rebels, but it's for just!"

"If it fits one's agenda, they can make any situation whatever they want it to be."

The corridor opened to more metal hallways and stairs. On a relatively empty floor, clear of the enemy, Madness and Cerene caught their breath.

"We're running in circles." Madness huffed. "Why is this place so godsdamned big!"

"Because the man who owns the place must feel very, very small."

A loud boom poured from beyond the walls.

"Count on Al to create a grand distraction." Light danced behind Cerene's eyes. "And Tobias to support it."

Madness felt that same pride in his brother and his best friend, the two bravely facing Lightning Saints and leading the protestors, but he felt unsteady. As if something had gone astray.

"Let's just hope they don't get carried away."

Footsteps gathered at their backs. A large group of Lightning Saints, their clothing slightly different from those of the guards and agents, sprinted past. These saints wore yellow and black dresses or tunics and pants but still bore a glove on their left hand.

Missioners.

Cerene and Madness followed at a distance. Missioners did little work, taking care of the local towns and spreading good deeds. They possessed some power from their god, but not as much as agents and guards. Missioners had little to no combat training, but often carried a wealth of information.

"Please, where can we find the Goddess of Dark?" He prayed his voice reached them. There was only so much more he could handle. "We've been ordered to stand post—"

It was the chill that stopped his pursuit.

He knew that darkening chill. No regular cold darkened a room and stopped mortal and immortal beings alike.

Down the hall, a massive presence with glowing red eyes loomed in the shadows. Its massive size consumed the space and drool dripped down its growing fangs.

"Baer?" Cerene ran forward.

Behind him, she stalked with shadows and ice surging with the might of ancient dragons. Her hair waved like the currents of a river, and her eyes glowed with the force of everything dark in this world. The clear, crystal walls seeped black-like blood through veins. He nearly fell at the sight.

All this trouble for one girl.

And once she was within his grasp, those black eyes receded to the gray Madness had come to know.

She took one look and cocked her head. "Why am I not surprised it's you lot causing this chaos?"

Cerene embraced Aurora, not even noticing Baer. The beast gave a row rumble of disapproval, so Madness gave him a good scratch. The beast purred with satisfaction. "You did well."

"You all came for me." Aurora smiled, but her eyes told Madness a different story. One that read she wished they hadn't come.

"Did you really think we would leave you here?" Cerene held the god's shoulders.

"I'm plenty capable of caring for myself."

Madness snorted, retreating back to his quick ways with her. "You were in a bind, and you know it."

"Ignore him. This was his idea." Cerene added in a lower tone, "He was worried."

"You? worried? for me?" Aurora pressed her hand to her heart. "Why, Madness Hunt, you flatter me."

"Yeah, yeah, don't get used to it." Madness turned, not wanting her to see the blush he felt rushing to his cheeks. "We need to get out of the palace and find Alfonso and Tobias."

"I assume they're the ones creating the fuss?"

Madness and Cerene peeled the Lighting Saint uniform off, and the four of them ran down the halls. Aurora froze any and all threats with ease. In the center of the palace, guards stood in defensive rows, but Aurora flicked them like a bug crawling up her shirt. Shadows rushed over the enemy like a swollen river.

She's stronger than the last time.

"You!" At the doors, the Lightning Saint of the Inner Circle they had conversed with prior ran forward. "I should have known!"

Her fist twisted with anger, but Aurora, with a simple flick of the wrist, froze the woman in a block of ice "That one felt personal."

"We improvised." Cerene pressed on.

I now understand why she was so revered. Why, when Tobias speaks of her, his eyes gleam. When Manda thought she would save this land. Aurora's power is … remarkable.

A week ago, Aurora could barely move. Now, she was a whole new being—an entire new god.

Outside the palace, the courtyard was lined with at least three dozen guards and agents. Aurora halted, forcing Madness, Cerene, and Baer to do the same.

Madness stiffened, fear choking his throat.

Because before them was not only an army of Lightning Saint and Bolt at their helm—but the God of Lightning himself.

And Alfonso and Tobias at his feet.

Chapter 12

Madness felt his heart sink. A closer look, both Alfonso and Tobias were bloodied and beaten. He inched forward, but The Pull—no—instinct stopped him. Aurora held power greater than any Madness had seen, that was true, but Blesk, the God of Lightning, was on an entirely different level.

And Aurora was once stronger than this?

The God of Lightning resembled the wizard: small, gray-haired, and powerful. Unlike the wizard, though, Blesk's face held long wrinkles and a cold glare. An evil, stiff and tempered, haunted the god, but Madness sensed he was not always this way. Something had changed the God of Lightning, and not for the better.

Blesk's golden, velvet robe spread behind him displayed like he had not planned to stay for long. His silk tunic and pants, both shades of gold, showed his status as ruler. On the robe's golden clasp, the lightning symbol was polished and forward.

The Fourth Realm really needs to step up its fashion game.

"I'm glad you're here to see me off, Blesk." Madness sensed Aurora's body shake, but she held her composure in the face of an equal. "I would have hated to leave without a goodbye."

"Get back in the palace, Aurora." Blesk was crass. "You don't want me to hurt these two, do you?"

Cerene nocked her bow, aiming right for the Lightning Saints' heads.

"Relax, mortal girl. I sense no magic from you." Blesk spat. "Your genes are empty—meaningless during this time, but these two have great power. Power to use at my disposal."

"Cerene," Aurora deepened her deep tone, "whatever you do, do *not* lose your target."

The archer narrowed her aim. "With pleasure."

Madness had thought Aurora would order Cerene to lower, to stand down, but no. The Aurora before him was different. It was as if the last week had brought forth her powers from the Old Age and, with it, an assured ruler. A dominant god.

"Those we found responsible for the little explosions across my darling city were almost dealt with in a gruesome manner, but these two stepped up. Took on the roles as the leaders." Tobias and Alfonso kneeled before a god that found them and all citizens of the Second Realm, nothing other than bugs to squash beneath his heels. Blesk ran his lean and wrinkled hands over Alfonso's face and gripped his cheeks. "A Weapon Wielder. Rare among Magicals, yes, but also a healer? Remarkable genetics! And then the other here, a Shifter." His wrinkled hand crossed Tobias' back. "An Ancient Magical, believed near extinct from our world . . . Aurora, how you crossed paths so quickly with these two is a mystery to me."

Shadows poured from Aurora's feet. "If you so much as lay a finger on them, Blesk, this town will turn to ruins that far surpass those of the Second Realm."

Madness swore Blesk flinched, but the Lightning God recovered. "Threaten all you want, Goddess of Dark, but your aids are mortals. Not to mention, you are not the god you used to be." Blesk turned to his advisor. "Ensure victory here. Yes?"

Purple lightning fluttered across the sky, and Blesk was gone.

"He's always been one to run from a fight, hasn't he, Bolty?" Aurora sashayed alongside the shadows.

"You're one to talk." Bolt's hand moved with green lightning.

"Does Lightning take pride in stomping out those we were designed to protect?" Lightning and shadow clashed in a ball of mist and green. "I'm pretty sure God's Code goes past just those mortals in our own realms."

The sparks were strong, but the darkness was deadly.

And the mortals moved. Cerene fired her bow and charged at a run with Baer at her side. Alfonso grabbed the Lightning Saint at his back and slammed him into the ground. The Weapons of Ore moved and transformed at his call. Tobias removed his cloak. His paws rumbled across the courtyard, chomping Lightning Saints between his teeth.

Lost in the midst of the combat, lightning flew toward Madness. It was going to hit, but razor-sharp ice flew, absorbing and breaking the ice.

"Get out of here, Mad!" Alfonso called out.

Madness was useless on a battlefield, he needed to hide.

"If only you'd let me help." The Pull tugged

"Stop it." He snapped out loud. "We are not doing this."

"But we could be great." It tempted. "*We could keep them safe.*"

Madness shoved The Pull and took cover behind some rubble. He watched his brother and friends fight against beings far greater in combat and skill, but their drive came from somewhere deeper than that of their enemies.

"Cerene!"

Alfonso called out, but Cerene was ahead of it. Like magic poured through her veins, Cerene's skills were unparalleled. Not even Lightning Satins could keep her at bay. She threw two daggers, hitting the Lightning Saints in the chest. She ran forward, propelling her legs into a split, taking both out in one hit. And as a cat in the night, she landed quickly and nocked not one, not two, but three arrows and released. They flew past Alfonso, right into the necks of the enemy.

Tobias and Baer tore through behind her, barreling the enemies down with teeth and claws. Alfonso finished them off with his hammer's might, breaking the earth beneath them. Madness marveled at his friends holding their own. At a group of *mortals* holding their own.

"See that?" Shadows twirled around Aurora like a song. "Mortals aren't what they used to be."

"Yes, but they are far from durable." Sparks passed between Bolt's fingertips. "No matter how this fight ends, the overall war will go in our favor!"

"There would be no war to favor if Lightning had not altered the spell!" Aurora shifted her weight heavily with each step. Pieces of cloth from her ragged black shirt and pants caught the wind. "If Lightning had not betrayed the Realms of Nelabac!"

Saints and mortals alike paused their battles. Not everyone, it seemed, knew Blesk had betrayed the Realms.

"Helena, deal with the mortals but don't kill them," Bolt ordered one of the saints. "We need some sort of leverage."

Madness watched Helena, one of the Lightning Saints, turn toward one mortal in particular.

"Cerene!"

The archer turned in time to catch Helena racing at her full speed. Helena shot forward, spiraling lightning, but Cerene fired an arrow directly down the electrical path. The charge split static through the air. Helena glanced as the shocks redirected to the sky, giving Cerene her chance.

And Helena screamed, reaching for the arrow piercing her shin, clean through.

"Mortal *bitch*!"

Helena pulled the arrow from her leg and took her fist against the stones, releasing a force of electricity through Cerene. Another Lightning Saint, an agent with black hair, moved to puncture the rod down Cerene's shoulder. Alfonso struggled through his battle, trying to reach her.

Aurora turned from her battle and blasted ice between Cerene and the enemy, allowing her to escape.

"To me!" Madness jerked for his friend. Cerene saw Madness and limped over. Her breath was heavy, and when she finally stumbled into his arms, she collapsed, gasping and sobbing for breath.

"You're okay." Madness pulsed some of his healing, did what he could to hold back the rage.

She was choking on tears, overwhelmed by the power of the enemy.

Madness saw Cerene wasn't the only one falling. All of his family were falling. They possessed greater skill than the immortals around them, but as Bolt stated, they were possessed mortal bodies. Killable bodies.

Tobias' and Baer's claws remained unsheathed, but their attacks slowed. Only Aurora could stand against the Lightning Saints, but she now fought Bolt and defended the mortals with her ice.

"Then why don't you help?"

Stop. Madness slapped his leg.

"Oh, Madness, let me come out and play. I'll be sure to let you keep control."

Madness screamed. "Stop it!"

"Madness, don't let it win," Cerene crawled from his arms.

"Don't worry about me." He held her tighter.

The ice wall broke free as Helena charged through, Baer at her back, a snapping, snarling beast.

Cerene broke free and ran forward.

"Baer!" The beast was already looping back to Cerene's side, and as they had practiced so many times before, Cerene mounted the beast and ran into battle.

"Cerene, don't!" Alfonso called. "Gods, damn you!"

"I'll do as I please!"

Alfonso continued to match the speed of his opponents, but he was losing traction. His weapons bled, too, a sign of his draining magic.

Madness gripped his chest. The pain they each endured . . . as he stood there! But Alfonso, if anything happened—

"Al!"

Madness unsheathed his sword, partially regretting not purchasing that sword in the Merchant's Quarters, and charged toward the saint closest to his brother, striking it down.

He would die to save them.

He would surrender The Pull and lose himself if it meant protecting them.

No. Don't unravel.

"What are you doing!" Alfonso shouted. "Madness, get back—"

"Fighting with Aurora is going to put me in these situations." Madness locked onto incoming Lightning Saints. "I've got this."

They had trained for these moments, and they were going to use everything in their arsenal. Madness would prove he could do more than heal and keep himself at bay.

But a scream rippled across the courtyard as Baer reared onto his back legs. An electric rod pierced his side, shocking both him and Cerene.

"Baer, stay steady!" Sparks danced across Cerene's skin, but she tried to comfort the beast. "Please, stay up."

But another powerful spark barreled right into Baer's side. The purple bolts sparked through the square, and Cerene leapt before Baer tumbled to the ground. So small, Baer appeared lifeless. Cerene scooped him in her arms. Her bow lay broken next to her. Helena now found her opening and seized the moment.

"Cerene!" Alfonso called out, but he was a moment too late.

A dagger, hidden in the electricity, shot forward, and all Cerene could do was block it from hitting her face was use her hand. Gut-wrenching wails echoed, and an ear-ripping roar followed.

Madness knew who it was—whose anger rang into the world. Not even the strongest of electrical shocks could stop Tobias as he barrelled for Cerene. The Shifter's eyes were set ablaze, even the silver markings of his glowed like minerals in the light as he fought the true beast lingering in his blood. There was no stopping a wolf determined to protect his pack.

"You may have gained back some strength, Aurora, but not enough to protect them and fight me!" Bolt curled over with a smile twisting in years of anger. "You gave up on the mortals a long time ago! Let them die with your legacy."

"Mortals have survived this war without the protection of walls, or saints, or gods. They have done more for one another than you or I could ever do for them." Aurora gritted her teeth. "Mortals were here long before us, and they will survive long after we are gone."

"Gods! You're so mind-numbingly difficult." Bolt threw back his head. "It's hard to believe you once held immense power. That you once bested every one of the gods. That at one point you were more powerful than your sister."

Lightning trailed through the ground and up Aurora's leg. Madness watched as she fought to use her immense power. He had caught glimpses of it that day, had seen the might of the darkness and how Aurora wielded as another limb, an extension of her very body and soul.

Aurora pushed back strands of her hair away as wickedness spread across her face. All the fighting ceased as dark winds circled Aurora's presence. Lightning became energy to fuel her power. Bolt took a step back, wary of the god.

"You've forgotten that I am the very essence of what makes this world. It will take more than sass and a little bit of electricity to defeat me." Aurora turned the rubble and rocks around her into impenetrable ice and darkness, and then she smirked. "I may be cocky, Bolt, but you'll do well to remember this: You, Blesk, and the others of the realms don't have a gods-damned clue what I'm capable of conjuring."

Aurora jumped, propelling her body off the blocks of ice and into the air. She crashed into Bolt, their meeting cracked the ground open. The sheer force rocked Madness on his heels. The key to stopping the Lightning Saints and escaping was stopping Bolt, and Madness watched as she put all her remaining strength into the final moments of the battle.

Bolt countered Aurora's attacks with matching speed and strength. Each blow weakened both the god and the saint, but victory lay with who made the first mistake. On who parried too early. Who tripped on the rubble. Who looked away.

It seemed Bolt had the same thought, and just as Aurora formed daggers of ice, Bolt rammed a fist into her cheek, sending Aurora through the courtyard. "Now's our chance!"

Lightning Saints pressed hard. Madness countered their attacks, but they were stronger, harder, and more charged. They were determined to take the mortals hostage and use them as leverage against Aurora.

Blood trickled down his skull. He had not felt the blow and had not felt his body hit the ground, pinned against the knee of a Lightning Saint.

His friends, too, fell victim. One by one, they were captured as Madness lay on the ground, feeling nothing but the ringing of his ears and the blurring of his vision.

But he saw Alfonso push through saint after saint to reach him.

No!

And like when running in a dream, Madness' body would not move. He had no sense of being as Madness lost everything. As a Lightning Saint elbowed Alfonso's face and punctured a sword through his lower abdomen.

Alfonso fell to his knees with a hand on the open wound. The Weapons of Ore lost their form. Madness swore he heard his friends call out to his brother, but the fire and the blood had taken him.

And Madness saw only a cold and empty sanctuary.

As Madness floated through his mind, his left arm sparked blue flames. He had been here before. He had been here in the lowest of times. In the scariest of times. In times when hope was lost and the end was near.

"Al."

"It can stop." The Pull pressed her scaly face against his and wrapped her leathery wings around him. *"We can avenge your brother together."*

"Avenge?" Madness trembled. No, did that mean Al . . .

All of it—of *her*—

"You can avenge?" Madness wanted her. She gave Madness the comfort he needed.

"Madness—no, no!" From beyond the vail of his muddled and clouded soul, Cerene's voice carried to him

"Don't listen to her." The Pull caressed, desperate to hold his attention. Their voices and minds and souls blended, becoming one.

Madness placed his head against The Pull's face and opened his eyes to feel their souls bleed as one.

"Let me in."

"MADNESS, DON'T—"

The madness within him stilled, and she unleashed his power.

His throat scratched raw as her voice screeched out into the world. It was haunted, not of this world. Madness' skin crawled and itched as it darkened and crackled and turned charcoal-black and red. The bandage covering his forearm burned to crisp ashes as an oil-black fire blazed across his skin. Madness gripped his bare arm as his curse mark loosened, and the demon bound to his body, heart, and soul unleashed.

"That's it, Madness." Her melodious voice floated in and out of his ear. Her chains unbound her from the prison she had lain. Madness felt her chains stretch around his arms and legs and even his neck. He latched to the subconscious of his own body.

He tore at his mind and body.

Even from within the prison of his mind, Madness felt every change. He felt his canines fall into fangs and horns curl on the top of his head. His white hair grew a long and straggly orange.

The spiral lines of the markings on his arm expanded and curled blood red. They traveled up and across his skin to his eyes. And as his eyes became the purest, richest, and darkest of reds, he screeched across all of Caris.

With the transformation complete, Madness felt relief. His hate of life and all that lived disappeared when She took control.

"Stay?" Madness whimpered. Everything was so hard when he was in control. With Her at the reigns . . . Madness could finally rest.

"Oh darling," she pressed against the chains of his mind. "What would you like me to do?"

He finally said, knowing that in this form, he could protect his friends, even if it was too late for his brother. If it was too late for him. *"Kill them all."*

Sometimes we don't have a choice when it comes to submitting to the monster within.

Cerene Misrinda

Part III

The Demon

CHAPTER 13

The sun rose high that morning, but Dark Manor did not need it to feel warm. Dark Saints danced about the manor, readying for the coming festivities. Guards returned from their missions, agents went from place to place until Aurora ordered them to stay put, and missioners carried baskets of food, crafts, and decor over the entire manor.

The Goddess of Dark peered at them from her kitchen window. For the first time in a year, the pieces of Aurora collected in one place again. The Dark Saints never dreamed of skipping out on the Summer Festival. Not because they would miss the fun but because they knew Aurora would freeze them into the next Summer Festival they so dared.

The Dark Saints came and went for months on end, only popping by Dark Manor for a day or two before venturing back into the Second Realm or other realms as ambassadors of peace. The Summer Festival put duties aside and gave the Dark Saints time to enjoy one another and remember their second chance at life. To embrace their immortality.

Missioners and guards moved back and forth from the main houses to Flower Meadows on the other side of the lake. The decorated handcrafted tables Aurora was gifted from the Earth Saints of the Sixth Realm. Their

legs were made of vines and roots. Flower blossoms and moss filled in the crevasses. Aurora used permafrost to keep them in an eternal bloom.

Her soul soared in the skies for the events to come, but when Aurora thought of the dreaded task at hand, her soul fell back to Nelabac.

Baking was not her specialty, but she had lost a bet to Tempton, one of the Dark Saints of her Inner Circle, and she was now charged with the task of preparing dessert for the Summer Festival. This year, the Dark Saints chose a bundt cake.

This will teach me to challenge a swordsperson to a duel ever again.

She moved about the kitchen cleaning while she still had sunlight to spare. Flour, sugar, dough, and flavoring covered the counter, sink, floor, and by some chance, the couch far on the far end of the living room.

"Gods," she sighed.

Usually, Aurora would clean immediately, as a dirty kitchen always proved a bad start to a new day, but that early evening Aurora kept her eyes on the setting sun. Feesr air rushed through the window. Aurora sensed a storm brewing, one prepared by the God of Lightning on the horizon.

Blesk is out of his mind if he thinks he's going to send a storm my way.

The apron stopped at her knees and tapped at her movements. Aurora felt silly shuffling across the floors, but she did not want to ruin her newly sewn dress. The pure white fabric with lace embroidering would easily stain. One of her eldest saints, Elaina, had sewn the dress for her to wear at the Summer Festival. Too excited to wait, Aurora went ahead and showed it off.

Strands of hair danced with the wind. It had grown well past her hips. Aurora preferred her hair braided in two, but that day Aurora left her wild and madly tangled. That day was more special to her heart than the Summer Festival. Strands of hair took to the fading light and danced until a steady knock echoed on the door.

She scrambled to remove the apron. "Come in!"

"Aurora!"

The door flew open. Her brow pinched. Squinting, Aurora spotted a man. His figure, dark yet familiar, was fading. She called after him, begging him to stay, but the figure disappeared like dust in the wind.

Outside, the sky was blood red. The flowers wilted and the lake ran dry. The wind picked up and shook her home, tearing it away piece by piece. The walls stripped away and Aurora sank in a pitch-black vacuum.

The screams of her Dark Saints echoed all around. Aurora called out, begging for any one of them to respond, but the dead did not call from beyond the grave.

The screams intensified the further she fell, and horror filled her being with the realization that there was no way out.

"Stop . . . Stop—"

But the Void kept going. Aurora watched as the last puff of air escaped her lungs and filled the frigid space. Through the unattainable tunnel of the Void, a shape formed. It was Luna.

The hate within her sister screeched through the space. A staff of crystals took form as Luna marched forward.

"Luna, stop!" Aurora called out, but she had no power in this domain. She, Mako, and Elaina were at the mercy of Luna.

The Dark Saints did not cry. They only looked at Aurora with eyes that read: *Don't worry about us. We're okay.*

With one swipe of the staff, Elaina's and Mako's heads rolled through the snow. Aurora felt what sounded like a scream bellow from the pits of her stomach. From the cracks of her soul.

I know this is a dream . . . but gods, does this hurt.

"I'm not done, sweet sister." Luna's voice carried on the snowy landscape. "My fun has only begun."

The mortals appeared. One by one, Baer and Tobias. Cerene. Alfonso, and finally, Madness. Unlike her saints, the mortals cried for mercy, for they had not yet lived.

And slicing an apple, Luna took their lives.

Luna's fingers danced on top of her staff, and she licked her lips like a cat teasing its prey as she looked at the remaining mortal. Her hand traced the outline of Madness' collarbone. Aurora felt so much fear.

The thought of losing them—losing everyone all over again—

Luna raised the staff, and Aurora's soul plummeted.

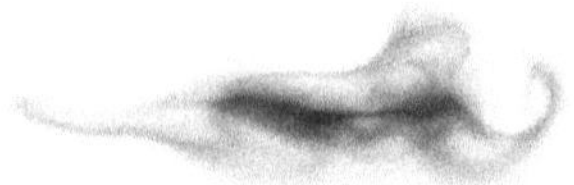

Aurora jolted from her bed, needing air, the wind on her face. Stumbling onto the balcony, the morning crashed into her. The ice, the cold, and the delusions disappeared with the wind.

The haunting dreams followed Aurora through the night since waking from the spell. The dreams always felt real, but last night's had been different. It was like Luna had entered Aurora's mind and teased her.

Darkness reached through the balcony. Aurora strained to reel it in. Only when Aurora had been more human than god had her powers struggled for equilibrium. Six-hundred years ago, she had the Dark Saints to guide her. Now, she had only herself.

The soft breeze across her face reminded her that this scene was real and she was not trapped inside the restraints of her mind. Aurora crossed her arms over the balcony and leaned against them, eyes on the few stars still twinkling in the morning dawn.

Is that you up there? Mako, Elaina? Looking down at all my mistakes?

At night, Aurora spoke to them, the millions of glistening stars. They were small beckons of hope in a world plagued by hopelessness and a guide in the haunted darkness.

Footsteps stalked from behind.

"Don't worry. I'm not going to jump" She rolled her eyes. "It's not like it would kill me anyway."

"I can never be too sure, Goddess of Dark." Aurora hadn't bothered to learn any of the guards' names. This one placed a breakfast tray on the table. "You're unpredictable, and your actions this past week have proven just that."

Aurora had nearly killed three guards and sent four agents through the shadows, letting them land where ever the void decided. She knew sending *herself* through the shadows was too dangerous . . . sending others was an entirely different scenario.

"I should be able to have a little fun while trapped in this tacky palace, no?" She popped a grape in her mouth.

The Lightning Saint said nothing as he returned to his post.

She sat at the table, eating and dreading the day to come. It would entail more sitting, waiting, and agonizing over what the God of Lightning had revealed about Nelabac and the current state of political affairs. That first day two weeks ago, Aurora had barely remained conscious during conversations but had remained lucid enough to remember the most crucial detail: It was Blesk who had betrayed the other gods and Nelabac.

Blesk paced the crystal floors around her defenseless bleeding body. He looked at her with a vengeance in his soul and fear.

"You don't care what happens to you people," Aurora spat. "You only care for your precious powers and keeping yourself from destruction. When Luna finds your Soul Keeper, don't think she won't use it. Don't be so foolish to believe she'll spare your life."

Blesk sent sparks through her body at that comment.

Their stings pricked at her skin.

"You're the last person I'd trust, Goddess of Dark." Blesk had peered down at her. "Luna's the sister with sense. With strength and numbers. If agreeing to destroy Nelabac and rebuild it from scratch is the way to keep me around, then I'll do it."

"You coward!" Aurora tried finding her feet through the pain and spilling of her blood. "Luna is wrong. The Diety created us to protect—"

"They have nothing to do with this!" Lightning soared. The room seemed small as the eye of the storm grew. "If They wanted to, They would have stepped in and stopped

Luna before any of this ever happened! It's over, Aurora. You have no power to control any of the gods or the affairs of Nelabac. Your plan failed. All that's left is sealing you away, so you don't try to stop us as we send Nelabac toward its future."

Luna's allies in the war were growing. Blesk had not revealed if any other gods had also sided with Luna, but Aurora knew it was possible.

I must reach Juvia as soon as possible.

After that, it took four days for her body to heal. Some of her powers had returned, as well. She could summon the dark and shadows and conjure ice, but the idea of using the Void kept Aurora confined to her tacky room. Tossing the Lightning Saints through it was for fun but also to test the limits of her power, and it had proved exhausting.

Since *Luna is coming for me, I need to save my powers to send myself through the Void when she does.*

Aurora had pondered Luna's darkness and how she had gone from wanting to protect Nelabac and Aurora to wanting them both destroyed.

She threw herself onto the bed, grabbed a pillow, and screamed. After, she rolled over and went for a bath.

Even the bathroom was tacky. The stainless-steel tub was slippery and frustrating to lay in comfortably.

The mortals would laugh at this place. The steel tub, draped curtains of golden silk, and the carpets of violet hues so bright they would blind anyone who stared long enough.

She was sure they stayed safe. Hopefully, they were tucked with the rest of the refugees outside the city. Maybe they had left and headed for Dandfol or the Fifth Realm.

Wherever they are, I know they're safe.

The bath water had chilled.

Blesk offered brightly-colored dresses made of heavy fabrics. They were far from her taste, so she picked the blandest black trousers and Madness' shirt.

It was a kind offering, one Aurora never saw coming. One she never knew would strike her core and spark such longing.

So many gods. So many motives. All humans, Magicals, and other beings alive one hundred years ago were dead. If some survived, as Tobias had, they were surely in hiding. It was a new generation of mortals and beings in Nelabac who only knew the betrayal of the gods. They only knew destruction and what happens when a god doesn't get their way—

She sat up from the pillow. A sound echoed off the balcony.

And she realized—

With claws unsheathed from his climb up the palace walls, *Baer* burst into the room. The panic in his eyes eased as he crossed the balcony threshold and into Aurora's arms.

"Oh, Baer!" He was a sight she had never thought to see but was so glad to behold. "How you managed that climb is a story we shall never know!"

They did not celebrate long, for Lightning Saints pounded the door. The noise was loud, an anomaly. Baer slid through Aurora's arms, his eyes and fur took the shape of the beast dwelling within his tiny body.

It was time.

At the call of the darkness, winds gathered, unweaving Aurora's braids. She grabbed the laces at their ends and tied them to her belt loop. The shadows laced over as Darkness and Aurora twirled in tandem.

I am the Goddess of Dark, and I have returned.

The darkness became her undoing.

Chapter 14

Aurora had seen death. She had seen bodies mangled in the fury of overkill. But she had not seen it like this.

No one moved or so much as breathed as guts and bones and the two halves of the saint's body dropped from Madness' jaws. A black and unholy substance burned against his skin. Hums crawled forth from the beast he had become and echoed through the square. Lightning Saints stared at the gruesome sight of their comrade dripping from Madness' hand and at the ancient creature he had become. Aurora knew Madness possessed a secret magic but never imagined it was a demon.

Madness not only revealed a haunting secret of Nelabac's past but a past believed defeated—*extinct.* Demons were a threat so sinister Aurora knew not even her would want to face them.

Cerene's eyes swelled with fear as she cradled Baer's unconscious body. Tobias' wolf eyes simmered with sorrow, his paws moving forward for his friend so slightly as Lightning Saints' charged the demon with electric rods, magical abilities, and other weapons unsheathed. Bolt and his Lightning Saints moved, refocusing on the greatest threat in all of Nelabac.

"Guard the town!" one shouted.

"Secure the palace walls!" another said.

"Take down that monstrosity!" Both echoed the calls of his comrades.

They knew if the demon left the secure walls of the palace, it would destroy Caris and every citizen within.

Lightning attacked with more wrath than ever, but it did nothing against the demon as it kept killing and killing and *killing.*

The demon stretched Madness' jaw well past human limits. Black acid flung from its mouth as it screamed, burning whatever it touched. Its sounds rattled saints and mortals alike.

But, behind those threatening, red, surging eyes, Aurora saw Madness'. He pleaded for help, for relief lost among the debris. It searched for relief in the debris below.

Aurora then knew it looked for Alfonso.

The brother lay in the rubble below the demon, unmoving. He appeared lifeless, but Aurora felt his soul. It was strong and stable, but the demon did not know that.

Cerene pointed, "Aurora!"

But Aurora saw the lightning before the mortals. It reached her fingers and at the moment of impact, Aurora redirected the lightning into the shadows.

"Bolt, we have bigger issues than the quarrel between us." Aurora crouched ready to pounce.

"I consider this all one big issue." Bolt opened both his arms, filling the space between them with electricity. "You and the demon are on the same side.

The demon moaned. Blood and goo dripped from its mouth and chard body as it spotted Alfonso.

Now that it has seen him, I need to reach Cerene and Tobias so we can stop it.

"Bolt, you're boring me." Aurora spread her arms up and up, ice and dark clouds gathering at her back. She had to use *that* power, now or never. "You've had time to take me down, and you've made it clear you're far from capable."

And Bolt's eyes sharpened, knowing what power she brought forth.

Aurora's enemies knew the battle was decided when she summoned the Wings of Darkness.

Tender black shadows thinned like the leathery wings of a bat but with the beauty of a hawk. Their ends fluttered like ribbons through the air and glittered in the sunlight. The Wings of Darkness created the phoenix of the night.

Aurora's back gave a little at their weight, but she held her own. She was not strong enough to wield their full potential, but Bolt didn't know that. Aurora surged the wings with the might of every muscle, and Cerene, Tobias, and Baer hunkered down as the winds gust past, blowing Bolt and his forces past and through the courtyard.

Aurora's feet teetered, carrying her to Cerene, Tobias, and Baer. They were cut and bruised from the Wings of Darkness, but they were okay. Aurora slid to their sides and embraced Cerene.

"Your hand." Aurora looked down at the mangled limb. Flesh tore clean up and through Cerene's middle finger.

"It's nothing," Cerene said. "We have bigger problems."

"How do we stop him?" Aurora grasped Cerene's shoulders. "How do we stop the demon?"

Aurora sensed Madness' soul confined underneath the demon's soul, searching to gain control of his body.

"You cannot stop him." Tobias was in his human form, securing his robe. "None of us can."

"This has happened before, no?" Aurora missed his smirk and his rose eyes. Watching the purest of red eyes, so full of hate and malice, take their place was unbearable. Even if they did disagree and were at odds with one another, Madness still came to save her. "Maybe if he sees a familiar face—"

"Rory, we can't." Cerene moaned, her hand causing agony. "We are not capable of stopping him. Only Alfonso can do that."

"I-I don't understand." Aurora urged. "Alfonso is stable, but he cannot do *anything* in his state."

Tobias returned to his human form. "Aurora, please."

"Just watch," Cerene added.

The demon sniffed and nudged Alfonso. Tears fell from the cracks of its eyes, and like picking up the thinnest of strings, a giant black hand reached over the hole in Alfonso's abdomen. Blue light twinkled and spun in the air as the wound stitched together.

Alfonso reached for his brother's head.

"Don't give in just yet, brother. We need you." Gently, he wrapped his hands around the horns and pulled his brother to his chest. "*I* need you."

Even with the demon in control, Madness' love for his brother conquered all other desires toiling inside his body.

The demon hummed, pulsing an ungodly power through its cracked skin. Its head jerked, fighting the turmoil going on inside the shared body.

Only when its eyes found Alfonso did the square glow healing, golden rays.

Two halves of one whole.

The fear and hatred seeping into the air disappeared. The black skin of the demon flaked in shades of silver, gold, and violet through the air. The horns receded into Madness' skull, and the demon's eyes dimmed.

They had Madness again, collapsed in his beloved brother's arms.

"Holy gods." Cerene was the first at their side. She rubbed dirt back from Alfonso's face with her injured hand. "Are you okay?"

"The idiot healed me before passing out from the transition," Alfonso responded. "Just what was he thinking doing that in the middle—"

"You know he has no control." Tobias interrupted, protecting their backs.

"I know, I know." Alfonso offered her a slight smile. "Nice set of wings, Rory."

Alfonso turned to Baer, cradled in Cerene's lap. He noted her hand, and his face twisted with rage. "Let me heal it."

"Never mind it." She pulled it to her chest. "Save what strength you have left. Those Lightning Saints will be up and attacking before we know it."

"She's right." Aurora shifted her wings. "I did what I could for us to regroup, but it will only keep the Lightning Saints at bay for so long."

"And we have to carry Madness around," Tobias added.

Alfonso tightened his grip on his brother. "Why does he have to be so damned tall."

Lightning blasted in every direction. The enemy stood in unified lines. The Void opened and closed, catching lightning that fired, but Aurora could only use it as a shield for so long. She spilled shadows, concealing them in smoky fog.

"We need a plan." Aurora kept her hands out, twisting the shadows.

"This situation has turned from bad to worse," Alfonso said.

"And from worse," Cerene added, "to terrible."

"Put Madness on my back." Tobias took the lead, removing his robe. "Cerene, hold him from behind."

"Right." Cerene handed Baer off to Alfonso. She also grabbed took Tobias' robe and placed it in her bag. "He'll want to be with you when he wakes."

A dull, blue light pulsed down Baer as Alfonso focused some of his power into their bravest companion.

The smoke cleared, revealing hundreds of Lightning Saints lined before them with Bolt at their lead.

But it was not just Lightning Saints that filled the space.

"Light Knights." Aurora stared in horror at their animal masks and empty, lonely bodies.

"We need to leave *now*." Cerene reached for a dagger at her waist.

"Right." Lightning flew past Alfonso's head. "But how?"

"Get behind me!" Aurora called. The mortals were drained. Alfonso could not use his Weapons or Ore, nor could Tobias hold the wolf form for much longer. Even if Cerene had a bow, she wouldn't be able to use it in condition.

It was her duty to protect them. She needed the power of the Altered Realm, but the scale of power required to get them out would destroy the city and put innocents at risk.

No. I would gladly sacrifice anything to keep them safe.

An explosion broke out, scattering the two armies.

"A delayed bomb?" Alfonso asked.

Tobias growled and shook his massive head, disagreeing.

Fires spread down from the enemy to Aurora and the mortals. Rock and rubble flew across the square. The walls behind them demolished at their backs demolished. Chaos ensued throughout the city, as well.

"You have caused quite the commotion." A voice laughed above the fight. "Forcing me to take a break from my book."

"What in god's name is happening now!" Bolt turned to the sky.

A tiny man observed them from above, smoking a pipe and reading a book. Tea boiled in a pot beside him. Lightning and crystals fired from the two armies, but a simple touch of man's finger absorbed the attacks.

His eyes peered up from the book. "I was just getting to the good part." He closed it softly.

As the fires spread and chaos consumed, Bolt struggled to focus his disoriented troops.

"*I can only hold them back for now.*" The wizard echoed through Aurora's mind. "*You all must get a move on. Let the fires guide your way.*"

"Who are you?" Aurora shouted.

"It can't be?" Cerene called from Tobias—"Aurora, I can explain later, but for now, we must trust him."

"*The girl is right.*" The wizard's voice stiffened as he urged them to leave. "*You all need to get a move on.*"

"No." Aurora fumbled over the words. "Besides, my people, those surrounding the walls, they will suffer consequences of this attack—"

"*Your mortal friends took care of most of them. I've ensured all on their way to Dandfol, even those who helped set off the bombs.*" The wizard moved above them, focusing on his attacks. "*It's time we all start to make a change in this war.*"

"But—"

"You are the ones who will purge Nelabac of the darkness it has fallen into!" The wizard's power split in waves of purple and red. *"Only you, Aurora, can defeat the darkening of this world before it is too late!"*

Alfonso pulled her hand. "Aurora, look."

A string of blue flames carried down through the rubble. Aurora didn't want to leave this new ally behind. Grounds Below, she had only met the wizard, but her soul told her he was a trusted ally. But he was someone else to sacrifice—die for her sake.

Her body hated every second of turning and fleeing as the wizard fought a thousand to one.

We won't let his sacrifice go to waste.

Aurora and the mortals sprinted down the path the wizard created for them. Cerene balanced Madness as Tobias sprinted with Cerene and Madness on his back. Despite her injury, Cerene held Madness tightly in her arms. Alfonso ran through with a Weapon of Ore in one hand and Baer in the other.

These mortals don't give up.

Lightning and Light Saints attacked, but Aurora blew them away with a good push of her wings. Citizens ran through the streets, screaming and escaping the mayhem. The effects of war, of battle and blood, had never reached those of Caris.

"There!" Cerene pointed at a hole in the walls of the city.

"Your handiwork?" Aurora asked Alfonso.

"It was all Tobias' idea," Alfonso said. The wolf grunted in response.

Their escape route was within sight, but rows of Lightning Saints waited. Their spears sparked with electricity.

Darkness gathered in Aurora's eyes, and black ice laced up her fingertips. Shadows poured from her limbs, and her magnificent wings glistened like obsidian crystals.

Aurora sauntered toward the enemy, ice and embers crackled with each step. The enemy shook, forgetting that Aurora was the great enemy.

"You saints forget your place."

One swope of the shadows and the saints were gone. Aurora gave them no voice. No mercy or warning. For a god owed no one grace.

Aurora was tired. Her powers were fatigued, but they were so close to escaping. So close to a near-clean escape to a near-impossible mission.

These mortals . . .

"Be aware of the Light Knights await on the other side." Aurora sensed enemy souls. "I'll be there soon."

"What are you doing?"

"I must secure our escape."

Shadows crowded the mortals as they piled through the gate. Aurora bent the darkness to will, preparing for the onslaught of enemies. The shadows slithered over the ground, swallowing the Lightning and Light Saints at will. In the Altered Realm—in knowing she was saving her friends—Aurora reveled in the screams.

With one final effort, Aurora flew through the gate, spinning and spewing the last of the Altered Realm. Darkness covered every crack and crevice with ice and shadow. The ice gripped the metal walls and spread the course of the entire city, doubling the tallest parts of the wall.

In the right light, one would see the embedded crescent moon. The blackened crystals glistened for those of Caris to know who was here, who was fighting, and who would win the wars to come.

Aurora landed before the mortals with no time to rest. Alfonso swung his ax in endless circles at the Light Knights while protecting Baer with his other hand. Tobias swatted his giant paws and snapped his teeth as Cerene held onto Madness from his back, gripping tightly to his black fur.

Aurora had not the time nor patience for delicacy, so she snapped her fingers.

Shadows covered the enemy. The darkness squeezed them into nothing. The ice drifted their remains to their master.

Aurora's body convulsed. The darkness was taking hold. She had dwelled in its power for too long. First, she released the Wings of Darkness, and as she did, Aurora felt her body return.

In this state, she felt every tear, cut, bruise, and ache. Every part of her wanted to rest but—

"We have to get to our side of the border."

They struggled through the refugee site, past the invisible fence, and into the Second Realm. Aurora felt the aching in their souls—the pain of the mind and body—but they made it. They crossed the border back into their homelands and collapsed. The sun was setting. There were no signs of looming Light Knights, and Aurora sensed pursuing souls. It was truly her and mortals. Aurora assumed Luna had called her soldiers back. For all Luna knew, Aurora was strong, fully capable of taking even her down.

Hopefully, my little show today scared Luna.

Aurora kneeled in the dirt and ran her fingers through it. The earth was different in the Second Realm. It was weak and dying, but it was her realm. She swore a few surviving blades reached around her fingers to welcome her home.

Arms wrapped around her back. Alfonso's glasses smashed so hard into her shoulder that Aurora heard them crack.

"You're sweaty." Her hand patted against his palms, letting him know she was okay. "And gross."

A giggle rose escaped him. "Worth it."

Aurora swiveled to face him. Baer rested in his lap.

"It's a sink," Aurora said.

"Yes," Alfonso agreed. "He's done this before, but not to this extreme."

There was a limit to how much magic a mortal could use. They could train to harness more, but there was an end to its source. Depleting so much as Baer had done often meant life or death, but Aurora sensed Baer's soul was strong, and the beast only needed rest.

Aurora looked to the other mortals to observe their injuries. The bleeding in Cerene's hand had ceased, though Aurora knew the pain remained. Tobias had scratched along his muzzle and legs, but nothing serious.

The demon. The hole in Alfonso's chest. Madness consumed in power. Aurora reached for Alfonso's chest. He was healed. She couldn't believe it. The tear in his shirt was the only reminder of what had happened in Caris.

That damned fool.

Aurora could not bring herself to look at Madness. Not because of the looming demon but because she refused to see him so broken. Aurora had known he possessed a dark past. His sharp tongue had come from the loathing for creatures like her because they were the same.

"They'll be chipping away at your work for days, Rory." Alfonso patted her back. "Nice work."

She tapped his hand. "Thanks, Al."

"This part of the Second Realm isn't secure," Cerene readjusted Madness' weight. Tobias ordered, padding into the forest. "The safe house is not too far from here."

And they were off, racing toward the unknown, praying to the gods that rest found them soon.

Chapter 15

The sky rested at dusk as they trekked through the forest. Cerene struggled to balance Madness against her chest. Alfonso had offered to switch places, but Cerene refused. With every passing second, her hand risked infection and permanent damage. Tobias did his best to keep an even pace, but he, too, needed their journey to end. With each step, his paws scraped against the soil, and every paw pressed harder into the earth.

"Let me walk, Tobias." Cerene ran down the side of his black and silver fur. "You're exhausted."

Tobias let out a low growl.

"Tobias," Cerene pleaded. Aurora did not truly understand the extent of their relationship. They were not romantic, but they shared a similar kind of intimacy. One that, without each other, they would collapse, and because of that love and respect, Tobias listened.

Soulmates.

Alfonso helped Cerene lower Madness and assisted her landing. Tobias morphed into his humanoid form, heaving on his hands and knees. Aurora sensed he, too, lingered on a magic sink.

Cerene pulled out Tobias' clothes. "Aurora and I can carry Madness."

"We are nearly there." Tobias dressed and found his footing. "Neither of you can carry him. Aurora is depleted, and your hand is mangled."

"Then let me carry him." Alfonso tried. "He is my bone-headed brother."

"And he is my friend." Tobias reached for Madness.

"I wasn't asking, Tobias."

Alfonso was carefree, always went with the flow, and followed his friends' orders, but when Alfonso had an opinion or demand, his friends listened without question.

Tobias hoisted his much taller and heavier friend onto one side of his back. Alfonso handed Baer to Aurora, then took the other side, shouldering the weight of their dear friend together. Madness showed no signs of waking any time soon. Dry blood caked his face. Whether it was his own, Alfonso's, or the demon's victims remained a mystery.

It was known throughout Nelabac that Terra, the God of Earth, had fought alongside elves, faeries, dwarves, shifters, wizards, and humans to defeat the demons. That was when Ancient Magicals had passed down their magic to human- and animal-kind. It remained a battle unrecorded, never transcribed, as Terra had forbidden it. The destruction, the gruesome outcome, and the sheer nature of demons were to leave Nelabac and never return.

So, how has this gone unnoticed? How many other demons are trapped in a human or magical body?

Cerene halted. "Tobias."

"I know," was all he said.

Cerene took off into the heightened undergrowth. Aurora gripped Baer a little closer.

In a clearing, four stoned paths lay surrounded by overgrown grass, thick underbrush, and dense forestry. A slight noise broke out, ruffling against Aurora's arms.

"Hey, buddy." Aurora rubbed his chin. The beast whined in pain.

"I'll take Madness from here," Tobias said. "Alfonso, please heal Baer."

"Only because of Baer." Alfonso passed his brother off to Tobias and claimed the little beast. Baer stirred, wailing at the transfer, but when his eyes met Alfonso's, a purr rumbled. A blue light summoned from Alfonso's arm and into Baer. "You'll be warm and in bed soon."

"Let's move so that can happen." Cerene took a step forward. "Just follow our lead, okay?"

Cerene walked not down a stone path but between the four and directly through the underbrush. Tobias followed behind, leaving Aurora and Alfonso in the clearing . . . contemplating.

"You also noticed they just kind of disappeared, right?" Alfonso asked.

"I sure did."

Her chest tingled, tense with aching.

Am I . . . nervous? Aurora eyed Alfonso. He eyed her. And, instantaneously, they clutched each other's hands and stepped forward into the grassy abyss.

The grass rose higher and higher in an endless maze. A magical element was at play, but Aurora did not know what Magical it hailed.

Aurora's free hand ran along the grass. It was a wall. In the grassy depths of the illusions, they were disguised, hidden from the outside world. The thick leaves brushed along her skin, thrusting her forward.

"*Alfonso,*" Aurora realized it was *someone.* "You keep pushing, and it *hurts.*"

"Well, *Aurora*, I may have glasses, but my eyes are shut because I'm *terrified.*"

"What are you so scared of?"

"Oh, what? Like you're not a little apprehensive!"

The two bickered back and forth through the foliage, only silencing when the *snap* broke from a root.

Alfonso tripped, taking Aurora went with him.

"Really?" She frowned, unamused.

"Blame the wolf and the archer!"

The moonlight shimmered as the wall of grasses thinned, and their feet met stone. The two came to a halt as the path reached a ledge, opening to a valley. Four paths of stone stacked in perfect ninety-degree angles, like a compass. At the base of the springtime valley sat a small cabin surrounded by a pond and land bridge.

"The stone paths were part of a spell." Aurora marveled, energy finding her again. "What we just went through is the power of a spell. One that allows an unknown space to exist between the pockets of others. That space happened to be the four stone paths. It can only be the work of an Ancient Magical, elves or wizards, maybe even faeries."

"You said a bunch of complicated things that just"—he whistled, flying his hand over his head.

A light waved back and forth by the cabin, seeming to call them, so Aurora and Alfonso bounded for it. Crickets and moths wandered up from the grass as they ran. Fireflies hovered in place, filling the valley with a sense of wonder and pure magic. The endless rows of flowers pulled at a loss of sense, time, and place. Aurora thought of the days spent with the Dark Saints when they strolled through their own magical meadow of flowers.

The cabin had its own touch of magic. Moss and vines covered the spaces between each gray stone. Some cracks and breaks held birds' nests and spider webs. Smoke poured from the chimney in the center of the round, red roof. Cerene stood near the wooden door, holding a lantern and a black cat with long, velvet fur. A jewel was crested above its piercing lavender eyes.

"So," Cerene said, one hand on her hip, "cool safe house, right?"

"Welcome, both of you." The cat, in Cerene's arms, greeted them.

"It speaks?" Alfonso nearly dropped Baer.

"*It* is Pan." Cerene giggled. "She's a beast like Baer, except she's been enchanted to speak."

"Woah." Alfonso leaned in close and rubbed the beast's head. "You're much prettier than this fur ball."

"Please,"—Pan pushed Alfonso's hand back with her paw—"do not touch me."

Alfonso blushed, embarrassed.

"The other boy and Tobias are inside." Pan jumped from Cerene's arms. The she-beast looked to Baer. "What a fool of a beast. Take him inside."

Inside, the cabin held more whimsical charm. The grass floor was silk to the touch. Water trickled from the walls and flowed into a tiny stream that hugged the interior walls to a small pond flowing to the one surrounding the cabin. Large mushrooms were furniture, and even smaller ones decorated the walls.

Not even my home held such charm.

Tobias lounged in his human form on the far side of the cabin. Cerene scooped Baer into her arms and joined Tobias. The three of them curled side-by-side. Tobias patted the beast, receiving a purr of satisfaction.

"We're safe," Cerene sighed.

Alfonso collapsed on a mushroom. His hands touched his abdomen, where a thick, twisted scar now existed. Aurora watched as he felt each edge of the raised and tattered skin. It was as if Alfonso finally grasped the extent of the injury.

He finally asked, "Where's Mad?"

"The boy is in the back bedroom," Pan called from the kitchen. "He probably won't be up for some time." Not needing to know more, Alfonso closed his eyes, satisfied with her answers.

Unlike the mortal, Aurora needed proof. She had to see that he was indeed okay. Aurora walked past the sleeping mortals and peaked her head around the hallway behind the kitchen.

"He's through the left door." Pan crouched next to the stove, watching water boil. "You like tea?"

Aurora looked around and back at Pan. "I'm a fan . . . yes."

"Kind?"

"Honey . . . and lavender?"

How . . . You know what, at this point, I'm not even going to wonder how a cat prepares tea.

Twin beds sat against the back wall. Madness lay on the one to the left. His blonde-white hair curled above the edges of his smooth jaw. Aurora also noted stubble on his cheeks.

The transformation must accelerate growth. If he often transformed as a child, that would explain his height.

Aurora pulled out a mushroom from a corner and sat at his side. She had never seen someone look so helpless and desperate to be saved. She had met Madness as someone strong and hard-headed. Watching the demon rip through Madness had been torture, and Aurora could only imagine what his brother and the others felt each time this occurred.

Cerene nor Tobias held the power to save their friend. Alfonso alone bounded Madness to this earth, to his mind and body. His love alone kept the demon at bay.

There was a fresh bandage on his left arm, and Aurora unwrapped it, revealing the demon seal. Black coils surrounded the seal, confining what lay inside. The seal was written in the ancient language. Aurora couldn't read the signs or symbols tattooed on his arm. The ancient language was known only to the elves and faeries from long ago.

Aurora stroked the marking with one hand. The other found his hair. She pressed her head against his chest to feel the rise and fall of each breath. To make sure he was still breathing.

He nearly died today. They all did, and there is no one to blame but myself.

Joy and anger filled her soul. She was furious the mortals had come back for her. She was furious this secret, one so dangerous, existed and was left in the hands of a mortal. Furious that Madness harbored so much pain, and she could do nothing about it.

Foolish, it was all so foolish.

Madness was unharmed, but he was hurt. He was always hurt. The demon within him controlled every emotion, and every day, Madness hated what he could become if pushed too far.

"Rory?"

Warmth filled her palm. His healing blue light sparked alive.

Madness brought his face into the candlelight. His eyes shimmered with a kindness Aurora had not yet seen from him. She did not understand this new-found likeness. Madness had welcomed her leaving, but she would take what he would give her.

"You're hurt," she said.

"It's nothing." Madness strummed his thumb across her knuckles. "How is everyone?"

"Cerene and Baer are injured but stable."

"Good." He squeezed her hand. "You put me and others through a lot, you damned girl."

Aurora held back a tear by covering them with a scoff. "Did I ask for a rescue?"

"No, but we thought it was necessary."

She paused a moment longer, then asked, "Why did you come back for me?"

Madness' gaze held such intensity Aurora swore he pierced her soul. "Your sibling is the one person you love in this world more than you love yourself. You would rather the world burn than live in a world without them. When I learned Luna was your sister, I understood a piece of you because no matter the cost, I would become a demon over and over again if it meant keeping Alfonso alive."

Despite her sister's terrible deeds, Aurora still loved her sister. Their bond—that love would always exist, and before Aurora killed her sister, she would learn the truth of her demise. But all the same, Aurora had to stop her, and she would do it with the mortals by her side.

Tobias Evergreen

CHAPTER 16

They still sat in the room, Madness in the bed and Aurora in the mushroom chair, though no longer touching.

"Mephista?" Aurora inquired. "She's the demon?"

"We reference her often as, The Pull." Madness wrapped back the bandage. "I can control her for the most part, but as you saw, not always. That's when she tries to take over my body."

"I thought demons were destroyed five thousand years ago?"

Madness lowered his head. "Aurora, if I tell you all I know and you tell anyone, especially another god, I'm as good as dead. Can I trust you with this?"

The history of the demons was unknown to all the gods except Terra. The battles were so grueling the God of Earth refused to discuss them. He wanted everyone to forget the demons and the power they once held over Nelabac, but it seemed he had failed. Part of Aurora had a duty to the gods and to Nelabac, but the other half to her companions—citizens of the Second Realm.

Aurora wanted the mortals and, most importantly, Madness to trust her. "You have my full confidence."

"In the aftermath of the First Gods War, the beings of Nelabac were successful in saving it from the demons, but not as they thought," Madness began. "There are two tiers of demons: lower and Ruling. Lower demons have little personality, no concept of consciousness, and obey orders. They were the bulk of the soldiers during the war and were slayed by the armies of the Nelabac. Their masters, Ruling demons, were slain, as well, but unlike lower demons, Ruling demons can be reborn. They spawn from the ashes in the Grounds Below and make their way up to Nelabac through the cracks that separate our worlds. Ancient Magicals and mortals learned the only way to truly defeat a Ruling demon was by sealing one within a host body. Those hosts became known as Demon Seals.

"In the war, humans had the least to give in the war against demons. Some were gifted with magic from Ancient Magicals, as we know, but many still wanted to prove themselves. Those humans were the first Demon Seals. These seals struggled to control their demon and their power. The whispers of demons are consuming . . . haunting. Many failed and went insane."

Aurora watched Madness steady himself. This was painful for him, thinking of those who were like him, trapped with a demon, but they had failed.

"That gave the Ruling demon within them a chance to take control?" Aurora tried to move the conversation along.

"Yes, allowing the Ruling demon to return completely."

"Where was Terra during all this?" Aurora asked. "Did he know of these experiments?"

"Terra had to rebuild the world, so for a time, he left Ruling demons to the issues of the people. To the Ancient Magicals and mortals of Nelabac. Dwarves, faeries, elves, and wizards controlled the experiments. After some success, they moved on to experimenting with their own races. When a suitable host was found, the idea was for the Demon Seal to control the demon's power and become an unstoppable weapon. With the world back in the hands of those who occupied it, among the Ancient

Magicals of Nelabac broke out. Terra only stepped in when he learned of disharmony among the beings of Nelabac. When he learned how Demons Seals could be used as weapons, he ordered their immediate slaughter."

"So, if the demon seal is killed, so is the demon?"

Madness hesitated but then answered, "If you were to strike and kill me now, yes, both Mephista and I would die. She would never be reborn."

"How do you know all this? I mean, you're not five thousand years old?"

"Sometimes I just know things about the demons or Mephista? Or the history of Nelabac?" Madness furrowed his brow. "I can access some of her memories because she's trapped in my body."

Aurora sensed how that unnerved Madness. As if that one detail made it all the easier for Mephista to take hold of his mind and memories and make them hers. Make *him* hers.

"Demon Seals who escaped the slaughter secluded themselves. Terra believed he had eradicated the demon race, so he stopped hunting. Over time, rumors of the demons disappeared completely. For all I know, I'm the last one. The last Demon Seal."

Knowing that a demon, even one, still roamed Nelabac was unsettling. It shook the very ice in Aurora's veins.

"How did you come to possess her?"

His nails pressed into the wrappings. The pressure surely broke the skin underneath. "Healers were specifically created to stop, seal, and contain demons; our powers are a gift from the Fae-folk. The faeries did not provide humans with magic during the war against the demons, so they provided a sanctuary to those who were lost to the demon's madness. Healers once existed everywhere in Nelabac, ready to spring their powers on a Demon Seal when needed. Each village of healers knew their true purpose was not to heal people but to keep Demon Seals under lock and key. Still, healers honed their skills in all aspects of the body and shared the wealth of their gifts."

"Is it not good they shared that with others? I'd never met a healer until you and Alfonso."

"It was for their protection!" His head fell to his free hand, the other gripped Aurora's. "Belief in the gods was not the only following, Aurora. Thousands of years ago, Damonism existed. A cult that believed in the Grounds Below and wanted to see demons as the rulers of Nelabac. Damonists slaughtered the healing clans until only the clan Alfonso and I are from remained."

"Then, how are you here?" Aurora couldn't stop the questions. "How did they not find you?"

"My mother and Alfonso's mother were the best of friends. Both healing prodigies. My mother married within the village, while Alfonso's mother married an outside traveler—that's why Alfonso carries the gene of both a weapon wielder and a healer." In every flinch and break in Madness' voice, Aurora knew this story was more painful than the last. "Both women ended up pregnant around the same time, though I am a few months older. When my mother gave birth, her seal broke. She went on a rampage. Mephista took over her body and destroyed everything. The closest living thing at the time was me . . . so the clan made the rash decision to seal sealed within me."

"How did they transfer her?" Aurora asked. "If it's in the ancient language?"

"The only way to transfer demons into another vessel is to ingest their blood as they pass." Madness was cold. Cut in the silence. "There is no spell needed. The seal appears once the demon is within you."

"Gods, Madness."

Cerene had mentioned the brothers had suffered a truly painful past.

"Through my brother's efforts, my father was able to gather enough of my mother's blood . . . It nearly cost my brother his life."

"You had another brother?" And it just kept going.

"When Alfonso and I were five, Light Knights discovered us. They killed my father and Alfonso's parents. My brother. Everyone in our clan died to help us escape." Darkness engulfed him. "The night I was born was pure chaos. It was madness—and my father named me for it so I would never forget where I came from or what I truly am: a dark, maddening demon."

The malice, darkness, and cold that drifted in Madness' soul made sense. It explained his temper and why he never fought on the front lines. It explained his hesitation to trust a soul he did not already know and feel safe with. If Madness gave Mephista even an inch, he could be lost forever like his mother and all the Demon Seals before him.

"Not too overwhelming, I hope," Madness grinned, but she saw through it.

"I've heard many tragic tales," Aurora tightened her grip on his arm, "but I think yours takes the cake."

Though Madness controlled his demon with great strength, Aurora saw the strain it held. The weight ate at him. The smart-ass comments were a way to push down the pain and pretend it didn't exist, which in turn only deepened his sorrow.

"What is it, Aurora?"

Aurora. The sound of her name on his lips felt like a cool breeze on a hot day. Aurora wanted more of Madness. She wanted to know his soul.

She moved to the bed. "Do you trust me?"

Slowly, she lowered her head to his chest and let his soul fill her being. At a distance, she felt only its outer edges, but with pressed against his chest, she peered deeper into its depths, feeling Madness' true nature.

Through the murkiness, there were two souls. One was large with rounded edges; it was good, full of passion and life, but also weak. A small soul with jagged, rough edges pierced the larger soul, leeching away its life force. It clung for support, feeding off every thought, emotion, and action the larger one made.

The large soul of Madness and the small soul of Mephista were in a constant battle for control of the body they shared. The pure goodness that radiated from Madness was the only quality that kept the Ruling demon from conquering Madness entirely.

"Even if we're cursed by different devils," her hands lay across his chest, and her eyes peered into his, "I know what it's like to have a power you never wanted.

Madness' white hair contrasted his brown eyebrows and freckles. Aurora wondered if he had always had snow-white hair or if it was caused by the torment within.

His soul beat stronger. "Alfonso and I never talk about the pas. Of our lives before. Of our families. Alfonso's family traveled a lot, so he stayed with my family often and never got to know his mother and father all that well. And my father . . . well, my father never loved me. He blamed me for my mother's death. Even though Alfonso stayed with us often, he never cared for my father because he never showed compassion. And my other brother . . . it's just too painful to talk about. For both Alfonso and I, we *can't* talk about him. We can't talk about *her*."

"Not many understand what it's like to have lingering darkness." Aurora folded her hands onto the lace around her belt loop. "To have the ability to . . . destroy."

That's what I've done. I've destroyed so much.

"I've never had anyone who understands that kind of destruction." Then Madness mumbled, almost too low to hear. "So, can you be there for me, as more than my god? As my friend?"

Shadows met roses. "Of course, Madness."

The god and demon faced each other as equals, both cursed by chaos.

"Rory," Madness said, breaking the silence. "Who's Mako?"

Aurora felt the hollow sounds of empty lungs gasping for air. Those were words she had least expected to hear him say. When she found enough composure, she asked, "How do you know that name?"

"Those first nights you stayed with us, I stayed by your side. You were so frail and weak. Delicate and broken . . . "Madness confessed. "In your nightmare's you call his name over and over—wanting him and that girl, Elaina."

For years it had been the three of them roaming and meeting the people of the new Second Realm to share a new age of peace, hope, and joy with the people of the Second Realm. The three had not just become one soul but one being. A true family.

Sorrow consumed her, but Aurora wouldn't heed its call. "I need to check on the others now."

She released his hand. Aurora did not want Madness or any of the mortals to see her in such a state. She was their god and had to be strong. She did not face all she had lost and suffered. It was something she did not deserve.

"Aurora—"

But Aurora closed the door before the shadows unraveled the chains bound to her soul.

CHAPTER 17

Aurora did not know how long she slumped against the door. She did not know how long she had held Madness, either. Or how long she let herself dwell in loss. She only knew it had been far too long.

"Um."

Aurora opened her eyes to Pan. The cat sat with her promised tea between her paws.

She swished her giant tail. "Are you done flirting? Or should I come back?"

Aurora took the tea. "You do know who I am, right?"

"Do I seem like I care?"

That cat is . . .

Aurora stood, tea in hand, and returned to the main room.

The mortals were up, picking at a display of food. It seemed they had not actually rested or recovered but rather eavesdropped on her conversation. Aurora tapped the side of her teacup and sipped. A final narrowing of her eyes had the mortals whistling and looking anywhere but toward the kitchen.

The green mushroom table displayed various types of bread, jams, and fresh cheeses. Most of the board had been devoured by none other than Alfonso. Aurora picked at the remains, taking as much of the remaining apricot jam as she could on top of a single slice of bread.

"Is there any food left for me?" Madness leaned against the doorway in a clean shirt and trousers.

"Nice to see you up." Cerene perched against Tobias, who lay in his wolf form.

"I heard my abilities were needed." He introduced himself to the ill-mannered Pan before joining his friends. First, he examined Baer, who purred in greeting. Madness ran his healing hands up and down, finding Baer's injuries.

"Baer, why is it that you're the one taking on the injuries these days?" Madness wrapped his hands between the beast's shoulder. A pop sounded, then a hiss and swipe. Baer licked his shoulder before jumping to Alfonso.

"Stopping the blood flow was more important than popping the shoulder back into place," Madness said to his brother. "You made the right call."

"I don't know what this group would do without me." Alfonso leaned back against the mushroom and stroked Baer. "My life-saving abilities, keeping you under control, *and* my constant humor? You all would be at a loss."

"We'd *definitely* have more food and sleep." Cerene turned to Madness, her injured hand up. "My turn?"

Madness inspected.

"I need to mend the ligaments, muscles, bones, and tissues. If I don't soon, you'll lose function." Madness took her hand between his. "You might want to bite down on something. This is going to hurt."

Pan brought a cloth from the kitchen, and Cerene settled it between her teeth. Tobias curled up tighter around his friend and nudged her as she screamed and beat her free hand against the floor. Aurora felt every soul reach for their friend, wanting to take her agony.

It was well past midnight when Madness completed the treatment. Cerene had passed out halfway through, which allowed Madness to work with a little more grunt and pressure. Tobias helped Cerene to the back bedroom and stayed by her side. In the main room, Alfonso and Baer lay on the soft, grassy floor of the main room. Madness leaned against a wall, appearing to sleep as well.

Aurora sighed. The mortals were safe and resting, and she knew that's what her body needed, as well, but her mind would not settle. The darkness had consumed her during her time in the Altered Realm, and it still fluttered, wanting her back. Air, she needed air.

"Aurora," Pan padded beside her, "you're more than welcome to the other bed."

"I'm just going out for a little." Aurora wanted to pet Pan but remembered how the she-beast recoiled to human touch. "I'm going to sit watch."

"You know as well as I do that it's improbable for anyone to find us."

"I know, but,"—Aurora looked back in the cabin—"they deserve to feel safe, even for just a night."

The mortals had proven their desire to follow Aurora on her journey. She knew this meant revealing the full truth of her sister's demise: Revealing the existence of the Soul Keepers. Still, if she rushed into sharing any information, it could prove deadly for them.

They were mortals in a war of gods, after all.

"Suit yourself." And Pan took off into the night.

A warm breeze flew through Aurora's tangled hair. She pulled at the lace ties and tied her back. Elaina had poured love into each of her dresses, evident in their details. No two dresses were ever the same. Each was unique in its fabric, embroideries, and color schemes. She stitched them to match the person they designed for, and the work always showed. Just like the Dark Saints, no two were the same.

The betrayal they must have felt.

Aurora braided her hair in two and tied them off with the lace.

"Sulking, I see?" Madness hovered in the doorway, lighting a tobacco roll. "I hope this won't be a continuous habit of yours."

"I should have known you'd come out here to smoke after such a day."

"It was fortunate Alfonso bought a fresh pack amid your rescue."

"And how fortunate, I get to enjoy the smell."

"Take your pick." He walked over the land bridge and sat with her. "Either the smell of tobacco or the smell of my burning flesh."

Smoke filled the surrounding air. They sat long enough for Madness to light a second. After such a groundish day, neither knew what to say.

"I'm sorry about earlier," Madness finally said. "For pushing you."

Aurora leaned her head against her knees. "It's fine, we were discussing you . . . it was only right you ask about me."

"And can you?" Madness added. "Do you trust me enough to share?"

"I don't know, Madness." She lowered to her back and leaned against her forearms. "I just don't think it's necessary."

"You know, it's okay to feel them." Madness pushed. "To talk about them."

"Again, I left the room *not* to talk about them." Her chest tightened. "Besides, they're gone. There's nothing to talk about."

Her heart ached, her body hurt, and her soul was tired. The heaviness of emotions was painful, and Aurora wanted it to stop.

Madness laid back on the grass with her, placing his hand inches for hers. "You never forget the people you loved. Gone is gone, but no matter what you went through, good or bad, a piece of them stays with you forever. Even if they destroyed your entire being, you still care. The willingness to give away pieces of your soul and expect nothing in return is what it means to truly love someone."

Elaina. Mako.

"Everyone in that house means the world to me, and if I lost them, I'd never be the same. But, Aurora, that being said, there are those people who come into our lives that we simply *can't* live without." When Madness called her *Aurora* and not *Rory*, she believed every word he said. "For Cerene, that person is Tobias, and for Tobias, it's Cerene. All they've shared connects them on a level we will never understand." Madness gleamed. "For me, it's Alfonso. Without him, there is no world to return to."

"Platonic soulmates." Souls connected on a level of intimacy that was not romantic, but the love was the same. Soul wavelengths, like a heartbeat, strengthened when around a soulmate. The soul settled and fell into perfect rhythm.

"For you, those people were Luna, the girl, Elaina, and that guy, Mako." Madness leaned on one side to face her. "They are the ones you thought you would never have to live without."

Aurora blinked to rid herself of budding tears. It was all too much. She refused to accept so much change so fast. Aurora knew she lived in a river of denial, but she would float down it for as long as she could.

"Rory, you said you've heard many tragic tales. I don't want you discrediting your own simply because you're immortal. Because you're a god. You can't go on bottling up your pain. What you lost—everyone you lost—that's something no one should have to go through. And that includes what happened with your sister—"

She sat up. "Madness, stop—"

"No, Rory, listen to me." He cupped the back of her neck. His eyes longed with not only anger but fear. Fear for *her*. "The only way to describe my life is misery, but those I love make life worth living. And I promise you, Aurora, you don't want to fall into darkness and have no one to live for because, at this point, you won't make it out."

Aurora wanted none of this. Madness was human, someone without the responsibilities of the world on his shoulders. He couldn't possibly understand her. "I don't get the right to care for anyone again. To love anyone—"

"Aurora—"

But Aurora made for the door, shutting out Madness, her emotions, and the rest of the world.

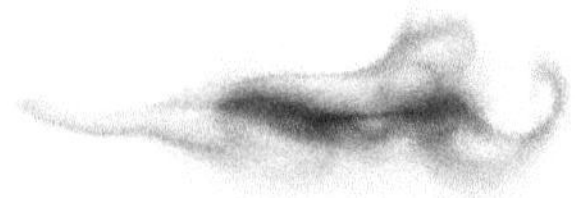

The following morning, Pan and Cerene cooked up a storm. Alfonso and Baer hovered nearby, snatching each pancake, biscuit, or piece of bacon as it cooked.

Cerene smacked at greedy hands and paws. "If you keep eating, there won't be enough for everyone else, and that *fluff* will only enlarge."

"This is far from fluff, my dear," Alfonso mumbled through the pancake and flexed his bicep. "It's all physic."

"Take that *physic* out of the kitchen." Cerene waved the spatula around. "It's getting over the food!"

"She's right," Aurora leaned against Alfonso. "It could prove a distraction."

"Rory!" Alfonso bellowed. "Pancakes?"

"No thanks," she said. "Good morning, Baer."

She scratched the beast's chin. In return rubbed, he rubbed against her hand but quickly turned his attention back to the food. Baer eyed Pan as Cerene continued to scold Alfonso.

Aurora surveyed the display of food on the counter. It was covered with crepes, eggs, pancakes, and other breakfast treats. "This is fantastic."

"Thank you," Alfonso mumbled, stuffing his face. "Made it all myself."

"I'm sure you did." Tobias echoed through the door.

Madness trailed in behind. "Alfonso is the last person in this room who could cook anything."

He moved beside Aurora, but she had nothing to say.

"Remember the one time he tried cooking?" Cerene rolled her eyes. "He nearly caught the whole camp on fire!"

"We're certain this happened only once?" Aurora inquired.

"Sad but true." Alfonso sighed. "They wouldn't let me touch a fire after that."

A crash sounded from outside the cabin door.

"Someone has found us." Cerene grabbed a knife from the kitchen and moved her arm in front of Pan. Alfonso turned to his ax with one hand and stuffed a muffin in his face with the other. Aurora also grabbed the closest kitchen utensil, which was a frying pan.

"You, who?" A sweet voice rang. "Anyone home?"

A woman with bright orange eyes peeped inside the cabin. Thick curly blonde swayed in the breeze, and flowers weaved in through a small braid. Similar to Pan, Aurora noted a diamond emblem crested on her forehead. Aurora sensed magic, pure magic flowing through the woman.

"BLOOMY!" Cerene squealed as she ran to embrace the girl.

"Cerene. You are here. In my home." Bloom's bare feet grazed the floor as she hovered inside the cabin. Her green tunic matched the grass, while her long, white skirt had golden embroidery. "Tobias, you too? Who are all these new people?"

"We've told you about these two, Madness and Alfonso. And you've met Baer." Cerene pointed to where the beast lounged with Madness. "And that lovely lady is Aurora."

"I see." Bloom took in each person in her home. Aurora noted her peculiar, aloof presence. Bloom walked over and leaned down to Madness.

"Hello," she said.

Madness side-eyed Cerene and then looked back at Bloom. "Um, hi?"

Bloom reached for Baer.

"Why are you all here?" Bloom floated to the ground beside Tobias. "You did not tell me you were coming."

"That's a rather long story to tell over breakfast," Tobias replied.

"The real question is how you got out of the Fourth Realm." Another voice, low and snarky, called from outside the door. "You don't need to convince me it was you lot that caused that place to become a gods-damned madhouse."

Cerene threw her hands in the air. "Alexen!"

A man close to Cerene's age approached the cabin. His reddish-brown hair looked like it had never seen a brush. A scar crossed his right eye and ran down below his white shirt. His dark gray pants bunched against his black boots, and a two-handed sword was strapped across his back. He held the strongest presence of anyone in the room, and to Aurora's surprise, he was utterly human.

Alfonso stood from his seat on the ground, pointing his finger at Alexen. "You!"

Alexen met Alfonso's gaze, and his smug face melted. "*You?*"

"You know him?" Madness pointed a half-eaten muffin toward Alexen.

"You bet I do!" Alfonso took a step. "He ran off with all our coin!"

Chapter 18

Tobias held back laughter. "So he's the one who took our money from you?"

"*Our money was stolen*?" Cerene and Madness scolded in unison. Cerene added, in *that* particular tone. "Why did you give him the money, *Tobias*?"

"His pockets were much more secure than mine. You know, since I turn into a wolf and drop my clothes from time to time." Aurora had never seen Tobias so relaxed. "I thought I would give him a chance to prove himself."

Alexen crossed into the cabin. "Seems he failed."

"Some girl fooled me when I was getting supplies before the distraction," Alfonso explained, "and *this* little shrimp ran off with it!"

"Who you calling, little shit?" Alexen spat.

"He actually said *shrimp*," Madness corrected. "Little shrimp, but the word you heard seems accurate enough." Alfonso approached Alexen. "Where's our money *and* your accomplice."

"Here." Bloom raised her hand.

"You?"

"I alter my appearance while Alexen thieves. It works on the careless citizens of Caris. Such as yourself."

"We only got out by using that same coin we took off of you to pay a dirty Lightning Saint to help us over that ice wall." Alexen moved to the kitchen and stuffed his face with food. "Some idiots decided to destroy Caris and blow up the entrance."

"Those idiots would, in fact, be us," Tobias said.

"For what purpose?" Bloom inquired.

Bloom and Alexen sat back, taking in all the details. Aurora noted Tobias didn't mention *why* she was a prisoner within the Fourth Realm, but neither newcomer asked why.

Bloom stroked Baer absentmindedly as if Tobias's story meant next to nothing. "I say it's rather a miracle we escape then."

"Lightning questioned anyone that didn't have a citizen pass." Alexen took a seat by his companion. "They were particularly interested in Magicals."

Aurora took a chance to better her relationship with the owners of the cabin they were in. "Are you both Magical?"

"She's Elvish." Alexen spat. "The diamond on her forehead should be a dead giveaway."

Aurora swore she heard him mumble, "*Idiot.*"

Aurora had only ever met one elf, Eden, Terra's advisor. The power an elf possessed varied from increasing battle skills and stamina to transformation and manipulation. Bloom seemed to possess a variety of skill sets.

"So, that's what the jewelry is all about." Alfonso pointed to the diamond. "It's beautiful."

Bloom said nothing, her eyes on Pan.

The room fell thick with silence. Aurora's ice was thinner than the tension filling the room. Madness eyed Alexen, while Alexen eyed Alfonso.

Three men with egos bigger than the Second Realm itself in one room? This should be fun.

All but Cerene paid any mind to the awkwardness. She beamed a smile big enough to break the tension.

"Isn't this great!" The archer draped her arm over Alexen's neck. "Everyone in one space! I've wanted this to happen for *years*."

Tobias leaned over to Aurora. "You see why that's never happened."

"It was about two or three years ago." Cerene went into how she and Tobias met Alexen, Bloom, and Pan. "Tobias and I were out with a patrol from Dandfol when a large group of Light Knights attacked us. Thankfully, these three showed up and helped out."

"Why do we not know about them, then? And the safe house?" Alfonso's brow pinched tight. "Is there a reason for not sharing that knowledge with Mad and me?"

"Bloom." Cerene angled her head toward the elf. "She asked us to keep them a secret."

Alexen offered a stern glare, one that read, *Ask any further, and you're dead.*

"When was the last time we were together?" Tobias directed toward Alexen.

"Three months." Alexen didn't hesitate to respond. He tore his gaze from Alfonso to face Tobias, softening. "Though, it's felt longer."

"That means we missed your birthday *again*." Cerene squeezed Alexen's cheeks. "What are you now, twenty-two?"

Surprisingly, Alexen allowed Cerene to pull at his cheek. "We have the same birthday. So yes, twenty-two."

Bloom sat with her back perfectly erect. "I thought we were expecting you in a few more weeks, no?"

"We had some change of plans."

Alexen held Alfonso's soul-piercing glare. "Sounds like four-eyes and company give you more trouble than they're worth."

"We have no choice," Tobias said. "We have to help Aurora."

"Why?" Alexen waved his hand at her. "What's she to you?"

Tobias was loyal to Aurora. He had proven that within their first few moments together. He knew who she was—who she had been one hundred years ago.

"Go ahead, Tobias." If he trusted Alexen, Bloom, and Pan, then she did, too.

He gave the shortest version of their journey thus far: How Aurora showed up and revealed she was the Goddess of Dark, that Last Hope was destroyed, and they traveled as Aurora's companions to end the war. "We're now steering the course for Dark Manor and then the Seventh Realm after."

Bloom did not seem fazed, her face the same neutral expression. Pan shifted uncomfortably, but Alexen's rage engulfed the room. No demon or magic lurked in Alexen, but Aurora was terrified. He was a man scorned by the state of the world, and he wanted her to know it.

"She's the reason my whole family is dead!" Alexen moved to his feet. "Why the Second and Third Realms were destroyed!"

"Alexen, that isn't fair," Cerene said, standing to face him. "Aurora is doing everything she can to fix it, and we're going to help her."

"And you trust her?" Alexen pushed back. "Cerene, you met her, what, less than a month ago and you're putting your whole faith in her?"

"She's done nothing but protect us while we've been together."

"What makes you think you can *keep* trusting her? She's a god." Alexen eyes were fueled with all the hatred of the world. "They left us and betrayed Nelabac."

"She's kept us safe, Alexen—"

"We can't trust her!" Alexen screamed.

And Cerene flinched. And the boys moved.

"Hey, asshole—"

Faster than the quickest winds, Alfonso was at Cerene's side. Madness was at his back, towering beside his brother.

"Alexen, calm down," Tobias moved, too, "please."

"And you?" Alexen turned to Tobias, his voice shifting from anger to hurt. "Traveling with her? After all you know about me? All you've been through yourself?"

Tobias reached for his hand, but Alexen pulled away.

"Don't act as if you're the only one who's experienced loss and betrayal." Madness overtook the room. "Everyone in this room has lost, and that includes Aurora. She's made sacrifices that none of us will ever understand."

Alfonso, Cerene, Tobias, and even Aurora, held their breath. Madness had gone from loathing Aurora for the same reasons Alexen did, to defending her against those who questioned her.

"She's the reason Nelabac is at war!" Alexen stepped fearlessly to a man twice his size. "What is she going to do now that she couldn't do then, hm? How do you know she's not going to turn her back on us *again*?"

"How can you stand there and blame one god—one *person* for everything that's happened?" Malice took his eyes. "You know nothing about her or what she's been through, so don't judge her off a few stories."

This is not going to end well.

"What's got you in such a tizzy, pretty boy?" Alexen poked Madness's chest. "Out of everyone, you should be the angriest. What about your family? How she and the Dark Saints weren't there to protect them? Or you? How your brother sacrificed—"

Alexen hit the ground in a flash, overpowered, unable to get in a single punch.

"That's enough, stop—please!" Cerene reached for the moving bodies. "*Alfonso*, get off!"

Alfonso and Alexen were the same in height and build, but it was Alfonso's fury gave him the advantage. Alexen thrashed around under the brute force Alfonso threw behind each punch. All he could do was throw up an arm to block and wait.

Madness pulled for his brother while Tobias gathered a bloodied Alexen. The two still reached for each other as their counterparts calmed them down. Bloom stood from the ground and moved over to Alexen, unspeaking but ever-present, glaring at Alfonso, and Cerene stood in the room, shaking, angry.

War raged outside the cabin walls, and if this group was going to fight alongside Aurora to stop those wars, they could not battle amongst one another.

"That's enough."

The room darkened and Madness and Tobias stepped back immediately. Alfonso took a double-take but put his fist down and stepped beside his brother. Alexen gazed, but not in fear. Aurora had to hand it to him, as all that poured from his soul was wonder, even awe. Bloom mustered a slight change in expression as her eyes widened.

"I'm sorry for what has happened to you because of my mistakes." Even though Alexen and Bloom needed to hear her more than the others, Aurora faced each of them for a moment. "I am going to do everything I can to fix what I've broken." She extended a hand. "The Second Realm is our home, and we each deserve the chance to fight and see it restored to its former glory."

Blood trickled from Alexen's hands, nose, and lip. Bruises covered his face, but he reached for Aurora's hand—

And he smacked it away, leaving traces of blooded left on her palm, yet Aurora paid no mind as she offered, "Join us, Alexen—Bloom and Pan. Join us in changing this world and stopping the war. See that I follow through on my word."

Pan gave a disapproving glare. "I've watched the beings of this world tear one another apart for decades. I don't know what you can do now that can change Nelabac's pain—to alter its histories . . . but between Bloom's enchantments and Alexen's strength, we would better your chances."

"Ha," Alfonso covered his mouth, "she said Alexen's *skills*." Madness chuckled along, "The fight between you two proved otherwise." Aurora shot them a look seeping of death. They silence/

"I fear Light Knights have seen us in our most recent comings and goings," Bloom tapped the pad of her index finger against her lip. "I'd rather not wait to find out if that's the case. It might be best for us to leave."

"N*o*." The panic in Alexen's eyes told his story. "We aren't going to risk our lives to help this fallen and pathetic god."

"Alexen," Tobias approached, "let's talk about—"

Alexen pulled back and stormed to the valley. Tobias reached, but Bloom stood before him.

"Let him go," she said. "You know how he gets."

The two held a bond that ran deeper than general affection, as Tobias didn't even show Cerene such tenderness. Glancing at the mortals, with seemed Madness and Alfonso were as surprised as she at their steady friend so shaken. It seemed Cerene understood the depth of the bond between Tobias and Alexen as her face twisted in empathy for her dearest friend.

"Bloom, do you still have that map?" Tobias shoved down whatever thoughts were on his mind and returned to the mission. "The one of Nelabac? We need to mark where we've been and where we're going."

With a snap of Bloom's fingers, the map appeared. It was dated by nearly three hundred years, but it had to do.

"Dark Manor is here." Tobias pointed to a section further to the north. "It's a good four weeks away, but if we take this path through the Mulga Woods, we can cut it down to two."

"I'm all for seeing the Dark Manor, Aurora, really," Alfonso said, his finger on the map, "but why are we heading to the Seventh Realm? I thought our goal was the Resistance?"

"We need allies," Aurora explained. "Immortal allies."

Mortals can try all they want, but they will never win alone.

"Light Knights consume the Mulga Woods, though." Bloom pointed out. "Should we just take the longer route instead?"

"No, there is no time to waste." Aurora declared. "Alliances are already forming, and we are falling behind in this war."

Time was not on their side, and delaying by even minutes could be detrimental. Besides, there was a direct link to Juvia's castle waiting for them at Dark Manor, but Aurora would only reveal the secret when the time came.

I'll tell them what they need when they need to know and not a moment prior.

She knew they had questions, especially Bloom and Pan. Aurora only thanked the gods that everyone accepted her word on the matter and moved on.

"Now that we've discussed our route and arriving, you all need to learn about God Society." Aurora stood above the map. "Even though both were mortals at one point, no immortal sees mortals as an equal—Ancient Magical, Magical, or human, all are the same in their eyes."

"Rory," Alfonso picked at his tooth, "I can't wait to meet all your friends."

"Yeah, they sound charming," Cerene chimed in.

"Thrilling."

"Most inviting."

"*All right.*" Aurora learned this type of banter was a habit of theirs. "In order to gain some respect, knowing a little about each's culture, traditions, attire, and ranking will make all the difference." She sat back down on the ground. "They won't fully accept you, but we can try."

"We know of guards and agents," Cerene said, "and missioners."

"Yes, but you don't know a thing about their behaviors or how to judge which realm they hail from or what to expect from each god and their saints."

Aurora flipped the map and asked for a pen, to which Bloom responded with a snap.

"We can skip Lightning since you are familiar." Aurora didn't go into more detail regarding the Fourth Realm. Besides, she did not anticipate political discussions or civil meetings with Blesk and the Fourth Realm in the near future. She drew out six figures, one for each of the other six gods and their saints. "In the Sixth Realm, the Realm of Earth, they wear hats made of bark and other belongings of the forest that they spin together with threads of spider silk." She drew out six figures, one for each of the other six gods and their saints. "They wear giant monstera leaves as clothes and embroider flowers for design. They are the oldest and proudest saints among the seven, and for good reasons. Terra has ruled Nelabac alongside Eden, his advisor, for over five thousand years. Together, they have saved it more than any other gods combined."

Elaina had always wanted to watch the tailors of the Sixth Realm to find out if they did make their clothes of spider silks. The child dreamed of carefully taking apart the leaves to see what they used to make such clothing. If the rumors of the spider silks, gigantic red oaks, and venom of basilisks were true.

And now she'll never know.

Aurora shook the thought and continued. "The First Realm tends to have more loose clothing. Often found in grays and blues, also some neutrals, though I doubt, we'll have any run-ins with them. They tend to be dismissive and aloof, not paying attention to the wars of this part of the world."

"What do you mean?" Alfonso asked.

"Lust's realm works differently than the others, as the First Realm and its lands are a mystery."

"What about the Fire Saints?" Cerene's face was eager. She leaned over to Bloom. "I've heard they leave little to the imagination."

Aurora laughed. "They wear very minimal clothing as they reside in the hottest part of Nelabac. What clothes they do wear are typically dark browns and warm reds with black and gold hints."

"They're also a very *fit*, yes?" Cerene raised her brows. "Muscular and beautiful?"

"All right, all right!" Alfonso cleared his throat. "Let's get back to the task at hand, shall we?"

Cerene and Bloom rolled their eyes.

"Oberon is a feisty god, though his advisor, Draken, keeps him level-headed," Aurora explained. "Oberon is kind-hearted, but he's not someone to tip off. He and the Fire Saints are not afraid to retaliate. Regardless if Oberon or Draken give a command, Fire Saints do not hesitate to protect their own."

Out of everyone, I hope Fire and Earth are on our side.

"We'll be spending a great deal of time with Water Saints." Aurora drew along the last figure. "They wear uniforms in shades of blue. Juvia is level-headed, and her decisions are never driven by emotion. In my opinion, Juvia is the one who leads the gods as a true, immortal being. Personal gain is never on her mind—only the benefit of Nelabac."

And that would make or break the war. If Juvia saw the benefit in aligning with Aurora to stop Luna, she would, but that also went the other way, as well. If Juvia thought allying with Luna and Blesk would better Nelabac in the end, she would not hesitate to do so.

"If for some reason you can't tell which saint belongs to which Realm by their clothes, and they do not display their powers, the best course of action is to take a look at their palms to find a god's sigil." Aurora drew sigils for each god below their drawings. "Each sigil is unique to its god and true to its nature. The symbol of Earth is a monstera leaf; the symbol of Water is three water swirls; the symbol of Fire is blazing; the symbol of Sir is gusts of winds; the symbol of Lightning is a striking bolt of electricity; and the symbol of Light is a perfect blazing sun."

"Rory, you're an artist!" Cerene admired. "I'll have you make a sketch of me one day."

"You missed one." Pan's tail flicked across the paper. "You did not draw *our* symbol."

Aurora's mind ran blank, then, she chuckled. "Oh, you're right." She thought of their faces. How happy many were when they saw the mark of the moon tattooed across their palms. "Well, it's not really relevant, right?"

They don't exist anymore anyway . . . I'm the last."

Aurora cast down her eyes, refusing to meet the faces of the mortals. If she did, she feared she would break.

"I mean . . . I'm the last."

A boutique of white roses—

Aurora's vision blurred. The cabin changed. The map filled with her symbol, scattering across the white paper over and over. The other figures were then covered in black—their faces hidden in shadows.

Aurora threw herself back against the wall. It—*they* wouldn't go away. Aurora lifted her head for the mortals. She couldn't breathe—

"I . . ."

She looked up to meet their faces, but they were gone—replaced by the beloved Dark Saints she had held so dear. The ones she had failed. Left behind. Sacrificed.

Murdered.

Alfonso reached for her. "Rory?"

"Don't touch me!" She threw out a hand.

Every blink, every glance—

She had to move—had to get away from the images flashing around the room, away from the images overtaking her friends.

The bedroom.

A tight and small space, she needed to feel secure. In the room, she kicked the door before anyone could enter and pressed all weight into it.

This attack was more than overflowing emotions, but this was an attack from her true self—from her soul. Aurora had detached from it since returning but had ignored the signs. Dark Manor was the only place to find answers, to connect back to where she felt most grounded.

"Rory?" *Cerene.* Her sweet voice carried over the knocking. "We are packing our things. We thought it would be best to get on the road as soon as possible."

Weight pressed back against the door.

"Do you have anything to pack?" Cerene asked. "What can I do for you?"

The silence said everything Aurora could not.

"You come out when you're ready." Cerene stood. "We're here for you."

Aurora leaned her head back and sighed.

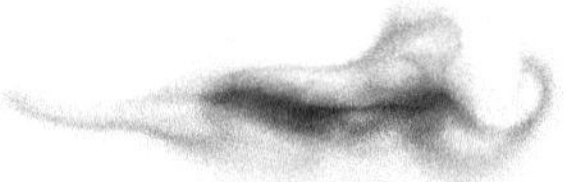

Aurora emerged from the bedroom, and when she did, the mortals proceeded as normal. Like they had not witnessed her have a breakdown. Aurora was grateful.

Cerene double-checked each pack once they were complete. Alfonso and Bloom discussed the best ways to pack all the food; he fussed as Bloom took a bite of each item they packed away and ignored each scolding.

Looks like Alfonso has some competition for who has the biggest appetite.

Baer ran back and forth as Pan ordered strict instructions on what to do around the cabin. Madness sat in a corner, packing medical supply Bloom had lain about the cabin.

"Where's Tobias?" Aurora asked anyone listening.

"He and Alexen had some things to sort out." Cerene put away the last of her belongings. "Come. I made you a pack.

Cerene had packed her bag with water, bread, and other baked foods on top and a blanket tucked at the bottom.

With the bag secured, Aurora straightened and faced the mortals. Tobias and Alexen had rejoined them, bringing all nine of them together.

Eight—eight mortals in my hands.

Each adjusted the straps of their bags and secured their weapons. Tobias and Alexen joined, as well. Their eyes were on her, and that's when Aurora realized they were waiting for her—waiting for her order.

"Our true journey is about to begin. Our true journey is about to get dangerous. We're about to journey to the heart of this war, and some gods will do anything in their power to stop us. They won't care if you're mortal and will stop at nothing to kill you." Aurora made eye contact with each mortal, searching for any small sign of hesitation. "When it comes to decisions, I won't be questioned. My word is law. I'm a god—your god. The decisions of the gods are never wrong."

For the first time in weeks, Aurora felt light hit her soul. The mortals were strong and hearty, and she didn't know what she had done to deserve such loyal companions, but as much as the moment before Aurora was a celebration, it was also an obstacle. Reaching Dark Manor and the Seventh Realm was not the end of their journey, only the start.

"We are at your service, Aurora, Goddess of Dark and Ruler of the Second Realm," Tobias kneeled. "Our weapons and souls are yours to lead."

Soul Keepers were a deadly secret, the one that was going to get the mortals killed. If either Luna or Blesk assumed the mortals knew anything of the Soul Keepers, they would torture them to death for that information.

When we are safe in the Seventh Realm, I'll tell them the full truth.

"What seems to be the issue here?" Pan asked, clutched tightly in Bloom's arms.

A bag slouched at Alexen's feet. It slouched as if Alexen had kicked it a few times.

Finally, Alexen said, "I'm not coming."

"I thought we decided you were coming?" Tobias stood shocked.

"Alexen, please come." Bloom flinched, giving away some emotion. "We need you by our side."

"I don't trust *her*." He pointed across the room. Aurora almost felt hurt, but if Alexen did not want to come, it was one less mortal soul to fret over. "If you all want to go and die then fine—but I refuse."

Tobias reached. "Alexen—"

"He has explained, and he does not wish to come." Mixed emotions wrapped around the she-beast's soul. "Let us make haste and waste no more time on the matter. According to you lot, time is of the essence."

Aurora felt her soul lighten, more confident in the decision to wait and say anything about the Soul Keepers. More mortals could decide to leave, and they would carry the dangerous burden.

Aurora traveled several yards from the cabin, giving the mortals the opportunity to say their goodbyes. Alfonso and Madness strode ahead, neither bothered by Alexen's decision. Cerene forced Alexen into a hug before joining Aurora.

Bloom and Pan faced him. Bloom extended both of her hands, and Alexen took them.

"I hope it's worth it." His gaze met Bloom's, longing with hesitation.

"The only way to find what you truly seek is to try everything until you find it," Bloom replied.

"You're so weird, Bloom." Alexen's eyes shot to Aurora. "Just . . . please, watch your back."

"Of course, we must, now," Pan said as Bloom turned from Alexen. "As that was your job."

Unlike the band of mortals Aurora had gotten to know, Bloom and Pan, and Alexen seemed wary of everything around them. The three hid secrets, that much Aurora knew, but what those secrets were remained unclear. They were quieter, more cautious of their every move and next words. Alexen was too distrusting, so much so, he refused to accompany his dearest friends. To him, risking it alone was safer than risking it with those he cared for by his side. It pained Aurora to think about whatever they had been through to create such skepticism and distrust.

The last to leave Alexen's side was Tobias. Aurora and the mortals stepped back further, watching from a distance as Tobias still tried to persuade Alexen to join them. The conversation ended with Alexen stomping inside the cabin and Tobias daring to place a foot back inside.

When Alexen finally slammed the door, Tobias withdrew. He padded out in front, dropped his clothes, and transformed.

Cerene went for him. "Tobias—"

But he was gone, bounding through the forest to mask his broken heart.

Bloom Holloworth

CHAPTER 19

The Mulga Woods' dangerous nature proved true. Light Knights crawled everywhere, seeking and hunting any living creature they encountered. When Aurora and the mortals weren't resting, they were on guard or in a fight.

With Dark Manor less than two days away, Aurora was on edge. She lay by the fire, cleaning her nail beds as the mortals settled for the night. Alfonso, Bloom, and Pan sat to her left, discussing magic. Baer and Cerene snuggled in close with Aurora, listening in. Tobias and Madness were off securing the area.

"So, how do your enchantments work?" Alfonso leaned against his side, munching on an apple. "Have you ever used them in battle?"

Bloom twirled the ends of her curly blonde hair, eyes on the fire. "If I tell, my powers lose some meaning."

It was safe to assume Bloom had spent many years on the run, hiding away and concealing her powers. She was cautious, only speaking when necessary and listening to everything. She kept those she cared for at a distance. Aurora had observed the she-elf to have a good soul. She was kind, too kind, it seemed, s even in that moment, Bloom was too considerate of Alfonso's feelings to tell him to back off. So the half-elf listened and responded to every question or comment he had within a boundary she felt comfortable.

The underbrush stirred. It was Tobias and Madness returning from a perimeter check. Tobias moved behind Cerene, settling in with Baer at his side. Aurora glanced at Madness as he sat next to his brother.

"But, Bloom, with the Water Wall of the Seventh Realm, would your magic be able to alter our appearance?" Alfonso shifted the conversation slightly. "Almost trick the magic and allow us passage?"

"Even Elfish powers do not exceed the powers of the immortals," Bloom said. "We would die before we ever got through the Water Wall."

Alfonso perched his lips as if disappointed.

Madness leaned behind his brother and whispered, "Is this man bothering you?"

Alfonso's brow twitched.

Bloom taped her lip and then bluntly stated, "Actually, yes."

"He's certainly bothering *me* more than usual," Pan hissed.

Alfonso collapsed on his side, pretending to take a sword through the side. "I never knew a cat's words could cut so deep."

"Leave them be—besides, as I've explained," Aurora assured them *again,* "reaching Dark Manor is the only way to reach the Seventh Realm."

Their eyes filled with questions, which they kept to themselves.

The fire's embers dimmed, and everyone turned in for the night. Baer yawned and extended his little paws onto Alfonso's feet. Then, he transformed and wrapped his giant paws around Alfonso, holding him like a child held gripped a stuffed animal. Their joint snores filled the camp in minutes.

"I'll take watch." Tobias began to transform.

"Tobias, no." Cerene walked to his side. "You've been on watch every night the last two weeks. Please, rest. Let Bloom and I take watch."

But Tobias ignored her concerns as his paws carried him into the woods. Cerene stared into the blackness of the trees where he had wandered off.

"Don't worry about him." Pan rubbed against Cerene's back. "He's trying to process how he feels."

"Mortal, Magical, or not: the species of *man* remains the same across the board." Bloom rolled her eyes.

"Right?" Aurora chimed.

"I'm tired of the sulking!" Cerene marched toward the woods. "Alexen left us *all* behind, not just him."

Bloom and Pan eyed each other and looked at Aurora.

"For *his* safety, I'd go get her."

Alone by the fire felt . . . odd. Those days, Aurora was *never* alone. She and Alfonso pulled pranks on their companions; Tobias and she traveled a little further back, mulling over the old days and smiling at the memories. Baer rode on her shoulders to observe from a higher viewpoint. And at night, Cerene cuddled close and talked up a storm. Their conversations often had no rhyme or reason, but Bloom lay beside them, giggling at the nonsense. The three only hushed when Pan had reached her limit and gave them a good hiss.

The mortals had carved a special place in Aurora's heart. It felt odd to sleep without them—not to have one closer to her side in the night. Their freeness and love of one another were admirable, and Aurora felt honored to have a place among them.

There was *one* option.

Across the fire, the flames and smoke obscured Madness, but Aurora knew he smoked a tobacco roll. The two had hardly spoken to one another since departing Secret Valley. Madness only if she was okay, and Aurora always responded with a yes, and they went their separate ways. Both knew things were left unspoken, but neither dared to utter the first words.

"Not going after the brooding wolf?" She craned her body over to rest her hands against her chin.

Madness looked up from his tobacco and then back at the fire. "In our time together, I've only ever seen Tobias that distraught a few times, and it's *always* after he and Cerene return from a run." He blew smoke. "Now, it seems I know why."

"He and Cerene really never mentioned them?"

"Tobias is one of my dearest friends, and never did he mention Alexen or Bloom or the temperamental cat," Madness said. "I can't believe he finds that asshole enjoyable."

"You almost sound jealous."

"Ha, yeah, because redheads are *so* my type."

Aurora's eyes darted to the empty space where Cerene and Bloom had been.

Am I this desperate? That I'm going to try and cuddle—no, not cuddle—but lay casually with Madness?

Silence filled the space.

Yes, yes, I am.

Her flimsy blanket proved difficult to work with as she wiggled across the glass like an inchworm. Madness turned his head to see her moving his way.

A grin spread across his face. "Are you a worm?"

"How did you know?" Aurora planted beside him and huffed.

His hands plopped to his lap," So, why did you *worm* your way over here?"

"Your jokes are nearly as bad as your brother's."

He gasped and held his chest. "You *hurt* me."

Aurora felt her soul lighten, felt her heart beat a second quicker.

His eyes peered into her as they had the other day. Like he fully understood the most intimate parts of her soul. Like he knew what she was going to say. And maybe that's why every time they spoke, the unspoken unraveled, and Aurora felt her chest was on fire and that everything else in the world didn't matter.

So she looked over and said what Madness already knew. "I don't want to be alone."

The fire died, leaving them with embers. Aurora lay on her back, star gazing. Madness looked at his tobacco roll, tossed it to the ground, and joined her.

"You do this every night," Madness said.

"What?"

"When everyone else has gone to sleep, you stay up last, watching the sky." His rosy eyes seemed a shade brighter in the moonlight. "Only when it's cloudy do you drift to sleep before everyone else, but never on a clear night. On those nights, you fall asleep with stars in your eyes."

"I did the same when I was younger." Aurora rolled to her side. "I would gaze at the stars for hours. Fall asleep under them. Luna would scold me and drag me back to whatever makeshift shelter we were staying in that night. Then, when Luna and I were drafted into the Second Gods War, I did the same."

"And what was that like?" Madness asked. "In comparison to this?"

"Organized chaos. Organized terror." Aurora shrugged. "The god war was gruesome . . . terrifying to face as a mortal, but on some nights, I didn't care, because I needed the moon."

"Luna?"

Aurora nodded.

His eyes found hers. "You really were mortal."

"Oh, yes, I fought for Juvia then—well, we didn't have a choice at that point, but that's another story." The memories raced. "When we were drafted, Luna and I were separated. Luna was already a strong fight, while I needed some training. At some point during the war's climax, we were reunited on the battlefield, and then we died. And then we came back as gods."

"It's hard to believe you were once like us."

"I meant it when I said I understand the pain of being mortal in an immortal world. I died for them. And, in turn, I became one."

A suffering far worse than death, it seems.

"How older were you?"

"Madness, it's rude to ask a woman her age," she joked.

"Oh, forgive my question Miss I-look-twenty-but-I'm-really-five-hundred."

She pursed her lips. "I was twenty-six, and Luna was twenty-eight."

Madness rolled and faced her. "Do you know why you became one?"

"I was never told. None of us were." Aurora looked back to the sky. "It was a life dealt that I don't believe any of us really wanted."

Part of her wanted to pull from the conversation, but this was not the time. Madness had lain his soul to her, and Aurora had—no—*wanted* to return the gesture.

"Luna has always protected me. Both in our mortal and immortal lives."

"And you never saw this coming?" Madness asked. "You never saw the darkness she wanted to spread across Nelabac?"

"I don't know what happened to her along the way. Like she became someone completely different . . . someone I don't know."

Aurora wasn't expecting Madness' next move. She wasn't expecting him to lean over, to feel him so close. To *want* him so close.

"As much as I hate you lost your sister"—his hand twirled along her hairline—"sometimes people don't want you to save them, and, in the end, they continue down the path they paved for themselves. In the end, no matter what we do, we can't save them."

The words lingered, and her heart frayed open. "Your sibling is your first and last best friend. The first people you learn to love for who they are. How can you turn your back on that?"

For a moment, Aurora thought Madness understood. That Madness grasped why Aurora wrestled with her duties as a god and her duties as a sister. Love was complicated, but when was it right to let go?

"You're right, but it's hurting you, Rory." Madness reached for her. "This relationship with Luna is hurting you."

"Don't act like you know everything there is to know about Luna or me." Aurora pulled back. "The other today, you said you understood me, right? You said you and I were the same."

"I know what I said."

"Then what in God's Realm is your problem?" Aurora stood above him. "Why do you have this constant desire to pick a fight with me? To counter how I am with my sister? Why do you care so much!"

"When you stop pretending that you're all fine and put back together inside when you're not!" Madness stood a head above her. "Luna wounded you deeper than someone who loves another should, yet you keep reaching for her. You keep protecting her—and what for? Why?"

"Don't speak to me like that. I'm a god, for crying out loud!" Aurora attacked, knowing it would hurt. "And don't act like you don't have your own problems. Don't act like you don't toil with the demons inside and the hauntings of the past."

She saw him stiffen but kept going.

"I notice how you don't sleep, and when you do, you wake up clenching your chest. You wake up holding back screams. I see how Mephista has a stronger hold on you than you let anyone, even Alfonso, know."

"Rory—"

"But the thing is Madness, you don't tell him because you secretly wish she would take over."

"Stop it—"

"You hate living, Madness, and you're just waiting for the day Mephista finally wins so you can let it all go."

Shadows danced. Black flames sang. Madness grabbed Aurora's shirt, pulling her close, but the darkness didn't like that. So ice lanced, stopping only at the skin of his neck. Both twisted with wickedness only known to those with powers beyond the worlds of Nelabac.

A god. A demon. Aurora truly didn't know who would win if they fought at full strength. The idea excited her.

"I said we were one of a kind." Red danced in his eyes. "But the biggest difference between you and I, Aurora, is that I'm human—mortal—and, eventually, I will die. Move on from this world, but not you. You'll grieve with your sins after Nelabac is gone, and that's a fate worse than death because you'll be all alone."

Aurora stumbled with the weight of his release, and Madness disappeared through the woods before Aurora had the chance to recover.

"Gods!" She peered at the grass through her knees and pulled the blades out.

"The nerve of that guy."

To the right, Alfonso crawled out from under Baer. The beast shifted and rolled over, not waking.

"You know, you two really need to work on keeping topics on the lighter side." He walked toward her. "You both have *way* too much going on to have conversations like that just yet."

"I said things I shouldn't." He heard every hateful word that had spilled from her lips. "I was frustrated and—"

"Madness will be in an even bigger mood once he realizes he doesn't have these to cool him off." Alfonso sat beside her and picked up Madness' pack of tobacco. "He probably realized by now that he left them but is too proud to come back." He took one out of the pack and rolled it around. "Rory, I don't know if you've noticed, but Mad isn't exactly the cookie-cut tough guy he tries to be. His burdens run into a past he can't let go of."

"He has a demon, but it's not the burden of all burdens." Aurora took the box from Alfonso. "I'm the one who threw Nelabac into the chaos it's in now."

"At least you *both* have the self-loathing thing down. Exactly why you constantly are at each other's throats." Alfonso pointed. "I know you and Mad have the whole cursed-power thing in common—"

"*All* right—"

"But you and I also have some things in common."

"Al, you and I are nothing alike." Aurora blinked. "You're kind and fun. You put others before yourself, never thinking twice about how decisions will affect everyone around you. You're the most considerate person I've ever met."

Alfonso was an earnest and kind protector, solely moving with every fiber to keep his brother safe. To protect him from absolute madness.

"You flatter me with such compliments!" Alfonso pretended to faint but gathered himself quickly. "But yes, we are alike, Rory. All your life,

I'm sure you've looked up to Luna as an invincible being, but even they have a weakness." His eyes changed. "For Luna and Madness, it's us."

Luna had always taken charge and made decisions on their behalf when they were children, all to ensure Aurora had everything she needed. Even if the trouble was an opponent was twice their size, Luna would beat them to a pulp if they threatened Aurora. Back then, Luna did anything to keep her little sister safe, no matter what it meant for her in the end.

"For Madness, when he sees you fight for Luna, the one who was supposed to be the one protecting you, *hurting you*, it breaks his heart." Alfonso tapped at his chest as if the pain reached through his very soul. "He knows she is to blame for your pain, and I don't blame him. We all feel that way about Luna and how she has treated this world and you. How you continue to save her. It's noble, yes, but as your friend, it's horrible to watch."

"Al." Aurora placed her hand on his, trying to calm the trembling. The Dark Saints had never been so honest with Aurora, and maybe she had willed it that way.

"But Madness, with him, it's different. He is always so worried about everyone else that he forgets his feelings are just as important." Alfonso trembled. "No matter how hard I try to get him to share and reveal how he feels, I never can. So, the fact he's found someone he's comfortable with is huge."

"I was so harsh with him just now. I don't think that's true."

"I'm the most important person to him, so he'll do everything he can to protect me. That includes protecting me from the parts of himself that he hates." He choked back tears. "It doesn't matter if it's his own self-pity feelings, he always throws his guard up. Even if Madness has to suffer because of it, he will say nothing to keep me safe."

Aurora hated the tango the brothers danced to protect one another. Their relationship was raw for anyone to see. A love that ran so deep it was beginning to hurt them both.

"I do what I can, but it will never be enough. I feel him crumble away a little more each day. I see him give in a little more each time she rears her head." Alfonso cried, desperate and searching. "Even if he's stubborn or sometimes cruel, something clicked in him that day he decided to trust you, Aurora. With you, he says *everything*. I don't know what it is or why, but he gives you feelings that he'll never entrust with me."

"Al, you already help him so much." Aurora wanted to comfort Alfonso as a friend, but he needed her as a god. He needed her to heed a promise. "Without you, Madness would have no reason to carry on. Grounds Below, without you, Mephista—"

"She has no name when talking to me. Call her nothing or call her The Pull."

"You can stop The Pull from taking over his body and taking him from us altogether." Aurora sensed the steadily-built anger in his soul, ready to erupt. "You are his beloved sibling, who knows Madness in ways only you do. Siblings have an invisible string linking them together for eternity. Your souls are one."

The siblings were a mirror. Both wanted to help, yet causing harm, only Aurora wondered, was if Luna wanted help. If she even wanted saving one hundred years ago.

Sometimes people don't want you to save them.

For centuries, Luna had put her sister's interest before her own, and the one time Aurora tried to do the same for her sister, the world fell to shambles. Aurora had destroyed the world for her sister but knew she would do it again. She would never regret trying to save her beloved big sister.

Hand still in hers, Alfonso laid his head on her shoulder and snored away. Aurora lowered him to the ground and lay her chest on his. As he claimed, Alfonso knew her well. He understood what it was like to be the ever-doting, concerned younger sibling, and what it was like to love someone so broken.

Bonds that strong sometimes cause the most damage.

Chapter 20

Aurora felt the fire before she saw it.

Her eyes opened to a hazy, smoke-filled forest. The raging flames poured from every part of the Mulga Woods. Bright and blue. Inextinguishable.

Fire Saints.

Alfonso slept next to her, unaware of anything happening. She shook him violently. Alfonso did not only sleep loud; Alfonso slept, and he slept *hard.* She finally had to take a hand to his cheek.

"Al—*fonso*!"

"I'm up!" He looked around. "Really? A fire?"

They scattered the camp for their supplies and friends. Alfonso went for his bag and Baer, but the sleeping beast had already taken off. Madness was also gone.

"Where did they go?" she noted his panic.

"I'm sure they went on to find the others." Aurora released ice to cool the blue flames, hoping to relieve some of the flames, but they did not go out. There was only one reason.

"Al, we need to run."

"Why?"

"It's as a feared." She grabbed his arm, Madness' pack of tobacco beside them, and sprinted as fast as her legs would carry her. "These flames are the works of Fire Saints."

As they ran, Aurora felt the animals' pain and panic. They fled as their world was annihilated. Aurora saved what little she could. In Aurora's current condition, her strength and powers matched the Fire Saints', and she was in no state to protect Alfonso and the other mortals. They would fall to the smoke and ash before they fell to the power of the Fire Saints.

Aurora halted their escape and focused for the souls of the mortals. On their shapes. Their familiarity. If they did not find them . . .

Gods, help them all.

She listened for the sound of their feet under the chaos. For their voices among the embers. Alfonso clung as close to Aurora as possible as the flames narrowed closer. Sheets of ice extended from Aurora's feet as she searched—

"Gods!" She ran her fingers through her scalp. "I can't find them!"

"Then we need to keep moving!" Alfonso took her hand and ran. "We've survived worse."

Through the forest, Aurora felt Alfonso grow heavier. He weakened the longer they stayed in the burning woods, so Aurora tried again to find the mortals.

There

"Left," she said, and Alfonso understood.

"Right."

"Straight—"

But a body, with a fast, painful force, slammed them against the earth.

Aurora shook, anticipating a Fire Saints.

"What in God's Realm"—Alfonso held his breath—"*Alexen*?"

Alexen scurried before them to something—rather the some*one*—he had thrown in their collision.

"They wouldn't back down!" Alexen coughed, his eyes clouded with worry. "They kept sending hottest flames I've ever felt—the thickest of smoke."

Tobias lay unmoving and in bad shape. Endless questions raced through Aurora's mind. Alfonso scratched his head, as confused as she, but it was not the time to ask questions. Alexen's breath went ragged as he struggled to lift Tobias. Carrying the weight of Tobias alone would kill them.

"Hey, let us help," Aurora offered.

"No!" Alexen shouted. "If we die, it's on my watch. *Not yours.*"

Reluctantly, they let Alexen push forward with Tobias. Aurora extinguished as much of the fire as she could, but Alexen moved so slow the flames caught up. Alexen's commitment was admirable, but it was going to get him, Alfonso, and Tobias killed, and Aurora would rather the mortal hate her a little more than lose a single one of them.

"Can't you heal him?" Aurora asked Alfonso. "At least enough to get us through the forest?"

"I'm not strong enough." Alfonso's head lowered. "This kind of damage is something only the best can handle."

The smoke thickened, and before they knew it, Alexen had staggered, dropping Tobias. He moaned in pain as he placed Tobias in his lap.

"I'm sorry," he whispered. No further words were exchanged, only a simple kiss on the cheek.

Like the Grounds Below we're leaving anyone behind.

"Alexen." Aurora walked over and placed her hand on his shoulder. "Alexen, please, let me help—"

"Don't touch him!"

Alexen was breaking—crumbling at the sight of someone precious to him dying right before his eyes. It reminded Aurora back to the Dark Saints. To watching Manda die in her arms. To the cursed look that Luna had given Aurora before she was sealed away.

"Tobias is important to me, too, Alexen!" Alfonso took him by the shoulders. "But, if you don't let us help get Tobias out of this forest and to Madness, then we *all* are going to die. You don't have to trust her alone but trust me. Trust me when I say this is the only way to get out of here."

And then a roar rang through the burning forest. A giant, feral beast loomed over their shoulders. The unusual blazing violet color of the black beast's eyes caught her attention.

"Are you all having a picnic?" Pan growled, unfazed by Alexen's presence. The sheer size of Pan's transformation was frightening, not to mention her thick, long fur added to her density. On her back was Bloom, eyes locked on her friends.

Another giant figure ran in from behind. It was Baer, carrying Madness. As the beast came to a halt, Madness jumped to their side. Aurora couldn't help feeling relief at the sight of Madness, and thankfully, everyone appeared unharmed.

"Here." Bloom jumped from Pan's back. She whispered an enchantment, and a thickness settled over their faces. "It will ventilate the smoke."

"The flames!" Pan hissed. "We must move!"

Alfonso lifted Tobias on the back of Baer while Bloom and Alfonso lifted Alexen. Before parting, Aurora caught a glimpse of their entangled palms.

"Where did he even come from?" Panic filled Bloom's voice. Pan lowered her body to the ground, making it easier for Alfonso to lift their injured friend. "Is he still breathing?"

"Yes, but barely," Alfonso confirmed pulling himself onto the Pan's back. Aurora noted the weapon wielder coughed. "Where is Cerene?"

Bloom pinched her lips. "We don't know."

Cerene was missing in the midst of a blazing forest, but they had to leave. Aurora's soul tightened, twisting in agony. And then she felt one.

It had called out on its own. She didn't reach for the soul, had not asked to feel its agony, but its pain was great enough to find her on its own. Aurora looked to Alfonso, realizing she didn't need to search further to find to whom it belonged.

Baer and Pan ran side by side, brushing against each other to encourage a steady pace. The smoke overwhelmed their line of sight, but Bloom's enchantment kept their lungs safe from further damage. The whole time,

Alexen forced himself to stay awake, asking of Tobias every few minutes. Bloom hovered, easing his worries.

The forest trees finally opened to the Wandering Plains, a vast stretch of open field that stretched to the northern part of the Second Realm. Dark Manor sat half a day's walk from them, but with their current circumstances, Aurora did not know how long it would take until they actually arrived.

"The fires are long behind us," Madness called out. "We need to stop so I can take a look at the damage on their bodies."

They possessed fewer belongings than before. There was one blanket, very little food, and a few pieces of flint. Bloom enchanted a tent from cloth in her bag, and they moved the injured inside, Tobias clutched at his chest, heaving and clenching in pain. Madness stroked his friend's head as a blue hue of healing filled the room.

"You'll be okay. You'll be okay." Madness repeated over and over. "Bloom, please, tell Alexen to calm down. He'll listen to you."

Bloom stumbled back. Her orange eyes blazed with emotion, something Aurora had never seen from the half-elf. She was scared, fearful at the thought of losing Alexen.

"I-I . . . I can't see this." Bloom shuffled out of the tent.

"Are you *kidding* me?" Alfonso shouted.

"Not now!" Madness centered the room. "Pan, you're up."

Low, anguishing moans poured from his lips. Alexen squirmed in Alfonso's arms, reaching for Tobias.

"Alexen, please, stop, stubborn boy." Pan ordered. "You mustn't put further strain on your body."

Alexen, who had acted selfish and cold up to this point, cared for those he loved rather deeply. He had traveled days on end to reach them and, unexpectedly, had made it in time to save the one he loved the most.

Aurora called to the shadows, and they lifted Alexen slightly off the ground and placed him beside Tobias. Alexen placed his head against Tobias' shoulder, and the shifter tilted his head against his lover's. And by the fate of the gods, that was its own medicine.

After the assessments, Madness reached for Alexen first. He guided his hands over Alexen's chest but was met with a grip even Alfonso would have a hard time breaking free.

"What are you doing?" Alexen wheezed. "Tobias first."

"Alexen, you're severely injured." Madness tried to reason. "You need immediate attention."

"He was off alone in the woods because of the horrible things I said to him!" Alexen thrashed against the healing hands. "I hurt him *first.*"

"Tobias was attacked, as he has some internal bleeding and bruising, but nothing beyond repair. I also need to clear his airway, but his injuries are not *immediate.*"

"Do I look like someone who gives a shit what you want or what I need?"

Madness hesitated a moment but then proceeded as wished. He moved his hands up and down Tobias' chest, fixing as he went. Tobias shifted his shoulders along the ground as Madness cleared the ash from his lungs and repaired his internal organs. Alexen whispered soothing words, doing what he could.

"See?" Madness looked over at Alexen. "Now, let me work on you."

"Yeah, yeah," Alexen coughed through a tough smile. He kept his eyes on Tobias as Madness moved through his body.

Aurora leaned over to Alfonso. "I feel like we're interrupting something."

"Right?"

Tobias lifted his hand to Alexen's cheek. "How did you find me?"

"I left three days after you. I don't want Bloom or Pan out fighting without me protecting them." Alexen explained. "But, Tobias—I can't be away from you anymore. I can't handle being without—"

Blood spewed from Alexen's mouth. His insides were breaking under strain. His body shook, and Aurora felt his weakened heart. Felt is mortal soul begin to fade.

Will he need to become a Dark Saint?

Tobias reached for Alexen. "What in Grounds Below is wrong with him, Madness!"

Aurora had to pin back Tobias' shoulders to prevent him from re-injuring himself.

"He has internal injuries from an unrelated incident." Madness pressed his hands against Alexen's chest. "Alfonso, remove Tobias."

"What?" Tobias moved his hand to Alexen's cheek.

"I need everyone else out." Madness paid his friend no mind. "Hurry."

Tobias fought back against Alfonso. "I won't leave him!"

"Do you trust me!" Madness pressed his hands harder to Alexen's chest but spoke only to Tobias.

Tobias' grip on Alexen tightened. "I just got him back. I can't—"

"Don't trust me as a healer," Madness gripped his dear friend, "but as your *friend* to save him."

Tobias was well over two-hundred years old and had lived through war, grief, and loss, but watching the person he loved die before him had stripped the warrior of all armor.

"I'll stay with him," Pan said. "The rest of you need to get out and look for Cerene."

Tobias blinked rapidly and said with a huff, "Cerene is missing?"

But before Tobias would respond any further, he passed out.

Aurora stroked Tobias' forehead. "Oh, our poor friend."

Together, Aurora and Alfonso lifted Tobias and laid him down on a clean blanket outside. Bloom watched their every move from a duffle bag she leaned against with Baer in her arms.

Alexen's screams echoed from the tent. Bloom's eyes budded with tears.

"Madness is doing all he can for him." Alfonso moved beside Bloom and placed his hand in hers.

And they waited, for news of the injured. For news of the missing.

The sunrise bled across the sky as Bloom and Aurora walked the Wandering Plains to start a fire. The one they had left behind was no longer visible. It was like it had never existed.

"Can you feel for her? For Cerene?" Bloom asked Aurora as they walked back their campsite with the few logs and twigs they could find. "Can you reach out to let her know where we are?"

Alfonso used his Weapons of Ore to spark a fire. He hovered over the flames, nursing it to life.

"Fire Saints could still be in the area." Aurora placed the wood in the fire. "It's too risky right now."

"What happened, Bloom?" Alfonso looked to Bloom. "Did you not hear or see anything?"

"Flames flew past the enchantment line, working in ways I had never seen prior." Bloom hollowed into a small ball. "The next thing I knew, Pan and I had lost Cerene. We found Madness and Baer right after. If I had had proper training . . . knew how to use my powers." This was the most emotion Aurora had seen the half-elf express. "Oh, Cerene."

"They must have had an elf among their ranks." Aurora crouched beside the elf and rubbed her back. "There was nothing you could have done."

"I guess this confirms one thing." Alfonso moved to check on Tobias. "The God of Fire is on the side of Light."

"Not necessarily," Aurora interjected. "Oberon loathed Luna. He despised the idea of killing mortals. He's the last one of the gods to side with Luna."

"Sounds like the God of Fire is playing by his own rules." Bloom clicked her tongue. "His own agenda."

"He better be ready to win." Alfonso didn't stutter with the threat. His eyes blazed with a fury Aurora had only seen amongst the darkest of creatures. "Because when it comes to the lives of my friends, I'll pummel gods or saints or the fucking Grounds Below if I have to."

As the day went on, everyone took turns resting. Aurora noted the weight of Bloom's soul. Between Alexen appearing and nearly dying and Cerene still missing, her soul was a wreck. Tobias slept on and off, only waking to ask about Alexen or Cerene. Both of which, there were no updates until mid-afternoon when Madness and Pan finally emerged from the tent.

"Well?" Alfonso asked.

Madness was paler than normal, his pink eyes were hollow. Aurora sensed his magic was near depleted, and his body hovered on the verge of a sink.

"He'll be okay." Madness took a seat beside his brother. "He received massive injuries from some other external source, and he inhaled so much smoke and ash, it's a miracle he pushed through for as long as he did. I expect long-term damage."

"Gods, Alexen," Bloom pressed her hands against her forehead. "What a foolish, foolish boy."

"The things humans do for love." Pan tucked her paws under her body and stared into the fire's flame.

"Speaking of which," Madness grinned, "help me move lover boy into the tent."

"Good point." Alfonso stood. "I don't want to be the one he snaps at when he wakes up out here instead of in there."

As the brothers moved Tobias to the tent, Aurora walked the Wandering Plans. Sleep called her, but there was no calming her mind enough to listen to reason. Her hair tangled, pulling toward the forest where Cerene remained, dead or alive.

Aurora thought of Cerene's potential capture by the Fire Saints. Of her running the Light Knights and being chased endlessly through the Mulga Woods. The *probability* of her death—

No, no, she's fine. She has to be fine.

Aurora crouched, placing her head between her knees.

"I haven't thought for a second that she's in serious danger."

Alfonso stood beside her, eyes on the horizon.

Aurora sat down and leaned against his legs. "How can you be so sure?"

"Because there isn't a single girl in all Nelabac like Cerene Misrinda."

Her soul fluttered. "You've got that right."

Cerene and the mortals had managed to pull off a successful rescue in the Fourth Realm. They had managed not only to survive in a world completely against them but fight back.

"She's the one that keeps us up at night," Aurora said. "The one that shares her dreams and ambitions. Her hopes for the future. Her love for her family and for the Resistance."

"She's got a heart of gold, that one."

Cerene called everything she wanted out of life a cliche, but Aurora reassured her it was admirable. After one of their late-night chats and in between Bloom's snores and Pan's hissing, Cerene pulled Aurora close and whispered, *I'm glad you found us, Rory.*

"I can't risk it," Aurora stood and marched forward across the plains.

"What?" Alfonso stumbled after her. "Where are you going?"

"It's nearing the night, and there *still* isn't a sign of Cerene." Aurora turned back. "We need to go out and look."

"Tone it down." Alfonso pointed toward the tent. "Cerene knows how to take care of herself."

No, not this time.

Alfonso called out again, but his words were lost to the wind.

Aurora had no plan. She had no true sense of direction at that, and she was exhausted, but that meant nothing. She would trade herself for Cerene if it meant her safety. If it meant the mortals stayed alive and well.

"Rory!"

It was Madness chasing after her now.

"I don't have time for you, Madness." Aurora swung her hands back and released ice as a warning.

"Rory."

"I can't risk losing someone else. I can't—"

"*Aurora,* will you stop!"

She turned and faced him. "What!"

He pointed past her to the horizon.

For a moment, Aurora thought it was another hallucination as she watched Cerene run toward her on the Wandering Plains.

"Cerene?" Aurora called out.

"Rory?"

Aurora felt like the wind as she bounded toward her friend.

As Cerene came into full view. Her clothes were torn, and she was covered in ash, but Cerene smiled brighter than the turning of the day. The weight of their meeting forced them to collapse.

"I was so worried." Aurora cried into the nape of her friend's neck.

"Hey, Rory, it's okay." Cerene comforted her friend. "I'm here, all in one piece."

"Please be more careful next time."

"On my life, as you as my god, I promise."

"As my *friend*."

Cerene smiled. "As friends."

Aurora pressed her forehead to her friend's. "You'll always be my friend before anything else because I don't know who else would keep me up gossiping all night. We both know Bloom isn't too good at that."

Their laughter became a cry. Aurora refused to loosen her grip on Cerene's hand. Her heart and soul longed to be with the mortals, and she would never let herself think otherwise ever again.

ALEXEN LUCK

Chapter 21

"Fire Saints had come from all around," Cerene explained to her friends by the campfire. "I distracted them the best I could for you all to get away. I then tracked Baer and Pan by their footprints, eventually bringing me here. It took all day, but I made it."

"Well," Bloom nearly smiled, "we are just glad you are here and safe."

Madness came out of the tent and sat next to Cerene. She hugged him tight. "How's he doing?"

"Tobias will be fine," Madness said, taking her in. "It's Alexen. I'm worried—"

"Wait, I'm sorry." She dropped the bread. "Did I hear that correctly? *Alexen*?"

"Don't waste good food in the name of bad company," Alfonso called from his bag, cradling Baer. "But, yeah. Somehow, Shrimpy found his way to us."

"Gods, I know Alexen is hot-headed and foolish," Cerene said, "but I didn't know he had a death sentence."

"Tobias would have done the same in his position." Bloom defended her close companion. "The lengths he would have gone to try and help him—especially with him coming out of nowhere, trailing us for days."

"It's probably a good thing it was swapped," Alfonso added. "Tobias is the most protective of us all."

"Idiot." Aurora felt the shadows rising around her.

"I don't know. I kind of get his line of thinking." Madness said before ducking back into the tent to check his patients. "It's not a surprise what people will do for those they hold most precious in this world."

Aurora volunteered for the first watch knowing she wouldn't sleep that night. Dark Manor was less than a day away. It was the only thought to fill her mind and haunt her dreams.

An early autumn breeze chilled the Wandering Plains. The grasses waved with the wind, and late-summer insects chirped in the night. Aurora strolled back to the fire and pulled her shirt down over her legs for warmth.

Aside from the snores calling from Baer and Alfonso, the camp was silent. Cerene and Bloom huddled close, with Pan at their heads, and Madness was in the tent with Alexen and Tobias. It was peaceful—restful.

I can only pray we don't run into more trouble with this short distance left.

The Fire Saint attack had been a warning. Aurora was certain the Fire Saints knew where she and the mortals waited on the Wandering Plains, and she was certain they allowed Cerene to find her way back to them. The game Oberon played concerned Aurora, but it had to wait.

"Hello."

Madness.

His limbs swayed with the breeze as he walked and sat beside her.

Aurora pulled her legs in tight. "How are the patients?"

"Healing." Madness settled in closer than Aurora anticipated. "They should be ready to move by tomorrow."

"You've worked tirelessly." She cocked her head in his direction. "You must be exhausted."

"I haven't felt this way since we raided an outpost near the Third Realm a few years back." Madness huffed. Aurora raised a brow. He added, "Don't ask."

"Fine, fine."

"But the exhaustion is worth it," Madness leaned back. "It's worth it knowing that when Tobias wakes, he'll smile."

"You're such a softy." Arora grinned.

"Yeah, yeah, don't go around advertising." Madness' smile faded. "His pain, it hurt to watch. To know that if I failed, my best friend would never forgive me."

"Both of them, really," Aurora continued. "Such love."

"I can't imagine watching someone you love like that suffer." Her words then refused to stop. "At moments, when watching Tobias reaching for Alexen, and Alexen cradling Tobias, I thought about how I would feel if it was you—well, I mean, any of you."

Gods.

Madness edged closer and the words split.

"Madness, how we parted before the fire . . . Gods, the way I spoke to you. If something had happened to you in that fire—"

"I know, Rory. I know." He hugged her then. Aurora froze, all dismay leaving her body. Against his chest, she felt his heart beat as fast as her own. Holding him, knowing he was safe, was all she needed.

"I'm sorry for pushing you." He cupped her face with both hands. His thumbs were so soft against her skin. "I, of everyone, should know someone should tell their story in their own time."

"No, don't worry about it." Aurora pulled away for a moment and fumbled through her pocket. "I grabbed these for you."

His face softened. "Of course, you did."

"Don't tell Alfonso, as he's actually the one who found them. I'm just taking the credit."

"Fine by me."

They cradled one another. Aurora sobbed into his chest. Madness strummed his fingers along the notches of her spine, and she stroked his left arm, where Mephista remained concealed.

Good. She didn't come undone in the chaos.

"We won't fight like that again." Madness declared. "I swear to you as my god—"

"*Friend,*" she corrected. "You are my friends before any other honorifics."

In a world of worry and madness, he was a haven.

His fingers traced around her palm. Aurora pulled in closer. "I like having you by my side."

"Me, too."

He leaned her back. "Stay?"

"Cerene will kill me."

"Just for tonight."

Aurora blushed. "Only because my blanket is with the mortal who hates me."

"I mean, I don't oppose stealing it off the shrimp." Madness grinned. "I'm sure Tobias would be more than glad to snuggle up closer with him."

Aurora told him to shove it.

They leaned back, holding each other close. Aurora held Cerene and Bloom this way. She and Elaina had held each other as well. Even she and Mako had shared a single night like this once but beside Madness, her soul felt different.

"Rory, remember when we talked about people we can't imagine living without?" Madness pressed his lips gently into the bristles of her braids.

"Yes," She knew what Madness was going to say, but still, her heart rumbled like lightning across a thundering sky. "I remember."

"Well," he kissed the top of her head, "I don't for the life of me understand why, but you're becoming one of those people, Aurora. One that I cannot possibly live without."

Chapter 22

The sun rose high that morning, but Dark Manor did not need it to feel warm. Dark Saints danced about the manor, readying for the coming festivities. Guards returned from their missions, agents went from place to place until Aurora ordered them to stay put, and missioners carried baskets of food, crafts, and decor over the entire manor.

The Goddess of Dark peered at them from her kitchen window. For the first time in a year, the pieces of Aurora collected in one place again. The Dark Saints never dreamed of skipping out on the Summer Festival. Not because they would miss the fun but because they knew Aurora would freeze them into the next Summer Festival they so dared.

The Dark Saints came and went for months on end, only popping by Dark Manor for a day or two before venturing back into the Second Realm or other realms as ambassadors of peace. The Summer Festival put duties aside and gave the Dark Saints time to enjoy one another and remember their second chance at life. To embrace their immortality.

Missioners and guards moved back and forth from the main houses to Flower Meadows on the other side of the lake. The decorated handcrafted tables Aurora was gifted from the Earth Saints of the Sixth Realm. Their

legs were made of vines and roots. Flower blossoms and moss filled in the crevasses. Aurora used permafrost to keep them in an eternal bloom.

Her soul soared in the skies for the events to come, but when Aurora thought of the dreaded task at hand, her soul fell back to Nelabac.

Baking was not her specialty, but she had lost a bet to Tempton, one of the Dark Saints of her Inner Circle, and she was now charged with the task of preparing dessert for the Summer Festival. This year, the Dark Saints chose a bundt cake.

This will teach me to challenge a swordsperson to a duel ever again.

She moved about the kitchen cleaning while she still had sunlight to spare. Flour, sugar, dough, and flavoring covered the counter, sink, floor, and by some chance, the couch far on the far end of the living room.

"Gods," she sighed.

Usually, Aurora would clean immediately, as a dirty kitchen always proved a bad start to a new day, but that early evening Aurora kept her eyes on the setting sun. Feesr air rushed through the window. Aurora sensed a storm brewing, one prepared by the God of Lightning on the horizon.

Blesk is out of his mind if he thinks he's going to send a storm my way.

The apron stopped at her knees and tapped at her movements. Aurora felt silly shuffling across the floors, but she did not want to ruin her newly sewn dress. The pure white fabric with lace embroidering would easily stain. One of her eldest saints, Elaina, had sewn the dress for her to wear at the Summer Festival. Too excited to wait, Aurora went ahead and showed it off.

Strands of hair danced with the wind. It had grown well past her hips. Aurora preferred her hair braided in two, but that day Aurora left her wild and madly tangled. That day was more special to her heart than the Summer Festival. Strands of hair took to the fading light and danced until a steady knock echoed on the door.

She scrambled to remove the apron. "Come in!"

She felt silly, fusing over an outfit and fixing her hair for one reason. For one person.

"Mako." Aurora smiled.

Mako bowed in her presence. He wore his usual attire of a basic black tunic and slacks. His jet-black hair had grown over the past month, curling just above his ears. She then traveled down to his eyes. Through the glasses' reflection, his brown gaze beckoned her forward. Aurora would stare into him for eternity if Mako ever allowed it—if he dared cross that invisible line between them.

"I've missed you." He was perfect in ways many missed.

Aurora wanted to rush for an embrace, but she resisted. Rarely over the last five-hundred years had Mako let down his guard, and the two spoke as intimate friends, but when they had, there was no other time or space. It was only Aurora and Mako. Only, time had continued, and as Nelabac grew, Dark Saints were created to protect the new Second Realm. Mako's duties as an Advisor became more demanding, and Aurora was the Goddess of Dark, the most powerful god in the Realm. They were a pair meant to exist yet destined to never be.

"I've missed you, too," Mako squared his shoulders, "Lady Aurora."

Five centuries had passed since they met, yet ice shattered every time he spoke her name. From the very beginning, Mako had stolen not only a piece of her soul but also her heart, and day by day, he took a little more.

"It's so hot out. Please, have a seat." She rocked from heel to toe like a child. Her sentences were short, choppy—and only worsened the more she spoke. "Take off your backpack and jacket. I'll get some green tea. I know it's your favorite."

"Thank you." His speech was always too formal around her.

Aurora grabbed the tea kettle and two cups and made her way to the couch. Sugar and honey already sat on the coffee table. Mako sat in the chair furthest positioned from Aurora's spot on the couch. No matter the times Aurora offered to share the same proximity, Mako consistently refused to connect.

Mako had been gone for a month, his longest trip over the last five centuries. He and several agents had scattered the realm, visiting every town, village, and settlement, learning what intel they could and ensuring all were safe in the current disheveled state of the realms.

Tension had brewed among the gods for the first time since Aurora and Luna's creation for some time. Aurora wanted her people to be wary when traveling between borders, but that was the extent of knowledge she would extend until she, too, had more intelligence on the world's affairs.

God and advisor sat stiffer than ancient trees on a still night. Neither made for small talk. Aurora would talk his ears off, but she would rather hear his mellow tone.

Aurora, you're a five-hundred-and-twenty-six-year-old god. Stop acting like a love-sick girl.

"How did the journey go?" She centered the conversation. "Have you a full report yet?"

"I was able to reach every registered settlement within the realm." Mako straightened in the chair. "We informed them of the current state of affairs within the realms. With minimum information, of course."

The gods were on the brink of war, but the people did not need to know that.

"Anything else?"

"I already check on everyone in Haven." Mako added a sugar cube and stirred. "It seems everyone is back in time for the Summer Festival."

Aurora scoffed. "You returned moments ago, and you already know this information?"

Mako tapped the spoon on the teacup. "Mona, Fredric, and I arrived a few hours now."

"Well then." Aurora uncrossed her legs, one hit the floors harder than she intended. "Since you've been back for some time now,"—She crossed into the kitchen and threw a pan into the sink—"I can only assume you've caught up on the changes we've made to Dark Manor and Haven while you were gone."

"Yes." The floors creaked at the weight in his steps. "Tempton gave me a complete update."

"The housing in the back part of the manor finished the week before last." The rag she moved over the counter held the sole purpose of distraction.

"Did you lead the charge?"

"No, Tempton did."

"He does well in my absence." Inches separated them.

"Ha, don't let that go to his head!" She swiped at cake crumbs. "We now have housing galore—"

Hands found her lower back. The rag stopped, and Aurora's heart raced. Never in all their time together had Mako touched or even dared to loom so close. Only once, when Mako became her first and most-trusted saint, had they been this close.

Aurora spun around. The calm she wanted to find in his eyes was gone. "What are you not telling me about this trip?"

He gently placed his hand on the nape of her neck, and naturally, Aurora arched into him. Cautiously, Aurora glided her hands against his chest, so she could peer into the soul of her favorite person. It was how exactly as she remembered, but something heavy lingered.

"We need to keep more guards posted in each of the villages and in Dandfol," he finally said, "and around the manor."

"What happened?" Aurora tried meeting his gaze.

"This has to do with protecting you." Mako released her and backed into the dining table. He leaned with both hands and head hung low. "It has to do with Luna."

"Protect me? Mako, I don't—"

"The rumors from before are true, Aurora." Mako gave a look that sent a chill even down her spine. "The mortals, they truly have created Soul Keepers for each of you."

Mortals working with dark and forbidden magic to create items capable of sealing the gods had circulated the rumor mill for months. The gods had met numerous times over the past year to discuss the details and sources to reveal the truth. Through it all, Luna had been the most fearful over the Soul Keepers, and Aurora had tried to soothe her sister, but Luna proved relentless. She urged the gods to consider an alliance and attack and put mortal-kind in their place.

"A Fire Agent—"

Aurora gave him a look.

"—A *reliable* one told Katerina and me." Mako took her hands in his. Both his symbols of the crescent moon symbols stared back at her. "We then called a meeting of advisors—*all* of the advisors."

"Even—"

"Including Sabelle of the Third Realm, and she confirmed it." Mako's eyes were haunted. "Luna, Goddess of Light and Ruler of the Third Realm, is going to war in preparation to end mortal and magical life."

Blood seeped underneath Aurora's nails. "Are we sure this is true?"

"Sabelle confirmed Luna's weapons, the training of the Light Saints, and recruiting new ones left and right."

We were created for peace.

Her powers circled through her veins. Luna was a fool that who relied on few and listened to no one. Not even her little sister.

"We were not created to throw it back out of balance and into chaos." Rage flurried.

"Aurora," Mako reached for her hand, a gesture she usually responded to with natural quickness, but her eyes were an endless sea of glistening obsidian. Her soul became a black, burning flame as ice spread from her feet. Shadows darkened the room, consuming light and all its darlings. Aurora's heart tore for her sister and for Nelabac as she failed them both.

"The faults of a few should not determine the outcome of the many. It breaks God's Code." Her body shifted to the Altered Realm. "As her sister, a contributor to this madness and a protector of Nelabac, I must bring her to her senses."

"And as your advisor and friend, I beg you to come back to yours." Mako took her hand. "The Dark Saints cannot see you this way. If they saw you trembling, they, too, would fear what is to come." Mako pulled her to him, their eyes reflecting the same forgotten emotion of fear.

"Please, if not for them, come back for me."

Her fury ran too deep for her sister. For the mortals of the Realms. For Mako.

And Mako, knowing her fury came from so many places, hugged her. Every inch of his soul and the depths of their silent love were there. It was something Aurora had wanted since the day they met, back when they were more mortal than ever. Back when Aurora and Mako had stopped surviving and fighting and embraced what immortality truly meant.

They knew what it was like to cower, plea, and fight. Both knew the harsh reality war would bring to Nelabac and all its people. They were victims of its cruel taste, having died from its hunger long ago. And now, centuries after they worked to end the Gods' War, they were to start another.

Aurora tried to stop her tears, but it was pointless. She was just as scared as Mako. Not knowing what would happen. How long the war would last. If they would make it out alive.

Love of her sister, of her people, and for her realm, Aurora knew, but this felt different. This rooted deep, twisting around her soul like an unwanted seed. The thought of a world without Mako swallowed her whole.

"Advisors will be meeting in the Seventh Realm at the God's Keep tomorrow morning." Mako took a step back, greatening the distance between them. Again. "I'll be back for the Summer Festival. I have matters to attend to before I leave—"

"Mako, no!" Aurora refused him. "I get why things have always been this way, but everything is about to change."

"Aurora," Mako stepped to the door. "You know we can't."

"Just stay with me, please." Her jaw creaked with tightness. The answer she wanted was for him to stay, but he never had in five hundred years of peace. Why would he now when the world was falling?

"Aurora, my darling, we will have an endless eternity."

"You and I have played this game, but I can't any longer!"

What they had kept on a tight tether lingered on an icy breath.

"I'm done putting duty before everything else! For once, I'm choosing what I want, and you should do the same." In all her immortal life, Aurora had never begged, but she did now for the one thing she feared to lose above all else. "Stay and love me, Mako."

The kiss was forceful and needy. Pleading. Like Mako, Aurora did not know what she was doing, but she knew she wanted all of it. All of *him*. Their mouths and limbs moved in a new pirouette. Mako embraced Aurora and placed her on the counter. She wrapped her legs around his torso and took him in. His hands moved, squeezing at her hips. Aurora released soft moans at his touch. Grinding her hips against his, she closed what space remained between them.

Five hundred years had led to that moment, and Aurora and Mako wanted it all.

Mako moved her to the bedroom and gently removed her dress.

"Elaina would kill you if the stitching tore," Aurora teased.

"And you'd have a fun time explaining how that happened."

She swooned as he leaned down and kissed her madly, his hands tangled in her hair as his nose tickled hers.

Mako leaned up and unbuttoned his shirt. He never learned battle techniques or trained with the agents and guards, so his body was less defined. Mako did not glow like a warrior, but all the same, Aurora found herself unable to take her eyes off him. All she cared about was Mako, the man she had loved for so long.

Mako sat back on his heels. Moving her hands across the bed, Aurora suddenly felt shy.

"What?" she asked.

"Nothing is wrong, darling." *Darling*, he called her again. "I've admired you from afar for so long, yet with you bare before me, I am further enchanted. No one has or ever will compare to the magic you have cast on me, Aurora. You are more than my god or my most precious friend—you are my light in the dark. My guiding moon."

Aurora feared the future, for what would happen to her realm, to her people, and to the Dark Saints in the war to come, but at that moment, all that fear seemed small compared to the terror she felt for losing the man she was finally able to love.

To no surprise, Mako had gone by morning. He had promised to wake Aurora before leaving for the advisor meeting, but Aurora had known he would not. Instead, she would see him in three days at the Summer Festival.

She rolled over in her sheets, recalling the previous evening. Mako had made Aurora feel alive in ways she had not known possible. It was like he had stroked the darkness and icicles of her soul into an abstract painting. She blushed, squeezing her pillow. It had been a space where they existed as one at their most vulnerable.

"I want that Aurora," he whispered with his limbs entangled in her own. "Until our last of days."

Aurora had never wanted thing more. "Always you, always me."

Her powers had sung as she and Mako held each other and talked of the life they would share once all with Luna settled. They had agreed to love one another and live in eternity and bliss, caring nothing of what others thought of them.

While lost in the thought of eternity and bliss, Aurora's hand found a piece of paper on Mako's pillow.

Darling,
Until our last of days,
always you, always me.
– Mako

Chapter 23

That day changed everything, and Aurora had relived it several times since returning, but that time was different. Instead of the past haunting her, it had come back to claim her.

"You okay?" Madness stirred beside her. His fingers pressed lightly against her spine.

Nice, Aurora. Dreaming of one man while sleeping next to another.

"Of course." She heaved, lost to a precious time and of a timeless night. "Being so close to Dark Manor is making me jumpy."

"You sure?"

"Yes, yes." She brushed off the dirt and debris. "Now stop pestering me."

Closer to Dark Manor, the more Aurora feared the waiting ghosts of the past. The memories only confirmed it was time to tell mortals about the Soul Keepers. It was wrong to let them go on without knowing what they were truly fighting and sacrificing their lives for.

"Rory, you're doing it," Madness said. "You're shoving it down—"

"Is anyone else awake yet?" She ignored him, not waiting for a response. "We have to get moving."

Her trembling hands straightened her clothes, patting away the dust. Aurora lightly tapped against her face. She expected the day to fill with more unwanted and painful memories.

"Oh man, oh man, look at that sun!" Alfonso sprawled across the ground, scratching dirt for his glasses. "Not a cloud in the sky! Who's ready for the bright and good day?"

But a small rock knocked the side of his head, tossing his glasses back into the dirt.

"Oops." Alexen walked out of the tent, accompanied by Tobias, in full wolf. His silver markings glistened in the morning. "I only meant to hit your head."

"You know," Alfonso said, picking up his frames, "if you did not travel us for days and almost *die* yesterday, I'd give you another good beating."

"I'd like to see you try." Alexen moved next to Bloom. "These fresh lungs got me feeling brand new."

"Oh, look at me, I'm Alexen," Alfonso pranced around. "I've got a hot Shifter for a boyfriend, a set of new lungs, and a cool sword."

Alexen's eyes shimmered. "You really think my sword is cool?"

Their banter reminded Aurora of the children in the neighboring towns. When time allowed, Aurora and Elaina would go to the beaches in the Seventh Realm with the children and play in the crystal waters of the Rula Ocean. Juvia had a soft spot for children and had always enjoyed their visits.

They played in the sand and swam in the ocean from dawn until dusk. Some children would cry when it was time to leave, but Aurora would coax them back home with a sleepover at her cabin. They spent the remainder of the evening baking and telling ghost stories and bad jokes. After the children went to sleep, Aurora and Elaina stayed up, sharing wine and discussing any and all on their minds.

Such a simple time with simple pleasures. Simple problems.

The group headed through the Wandering Plains. Aurora walked alongside Bloom and Pan, Madness traveled with Tobias and Alexen, and

Baer trotted in his beast form, racing Cerene through the grass. Alfonso followed suit and jumped on the back of Baer.

"Cheaters!" Cerene called out.

They bounded through the open field without a care in the world.

A time left far behind, of a time ceasing to exist.

"Luna and I grew up in an area like this in what is now the south of the Seventh Realm," Aurora linked her hands linked. "We often played like that."

Despite growing up in the midst of war, we managed to make lasting memories, right, Luna?

"I once played more and cared less." Bloom skipped, her blonde curls bouncing with each step. "So much has changed."

"Times were simpler," Tobias added. "Peace was real."

"We had little, but at least I had known what to expect."

Both Bloom and Tobias had been alive during her reign, and she had failed them both. They, too, had lost everything they had once loved those centuries ago.

Tobias surveyed the landscape. "Many battles were fought across the Wandering Plains during the Great Saint Wars."

As if cursed, Aurora's foot hit a helmet. She rubbed away the mud with her foot, revealing the insignia engraved on the front. The helmet had belonged to the Fire Saints.

"How many?" Aurora did all she could to keep the question from catching. "How many battles were fought and lost across my lands?"

How many mortals and immortals alike fought and died for her sake?

Bloom's face hesitated with a forming emotion, but as quickly as it appeared, Bloom took off. Aurora's hand reached out, but she said nothing to stop the half-elf.

"She's quiet," Aurora said, "so quiet about herself."

"Bloom has spent far longer than me trying to heal from the past. A past she has never shared, not even with Alexen," Tobias said. "Trying to heal from all that has wronged her . . . do not take her silence or few words to offense."

"I never mean to push her—or you, for that matter." Aurora placed her hand on his shoulder. "I only just wish to know what I've missed. To know the pain I've caused."

"It does not pain me to tell the one I've waited a hundred years for about what happened in her absence." Tobias' gaze was true. "I never imagined I'd one by your side. It is an honor, Goddess of Dark."

They shared a space of agreeance and respect. Aurora felt that Tobias would have been part of her Inner Circle, serving her as the most loyal of them all.

"The first battle, the First Great Saint War, was fought inside Dark Manor. I left the legions after that, for I was much too young at the time to stay." Tobias shared as they carried through Wandering Plains. "The following battle became known as the Second Great Saint War, when Fire, Water, and Earth Saints still protected the Second Realm and its people from Light Knights. Water Saints fought side by side with Fire, pushing the Light Knight Army back into the remains of the Third Realm. Their efforts proved just, but the war after was their doom."

"Was there one after?"

"The Third Great Saint War ended all alliances across the realms," Tobias explained. "Fire and Water Saints still resided in the Second Realm. However, the Light Knights had, somehow, gained numbers and followers. It was a slaughter. Fire and Water Saints returned to their realms, leaving the Second Realm to demise. That was thirty years ago."

Across the plains, Aurora felt them. She felt the hundreds of souls of saints who had died on the Wandering Plains. She felt the souls that never found peace, those still wandering, waiting for the day they found rest.

"How did you move on after?" Aurora dared to ask. "How did you keep living after so much loss? How do you know what remains is worth fighting for?"

"My mother was the most beautiful wolf I'd ever seen. She was white with golden stripes. When she ran, the sunlight caught and chased her through the winds. She was the starlight of day." He stopped and faced her, loss reflecting off the sun in his eyes. "You never really move on from loss, Rory. You learn to live with it a little more every day, and the pain becomes easier to bare."

Sorrow was what Aurora had given Tobias—what she had given him and Bloom. Despite building a new life for themselves, they still held onto the past and the ones they loved and lost forever.

"Hey!" Cerene called from the back of Baer. She had managed to wrangle Alfonso off the beast's back. A sight Aurora was sure the gods hid from them for a reason. "I see a giant hill that circles itself?"

Aurora lowered. "We've arrived."

The hillside Cerene spoke of was a crater formed long before any gods, humans, or Magical wandered Nelabac. Aurora had chosen to place her home inside the valley for its serenity. It was a steep incline, but once they climbed the hillside, they would enter Dark Manor.

"This is, as we called it, Lil' Hill," Aurora said, gazing up at the side of the crater. "Agents and guards gave it that name as more or less a joke."

"You don't say." Alfonso waited at the bottom of the crater with Baer and Cerene, then looked up at the climb ahead of him. "Are we going to make it?"

"We will." Alexen began the climb. "I don't know about you, though."

"There is a back entrance we carved out as a flat, walkable path for the neighboring mortal towns," Aurora confessed. "But the climb feels more exciting."

"It does not!" Alfonso protested, but the ascend had already begun.

Aurora heard the mortals heave and complain as they climbed, but they pushed on as their countless moments of danger, and near-death experiences were about to pay off. The ground was slippery with leaves and mud. Of course, the first to fall was Alfonso. The sight reminded

Aurora of when new dark agents and guards trained with their strict and fearless instructor and also a member of Aurora's Inner Circle, Tempton.

Tempton, like Aurora, had served in the human armies during the Second Gods War, and he retired when the war ended. Aurora found Tempton a few years into her years as a god after he was trampled by his cattle. At forty-five years old, Tempton still wanted to work and help as he could in the newly formed Second Realm. He became Aurora's first Guard and the third member of her Inner Circle. He was hot-headed and stuck in his ways, but he was a great cook and loved his realm.

Tempton. Elaina. Mako. Who else will call me home today?

Her chest tightened, spreading a faint heat through her upper torso. One small part of her heart still believed the Dark Saints were waiting for her. She prayed they would greet her with grace and hugs and a feast so grand it would last for days. She imagined feeling like herself again—feeling like the god and being she once was.

The mortals and other citizens of the Second Realm never knew the realm in its glory. They never experienced the joys of the Dark Saints, their gifts of friendship and protection. They never knew what it was like to be under the watchful eye of the strongest god across Nelabac, a god found and made in the darkest of times.

Now, Aurora's people thought of her and this place—her beloved home—as a glooming, haunted dome of war's miseries.

Alfonso reached the top first. He took a long look at what lay below. "You really lived here?"

His tone gave no indication of what he saw in the valley. To if it was blooming with an abundance of flowers or if it had fallen to desolation. One by one, the mortals joined Alfonso on the ledge, first Cerene and Baer, then Madness and Bloom, and finally Alexen and Tobias.

Aurora paused before joining the mortals. Once she peered into Dark Manor, the last six-hundred years would fade like yielding shadows. Not the moment she woke up in Manda's cabin or when she released her powers in the Fourth Realm. It was now, in the place she once lived and breathed with those she loved so dearly.

Through the glare of the sun, Aurora stepped to the edge of the rocky ledge. When her sight cleared, Aurora found herself peering at a sight more magnificent than she had ever anticipated.

Flowers stretched across half the valley, down the way to the sparkling pond. Through the trees where the flowers stopped, Dark Manor lay in wait. Aurora wanted to second guess—believe it was another illusion or fantasy, her mind playing cruel games, but no.

"Yes, Alfonso, this is my home."

Dirt and pollen fluttered under her each step of Aurora's boots as she bounded down the side of the crater. The bliss and joy—Aurora had not felt anything like it in centuries.

Pollen and bees buzzed in the valley. No matter the moon or season, flowers always bloomed in the flowering field. Daisies, daffodils, pansies, and so many Aurora did not know the names of sprouted forth. Butterflies, bees, and dragonflies flew around, calling the stems home.

Rabbits and birds scurried from their nesting spots among the brush as Aurora raced through. When she reached the middle of the field, she fell into the flowers. The pollen sent Aurora into a sneezing fit, but it mattered not. Aurora was free to enjoy—free to feel herself again. She giggled, kicking her legs like a child. She was happy, unconfined for the first time in a hundred years.

She moved her arms and legs, like making a snow saint, among the flower stems. Aurora thought she could stay in that endless space forever. Remain stalled, lost in a riff of time where nothing but memories remained.

Her hand stung then. A sound resonated, one resembling the clanging of metal. Rolling to her belly, Aurora cleared away the stems and dirt to find it was indeed something made of metal. She took a strong grip and yanked forth a rusted soldier's helmet from its resting place.

The First Great Saint War was fought in these flowers. Light Knights against the Soldiers of Night. Hands shaking, Aurora rose to her feet and scanned the rest of the field. Armor, weapons, and war drums scattered the ground like weeds among flowers. A war fought for Nelabac, the Second Realm, for her, the Goddess of Dark.

The mortals stared, captivated by the flowers and the past in their undergrowth. Tobias was in his shifter form. He padded further into the field, held his massive head to the sky, and howled.

When this is over, I'll find the proper way to honor those who died on this battlefield. To those who gave their lives to rise against the light lost in darkness and fearless of death.

Madness placed a hand on her shoulder. "It's amazing, Rory. Your home is lovely."

Madness looked past the halo of gloom, and Aurora was grateful.

Water lapped the sandy pond's shore, each ripple carrying memories. The endless number of days Aurora watched the Dark Saints swim and run through the meadow. The number of parties and celebrations held each year. The time Aurora raced Tempton from the far side of flowers, through the lake, and around the crater to see who would cook dinner the following night. Aurora lost, but she enjoyed each second she spent making soup and pies alongside him.

When she and Elaina drank too much wine and went skinny dipping and woke to pounding heads the next day.

When Elaina made a crown of flowers for all four-hundred saints, and in return, they each picked a flower for her. Her bedroom was covered in pollen for a week.

When she, Mako, and Elaina stumbled across the crater, and knew it would be where they hailed home.

The crater was Dark Manor, but the Dark Saints had given the village they resided in its own name, Haven. The homes of Haven were constructed of stone and wood. Dark Saints could claim a home as their own or share it with others. Aurora never wanted roads carved or paved through Haven and the rest of Dark Manor. She wanted their paths to form naturally, to let time and dedication pave the way.

The relics of the war scattered Haven, too. Windows were shattered, and doors were ripped off their hinges. Some homes were completely demolished. Armor rusted in piles outside the homes the Soldiers of Night had inhabited during the First Great Saint War. A war fought and lost.

Madness and Alfonso weaved in and out of the homes, picking up trinkets from the war here and there. With Tobias at her back, Cerene dug through the piles of weapons, which Aurora assumed for a new bow. Alexen, Bloom, and Pan walked to the other side of Haven.

Baer rubbed against Aurora's legs. She scooped up the beast. "You tag along with me."

Aurora had wanted her home to resemble her human life. When it had been just her and Luna. Carpenters had asked to build something grander, more appropriate of a god, but Aurora had refused. She wanted a simple cabin, and to Aurora's surprise, her home looked untouched.

She ran her fingers along the edges of the wood. The carpenters had also insisted on sanding the wood and refining the details, but Aurora had said no. She found the rough edges of the wood defining and erasing that would only take away the home's character. She did not mind a splinter or two as the wood smoothed out, as it eventually did.

Aurora walked up the porch stair. With an encouraging nod from Baer, Aurora breathed and opened the door.

The only new inhabitants to her home were leaves, dust, and creaking floorboards. The countertops had collected grime, and some of the glass cabinets and windows had shattered, but everything had remained right where Aurora had left it.

Baer jumped off her shoulder to explore the cabin, leaving Aurora to remember alone.

Aurora pushed open a broken window above the kitchen sink, letting the breeze blow through. To her, there was no greater view: the sun shimmering over the lake and her friends alive and well.

In the living room, the leather couch's wooden frame had peeled and chipped over time, but its cushions and cloth remained. The colorful rug the missioners had knitted for the living room was now faded shades of brown.

The last I was here was with the Inner Circle: Mako, Elaina, Tempton, Fauna, Mona, and Fredrick. We went over the details of Luna and her war on the mortals and the Soul Keepers. Hours later, I condemned them to die. And they were okay with it.

Aurora clenched her jaw, needing the pain. She longed to feel anything over the dread and hauntings that came with looking around her home.

Baer padded out of the bedroom and placed his little paw on her leg, His tail waving back and forth furiously.

"Okay, okay, I'm coming."

To the right of the kitchen sat her bedroom. It had an exceedingly large bathroom and closet. Those were the only two rooms Aurora demanded to have on the larger side. Indulging in a nice tub and great clothes were two luxuries Aurora had never shied from. The white paint peeled off the door to her bedroom, and the once-red rug was unrecognizable. Aurora's bed had fallen apart, along with a little side table. And all her books had molded. Stories and recordings she once adored were gone.

Portraits decorated her walls, but their paint had faded from the elements and time. The faces within them were unrecognizable. Her fingers stroked along the one that had been of her and the Inner Circle.

All of them smiled ear to ear for hours so I could paint that portrait.

Baer sat on the bed with a note in his mouth. The paper had aged like the rest of home, but the words inside the folds were still legible and meant the same as they had that evening one hundred years ago.

Aurora screamed and cried and trashed in her grief because no matter how much the Goddess of Dark tried to hide or pretend, she truly had lost everything she had ever loved.

CHAPTER 24

Shadows patrolled the cabin, consuming it in a tornado of glistening alabaster crystals. Darkness had come alive from within Aurora, seeping out of her broken parts. She lay on the bed, cocooned in darkness.

In such a deep and unreachable place, minutes passed like days, and seconds felt like an eternity.

And that's what she wanted. What she deserved. Aurora deserved to sit in the pit of rotting darkness for as long as darkness existed. For as long as she existed, there would be no escape, no way to erase what lived within.

Shadows fluffed like a dusted curtain and spewed over the floor like living tethers of her soul, weaving back and forth, wrapping her in a shell. Black marks coated her skin, and Aurora welcomed them. The darkness could take her body, being, and mind as long as the aching lasted. It could take every part of her because the aching let Aurora know it was real. That *they* had been real.

Voices muffled against the shadowed shell. Loud clangs pounded against it. Aurora stirred, hoping, praying it was the Dark Saints.

It was only a mortal, Alexen. His sword swatted at the shadows, trying to blow them off, but they fought back, striking like snakes.

"Rory!" The darkness tightened, forcing him back. "Snap out of this!"

This must be what happened to Luna all those years ago . . . Getting dragged down without knowing or wanting the way out.

"You claim to be the kind of god that fights and wants to help the Second Realm. How in Grounds Below are you going to be able to do that if you sink into the darkness yourself?"

Alexen fought his way to the bed, reaching to for Aurora in the swirling shadows of the living void.

"When my family died during a raid on our village, my mother said you would come back and save Nelabac. I thought, as my family and friends died, how the Grounds Below could a god of good let evil pursue?" Alexen cracked at the shell. "We push back grief and suffering, saying we'll deal with it later, but in reality, sadness doesn't work that way. Me blaming you for their deaths doesn't help. And blaming yourself for the death of the Dark Saints isn't going to save you."

More sounds echoed through the shell. It was all the mortals. Aurora felt their souls fight for her, their god. Their friend.

"Rory—"

"Stop it!"

Someone took hold of her arm.

"Rory . . ."

She could not hear. She did not see. Had forgotten to *breathe.*

Aurora reached her arms out for an escape, but they kept coming, over and over and over.

Elaina, Tempton, Fauna, and so many more. She threw her hands against her sweat-soaked sheets and clothes.

Aurora only stopped when giant fists grabbed her own and wrapped her with warmth.

"Feel our souls." Someone—a man's voice, soothed. She knew that voice and the tall, irritating man that carried it.

"I can't."

"Feel who is with you." *Bloom.* "Where you are."

"After all we've been through, you're not going out like this." *Alfonso.* "Our journey is just getting started, Rory."

No.

Aurora shoved them with a wave of power. "I met you all too recently for you to care for my troubles."

"The length of time you spend with a person does not determine the strength of the bond." *Tobias.* "The ability to connect through our common interest and goals—through our struggles and our joys, that's where you find true strength and friendship."

"We love you, Rory." *Cerene.*

Aurora peered through the murky waves of darkness and saw Madness. He had been right. She had not dealt with the pain of losing her saints or the man and best friend she had loved.

"Aurora."

Madness.

She felt his soul—

"Look at me." He took her arm.

She refused—

"We have all lost someone dear to us, but Aurora, the last thing they would want is for you to blame yourself for their death." His rose eyes were sweeter than all the flowers in the meadow—purer than any color on the wheel. "Above all, they sure as Grounds Below don't want you to give in to the one thing you fear more than anything in this world."

Her voice, haunted and cruel, said, "And what's that?"

"The Darkness."

Aurora grew up watching evil and darkness plague the world. When Aurora and Luna were summoned as gods, Luna was to fill the earth with good and spread light, while Aurora was to guide the dark and cast it far from the souls of others. The two were empathy embodied—and when Luna turned her back on the light, Aurora felt a hole in her heart that would never heal.

A light that would never return.

"I let them all die for her!" The ice shattered. "They died to protect her from what I was trying to save her from all along! It's all my fault!"

Around the room, the shadows dissipated and receded to their master.

In time, Aurora would allow herself to share with the mortals—her new family and friends—how she felt. Let them be there for her in her pain, and help her heal.

But for now, all the Goddess of Dark needed was to cry a century's worth of tears.

Chapter 25

It was sunset when Aurora stood from the bed, head pounding from the crying. Her eyes were nearly swollen shut.

She rose from the bed and looked around. Mako's note was tucked between her hands, so she took it and secured it in her undershirt. Only when the war was over, and Aurora had time to grieve him and Dark Saints properly, would she burn the letter and let them go forever.

In the kitchen, she looked through the window overlooking the lake. The mortals were out there, chatting away. Aurora smiled, ready to join them.

On the front porch, Alfonso sat on the steps. His head leaned against the railing, snoring.

"You know, you're not doing a very good job of guarding me." Aurora nudged him with her foot, and Alfonso jerked awake.

"Rory!"

Aurora embraced him. "I'm glad it was you out here."

"Everyone is by the lake." He gave a slight squeeze before letting her go. "Alexen is cooking dinner."

"Alexen?"

"Fish." They walked arm in arm. "He's surprisingly a good cook."

"I'm sure Baer is dying for that meal."

"Believe it or not," Alfonso pulled her in close, "so is Pan."

Indeed, Baer and Pan waited by the cooking fish as Alexen swatted their impatient paws. Madness and Tobias sat by the fire, chatting and passing a small jug of what Aurora assumed was liquor, and Cerene and Bloom swam in the lake.

This is the peace we all deserve.

After dinner, Aurora sat at the edge of the pond, listening to the water hit the shore. Bloom joined, wiggled her way into the sand, and laid back.

"Cozy?" Aurora leaned back with her.

"Very." Bloom kept her gaze on the stars.

"I'm sorry if I upset you earlier on the Wandering Plains," Aurora said. "I'm guilty of asking others about their past without wanting to talk of my own."

"Sharing more of myself seems a curse to those around me." Lightening bugs danced in Bloom's blonde curls.

"What do you mean?"

"Everyone I tell my past to ends up dead." Bloom did not flinch. "One way or another, death finds and claims them."

"I'm sure you're not cursed, Bloom." Aurora reached for her hand.

"Rory, I'm going to tell you something no one living knows because I know you cannot be killed. Can I trust you not to tell anyone, for their sake?"

If Bloom truly believed she was cursed, Aurora wanted to assure the mortal that her secrets were safe. So, she nodded.

"I'm half elf, half human, as you know." Bloom adjusted herself in the sand. "My mother was an elf, and she kept me sealed from humans and elves alike because if anyone knew the truth of where I came from, I would be dead. Halfbreeds were not exactly welcomed. She raised me to fear most and true no one.

"But, when I was still a child, I escaped my home and wandered into a village located in the northern mountains—the ruins are in the Sixth Realm. That was when I noticed how different I was from others. My ears were pointy, and no one else had a diamond seal." Bloom spoke so fast that Aurora had to concentrate on keeping up. Bloom's past had been bottled for so long that she had to get it all out in one breath and share her life and story. "Eventually, as I wandered about, the townsfolk took notice, and I was captured. Elves were rare then, even a thousand years ago, so finding a young one, alone without a clue of what the world was like, was a golden opportunity."

Did she say a thousand years?

"I was kidnapped and placed in a steel cage made for small creatures. Since I'm a half-elf, my mother was unsure if I would ever develop powers, so she never trained me. The men fought like wild beasts over a scrap of meat to claim me. To use me for gold, glory, and gods knew what else. Eventually, one claimed victory. He said he was going to take me south for experiments."

"A wizard, I presume," Aurora said.

"Yes, a wizard." Bloom's eyes filled with tears, but they did not fall. "There was a darkness that once covered Nelabac, Damonist."

"Madness told me of them," Aurora said. "They worshiped demons and believed they were to rule Nelabac instead of the gods."

"And they believed sacrificing the magic of those who eliminated the demons would bring them back," Bloom said. "Using blood magic and sacrifices of Ancient Magicals would bring back the demons. This wizard was a Damonist that meant to use me as a sacrifice, but my mother found me first."

Gods.

"My mother was an old and powerful elf. Strong in wits, combat, and magic, and she used those talents to hunt and kill that entire village and find her way to me." Bloom was void of any emotion. "Her and the wizard fought while I stayed locked in that damned cage. I was helpless in aiding her. When it was over, my mother was victorious. She ran to my crate and pulled me from it. She made me promise never to disobey her again and to never trust anyone with who I truly was, and I promised.

"When we returned home, I never left again. My powers developed, and my mother taught me to use them. Despite my human blood, I was gifted in all aspects of elvish magic. My mother was proud. I eventually reached adult age, and my mother knew it was time for me to depart, as she could not keep me confined to our home forever. When I decided it was time to leave, she cast a spell of protection—or so I thought.

"When she was done, my mother collapsed, breathless and dying. Elves do not die of old age, only of injury or magic. As I held her in my arms, she explained she cast a spell—a *curse* that would kill anyone who learned what I truly was and where I came from."

Aurora had no words as Bloom faced her, waiting for something.

"Being more than one thing is unnatural in this world. Mortals, especially humans, like order and categories. When you cannot fit into one box, you become an outcast. Mother told me never to trust humans with the truth and to avoid elves at all costs. After many failed relationships with mortals and immortals alike, I secluded myself for centuries."

"Until you found Pan and Alexen?"

"My life changed after them. They never asked questions or pried into my past." Bloom grinned. "Tobias knows something larger is at play. He knows that Ancient Magicals and our powers work in mysterious ways. Cerene asks, but I shut her down every time."

Bloom hid an invisible pain, one she could never share, and that, Aurora realized, was agony in its truest form.

Suddenly, Bloom leaned over and stared, placing her hands against Aurora's chest.

"What?"

"Fell nauseous? Ill in any way?" Bloom blinked, eyes wide. "Like you might die of hunger or famine or that you've been stabbed?"

"Fit as a fiddle."

"Good." Boom smiled. "It seems curses don't work on gods."

Aurora wanted then to tell Bloom then how she felt the gods were curses themselves, but it was not the time.

"Do you think there is a magic there that could break it? A magic of the gods, perhaps?" Bloom's orange eyes were tight, twisting with centuries of pain. "I've sought wizards over the years with no luck . . . I've never had the opportunity to present myself to a god. I just want to be free, Rory. To care for those around me without consequences."

"Our magic work that way, Bloom." Aurora pinched her lips. "But, when this is all over, I promise I'll help you break this curse."

Suddenly, the pond water rose and fell like waves. Aurora and Bloom stood and backed away from the water's edge before their clothes soaked through.

"What in the Grounds Below is happening?" Alfonso was the first at her side.

"I was hoping for more time before they came for us," Aurora confessed.

"Before, *who* came for us?" Cerene asked.

"Remember how I mentioned there was a way to the Seventh Realm from Dark Manor?" Aurora kept her eyes on the water. "Well, this is it. This is our way to the Seventh Realm."

A waterspout shot high into the sky, sprinkling droplets in the moonlight. The water released and fell back into the lake. Concealed within it had been a woman.

She stood on the water as it settled. Her skin was pale with light blue undertones, which complimented her long, pin-straight black hair. Her straight bangs were shaped nicely around her chocolate-colored eyes. She was stunning in a tight blue and white uniform that showed every generous curve.

Aurora waltzed over to the woman. "Nice to see you, Katerina."

"Lady Aurora, long time no see." Katerina glided over the water and planted onto the sand. "We've been waiting for your summons."

"I did not realize I *had* summoned you. I don't remember touching the waters."

Katerina leaned back and smiled. "We enchanted the sand."

Crafty.

"Either way, it took a little longer to reach Dark Manor than I had anticipated." Aurora stepped toward Katerina. "I must say, I am rather disappointed she did not greet me herself."

"You know Lady Juvia never leaves the castle's grounds." At nearly a head above her, Katerina was much taller than Aurora recalled. "She sent me to pick up you and your companions."

Tobias growled from the fire. "Can we trust her?"

Saints the mortals had faced over the years had only tried to kill them.

"I've heard rumors you were traveling with a group of mortals." Katerina walked and inspected the mortals. "I just did not think it true."

Aurora crossed her arms. "How did you gather that intel?"

"After we heard of your encounter in the Fourth Realm." Katerina popped some of the smoked trout in her mouth. "Oberon also told us of your encounter in Mulga Woods."

If the Seventh Realm had contact with the Fourth and Fifth Realm, it could mean they were working together.

"What does Juvia want with me?"

"She has information of interest." Katerina ate the last bit of fish. "About your sister. About the war."

Aurora couldn't resist. "She's found a Soul Keeper? After all this time?"

"I am not allowed to say. Not here." The advisor's eyes glanced at the mortals. Aurora would only get her answers from the Goddess of Water herself.

"I'm sorry, but"—Cerene stepped forward—"what's a Soul Keeper?"

"I've been meaning to tell you all for some time."

Katerina spoke up, "It's best—"

"You forget your place, Katerina." Aurora flashed her shadow over the pond, startling both the advisor and the mortals.

"I mean no harm, Lady Aurora," Katerina bowed, "but should you really be sharing such secrets in front of mortals?"

"They may be mortals, but they rank much higher than that. You'll do well to remember and relay that information. Understood?"

It was a statement, not a question.

Aurora turned back to the mortals. "You know we sealed Luna away, but I never told you *why* Nelabac was on the brink of war to begin with."

"I thought it was simply because she was, you know,"—Alfonso spun his finger around his temple—"she lost it."

Alexen let out a snort.

Aurora ignored the comment. "Magicals and humans came together and formed weapons against the gods known as Soul Keepers. They did not want another godly war, so they crafted a way for the immortals to feel fear. A way to seal the gods away for good. When the gods learned about the Soul Keepers, we were divided on what to do about them: start a war on the people of Nelabac or try to destroy the Soul Keepers. Ultimately, we decided that finding peace with the mortals was the best option."

"And it's safe to assume Luna was not too happy about that?" Alexen asked.

"Luna did not care what the gods had agreed on. She was fearful of being trapped inside the keeper created for her," Aurora shuttered. "She went to war, killing thousands of humans and Magicals and saints that stood in her way. That's when I came up with the spell to seal Luna and take away her powers—"

"And as we know, that did not go as planned." Katerina was there that day, the day everything changed. "Over the past one hundred years, the Waters Saints and I have focused all our efforts on finding the Soul Keepers."

The mortals said nothing. Their eyes were empty. Aurora had not placed all her trust in them as she had promised, and it hurt them.

"Why didn't you tell us?" It was Madness that spoke for them. "You said you would tell us everything."

He trusted Aurora with his deepest secret, yet she still, after so many chances, had not done the same. He felt betrayed, and Aurora didn't blame him.

But still.

"We were constantly on the run, fighting and surviving," Aurora confessed. "Cerene went missing, for gods-sake. I never knew if one of you would leave, and having that information would be deadly if the wrong saints found you. There was just never a moment . . . "But Aurora swallowed her pride. "I should have said something sooner, and I'm sorry. I know nothing more about the Soul Keepers than what I've said here."

Aurora was mortified as she apologized to mortals in front of the Advisor of Water. It made her weak, and Katerina would tell Juvia of her affection for the mortals and use it as a weapon. Aurora could only hope her answer satisfied the mortals, as the next challenge provided their full attention.

"You can discuss this further in the Seventh Realm." Katerina tapped her heels together. Water sprayed, and bubbles floated through the air. "Gather your things, secure them tight, and stand in a line. The pond will have us to the Seventh Realm in a moment's notice."

"And," Alfonso gulped, "the magical pond?"

"Now," Aurora sighed, "I *did* purposely forget to tell you about that."

Katerina gleamed and lifted her arms toward the sky. Water splashed and caved into a raging whirlpool. The advisor's connection to the element was remarkable. The water moved with ease at her fingers, bending at each command, the two as one.

Aurora was excited for the mortals to witness the power of the Water Saints.

Lightning isn't the only element that dazzles a crowd.

"All the gods have a pond such as this one. It acts as a portal to reach one another." Aurora explained. "It's kind of like my Void, but it's more intricate system."

Only the side effects leave you dizzy and nauseous, wishing for a bucket to hurl into, but Aurora kept that to herself.

"So,"—Katerina towered her torso above their faces, looking down with a wicked grin—"who's first?"

"I'll do it."

Alfonso looked around, a little sheepish and not fully grasping what he had volunteered for, but from his puppy eyes and rosy-red cheeks, the reason was written all over his face.

Katerina waved him onto the pond. Alfonso was mesmerized by the advisor and not the fact he walked on water. Cerene rolled her eyes, letting out a soft yet deep grunt. Tobias leaned over to her and whispered something low. She Let out a *tsk* and stomped to the other end of the line beside Madness.

Alfonso's happy and swooning gaze turned from Katerina to the water funnel, flooding up his waist. His screams muffled as the water lifted him in the air, spun him up the tunnel, down the whirlpool, and out of sight.

Aurora glanced down the line at the faces of her friends: they resembled Alfonso's the moment before he disappeared.

Alexen foolishly took a step. "Where'd he go?"

"Oh good,"—Katerina guided the water around Alexen's waist "another volunteer!"

"Like the Grounds Below—"

He flailed his arms, demanding she put him down, but in seconds he was swallowed and out of sight. After Alexen, it became a down-the-line system. Bloom went with Pan, then Cerene and Baer, neither beast appearing happy about the mode of transportation. Tobias went without a single complaint.

Only Aurora and Madness remained.

"How can he remain stoic as he's swallowed by water?" Aurora laughed, trying to break the tension.

But Madness said nothing.

We've come so far, and this *is what he chooses to hold a grudge against? My right to secrets?*

Without a moment's notice, water wrapped around Aurora's waist, sucking her through the deep blue. All around, water spiraled. The colors of the tunnel changed rapidly from violets to aqua blues and colors unknown. Aurora felt her stomach nearly rise out of her mouth, but as soon as the joy ride began, it ended, and Aurora landed gently on an exquisite fountain's edge in the heart of the Seventh Realm.

Juvia did not live in a simple forest cabin or have one palace to call home. Not even Blesk's palace compared to the grandness of the Goddess of Water's running waters and marble castles.

The fountain portals were located in the rear of the castle's grounds. Twenty fountains in the space, all of which led to different parts and realms in Nelabac. Only Water Saints and Juvia had the ability to pass through at will and to allow others to come and go through. It was a powerful magic, one Aurora and the other gods envied. Some of the top-ranking members of the Dark Saints could travel through shadows, but not all. Juvia's portals were a weapon of peace or a weapon of war, either of her choosing.

Aurora stepped onto the marble floors. The grassy estate stretched before her for acres. Statues and trimmed hedges and gardens filled the groomed grounds. Water spewed down the sides of the castle like a waterfall into the floors and out into the grassy estate beyond. The tiled floors were squares, perfectly trimmed with grassy patches between them.

Water Saints passed by under the walkways and arches above and below the main castle. Many wore blue robes and slacks or dresses resembling Katerina's uniform. But, when the Water Saints saw Aurora graced before them, time stopped. They took the goddess in and bowed.

Aurora broke from the stares of Water Saints to the mortals at her feet, each moaning over their stomachs. A splash called from their backs. Madness arrived, though not as dry as the rest of them.

"Oh, dear." Katerina appeared from the waters last. "I forget the moment I stepped through the portal all the magic focuses on me. My apologies, human."

"It only took a month, but you've finally made it."

The voice was feminine, low, and mighty. A woman who appeared in her early to mid-thirties walked toward them with a halo of Water Saints at her back, each covering their faces with the hoods of their cloaks. She had a pixie haircut rich in blue and gray hues that matched her ocean eyes. The deep, royal blue cloak dragged behind her, spreading out like a tidal wave. It showcased her power and rule of the Seventh Realm.

Aurora squared her shoulders and faced the Goddess of Water, her equal. "It's nice to see you too, Juvia."

Chapter 26

The Goddess of Dark and the Goddess of Water glared at each other. Power filled the silence. Words unspoken were reached. Only the sounds were water sprouting from the fountains. Aurora tested the waters, waiting to see if Juvia would speak first, but she knew that was a lost cause. Juvia possessed the eyes of a sea serpent and a heart cut from the finest diamond slabs. A lethal weapon wrapped in fine silk.

Instead, Juvia walked, expecting not only her Water Saints to fall in behind but also Aurora and the mortals.

I'll let her have it for now.

"Come." Aurora beckoned, and they proceeded through the castle grounds.

The mortals gazed at the castle structures, taking in its one-of-a-kind craftsmanship. The castle, rather castles, stood in the shape of a heptagon. Seven towers for the seven gods. Six were the same in size and height, stretching up nearly ten stories, but the seventh tower, where Juvia lived, was grander. Her tower housed all ten thousand Water Saints, a ballroom, large kitchens, libraries, and an endless list of other luxury rooms. At the top sat God's Keep, where the gods gathered and discussed the matters of Nelabac.

"Man, Rory." Alfonso patted her shoulder. "You need to spruce up your manor a little bit, do some decorating."

"It's kind of the dumps when comparing it to this place." Alexen joined in the banter.

"Agreed."

"Adding some color might help?"

"That would be lovely," Tobias added.

"Yes, it *is* quite the dump."

Baer meowed. Aurora assumed he thought the same as his vocal companions.

"*All right,* I get the point!"

"The mortals are rather . . . opinionated." A Water Saint by the name of Samuel joined them. Samuel was a member of Juvia's Inner Circle and Katerina's biological brother. "Lady Juvia, the Second Tower has been cleaned."

"They are much like their god," Juvia said. "Thank you, Samuel, for the update."

"Of course," Samuel bowed and straightened. "Lady Aurora."

"Do I"—Tobias spoke up—"Do I know you?"

The Shifter spoke to Samuel, who expressed little reaction. Everyone stared back and forth between the two, waiting for a response.

"I doubt it, mortal. I rarely leave the grounds of the Seventh Realm these days."

"Right, but you look—"

"You *don't* know me."

The distaste in his voice was no surprise. Samuel had greatly opposed the spell to seal the gods and had proposed gods work together to eliminate Luna. Samuel was a dedicated, devoted saint. Losing Juvia was sure to have struck him hard, and anyone or anything to do with Aurora was sure to sting.

"Samuel, be polite to our guests," Juvia said. "They may be of the Second Realm, but they are honored guests of the Goddess of Dark. Do well to remember that throughout their stay, yes?"

Samuel glared, but it was unclear if the look was for Aurora, Tobias, and the mortals as a whole or for strictly Alfonso, who kept his eyes solely on his sister.

They proceeded through the connecting archways of the castles. The gardens were trimmed to perfection and covered in hundreds of plants and flowers. Stained-glass windows moved with a current of tiny droplets of water within them. Missioners tended to the castle grounds, moving about for their daily duties.

The Second Tower was carved from levadian black marble, mined from the Mountains of Ore found deep in the Seventh Realm. Above the high arch hung a crystalized crescent moon forged from black diamonds. The stairs seemed endless as they climbed. Circle-top windows were scattered along the way. Their view displayed the vast courtyard or the Rula Ocean.

At the top of the stairs, a closed, winter-white marble door sat, waiting for Juvia's touch.

"It should be as you last remembered." Her hand pressed to the door, and an unseen layer of water rippled the door open.

The living room was plastered with olive-green wallpaper. White furniture with rounded edges sat on the crystal floor and a wove rug of tiger orange and royal blue. Side-by-side doors led to the balcony, overlooking the entire estate. The fire burned against artificial logs. Two hallways dispersed on either side of the space, opening to the bedrooms, bathrooms, and studies.

The mortals dispersed the apartment. Tobias curled up by the burning fire and snoozed, while Madness opted for the balcony. Aurora walked down the hallway to a bed where Cerene and Bloom jumped on a mattress that easily accommodated four people. Aurora only grinned and left them to play as the children they never got to be.

At the end of the hall sat her suite. A black sheet of ice covered the door. Aurora raised her hand to the center, dissipating the ice.

She always marveled at her room, at the grandness of it all. Aurora threw her wretched shoes aside and slid across the marble floors to the round bed. Opal drapes surrounded the bed, cocooning it in shades of peace.

Aurora then remembered: the closet. The closet of which held stunning gowns, coats, and blouses she only wore when in the Seventh Realm. Aurora would go through them once she rinsed off grime and sweat in the giant bathtub.

A full, functioning *bathroom.*

Water sprinkled under the doorframe separating her suite from its private balcony. Aurora stepped through—her skin and clothes remaining dry—to the beautiful view.

The balconies in the other rooms overlooked the courtyard or large estate, but Aurora's viewed the Rula Ocean. The moon glimmered off the surface. Aurora begged to touch the treasured moon she had so often found herself at one with.

"Beautiful, yes?" Juvia rose from the water running through the castle and took a seat on the balcony railing.

"Just as I remembered." Aurora was no longer a girl on the run but a god trying to save the world. "As if nothing changed."

"Oh, but everything has."

"Is this invite to your home a hostage situation?" Aurora leaned against the railing. "Or are we truly, as you put it: honored guests?"

"That remains to be determined, dear Aurora."

"Fine, then, let's start on neutral grounds." Aurora played the game. "What happened while we were gone? What happened with the Seventh Realm?"

"Where to begin?" Juvia's eyes were the deepest of waters, the strongest of currents. "Katerina told me of the Saint Wars and how saints and mortals from every realm and side perished. Many of my saints of the Inner Circle are now dead because of that carnage. After what they called the Third Great Saint War, Katerina took it upon herself to build the Water Wall to protect those within the Seventh Realm." Juvia was annoyed, but Aurora sensed it was not because of her but rather because of the disarray throughout the realms. "And now, with my return, I have rebels wrecking uprisings and chaos."

Aurora scanned the ocean. "How are the other realms?"

"Dealing with the same issues." Juvia turned to Aurora, and added, "All are furious with you."

"As you know, Oberon attacked me on my way here." Aurora rolled her eyes. "Blesk tortured me and then held me hostage."

"Oh, I'm aware. Blesk was here a few days ago." Her melancholic tone remained. "He told me about the attacks and what happened in the capital. That was gutsy of you, but I guess you're just a gutsy god. Taking chances without knowing the full extent of the consequences. If you ask me, you got what you deserved."

The harshness stung, but Aurora understood. Losing ten thousand pieces of her soul had carved Juvia into the most immortal of the gods. The good or the bad, and the wanted or unwanted—Juvia had lost most of her humanity to gain power in numbers, power in wits, and the strength of a clear head. She had ventured farther than any god had dared, and eventually, she would be carved into nothing but a living, graven relic.

"You're mad at me, too, I presume?" Aurora asked firmly.

"I left this world a century ago, knowing not to hold a grudge against you in this lifetime. "Juvia corrected. "Most of my humans are safe, and the loss to the Water Saints was few—roughly two thousand. The ones who lost were a part of the Solider of Night. It was their own fault they lost their lives."

"All the same, I'm sorry for those you lost." Aurora defended those who died for her. "They died for a god who could not keep her people safe."

"Fortunately, I did not lose any of my abilities. Seems like that part of the spell worked, but it seems you lost everything." A hint of lingering pity. "Just as the spell said."

"I can thank Blesk for that." Aurora spat. Juvia's eyebrow raised. "I'll fill you in on his betrayal later."

"Very well." The Goddess of Water agreed. "What a shame, though: The god who once cast such a wide shadow above the rest of us has fallen to the light."

There it is.

Juvia wanted Aurora to feel weak, to know she was virtually powerless. The Goddess of Water preferred mental games to physical attacks, as she knew words often cut deeper than any physical wound.

"A feast will be ready shortly for you and the mortals." Juvia moved from the railing to make her leave. "We can discuss what you came here for afterward."

"They are more than just *mortals*." Aurora corrected. "As much as they've done, don't belittle them."

"It's what they are, Aurora." Juvia did not face her. "They deserve no other title."

"Refer to them as Honorary Saints," Aurora asked.

"You've always been so devoted to those who care for you." Juvia laughed rather plainly and disappeared into the waters.

Relief flooded her at the Goddess of Water's leave. Standing up to Juvia was difficult, especially after she had proved just how weak Aurora had become. Aurora was thankful she had not walked into a trap because if they had, Aurora wasn't so sure anyone would have survived. Herself included.

She rubbed her fingers over one another, forming spirals of ice. The other gods no longer saw her as an equal. Traveling with mortals had not helped her situation, but that was the only fact of the matter that didn't bother her.

They already have the souls of darkness in them. They have their will. They don't need a piece of mine to prove who they are to me.

"Aurora."

Madness' voice hit with the chills of the salty air. He was in a black tunic and pants, though the shirt appeared a bit snug against his tall frame.

Aurora wanted to make a snide joke, but Madness' mind was far from where they stood.

His eyes were feral, beaming red. "When were you going to tell us?"

The Soul Keepers.

Aurora cut away and moved across the balcony and back into the bedroom. "I see you got some new clothes."

"Aurora."

"As I said, it never came up." Her fingers strummed across her bedsheets. "There was never a right moment, Madness."

"There were plenty of opportunities!" His fists clenched. "When we were at the hideout or your manor—or perhaps when you came to us and took you in? When I shared my biggest secret, you should have done the same!"

"I didn't want any of you involved to begin with!" Aurora spun around to face him. "You and the others chose to come on this journey. To make me a part of your lives."

"The moment you brought those kids back to camp, you invited us into your life." Madness shook his head. "More than once have almost died for you—we *still* could die for you! The least you could have done is told us the truth about what we would have died for."

"Truth of what?"

"You're stilling play dumb—unbelievable." He took a step towards her. "The Soul Keepers, Aurora! Those are what you were after all along, and you needed Juvia to find out more so you could start hunting them down, but you didn't want to involve us . . . even after everything we've done for you."

If any of them were to put their lives at risk again and maybe even die because of Aurora, she could not go on. Their lives were more important to her now than any stupid Soul Keeper and the war. Gods, even Luna.

"I'm doing it to protect everyone."

Aurora could not die on the journey to end the war, but the mortals would.

"You? Protect us?" Madness stood inches from her. Malice consumed his gaze, "Aurora, if it was not for us, you would never have made it this far. You can barely protect yourself, let alone eight others! You call yourself a god, but are you really? You have no saints, little power—Ground Below, mortals came your rescue!" Aurora refused to flinch. "You want to know what else was taken one hundred years ago? What else was injured? Your entire soul was shattered. You lost everyone. You're a pathetic god who lost everything for someone who never cared the same for you—"

"Who do you think you are speaking to me like this?" Aurora countered. "Do you speak to all your 'friends' this way or only me?"

"You've made it clear we are *not* friends, Rory." Madness stepped back. "From day one, you've reminded us that you're a god."

"The minds of men really never change despite the century." Aurora felt she was going in circles. "Just because we shared a few secrets does not mean you are entitled to know all of mine."

"You still don't get it."

"*Enough*!" Her powers swirled the room, dimming all the natural light. "I meant it, Madness Hunt, when I said I cared for you, but that does not mean you can trample all over me. I am the Goddess of Dark and Ruler of the Second Realm, and it will serve you well to remember that." She grabbed his tunic. "It will do you well to remember the vow you made me when we set out from the secret valley—it will do you well to remember I can destroy you or cast you out as fodder for the Light Knights! Do you understand me?"

She was sick of hearing she was weak—that she was not enough. Gods she was weak, but there she stood, struggling to stand, struggling to fight a war. Struggling to keep her new found-family together. Struggling to keep on fighting.

"You never planned on keeping us all together, did you?" Madness' voice cracked. "You're planning to leave us behind."

But Aurora had had enough.

She stepped back to Madness, took his cheeks between the palm of her hand, and spat, "If you ever speak to me like that again, I'll show you exactly what it means to be a god."

Like the rest of the castle, the great hall was grand. Water poured from the walls into the pond surrounding the table carved from the finest woods of the Sixth Realm. Sea turtles and coy fish swam, diving in the seagrass below.

The days of berries, bread, and undercooked fish were behind the honorary saints as exquisite roasts, casseroles, wines, and desserts spread across the table. All the mortals were at the table except for Madness. She understood his pain and frustration with her, especially after Madness had shared how important she had become, but Aurora was a goddess and owed Madness nor any mortal an explanation for her actions and decisions.

The mortals ate ravenously, like vultures on carrion. Juvia and a few of the Water Saints darted their gaze toward Aurora, but she ignored them and took liberty in throwing her feet on the table.

Samuel cleared his throat. "Seems you all haven't had a proper meal in some time."

"What would you expect?" Alexen joined. Mud from his boots flaked onto the table. "We've eaten berries and slept on the ground for weeks."

"Don't remind me," Cerene sighed. "I'm so full, I don't think I, can eat another bite."

"Cerene," Bloom chimed in, "you're *still* eating."

She stared at the chicken thigh in hand. "Then this chicken leg and the rest of the rotisserie will be joining me upstairs."

"Eat and sleep as much as you like." Juvia stood, dismissing herself. "Aurora finds you all of value. Her guests are my guests."

The mortals were smarter than Juvia or any immortal gave them credit for. They deciphered the snide comment, knowing its derogatory nature was intended. Aurora knew Juvia came from a place of neither harm nor intent, but the mortals didn't know that. Even if Juvia protected mortals, it did not mean she appreciated or respected them. Aurora only hoped this group of mortals kept their mouths shut and did not provoke their host *more* than they already had.

"I speak for everyone in saying we appreciate the meal." Aurora rose to her feet. "Not only that but also your hospitality, Juvia."

"It's nice to be at peace," Tobias added just enough emphasis on *peace* for his companions to get the hint.

The corner of Juvia's lip curled. "Why don't my saints give you a full tour of the castle tomorrow?"

"That would be wonderful!" Cerene jumped to her feet, playing along. "Your home is so beautiful. I'd love to see it all."

"Perfect." Juvia smiled, which Aurora believed to be genuine. "Samuel, I want you and Grayson to give the mortals their tour."

"Of course, Lady Juvia." The Water Saint pushed back his glasses. "I will inform Grayson right away."

"Lovely." Juvia went to make her leave. "Aurora, we can speak more tomorrow."

"But, Juvia, I'd rather we speak—"

But Aurora did not have time to wager as Juvia, Katerina, and Samuel stepped into the surrounding pond and disappeared.

The mortals sat around, looking at one another.

"Well," Alexen said, picking up more food, "that went exceedingly well."

"It could have gone a lot worse," Alfonso chimed in. "You could have gone off the handle."

"Or the demon boy," Alexen said. "Good thing he was not here."

"Alexen." Bloom looked at her friend.

"What?" He shook a chicken leg. "We're all friends now, no?"

One by one, they filed back to the Second Tower. Pan fell asleep in Bloom's arms, while Baer did the same with Cerene. They deserved the rest. The two beasts were placed in bedrooms so the noises of the evening didn't disturb them.

We owe them our lives many times over.

By the fireplace, the crew enjoyed tea or red wine. Madness hovered near but did not settle in a seat. Aurora was glad. The last thing she wanted was to deal with his nonsense.

Some, like Alfonso, enjoyed the wine a little too much.

"Well, I'm off to sleep." Tobias' hands hit his knees, and he turned to Alexen. "Ready?"

"I could not be more ready for a soft bed." Alexen stretched his legs.

"A soft bed," Alfonso teased, drunk off his wine, "or a nice snuggle?"

"Wouldn't you like to know?" Tobias winked and followed Alexen to their room.

Cerene reached for an almost-empty bottle. "Must be nice to have someone to love."

"To have someone to care for your woes." Bloom lay flat against the floor closest to the burning fires. "To share your dreams with."

Aurora tapped the note tucked in her tunic.

"Oh please," Alfonso slurred. "Love is for fools. Why would anyone want to be attached to the same person for life? Life, it's too exciting—too vast to live one with such boredom."

Aurora, Bloom, and even Madness eyed Cerene. The archer's face held a stare that scared even the darkest of creatures in Nelabac.

Grounds Below.

"Cerene," Alfonso held his hand out, "you gonna finish that bottle?"

Bloom pinched her brows. "Gods help him."

"You know what, Al—"

"Here we go." Madness chugged the last bit of his glass.

"You're just jealous that you don't have anyone special to share a bed with." Cerene pointed the bottle at Alfonso's head the entire time. "And you probably never will!"

The door slammed loud enough for Juvia to hear it from her chambers in the highest tower across the castle.

Alfonso squeaked, dumbfounded. "What's her deal?"

"Al, I believe it's time for bed." Madness stood and guided his brother to his room.

"I second that." Bloom departed. "Night, Rory."

Aurora waved her friends off, and she sat by the fire alone. Madness reappeared from Alfonso's room. Aurora heard as he lingered outside. She thought she heard footsteps backtrack, but instead, Madness slipped into his room without another word.

They all deserve a long and uninterrupted sleep. No running and jumping through forests to see the next morning. Tonight they'd sleep like the ancient kings and queens.

After a little more time by the fire, Aurora dimmed the embers and made for her room. On the balcony, the salty breeze brushed against her skin like the little shards of ice that used to be in Aurora's full control.

Her hand felt the air, freezing particles floating in the night. Black ice swirled around her hand with intricate designs. She peered into the ice, seeing the cracks. Fragile, that was all she was these days. She balled her hand, releasing the power from her hold.

Useless.

Her powers were deemed to never return to their prior strength.

"Madness is right," Aurora said to the night. "I don't deserve the title of god."

"Don't feel that way, Aurora."

The voice belonged to a long, forgotten soul. To someone once so dear and precious to Aurora's heart and mind, it had to be a trick. Her heart feared whatever place her mind had taken her. Was she dreaming, captured in a spell?

The voice was of the friend and Dark Saint that had guided Aurora through each and every decision with wisdom beyond even her immortal years.

Aurora strained as she turned to look and see if it was her mind playing tricks. If it was giving false hopes in times of need, but standing before her was a sight more beautiful than any ocean or manor or victory. A girl, now six-hundred-and-eighteen, stood in a white summer dress that had a twin—*the* twin Aurora had torn the lace from and wore in her braids to remember her beloved Dark Saints.

"Elaina?"

Chapter 27

The sight before her was quite terrifying but all the more beautiful.

"Is this-is this real?" Aurora choked back tears. "Are *you* real?"

Aurora and Mako had found Elaina after a storm, stuck under the weight of an overturned carriage. Her family and the horses were dead. Once Aurora examined Elaina's extensive injuries, she offered the girl death or immortal life. Elaina accepted sainthood and became Aurora's second saint and member of her Inner Circle. Aurora had gained no greater friend since.

"It's me." Elaina hugged Aurora's neck. "I'm alive, Aurora."

With Elaina so close, the smell of flowers in bloom pressed against her, Aurora knew it was her.

"How?" Aurora brushed back dirty blonde hair and gently stroked Elaina's cheeks. Blue, hollow eyes staring back. "Everyone else is gone—*you* should be gone."

There should be nothing left.

"After everything . . . I somehow remained." Elaina's voice was low, empty. "Katerina came to Dark Manor days after and invited me to live in the Seventh Realm. I've been waiting, like all the rest of the saints, mortals, and residents of Nelabac, for the gods to return."

For Aurora, the last one hundred years had passed like falling and waking from a night's sleep. The thought of Elaina waiting on her to return cut deeper than any wound. It was cruel.

Elaina's hands ran down Aurora's hair, stopping at the lace tied around her tunic.

"The dress." She touched her own. "You kept some of it."

"I was able to save some of the lace," Aurora said. "The rest of the dress . . . well, it didn't hold up very well."

"I'll make you a new one." Elaina smiled, weak. "I know how much you love dresses."

"I love *your* dresses."

So many questions raced through Aurora's mind, but they would wait. For now, Aurora only wanted to catch up with her dear friend, with her last loved one of the past. Elaina was a gift from the gods, and Aurora was going to savor it.

After their tears subsided, Aurora rinsed off in the marble bath, dressed in a black silk nightgown, and tucked herself in bed with Elaina. They exchanged tales of Elaina's adventures with the Water Saints and of Aurora's journey with the mortals to reach the Seven Realm.

"The mortals sound like quite the bunch," Elaina giggled.

"They certainly keep me on my toes." Aurora propped her hands against her cheek. "They're far more of a hassle than the Inner Circle ever was."

"They were always too uptight." Elaina braided her hair. "You need a reminder or two on how the average person behaves."

"What do you mean?"

"I don't recall anyone ever saying *no* to you."

"Well, I *am* a god, after all." Aurora rolled her eyes. "Besides, that's not true—I recall a rebuttal here and there."

Elaina raised a brow.

"Okay, okay—maybe everyone was a little *too* reluctant to question me, but never you or Mako." Aurora laughed. "You both always called me out."

"Of course we did!" Elaina threw her hands up. "Half the time, you never thought anything through! You're so stubborn and hard-headed."

"Well, now I'm paying for it—times *eight*!" Sat up. "The mortals disagree or argue with me and each other every step of the way!"

"It's good for you—reminds you to always stay one step ahead." Elaina smirked. "I heard them nagging and gawking earlier. They sound like a hoot."

"You heard us earlier?" Aurora sat up. "Why didn't you come and say hello?"

Elaina took a breath in. "I got nervous."

"They are the last group to get nervous around. If anything, they end up embarrassing themselves."

"Yes, but . . . what if they don't like me?"

"Oh, Elaina, never." Aurora grabbed her friend's hands. "How could they not?"

Elaina had been spared, but she had lived the last one hundred years alone. She was surrounded and protected by Water Saints, but they were not her family, nor would they ever be. She had spent one hundred years surrounded by beings in complete isolation.

I'll never let Elaina fear being alone again.

Elaina fell asleep quickly, but Aurora's mind refused to settle. Her mind, body, and soul ached, longing for relief. It had been that way since she returned. Her soul was restless, her emotions endless. Creating Dark Saints numbed human emotions and motives, taking not just a piece of Aurora's power or immortality but her humanity. It gave gods the ability to look past what made them mortal and allowed them to think logically as higher beings. The only option to survive the spell was to take back those pieces of her—to sacrifice the Dark Saints.

Saints existed solely through their god, accepting a piece of their humanity, soul, and power. The more saints, the further detached from humanity a god became. The more than became a truly immortal being. When all five-hundred pieces of Aurora's soul came flooding back, she felt like a true twenty-six-year-old mortal again, like the last five-hundred years as a god never happened.

But some piece of Aurora had resisted the call. A piece of her was so mighty it had dictated its destiny, and Aurora was thankful for its refusal to yield.

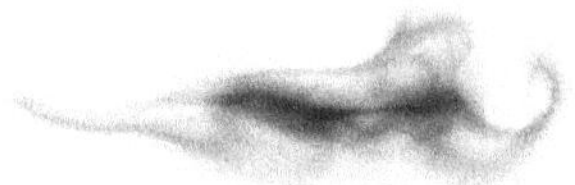

Shrills woke her, shrills as Elaina held on tight to a cat—to *Baer*. She nuzzled him close, and the cat stared back at Aurora with eyes that read, *help*!

The black doors connecting the bedroom to the rest of the apartment swung open. Alexen and Alfonso stood weapons at ready.

Alexen cocked his head. "Who's the girl?"

Alfonso didn't wait for a reply and charged, but he was met with ice. He stood, frozen neck to toe. Alexen looked to Aurora, then Alfonso, and then to Elaina.

"Hi." Elaina released Baer and extended a curtsey. "I'm Elaina."

There was no need to explain just who the girl was.

"Just when I think we are catching up on surprises." Alexen smiled—but his expression and tone changed and redirected toward Alfonso. "Why did you charge in like that? I thought there was a serious danger in here!"

"It's not my fault I heard Baer squeak!" Alfonso shivered as the ice was released.

"It entirely is." Alexen headed out of the room. "You not only scared the new girl but also woke me up unnecessarily."

Alfonso chased after the swordsmen. "Hug me. I'm cold."

"The real question is, why is it just you two in here?" Aurora stood from the bed. "Where is everyone else?"

"They went down earlier for breakfast." Alexen extended a hand, pushing back an uninvited embrace. "Alfonso wanted to wait for you, and Tobias left me to sleep in."

"The poor boy's wounds are still healing." Alfonso reached for Alexen's cheek, but a quick hand slapped it away and found Alfonso's cheek instead.

"Hey!"

"We're *really* edging toward our rematch."

The weapon wilder smirked. "It wouldn't be much of a fight with you still all bruised and battered."

"Oh, it's more than fair. You don't have that big brother of yours this time."

"It's hardly daybreak, and you two are already giving me a headache." Ice shot across the floor and kicked Alfonso, Alexen, and Baer out the door. Aurora heard protests from the other side but paid them no mind. "We'll see everyone at breakfast!"

She locked the doors—with the lock itself and ice and shadows—and turned to Elaina. Her face was long, grinning, and on the verge of laughter. "Oh, Aurora, what have you done to yourself?"

"Not another word." Aurora pointed to the bathroom. "I'm just . . . going to get dressed."

Great first impression, boys.

Aurora opted for a simple long silk, black skirt, and a flowy, long-sleeve blouse for the day. Elaina remained in her white dress. Aurora left her hair down and tied the two pieces of lace to her wrist, and tucked Mako's note into the ruffles of her undershirt. Once ready, the two headed for breakfast in the main hall.

The breakfast table was filled with a variety of pastries, fruits, and meats. The mortals wore matching jet-black leather uniforms that resembled the Water Saints'. Tobias wore black robes. Madness was the only one who remained indifferent—both in clothing and toward Aurora and Elaina. He sat brooding at the far end of the table. Aurora felt a tug to speak with him but then thought against it.

There were no Water Saints in the main hall, and Aurora was relieved. It meant Juvia trusted her, and in the current state of the world, Aurora, the mortals, and the Second Realm needed every possible ally.

After proper introductions, Alfonso, Cerene, and Bloom bombarded Elaina with endless questions. Baer and Pan even leaned in to hear what the last Dark Saint had to say. All the mortals wanted to learn not only more about Elaina but more about Aurora.

"What was Aurora like back in the day?" Alfonso asked. "Stern?"

"Noble?"

"Honorable?"

"Cunning?"

"Indecisive?"

"A pain in the ass?"

"*Okay*." Aurora ended the chatter. "Enough about me."

Elaina giggled.

"Aurora has a point," Pan said. "What is your favorite animal, Elaina?"

"Well," Elaina looked down at Tobias, "I've always been rather fond of wolves."

"You honor me, Elaina." Tobias bowed his head slightly. "Maybe we can all go out later, and you can show me the Goddess of Water's castle grounds from my back?"

"Everyone is getting along and is beyond cheery," Alfonso whispered. "Is she a prophet?"

"Even you and Alexen were chummy this morning." Aurora cut into her ham. "It seems she's what this group needed."

"I wonder what will happen next." Alfonso leaned back in his chair. "Alexen smiles? Madness speaks to you again?"

The shadows tipped back his chair just enough to tip over.

The doors to the hall opened as Samuel and another Water Saint, Grayson. Aurora had always liked Grayson. He had an impressive knowledge of military strategy and was always friendly. He moved about the table introducing himself to the mortals. His green eyes and curly brown hair complimented his genuine gaze. He was different from the other Water Saints, like he had received the warmth that once filled Juvia's soul.

"Grayson!" Elaina perked up at the sight of him. "How are you this morning?"

"Elaina," he was cheeky. "Better now."

She was beaming, and Aurora raised a brow.

In the five hundred years I've known her, she's never once been swooned.

"Lady Aurora." Samuel summoned from across the room. He did not look pleased to see her. Then again, Samuel never looked appeased by anything. "Lady Juvia is awaiting you in her chambers."

Aurora noticed Tobias focus on the Water Saint. She recalled Tobias seemed to know Samuel, yet Samuel had no knowledge of the Shifter.

"While Lady Aurora meets with Lady Juvia," Grayson clapped his hands, "Samuel and I will escort our guests around the castle grounds."

"I will be joining Aurora," Elaina said.

"Your presence was not requested, Elaina." Samuel snapped.

"I'm God Aurora's last surviving Dark Saint and member of the Dark Inner Circle." Elaina rose from the chair. "I believe my *presence* is necessary."

"If it was necessary, I believe Lady Juvia would have requested you."

"Will Katerina not be at this meeting?" Elaina crossed her arms.

"She will, but again, if Lady Juvia wanted you there, she would have instructed me to bring you."

"Now, Samuel." Aurora stood and crossed her hands behind her back. "I believe Elaina has a point. She is my last Dark Saint. I would like her with me."

"Does she have the Advisor's mark?" He pushed back his glasses. "Does she have the symbol of the Goddess of Dark marked on *both* her palms? I believe not."

Elaina slammed her hands on the table. "That matters—"

"Mako died, yet you, who lived, were not made Aurora's advisor, Elaina." Samuel walked toward her. "You are no more important to her than you were one hundred years ago."

"*Samuel*," Grayson said with iron in his tone. "We were sent to fetch Aurora and escort her companions—not insult them."

Elaina's head hung low to hide silent tears. The mortals looked at Samuel with disdain.

"Where does someone like him get off on hurting feelings?" Alexen gripped his knife with such strength tight that Aurora thought he would throw it at the Water Saint.

"For once, I agree with my hot-headed swordsman." Aurora let her power seep and darken the room. "You were never told to insult a god, correct?"

Aurora half expected another remark, one she would gladly return with more than words, but Samuel acknowledged he was outnumbered, even among his own.

"Grayson," the Water Saint made for the door, "bring everyone to the courtyard when they have finished their meal."

And he was gone.

Everyone, Madness included, turned toward Elaina. The mortals knew their place with Aurora, but when it came to Elaina, they understood there was a deeper bond.

"Are you all right?" Aurora placed a hand on Elaina's shoulders. "He's always been cruel."

"No, it is more than that." Elaina straightened her shoulders and wiped her tears. "Let us not dwell, yes?"

"I will speak to him," Grayson said.

"No," Elaina gripped the Water Saint's uniform. "Don't make a fuss over me, please."

"Someone like him needs more than words," Alexen spat.

"I agree with shrimpy here." Alfonso reached for a Weapon of Ore. "Wanna team up?"

"Just this once?"

"This *once*—"

"Yes, yes, we all agree Samuel is an ass." Aurora ended a dangerous pact before it made any moves. "All the same, you all will accompany him on the tour of the grounds—

"But, Rory—"

"With Grayson,"—Aurora withdrew the darkness in the room—"and you will *play nice.*"

Both opened to protest.

"*Play nice.*"

They wanted to argue, it was written on their faces, but Alfonso and Alexen complied.

"Key words, Aurora." Alexen crossed the room and quoted, "*play* and *nice.*"

"Shrimpy," Alfonso followed behind, "I'm glad you came after all."

"Watch them." Aurora pointed to Cerene and Bloom. "Please."

"I don't know. Maybe they have the right idea." Bloom danced out the door, both Pan and Baer hot on her heels.

Cerene briefly hugged Aurora before departing and whispered. "You know it's probably a good idea when Bloom comments on the matter."

Only Tobias, Grayson, and Elaina remained in the dining hall. Elaina appeared broken, desperate even to stay by Aurora's side. Aurora eyed Grayson, who seemed concerned for the last Dark Saint.

"We mustn't keep our gods waiting, Elaina," Grayson remembered he knew his place.

"Come." Tobias extended a hand. "I would love to hear more about you and all you've experienced."

Elaina was rather hesitant but accepted the gesture.

"You'll have fun," Aurora reassured her dear friend. "I'll see you in a few hours."

"Right." Elaina gave a weak smile. "It'll be fine."

Tobias led Elaina out of the room, but Grayson lingered.

He asked, "Doors closed?"

She slumped back in her chair and pinched her brows. "I need a moment alone."

"Of course."

"Grayson." Aurora called out before the Water Saint shut the doors completely. He paused and looked up. "Watch out for them, yes? Especially Elaina."

"No need to ask, Goddess of Dark." Grayson's tone shifted then, in a protective, feral nature. "It would be my great honor to watch out for the last lights among the darkness."

The doors shut, and she grinned.

Her eyes looked to the high ceiling that opened to the clear blue sky. The clouds floated so far away. Aurora sighed, letting the weight of it all press against her chest. The sun's rays rained warmth through her clothes and skin, not that she felt it. Besides the running waters, the room was silent and still.

Those nine . . . Whether by battle of the mind or battle for life, they're going to be the end of me.

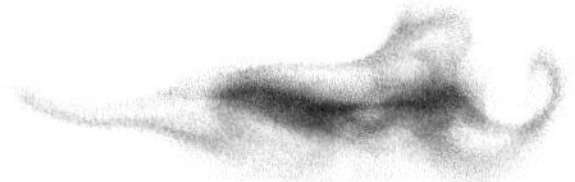

The entire castle was glorious, but Juvia's tower, the Seventh Tower, took the term to an entirely new level. The cement structure was covered entirely by running water. Each step passed through the waters like hands through air or feet through grass and mud. Aurora walked the grounds before making her way up. She passed many saints dressed in light blue uniforms. Some pulled the hood of their cloaks over their heads, but all bowed at Aurora's passing.

I need to tell Juvia to ask the Water Saints to quit with the formalities.

The solid iron door on the upper levels of the Seventh Tower led to Juvia's private quarters. It was one of the few structures without water pouring down it. Instead of knocking for permission, Aurora let herself in. The glass floors covered a pond with swimming ocean life. The furniture was muted pastel of blues and greens, and the walls were murals of an ocean, a river, and a lake, different bodies of water brought to life with the dripping of water.

Aurora peered through the open doors to the balcony to Juvia. The Goddess of Water sat overlooking the courtyard in a violet-silk gown and tea in her hand. Aurora tiptoed behind—

"Is that godly behavior," Juvia's eyes never pried away, "Goddess of Dark?"

Aurora slouched into the chair next to her. "I'm guessing the answer is no?"

"You've been around humans for too long," Juvia placed her cup of tea on the balcony floor. Aurora watched it disappear into the waters. "You've picked up some of their bad habits."

"There mortals have fun, Juvia." Aurora teased, "Do you even know what fun is?"

Juvia simply replied, "Once."

The balcony had the best view of the massive estate. Rows of grapevines separated the yard into multiple sections. The grass was the perfect dark shade of green and trimmed to perfection. Large oak and sycamore filled the forest beyond the courtyard and led to a divine waterfall. The water was crystal clear and never too warm or cold. Diving into the soothing waters was Aurora's favorite part of visiting the Seventh Realm.

I'm sure there enjoying it now, the mortals and—

"Elaina." Anger flooded her. "Why was she not the first thing you had Katerina tell me about?"

"I thought you would be happy to see the spell did not go as planned in a *good* way."

"*Mm-hm.*" Aurora sneered and moved on. "How was it even possible? For her to still live?"

"Maybe the Dark Saints chose who lived in the end. Maybe it was your will and devotion to them." Juvia sat up. "Only the saints know how it went down once we departed this world and became one with it."

"Do you remember any of the time away?" Aurora asked.

Juvia's eyes softened, almost sad. "I remember those final moments after the spell and feeling my body liquefy. I remember watching Lust turn to air and Oberon become flames. I watched my fellow gods become their very element." She leaned on her knees, her pointed fingers pressed against her lips. "There were moments over the years when I felt myself flowing through the currents of the rivers and oceans of this world. I recall the animals and creatures below the water's surface communicating, but I mostly remember the time. The long, aching time."

Aurora flinched. Juvia's tone held anger—held an emotion.

"I woke outside the estate, and Samuel found and carried me back home." Juvia sighed. "All that time, I heard Nelabac. I heard her pain and suffering . . . yet there was nothing I could do."

Aurora recalled nothing of the hundred years away. The past months, she had pitied herself for it, but it sounded like she was fortunate on that account.

She leaned back in the lounge chair. "I need a drink after that one."

"Such an elegant response." Juvia's eyes held a knowing. "I thought you would take to talking about yourself, but I guess that means your time away was not as . . . thrilling."

"No." Aurora held her gaze. "No, it was not."

Aurora saw what looked like jealousy and pity flash across the Goddess of Water's face, but the emotion was gone as quickly as it appeared.

"We don't have time for drinks or even the thoughts of them with the state Nelabac is in." Juvia then asked, "Do you have anything you can share?"

"Well,"—Aurora crossed her legs and arms—"I've been hunted, beaten, and held captive since my return."

"Yes, as I explained yesterday, Blesk explained the details," Juvia cocked her head. "It was rather impressive mortals came to your rescue."

"They've got guts." Aurora was proud of her mortals. "So you've spoken to Blesk, which means you probably know he has sided with Luna—"

"And he's the reason the spell did not work?" That anger flashed again. "Yes, I know all about it."

"Do you know anything of the others? Terra? Oberon? Lust?" Aurora braced herself. "What of the Fifth Realm? Fire Saints attacked us—nearly killed three of mortals on our way here."

"I've had contact with the other realms." Even the mention of the God of Fire sent Juvia into a fuss. "The *pyro* is fine. He's just being *Oberon*."

At least I got Oberon out of the way.

"The First Realm had no casualties or changes over the last one hundred years," Juvia explained.

"That's no surprise." Aurora rolled her eyes.

"Yes, but he's still angry with you," Juvia's tone shifted then, "because of what happened in the Sixth Realm."

"The Sixth?" Aurora furrowed her brow and circled her finger in a circle, encouraging Juvia to continue, but the Goddess of Water was troubled. She gathered her gown and leaned on her balcony. "Juvia, what happened?"

"Two weeks ago, Luna and an army of seven thousand Light Saints—well, Light Knights—marched into the Sixth Realm."

"*Seven* thousand?" Luna had more than doubled her army in a few, short months.

"There was a full-on battle." Juvia's eyes held truth. "Half the Earth Saints were slaughtered . . . and Terra, unable to defend his territory, lost it to Luna. She took half of it."

Aurora rose to her feet. "What do you mean, *took*?"

"She split the land, Aurora." Juvia turned, tears swaying in the air. "Luna took half of the Sixth Realm, separating it from the rest of Nelabac."

"What of the mortals who resided in that part of the Sixth Realm?" Aurora felt breathless, like no matter how much she breathed, there would never be enough. "What has become of the stolen land and the Sixth Realm that remains?"

"I'm sure the humans told you the state of affairs in the Third Realm long ago."

"It's a barren wasteland," Aurora said, "but, what does that have to do with breaking off half of the Sixth Realm?"

Juvia paused, having to center herself. She rarely lost her composure. "Aurora, I don't think you understand the calamity of your sister—the true *monster* she has become."

"What did she do, Juvia?" Aurora gripped the Goddess of Water's shoulders. Her heart screamed. "What did my sister do?"

"Luna's powers are greater than anything I've ever seen." Juvia trembled. "Her powers are beyond what yours ever were. What any of us could hope to be." *Trembled.* "The Goddess of Light has obtained powers beyond what any of us gods could begin to stop."

Aurora knew in her heart of hearts that Luna was gone. That her beloved caring sister had faded from this world. Something had enwrapped and stolen the light of Luna's soul and made it theirs, and there was nothing Aurora could do to save her—no matter how badly she wanted to.

"Juvia, tell me what I have to accept in order to destroy her."

"She *claims* souls." Juvia revealed. "It's why the Third Realm is nothing but ashes and dust. Luna wanted more power—more souls, and she took everything from the Third Realm in order to do so. She stole half of the Sixth Realm to gain more. Luna has found power in stealing souls from every animal, human, Magical, and life force she can get her hands on and makes them her mindless, soulless following soldiers that she will lead to end this world and use to remake the next."

Aurora staggered, grasping the railing. Grasping for air. For sanity. Never would a god imagine performing such strange and evil magic. The soul of a mortal made them who they were, and if removed entirely . . . the consequences were catastrophic.

"We've coined the term Soulless for these creations." Juvia continued, "They feel nothing—no pain, remorse. They don't die easily, either. They can't think or speak for themselves. They only follow orders given by Luna or those of her Inner Circle."

"Those twisted beings can control them, too?"

"Are you surprised?" Juvia questioned. "You know saints reflect the soul of their god—some of their desires and personalities."

"I know." Aurora pinched her brow. "I've seen Light Saints throughout the Second and Fourth Realm. Their movements and powers were strange. Could those be Soulless?"

"Luna's army has been broken into two factions: the Soulless and the Light Saints. Together, they make the Light Knights." Juvia explained. "Soulless are those of the Light Knights' army that wear the mask. I believe it is because their features have become unsightly. They are the front soldiers now, as killing them proves a challenge for several reasons."

"Because they are technically still mortal." Aurora realized. "It goes against God's Code."

And I've killed some before—back when we escaped the Fourth Realm.

"To some extent, yes, they are, but again, it's like they are empty bodies to do Luna's bidding. Vessels she can easily replace with the next town her army destroys. She's building an army of Light Saints and Soulless." Juvia paced around the balcony. "Her goal is to obtain as many disposable bodies as possible to eliminate every being in Nelabac."

"Even-even if it came to war," Aurora paced, "it's not like the Soulless can defeat the saints. I mean, they can't kill them . . . right?"

"They can, Aurora. I don't know how, but they can."

"How many does she have?"

"Her army of Soulless stands at thirty-thousand," Juvia said. "That doesn't include the Light Saints or Blesk's Lightning Saints."

"Thirty-thousand human souls and bodies at her disposal."

How much worse can it get?

"Even if all of the gods joined together to fight, we would be outnumbered. We could never slaughter the Soulless. It's against everything we were created to do." Juvia placed all her weight on the railing. Her ferocity rippled the water around it. "Even if Luna, as well as

Blesk, have turned against us and what we stand for, we cannot. The five of us left must protect what we were created for."

"Are they human if they have no soul?" Aurora asked. "If they have no sense of right and wrong? Of having a choice? Will the other realms even join us for the war—"

"You lose yourself, Goddess of Dark."

"Of course, I am!" Aurora spun around. "I mean, we ended ourselves and our reign one hundred years ago, and all we did was make everything *so* much worse!"

Aurora watched Juvia toil with that same thought—the same regret. Soulless were mortals and Magicals—beings of Nelabac the gods were meant to protect—fighting for the other side, yet they had no soul, no consciousness when it came to their actions. Aurora had killed some at the border—she knew what the right choice was at the time, but was it really? What were the right choices in the war this time?

Luna had fallen too far. She would be after Aurora at every turn to stop her from putting an end to her plans. Luna would use humans as a means to destroy Aurora. The Goddess of Dark feared she would have to face the rest of the journey on her own, even if she did not want to.

"Luna, what have you become?" Aurora prayed for her words to carry across the winds. "How can I help you?"

Baer

CHAPTER 28

Aurora crossed through the estate to find the mortals. She expected flying limbs and arguing, but instead, she found them training alongside the Water Saints.

A leopard shifter instructed Baer and Pan as a fighting pair, and the two move in tandem, using their body movements to create a unique language for combat. Bloom flipped through books of ancient spells and enchantments, whispering them under the breath of the winds at the trickery of the language. Aurora watched her eyes sparkle when she succeeded.

"Ugh! I can't get it!"

Frustration called from Cerene. She held a new bow and arrow and aimed toward far-away targets.

"You must trust the bow." Elaina encouraged. Elaina had insisted on learning to wield a weapon in the early years. When Tempton joined the Dark Saints, he figured a bow and arrow suited her best. Dark Saint had Cerene firing multiple arrows at a time without allowing the time to aim. The task seemed to get the best of the archer.

"Learn how it moves," the Dark Saint explained. "Understand where you want the arrow to go and trust your instinct."

"I can hit my target if I have time to aim. Plus, this would be so much easier with *my* bow." The bow had been left behind in Caris when it was crushed under the weight of Baer. The new bow, a gift from the Water Saints, was plated in gold and scripted in protective charms. The string was made of ancient irons, making it impossible to break. The tips were carved sharp as daggers to use a second weapon. It was truly the perfect weapon for Cerene.

The archer closed her eyes and held a breath. In the next second, Cerene pulled the bow back and released. One arrow hit its target, while the other hit the ground at Alfonso's heels.

"Cerene!" Alfonso swung around to face her. "That one was on purpose!"

"Was not!"

"Focus, four eyes." Alexen kicked Alfonso in the back, knocking him over.

Who made this match-up? To the left, Aurora saw Tobias and Madness chuckling on the ground, taking bets. Both bet on Alexen to win the spar. To Aurora's surprise, Samuel observed, training the two mortals.

Of course, they did.

"Betting against your own brother?" Tobias asked.

"I know my brother a little too well," Madness said. "He can only fight when his life is on the line and never in a sparring match."

Aurora sat down next to Tobias. Madness paid no attention to her arrival.

"My money's on your brother," Tobias grinned. "Alexen has too many eyes on him. He's totally going to choke."

Samuel moved between them. "Alexen, you're agile and slim, and Alfonso, you're a brute, built with the muscles to carry that ax and hammer. You two are perfect matches for this training exercise, practically designed for each other."

"Designed for each other?" Alfonso leaned against the hammer. "This one was designed for a more calm and wise kind of guy. I'm too much for him to handle."

"I'm going to have to agree on that one," Alexen snickered. "I'm more into intellects."

"Ha! I guess that is something you need." Alfonso swung back around. "You need someone to balance those empty thoughts."

"At least I have thoughts. And someone to share them with. You, on the other hand"—Alexen swung his sword, colliding it against the ax—"just keep screwing that up."

Aurora gapped. "Did he just reference?"

"Yes, he totally did." Tobias kept his grin on Alexen. "He's not so bad, is he?"

Madness said, "Not bad at all."

One for Alexen.

Alfonso charged with his ax over his head to strike down, but Alexen blocked. The two sparred back and forth. Alexen moved with astonishing quickness. A closer look at the two-handed sword he wielded showed that he no longer used his sword, but he, like Cerene, had been gifted a new weapon.

The blackened steel glistened with midnight blues. A pattern resembling a rushing river ran along the edges, and like a rushing river, it moved quickly and balanced well in Alexen's hands.

She had watched the mortals spare in the Fourth Realm, but it had not been with such vigor and determination. Sweat beat down their backs, and it looked like they had been at it for hours. Glancing over at Tobias and Madness, by the looks of the dirt on their faces and a few cuts, they, too, had participated at some point.

They know we are not staying here for long, and they want to be as prepared for the next leg of the journey as possible.

Back and forth, Alexen and Alfonso shuffled their feet in a dance. Alfonso moved much quicker because of his magic. Alexen was like Cerene, a true, mortal human, but Alexen had steady hands and greater wits. The two created a theatrical play of weapons.

Samuel's eyes glanced down from the spar to Aurora. Samuel was a Think, which allowed him to peer into minds and catch glimpses of a person's thoughts and emotions. Some could penetrate deep into the minds of their victims, see memories and read their running thoughts, but there was only one Think who could do that, and Aurora wanted to avoid her coming across her for as long as possible.

Samuel's eyes narrowed as he reached for her mind, but Aurora pushed him out.

I must teach humans the use their souls to shield their minds.

"Tobias," Aurora whispered, "have you figured out where you know Samuel from?"

"Not yet." He batted his eyes. "I know I've seen his face. That we've interacted. My years as a young child escape me, but I swear I know him from—"

"Had enough yet, tubby?" Alexen waved his sword around.

"Don't be jealous, Alexen. I know you're jealous of the muscles I have to spare," Alfonso lowered. "Come to think of it, just *what* does Tobias hold onto when the two of you cuddle?"

Blood trickled down Alfonso's cheek. The sword moved so fast that no one saw as Alexen made contact with Alfonso's cheek. Alfonso, a little surprised, jumped forward and swung the ax at Alexen.

Spikes flew out from the hammer, nailing Alexen. He fell over, holding his bloody face in his hands, spiked iron needles stuck to his skin.

"Alexen?" Alfonso changed his Weapons of Ore to their iron from the moment he saw Alexen on the ground. Friendly banter and bets were off as they raced to their friends.

"Couldn't help but take up the opportunity, could you?" Tobias growled, bending over Alexen. Madness worked to remove the countless spikes.

"You and I both know that I would never hurt any of us on purpose, even shrimpy." Alfonso pointed at the ground and the spikes. "I don't even know how that happened!"

Even if he and Alexen bickered, he would never hurt him. Tobias' seemed to simmer as Alexen sat up and pointed at Alfonso.

"How the in the Grounds Below do you not know you can shoot small, *painful* needles from that thing!" Alexen groaned.

"Even though you caused injury, that was impressive." Samuel's voice carried over their internal quarreling. "Learning a new magical skill like that at such a late stage in your human life is uncommon. Most weapon wielders never learn their true power. I'm sure it would never have developed if it was not for the peril you've faced. For this war."

"We got it from here, Water Saint." Madness sneered. The mortals had faced war and danger their whole lives, perfecting their skills to protect not just themselves but others around them because they were gifted. Samuel stated Alfonso's skills on circumstances and not on his natural gifts diminished his identity to nothing more than a mortal surviving.

"It also seems the wielder is not the only one of this odd group learning to control a powerful force within." Samuel turned from his general group observation to a person of interest. Water sprung from grass blades and encircled him. "Only this power is dark and deadly, so much so its darkness wasn't even allowed on written record."

How dare he.

"Samuel, stop," Aurora commanded. "You will not attack my companions any further."

"No, Rory, it's fine." Madness tapped the Water Saint's chest. "I want to hear what he has to say."

Samuel's eyes sparked alive with knowledge he was never given. Personal information he was not entrusted with. Personal information he had stolen. "You possess a terrible creature in your body. A creature that was believed cleansed of Nelabac long ago. One that is slowly, ever so obviously, consuming your mind, body, and soul.

"It's so powerful," he challenged the monster lying in wait, "that I should strike you where you stand to save everyone from its impending destruction."

All the mortals, even Alexen, with needles still protruding from his face, bared their fangs and weapons. They had spent their whole lives running, defending, and fighting against saints. Samuel's threats were no different.

"We may only be mortal, and we may not be able to kill you, but we'll beat you or any saint all the same." Needles flew from Alfonso's hammer. "Mortals are not what they used to be."

"Don't fret, you've demonstrated that." Samuel waved off the water dancing around him and faced Madness. "If you can learn to control the demon, as your brother has learned to control those needles, its power will be an asset and not a burden. It can be something used to defend and save you, your brother, your friends, and your god if the time ever arises. Be used to save this world instead of burning it to a crisp."

"For twenty-seven years, I've worked to get this *bitch* in my body under control, but it's all failed!" Madness grabbed Samuel's uniform. "What else am I supposed to do?"

Madness' eyes were pleading, but Samuel held little sympathy.

His eyes were colder than the stillest waters in the northern seas. "If you don't succeed, then the people you hold dearest will die by your hands."

Aurora sensed that for once in Samuel's existence, he was trying to help someone besides himself, his sister, or his god, but she had enough of his sharp tongue.

Something he and Madness have in common is that drive to protect those they love, no matter how harsh they seem.

"Madness, release Samuel," Aurora ordered.

But Madness squeezed Samuel's uniform closer. There was so much unspoken pain in those pink eyes, but they remained pink.

Finally, Madness released Samuel's tunic and stormed away.

Even if it was cruel, he needed to hear it. Sometimes we need to hear the things we hate most about ourselves from others. It's often the only way to accept our flaws and move on from them.

Aurora felt Samuel's soul. He wanted to help Madness and the mortals, but he did not know them. He did not know their fears or ways of living. Even if Samuel read their minds and viewed their pasts, he did not share their grief and their pain. Just because one was familiar with the stories, it does make them a piece of their history.

"Samuel, take Grayson and leave at once." Aurora faced the Water Saint. "Speaking to my Dark Saint with such haste is one thing, but if I ever catch you speaking to the mortals in such a way again, there will be consequences. Ones you will regret."

"Goddess of Dark, I—"

Ice and shadows poured. "*Leave.*"

The Water Saint hated her—she knew that. She had watched as Samuel begged Juvia not to go through with the spell and to find another way to stop the Goddess of Light. And now, with a band of mortals devoted to Aurora and her cause at her side, ready to give their lives away, Samuel only resented her further.

He's a good saint.

Reluctantly, Samuel bowed and left with Grayson. Once out of sight, the mortals relaxed.

"You know, about ten needles are *still* embedded in my cheek." Alexen cleared his throat. "So yes, please, go after your brother so he can get them out of my face."

"Gods," Alfonso said, "let me go fetch him."

"No, let me go. I might be a better reasoner at the moment." Tobias placed his hand on Alfonso's shoulder. He turned back to Alexen and winked. "You stay and help the fallen."

Aurora also yearned to follow after Madness, but she stayed, as she was the last one he would want comfort from at that moment.

Cerene and Bloom suggested they return to the second tower for a late lunch. Over food, the mortals discussed their training and what they needed to improve on over their stay in the Seventh Realm. Aurora sat quietly, soaking in the conversation. She had believed in the mortals every step of their journey, but there was a war coming, and now, after all she had learned from Juvia that morning, Aurora wanted nothing more than to keep them safe.

A gentle hand found hers.

"Can we go for a walk on the beach?" Elaina leaned over Aurora's shoulder.

Her jaw released tension. Remembering Elaina, a piece of light in the darkness, lifted her soul. "Of course, we can."

They waved by the mortals and made their way down through the Second Tower to where it met the sand dunes connecting to the beach. Once there, Elaina sprinted across the sand, chasing seagulls along the coastline and kicking up water.

If faeries still existed in this world, she'd be their queen.

"Aurora! Come on!"

Aurora laughed as she walked over. "What will the Water Saints or Juvia think of me if they see the Goddess of Dark frolicking through the waters like a mortal child?"

"Aurora, we've discussed this." Elaina placed her hands on her hips, dampening her dress in the process. The winds pulled and tangled her hair. "What's the point of immortality if you can't have fun?"

Aurora skipped down after Elaina and joined her by the shore. They kicked and splashed the ocean water, played in the sand, and built castles. Aurora's blouse and skirt were soaked in water and sand, but she did not mind. Elaina was right: What was the point of eternal life without bliss?

With her clothes soaked and the chill of an autumn night, Aurora was ready to head back to the castle, but Elaina kept building castles. She patted the towers. She smoothed walls. She dug at the sand for deeper and wider moats.

"Are you ready to head back?" Aurora asked.

"Almost." Elaina's eyes stayed on the castles. There were three castles. Two were equal in size and shape, while the center castle was larger and sturdier. Elaina focused on that one over the others. The one on the left was collapsing. The one on the right had already collapsed into the sand and ocean.

"You should take a long shower when we get back." Aurora pushed back Elaina's hair. "Salty air always tangles your hair."

But Elaina's mind was not with Aurora on that beach, nor was it on the sand castles she meticulously constructed Her mind was on who they were.

This might work.

"That Grayson sure is a sweetie." Aurora tipped her head to one side. "It's rare for saints to date outside their realm—not unheard of—"

"*Aurora*!" Elaina snapped, cheeks blushing. "Grayson is no more than a friend."

"Yeah . . . *friend*."

Elaina lightly flung sand.

"Since we're close in age, he's been a good friend all these years. He's been my only friend through the loss." Elaina finally removed her hands from the castles. "In the beginning, I never left the Second Tower. He would bring my meals. Brings books or art supply. I finally told him I liked to sew, so he brought fine fabrics and silks and asked that I teach him. Eventually, we started going on adventures through the realm. He made me feel normal again."

A single tear rolled down Elaina's face. "He's been my one and only light among the dark."

They scooted closer and watched the moon fill the sky.

"The Water Saints have been very kind, but they are not home." Elaina kept her eyes on the moon. "They will never be home."

Aurora wanted to talk about them, too. She had yearned to talk about the past but only with someone who understood. Someone who was like her.

"Did you visit at all while I was gone?" That someone could only be Elaina. "The Second Realm?"

"After the First Great Saint War, when the Soldiers of Night fought against the Light Knight army, I never went back," Elaina explained. "The carnage, bodies, and memories . . . they cut too deep."

Aurora pinched her lips. "Katerina told me she found you."

"Yes, she came with the Soldiers of Night to prepare for the battle."

"Katerina fought in the war?"

"No, as much as she believed it was right, she felt it went against Juvia," Elaina nodded. "It was Samuel who led the charge."

Aurora held her breath. "What?"

"That's why he is so intent to make his point with you, me, and the mortals," Elaina explained. "Samuel fought for the Soldiers of Night—for the Second Realm when no one else did. He fought more for Nelabac than any other being across the realms."

That is how Tobias knows him—he knows him from the war.

"I thought all the Soldiers of Night were slaughtered?"

"He won't talk about it," Elaina said. "I've tried, but Samuel only pushes forward with ending the war now."

Aurora had so many questions, but Elaina did not have the answers.

But she might have the answer to one question.

She breathed in and let go. "How are you alive?"

The lapping waves rose higher with the tides of the moon, a true force of darkness.

"I watched them die." She stared into the ocean's depths. "I watched as their souls fled to the sky. Each of them turned to crystallized ice. I cried when it came down to just the last few of us. Mako, he . . . he held me until the very end."

Just the mention of his name set Aurora's soul to another plain of existence. To a hole never to be filled. Not only had Elaina watched each and every member of her family die, but she was with Mako at the end of it all. Tingles filled her nerves. Aches creaked through her bones.

"He told me not to cry," Elaina said with a face full of tears. "He died knowing we would have each other again someday."

Under the moonlight, the two remnants of the Second Realm held one another. The smallest castle washed away the tides, but the two larger ones remained.

Aurora pulled Elaina closer. "I never wanted this for you—for anyone."

"We do not control what happens to us." Elaina wiped her tears. "We can only control what we do with what we are given."

Aurora grasped her knees, trying to stop the thundering of her heart. "Elaina . . . what would Mako have me do now?"

"He would tell you no person or persons are more important than your duty as the Goddess of Dark. You have to win so Nelabac can live again."

Elaina's heart and soul were more courageous than any other that walked the earth before and after her time. Aurora was fearful of the future and scared of losing Elaina all over again, but she knew what had to be done.

She could not bring the young, frail, and innocent child with her, no matter how much she wished. No one would come with her. The journey ahead was hers and hers alone.

One sand castle remained.

Chapter 29

A month had passed since their arrival in the Seventh Realm. After Aurora explained the dire calamity of Luna's army, the mortals trained longer and harder, pushing their bodies, minds, and souls to the breaking point every day. They began to move like shadows of the night, preparing for the journey to defeat Luna, find the Soul Keepers, and end the war. But only Juvia, Katerina, Samuel, Elaina, and Grayson knew Aurora's plans to face Luna alone.

Madness asked me to stop keeping secrets, but I don't think that's possible in this world.

Those the Seventh Realm warned Aurora it would end with her death, and all hope for Nelabac lost with her. So Aurora pushed back, training her body like the mortals. Darkness and shadows still did not answer her as they had one hundred years prior, but her body strengthened, and her stamina to withstand the powers of darkness greatened. Aurora challenged Juvia at the beginning and the end of every day, and every outcome was the same: Aurora left soaked to the soul.

When Aurora was not training to wield the shadows and ice, she watched the mortals, assessing their improvements. She wanted to feel absolute in her decision to leave them behind. They trained side-by-side, coaching one another on strengths and weaknesses. They plotted weapon combinations and compatibility. They laughed with one another and encouraged one another the whole time. The mortals leaned on and supported one another, eager to succeed, all but Madness.

After Samuel's confrontation with Madness, the two trained explicitly together. Every morning, Samuel waited for Madness at the base of the Second Tower, and they traveled deep into the woods. Long after everyone had gone to bed, Madness would return. No scars, no open wounds. Not a single word.

To Aurora's knowledge, Samuel had no credibility in training Madness or demons. She had voiced her disapproval on the training, all the mortals had, but Madness ignored them. They feared what would happen if Mephista was unleashed and Alfonso's wasn't close by, but Madness refused to listen to reason.

Madness seldom spoke when he was with them. His mind was off, out somewhere else. His eyes were hollow and shadows haunted his face. Alfonso received words here and there, but the two had yet to hold a real conversation over the last month. Cerene had called a meeting to chat with Madness and to end his training with Samuel, but Alfonso told them not to worry and to let Madness work through whatever he was toiling over on his own.

Samuel had awakened something in Madness' soul, and only time would tell if it were for the greater good or if evil would overcome.

Aurora sat at the dinner table, unable to eat. It had been that way since learning of Luna's crimes. Her mind remained lost on hunting and defeating her sister, but around the table, the mortals remained oblivious to the dilemmas at hand.

They laughed and enjoyed one another. They knew change was coming but not when, so their souls remained free of worry and enjoyed the bliss of life as it existed. Here, where they were safe . . . Aurora had never seen the mortals so happy.

Here, they're protected. No one can harm them.

Absolutely no one.

"I'm finally getting the hang of this new bow," Cerene called Aurora's attention. "Thanks to a certain little saint."

Elaina giggled, satisfied and proud of her work. She loved the mortals, already feeling at peace in their presence. Aurora was not surprised. The mortals had a way of welcoming anyone the met, making them already feel a part of such a tight and close family.

"I'm not surprised," Aurora smiled. "Elaina has a gift for teaching."

"Maybe she can teach this one"—Alexen pointed his meat-tipped fork to Alfonso—"to control his needles!"

"Look," Alfonso shrugged, "I nail my target about sixty percent of the time."

"We need at least ninety."

"*Ninety*?"

"Maybe that just means you need to work on your defense." Tobias tipped his head at Alexen. "You know, just an observation."

"Oh, look," Alfonso chuckled, "trouble in paradise."

"Oh, piss off, Alfonso." Alexen chewed his food. "I'll show you who the better swordsman is tomorrow."

"Why wait until tomorrow?" Bloom chimed. Everyone turned in her direction, even Pan and Baer. "Nothing like a moonlit duel to the death!"

"Bloomy!" Cerene laughed. "That's so dark of you!"

"Speaking of dark." As the others bantered, Aurora leaned over to Alfonso. "Where is your brother?"

"Doom-and-Gloom took an early dinner." Alfonso rolled his eyes. "We asked him to join us, but he refused."

"Sounds about right."

He leaned so only Aurora could hear him. "I think because of you."

His feet froze on the marble floors.

The room rang with laughter. Elaina's was the loudest. Her sweet voice captivated everyone. The symbol of the moon on Elaina's hands reached Aurora's eyes. If anyone had to be protected, it was Elaina.

"How about the duel, then?" Alexen jumped from his chair. "I've figured out how those needles work."

"I thought their accuracy was *too* low?" Alfonso broke his feet free.

"I think he's just admitting he needs to work on his defense." Tobias teased.

Alexen playfully grabbed Tobias' cloak. "One more peep out of you, and you're sleeping on the couch!"

"All right, save the public affection for after I whoop your ass." Alfonso moved out of the room, the mortals trailing in behind. "You'll need all the comfort you can get."

"Alfonso's not going to win this one. I mean, he ate half of the meal!" Bloom whispered to Cerene, who leaned over and added, "I agree. He's going to be so sluggish."

Aurora lingered at the table. She wanted to join, but there were many plans to map. Too many decisions to make.

Then, she felt a hand on hers.

"Aurora." Elaina was there with Baer in her arms and Pan at her feet. The beasts had taken a liking to the Dark Saint. "Are you joining?"

"I have much to attend to." She pushed back her chair. "But I'll walk you three to the training yard and stay for a few minutes."

Elaina beamed. "Perfect."

As they walked, Aurora turned to Pan. "What has gotten into Bloom lately? She's so—"

"Rowdy?" The beast snapped. "I was thinking the same."

"I was going to say *funny*," Aurora laughed. "But *rowdy* is one way to put it."

"Those mortals." Elaina gleamed the happiest Aurora had seen her since their reunion. "They really do have a way of affecting you."

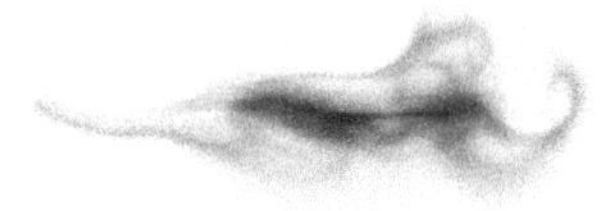

After watching Alfonso and Alexen battle back and forth, Aurora took the forest. The air was cold, and her feet crunched on fallen leaves. Autumn had arrived.

She arrived at the waterfall, hidden deep in the castle grounds. The swimming hole ran twenty-feet deep with crystal clear water. Aurora contemplated jumping in, but she liked her dress too much. Instead, she climbed to the jumping ledge and dangled her feet over the edge.

I have to decide. I have to decide what to do about the mortals.

The mortals knew their protection and safety were not guaranteed if they traveled with Aurora. Those were terms Aurora had explained in the secret valley. As their god, Aurora admired their hearts; as their friend, she deemed them fools.

"It's night time." Juvia appeared through the waters in a blue blouse and trousers. Her hair almost matched the color of the cool waters. "And your mortals are battling it out in my training yard."

"Who's winning?" Aurora patted the earth beside her. The water guided Juvia to her side, and she sat.

"They were wrestling when I was watching so . . . it could go either way." Juvia planted beside and dangled her feet. "My bet is on the one with the scar."

"No way." Aurora cocked a grin. "Alfonso's got him beat."

They sat in silence a moment longer.

"You seemed in thought," Juvia questioned.

"Not really." Juvia did not care for trivial conversation, nor did she agree with the mortals being in Aurora's presence. Aurora knew for certain she would not agree to them accompanying her on the mission.

Juvia raised a brow. "Aurora, I've known you for hundreds of years—I even consider you a friend."

Aurora leaned back on her hands. Juvia surprised her. Genuine words from Juvia were rare, so Aurora embraced them. "Do you ever recall your previous life? Of when you were mortal?"

The two had shared their past lives together, but only once. And never since.

"In moments when I'm alone and the loneliness of eternity sinks." She confessed. "Yourself?"

"If I do, but only of when it was Luna and me," Aurora said. "Everything else is hazy. Like it never happened."

Juvia pulled her legs in tight. "I think more of that particular day than anything else."

Aurora knew what day she inferred: The day she became a god. The day they were chosen to save Nelabac was always the most vivid. The day they were chosen with little reasoning and great expectation.

"I think of how it happened—of how I was supposed to meet the man I loved by the river. How he never showed, but drunken men did. I think of how they held me under the river's currents because I refused to give them what they wanted. I think about how I was dealt a fate crueler than death." Juvia's eyes became one with the waters below. "I'm cursed to serve the very element that killed me. I'm cursed to move it, control it. Nurture it. I'm forced to weave it through the six realms that remain and to keep its people, animals, and plants alive."

"Luna and I died fighting in your armies. In the Second Gods War." Aurora and Juvia had discussed this centuries ago, back when Aurora was a new god and resented Juvia for forcing mortals to fight a god's battle, but since, the two had moved on. Had gained understanding. Had become friends. "I often wonder if the gods were not at war, I might have died six hundred years ago at a decent age. Had lived a human life."

"If I had not been so love-struck and foolish, I might have had the same," Juvia claimed. "Then again, maybe there was no other path. Maybe we were meant to be gods, and no matter what happened, we were destined to end up here, talking above this waterfall with the fate of Nelabac in our hands."

The seven gods were never given a choice, but the mortals of the world were not destined to suffer because of them.

"I don't want to place the mortals in unnecessary danger, Juvia."

"They will be called the Land of the Deserving when their time comes, Aurora," Juvia turned. "We cannot change destiny."

"But what if we tempt fate with the decisions we make?" Aurora touched Elaina's lace. Tapped Mako's note. "How do we know the choices we make are not hurting those we love? The ones we want to protect?"

"The water has a way of soothing the soul of all kinds of worries. Worries of the past, the future, and the now. The worries of my realm, my saints." Juvia took her gaze to the falls. "Even if it claimed my life, the water shows an everlasting connection to every living thing in this world. Exactly what we represent, what we must be."

"Even those like Oberon?" Aurora cut her eyes. "Even those you loath most in this world?"

"Like water, we are connected." Juvia held Aurora's hand, a gesture the Goddess of Water offered sparsely. "I have to think of him because he's important to me—Nelabac is important to me. My soul and emotions have chipped away with each Water Saint, but it's well worth it. They keep this world safe, and even if the emotions I have are gone, what I value and love are not." Juvia palmed her hands against her chest. "Everything I do is to protect what is sacred to me. I will sacrifice every piece of myself to keep what I love and value safe."

"I want them not simply to survive but truly live." The shadows of her soul stirred. "We were chosen to protect mortals and Magicals from suffering, and that is all they have done . . . I failed them."

"Remember what the Deity said when they picked us?" The waterfall poured faster and tingled the air around them. "Those who have experienced and suffered the most in this world are most fit to change its course."

Aurora's soul said, *leave*, while her heart said, *stay*. But unlike the last time the two battled, Aurora listened to her soul.

I either win this for them and this realm or fall into the depths of darkness trying. "I don't believe Nelabac has a third chance."

The suite was quiet, but the presence of the mortals lingered. Crackers lay on the floor. Fresh red-wine stains tainted the carpet. A chair clung to life on three legs from a quarrel between Alfonso and Alexen nights prior.

Aurora walked the rooms, pausing before Madness' door. Her hand hovered the knob. She wanted to at least tell him goodbye. To tell him she was sorry for hiding secrets and for not being able to keep her promise. For tempting his fate with her destiny.

But she walked away.

In Aurora's room, Elaina sat on the bed. A bag lay packed at her feet. Somehow, the little Dark Saint knew today was the day. Maybe it was their connection, the sharing of the soul.

"I have to go." Aurora approached. "I'm the only one who stands a chance in stopping Luna."

"And what if she tries to kill you, Aurora?" Elaina stood. "What will you do when the person you love the most tries to take your life."

"We don't know—"

"Cut it out, *Aurora*!" Ice flew from the Dark Saint's hand. Elaina rarely used her powers, let alone in front of Aurora. "Luna wants you dead, she's waiting to take your life."

Elaina approached and took Aurora's hands in hers. "Please don't leave me when I've only just got you back."

Aurora pulled the girl in close. Elaina cried, softly. Quietly. It was like a plea to stay, but a knowing in her heart of hearts that Aurora had to leave.

"I have to do this, Elaina." Aurora lifted the weeping girl's head. "You know it as I do that if anyone can stop her, it is me."

"And if you die?"

Aurora paused and then said. "Then it was my time."

"You're so difficult." Elaina pinched her lips tight. "I packed your things. Some food, your favorite tea, and a change of clothes. The pair on the bed will be good for your travel."

Aurora changed into the red pants and top. They were crimson red with golden lining along the hems and seams. Aurora also put on matching gloves that stopped just below her elbows. After lacing up her boots, Aurora tied a thick, orange scarf around her waist and draped a black cape over her shoulders.

On the balcony, Elaina looked up at the moon. Elaina's soft features caught the light. Her eyes were as bright as flowers, and her hair was like gold.

"How do I look?" Aurora said. She did a spin.

"Like a god on the run."

"Tell the mortals I went to bed early and only give them this in the morning." Aurora pulled out a piece of paper and handed it to Elaina. "Do you have the items I asked for?"

"Okay." She rocked on her feet. "Their gifts are ready."

"Already?" *Juvia knew, too.*

Elaina pulled out a black velvet bag and dumped the items on the bed. Eight golden ear cuffs and two golden collars spread out on the bed. The cuffs were on the large side. Their edges shifted into points. The golden collars were thin and circular.

"When you wear yours, you'll be sharing a piece of your soul," Elaina said. "Just as you requested."

"It won't make them immortal or let them draw forth ice or shadows, but it will shield them and provide an extra layer of protection." Aurora's hand hovered and called forth darkness. "This way, I can always find them. And they can always find me."

The golden jewelry rattled as the shadows entered, and Aurora's soul bounced, igniting as it had when she made a Dark Saint. Her body bounced and suddenly felt lighter.

"It's done," Elaina adorned Aurora in her cuff. "You can always protect them."

"That's your job now." Aurora placed Elina's on her ear. "Keep them safe."

"I'll miss you." Elaina buried her head into Aurora's chest.

"I'll miss you, too, but no matter the distance, we will always share a piece from the same soul."

"Nelabac will always connect us."

Aurora turned out the door and dared not to back. She thought only of those last words and how they would never be enough as she finally understood what Madness meant all those weeks ago.

No matter how someone leaves, gone is gone.

CHAPTER 30

Aurora imagined Alfonso's needles felt something like the rain as it beat relentlessly against her back. The dreary weather that carried through the swamps went on for miles. The swamp surrounding the castle grounds was designed as a defense mechanism during the previous war. It seemed never ending. The overcoat Elaina had packed did what it could to keep the rain out, but it was not enough to stop the clinging and moist textures from crawling over and seeping into Aurora's skin and wrinkling her like a raisin.

By that point, there was no doubt the mortals knew she had left. Aurora was certain they argued over the note and what to do about it, but even if they chose to come after her, there would be no getting past the posted guards—or Samuel.

Aurora reached the gate to leave Juvia's ground and was faced with Samuel.

"Here to see me off?" She waltzed by him, stopping, so they faced opposite directions.

"Not my choice, of course." He pushed back his glasses. "Lady Juvia insisted."

"Samuel, you have a connection to them. Don't let them follow me or allow anything happens to them." She gulped down the last words, "Even if Madness… "

"Your mortals have a will of their own, Goddess of Dark, but I will do what I can," Samuel reassured her. "And Madness, he's made much progress in the past weeks. Staying here is best for him . . . For all *of them."*

Aurora nodded and walked forward, ready for her leave. Ready to stop her sister.

Samuel called out, "I hope for the humans' sake, above everything else, that you succeed in bringing this world out of the darkness you brought it."

Lightning cracked, followed by roaring thunder. The further Aurora trekked through the swamps, the harder the rain poured and the louder thunder echoed.

Juvia produced terrifying storms, but the rumbles and grumbles of the sky were beyond her abilities.

"Blesk must be hounding the area,"—Aurora screamed at the sky—"because Juvia is harboring a *fugitive*!"

Aurora had removed her boots earlier to prevent ruining them in the deep mud. The mud wiggled between her toes.

And with one step—not lifting her foot high enough—

She tripped.

"*Gods*!"

Her fist hit the water and mud over and over and over.

Her eyes shifted back and forth through the swamp, searching for any shelter—any relief from the wetness and misery—if only for a moment.

And there—she saw it. Between a giant tree, a carved, open space, large enough for her to squeeze into appeared.

"Ha *ha!" I'm losing my mind.*

Lifting her knees high through the waters, Aurora made her way to the hideout.

Aurora knew the space, as she had been part of the human unit in the Second Gods War to invade them. Water Saints had used the open tree space as bunkers in the swamps to hide, seek, and hunt their enemies. Like Juvia, Water Saints could sink into the water's depths, swallow an enemy whole, or bring their own troops in by the masses. To attack the Seventh Realms was a fool's move, and it had gotten Aurora killed.

The bunker was barren. The chairs and tables carved and chiseled from the inside of the tree were the only—and unmoveable—objects. There was a small loft with a bed. Dust and cold, humid air filled the rest of the space.

Aurora considered settling in the chair or climbing up the loft, but she curled up on the floor. Her eyes ventured to open space and watched the rain pound against the swamp.

Aurora felt one with the earth, taking on all the pounding, pain, and worry. Caring for the lives of every person on her back. Like the earth, she was never allowed to crack for even just a moment, for if she did, they would fall.

Gods dammit, I can't feel this way again.

"I was wondering when you would get here."

Ice cased her fingers, ready to attack the familiar voice.

She did not want them here. She wanted to send them on their way—away from her and the danger, but that was an unlikely scenario.

"You followed me?"

"No." Madness jumped down from the loft, his hair wet. "Samuel sent me."

Even in the tiny, hollow space of the tree, there was so much distance between them.

"I overheard you and Elaina in the bedroom before you left." Madness leaned against the back of the tree. "I then found Samuel, and he told me where you might be headed."

"He assured me he would not let you follow."

"Samuel and I have only known each other a short while, but he knows that I'm going to go where I'm needed. He knows I'm always going to pick those I love."

There was hurt in his voice.

"I'm doing what is best for the group, Madness." Aurora took a step toward him. "What's best for Nelabac."

"You're doing what you think is best for *you*!" He moved. "You think you can take on the Goddess of Light—*your sister*—by yourself? You really think you can do that?"

The hurt was not because she left the mortals behind—but because she left *him* behind.

"Light Knights, Soulless, saints, and gods can *kill* mortals and Magicals." She moved toward him. "They'll do it without a second thought."

"So, you thought a little ear cuff is good enough to keep us safe now, Rory?" Madness pointed to his ear.

"If you all come with me, you all can and will die! I am the only one able to defeat and stop Luna."

"No, you're not, Rory." Madness took her shoulders. "Your greatest weakness is the ones you care for and love. Your friends, your realm, Elaina, and above all, you love your sister. You love Luna. Facing her alone is not going to make killing her any easier—"

"Madness—"

"No matter what you may think, no matter what you do." His hands found her cheeks. "Luna will succeed in killing you, and unlike you, she won't feel sorry or cry when she does, Aurora. She will rejoice."

The darkness in the Goddess of Light was deeply rooted. It had twisted her soul into an unfamiliar fracture of light. And no matter how painful it was to admit, Luna would kill her sister and, as Madness said, be glad of it.

"I gave everything up for her!" Aurora threw her fist against his chest. "My realm, my saints, my best friend . . . If it was all for naught, then what kind of a god am I? And what if you all died while helping me do this?" She felt everything in her begging to collapse. For some release. "Gods, if it happened again—lose what is most precious to me—like the ice I command, I'd shatter."

"Dammit, you can't save everyone in Second Realm or in Nelabac alone." Madness combed back the tears. "Even if you are a god, you do not deserve the blame of the world on your shoulders."

She nuzzled into his chest. "If anything were to happen . . ."

"Okay, how do you think I would feel if I lost you?" His forehead pressed against hers. "Aurora, I meant it when I said you were becoming someone I cannot live without. Without you, I, too would shatter."

His lips were soft and inviting. They were reassuring and strong.

"So, if you're going to die, let us do it with you. Let us fight for you and the Second Realm." He pulled back. "I am with you. We are with you."

Madness was the eye to her storm—and she to his, and it was a mistake ever to think otherwise.

The Second Realm was *their* home. This fight was as much theirs as it was hers. They were mortals with free will, and with it, they wanted to save their home. There was nothing more admirable.

"We will be there until the end." His pink gaze felt like coming home. "Until we see the win."

Madness, along with the rest of the misfits and Elaina, were with her. Until all the wars against all realms came to a permanent end, they'd fight to the moment peace and life became victors.

"Hurry up, you runts!"

Aurora and Madness ducked.

"No one should be out this way," Aurora whispered.

Footsteps by the thousands marched in their direction.

"Order your own, Bolt." Another voice called. "Mine listen to only my commands."

Aurora felt her heart skip.

No-no it can't be.

"Those with the mask don't listen anyway!" The first voice—Bolt—called again. "What's wrong with them anyhow?"

The woman leading the charge had short, pin-straight silver hair. The uniform she wore was white as snow with gold lace stitching.

"That's Sabelle." Her eyes locked on the woman. "Luna's advisor."

Behind her, an army of Light Saints and Soulless marched toward the castle, followed by Lightning Saints.

"That explains the heavy storm," Aurora said. "Light and Lightning have officially teamed up, and they're marching to attack the castle."

"They're declaring war." Aurora felt Madness' soul flutter in fear. "We have to get back and warn them."

Bolt came into view. His twisted scar kept his facial expression to a minimum. He and Sabelle marched their troops forward across a frozen swamp—courtesy of Sabelle and her powers—and before long, they were gone.

"How did they even know we were here?" Aurora stood, adjusting her bags.

"We can worry about that later." Madness moved to the back of the tree to get his belongings. "For now, we need to focus on getting back."

Juvia had no idea of the onslaught headed her way. They were the only ones who could warn them.

"It's still night," Aurora explained. "I can carry us through the shadows to the main square, and we can beat them there before the attack—"

"No." Madness snapped. "As much as we need to reach the castle, you can't waste any of your strength. We are going to need your power."

"It's a surprise attack, Madness!" Aurora urged him. "Eight thousand of our enemies' troops are marching right up to the gate. The Water Saints will be slaughtered. Our *friends* are in danger."

"If we lose any of your strength, we're all dead." Madness remained in his resolve.

The army would reach the castle before them, but Madness was right. Aurora's full strength was needed during the battle. Eight thousand Light Knights and Lighting Saints marched toward the castle. Juvia possessed eight thousand Water Saints, but nearly two thousand were missioners and untrained for battle. Only Katerina or Samuel stood a chance against Bolt and Sabelle, while Juvia defended her people.

Aurora had foolishly left her friends behind, and now an army of saints and Soulless were marching toward them, teething to take their lives. Bolt and Sabelle were after to slaughter all those she Aurora held dear.

I can reach them in time before the army reaches the castle. Sabelle won't touch a single one of them.

Sabelle's snowfall and the frozen swamp were gone, and the rains poured heavier than before. Both Aurora and Madness ran as they could, but they were too slow.

"Did you see all the masks?" Madness asked. "All the Soulless?"

Aurora nodded. "How could you miss it."

Of the eight-thousand troops, five thousand appeared Soulless. Luna did not care if she lost any in the battle, as she knew their numbers were easily replaceable.

Aurora flicked ice in her palm, testing the strength in her body. The past months had indeed strengthened her mind and body. Saints would prove easy work, but if another god were to join in the battle, Aurora was not too sure of the outcome.

What if Luna . . .

A pain ran through her chest, and Aurora collapsed. It was tight, like she had eaten too much too fast, but more gut-wrenching and painful. She grasped her chest, screaming for the agony to stop.

What is this!

"Rory!" Madness kneeled. "Are you okay? How can I help."

The pain subsided. Aurora's chest felt heavier. Like the shadows within her had shifted.

"Yes . . . I'm fine. Madness—there is not much time." She found her feet. "We will run a little further, and then I'll call on the shadows."

"Aurora, they will be fine. Please, let us run a little farther, especially after whatever that was."

"Madness, we are still a mile out!" Aurora shouted. "Running in this water in this insane weather will take at least another hour. We don't have another hour!"

Aurora had lived and watched how quickly battles came and went. Madness and the mortals had learned to survive by strength but had not fought in a proper war battle.

"The Void almost killed you last time!" Madness snapped. "I won't allow it."

The Void. Madness had watched Aurora painfully take Bolt through her shadows. She admired him for not wanting her to suffer again, but to be part of that pain, but it was a risk they had to take.

"We need the shadows." Aurora reached for his hand. "It will be okay. I'm much stronger now. I can handle it."

Something of Madness had changed over the last month. He was vulnerable, more openly emotional. Aurora felt it not only in how he spoke to her but in his soul. It was stronger and had its own willpower and desire. Mephista was shadowed by its strength.

I understand why Samuel wants Madness to stay here.

"All right." He finally agreed.

Aurora called on the Altered Realm. Ice crawled forth, forming intricate layers over her arms. Madness stepped close to Aurora and interlocked his fingers with hers. Shadowy vines poured from her back and wrapped around them both. They reached down into the muddied water and plunged them into the darkest shadows. Into the Void.

Aurora thought of the gates to the castle's grounds—and in a moment, they arrived.

It was horror.

As when Aurora had existed and died as a mortal, water, lightning, and light clashed. Aurora felt slightly paralyzed, stuck in a moment in time, but Madness squeezed her hand.

A Light Knight—a Light *Saint*—hurried at full speed. With a skim of her fingers, Aurora brought ice to the tips and sent them flying into the Light Saint's chest. He flew back, dropping his sword. Aurora reached down and tossed it to Madness.

"Nice work," Madness called as they raced onto the battlefield.

"I'm just glad it was a Light Saint and not a Soulless," Aurora didn't know if she could bring herself to kill one. Even though the soul was gone, Aurora did not believe she could kill the body of a mortal.

Aurora watched saints from each side fall in defeat or death. She wanted them to stop and remember the five-hundred years of peace they had experienced, but it was useless now. Alliances were broken and relationships were in ruins. The Third Gods War had begun.

In the courtyard by the fountains, the battle surged. Smells of blood and torn flesh and cries of the dying bellowed through the arches and walkways of the castle. It seeped into the memories of Aurora's soul.

"We won't find anyone at this rate if we stay together." Aurora pressed her back to his. "We must divide and conquer."

"I'll go into the courtyards," Madness said. "You check the suites."

"Right." They split, but Aurora reached for Madness before he was too far out of reach.

"Find your way back to me."

And he was gone with the masses, and Aurora was alone with her power. She grew up as a child in the God Wars, learning to fend for and fight for herself. When Aurora was human, she was useless in battle, but when she became a god, Aurora had found her calling.

Aurora pushed along ice underfoot, gliding through the castle grounds. She passed the fifth and sixth towers, making her way to the second. She would make sure no one was there, trapped or hurt. Bodies swept the narrow spaces. Light Knights tried to take Aurora on as she glided past, but she swatted them with ease.

She kept her eyes peeled for Juvia or Katerina, and even Sabelle or Bolt. Aurora would only make a move on the two advisors once Juvia was at her side. Although both advisors were strong, with a powerful connection to their element, it was Sabelle she worried over. Sabelle was a Think, but unlike Samuel, she played twisted games. Sabelle relished in driving her victims mad. .

If Sabelle got her hands on any of the mortals . . .

Snow, as dense as crystals, skimmed her field of vision. A few crystals cut her lip. Aurora stopped and faced her attacker. It was a Soulless.

The dog mask and white uniform were soaked in blood—whether its own blood own or its victim's, there was no telling. Luna saw the humans as animals and decorated them as such, and they acted accordingly.

The Soulless charged, spiraling through the air with light and snow. White crystals flew from its hands, slicing Aurora's arm and left cheek. She fell backward, stunned. Even though Luna took the soul of the mortal rather than giving away a piece of her own, they still harnessed her powers of light and crystals.

It was impossible—yet taking the soul of a human was an unheard practice until Luna took it upon herself to be the first to do so.

Aurora threw up the defense. Shadows blocked the light and crystals, pushing Aurora back against the castle wall. The Soulless swung, and Aurora ducked.

I-I can't attack.

Aurora was unsure if it was because the opponent was a mindless human or because they harnessed Luna's power. All she could do was dodge and hope for an opening of escape.

Its gurgling stirred her senses. The Soulless' mind and body that remained reached for something. It was not attacking her willingly, and even without a soul to feel, Aurora knew the creature wanted peace. Black ice laced across her fingers like knives, and Aurora mustered the strength to stab its abdomen.

"What?"

It was a fatal blow to any creature—human, Magical, immortal—but not a Soulless. Dumbfounded, Aurora went back on the defensive. Even when pleading for it, the Soulless seemed invincible to death, even from a god.

Then, it's head at her feet.

"Only way to kill the empty bastards is with a clean sweep of the head!"

The corpse collapsed backward, and Alexen swung his sword to his back.

"I never thought I'd be happy to see you," Aurora stepped toward him.

"Likewise."

Aurora thought she saw him smirk, but more Soulless gathered.

"Where is everyone else?" The two moved back-to-back.

"Half are in the estate. The other half, no clue." Alexen jabbed his sword through one's head and back out. "I *did* pass your boyfriend on my way here—duck!"

There was no time as Alexen's sword swung. Aurora lowered and heard his sword crash through another Soulless' skull.

Aurora gathered herself and stood back up. "And where might yours be?"

That time, he *did* smirk. "Tobias was upstairs with Bloom and Pan before the battle. I was on my way there, but the enemy came out of nowhere."

Good, Elaina's not alone.

"Then that's where we're headed."

They raced past the fourth and third towers with little conflict. Saints and soulless attacked along the way, but Aurora and Alexen took them down or dodged with ease.

"Now imagine how great we could be if you actually liked me."

The base of the second tower crawled with Soulless. Alexen moved along the stairs, killing them as he could. Aurora was useless and did as she could to defend Alexen from behind.

For a mortal, Alexen's soul is rather mighty.

Alexen beheaded the last Soulless, and they were faced with blood—lots of blood against the giant, icy door.

"Elaina!"

Adrenaline pushed them through the living room. Two bodies that lay inside were Light Saints.

"Bloom! *Tobias!*" Alexen raced to the bedrooms. Aurora looked around the main room for more bodies, but there were none. Alexen remerged. "Their rooms are empty—they left before it started."

"But this blood is from someone other than the Light Saints." Aurora stumbled toward her room. "Did you check my chambers?"

His face went white. "No."

The door was open. Someone had forced their way inside the impenetrable door.

Aurora's feet carried her faster than they ever had before. She had to make sure no one was inside—

The headboard was smeared in fresh, hot blood. Along the walls was the symbol of light—

"*ELAINA!*"

Below the symbol of light on the balcony—

Blood still trickled down her throat. Her clothes were drenched in her blood. Elaina's final gaze was on the ocean, her face soaked in blood and tears.

Elaina died alone, sitting in her favorite spot, looking at her favorite view, waiting for her favorite person's return, again. Their linked ear cuffs in the palm of her bloodied hand.

Aurora shook. She believed she screamed, but there was no noise. No sense of being. No plane to steady her.

Aurora cradled the Dark Saint's body. She had loved Elaina as her own flesh and blood, and her true sister had taken her.

"Aurora." For once, Alexen's voice was soft. His hand touched Aurora's shoulder like grabbing sheets of ice. "Aurora, we need to move."

"If-if I had stayed." Aurora heaved. Her hands pushed back Elaina's blooded hair. "Alexen if I had *stayed*."

Alexen lowered his weapon.

"*What do I do?*" She needed advising—a guide among the swarming darkness.

His hand fell along her back.

"Avenge her, Aurora. Awaken Darkness."

And she listened.

It was then Aurora realized she had felt when Elaina died: It was as she and Madness raced through the swamps. Aurora had felt the that last, stubborn piece of her soul return home. Shadows gathered in a fury Aurora had not felt in centuries as they lusted for battle and vengeance.

Aurora did not know if it was the pain or if it was Elaina's tiny soul returning to its place within her, but when Aurora walked down the stairs with Alexen at her back, the roaring silenced, and the rage of Aurora's soul erupted. The shadows and murky darkness stretched crossed the stairs, the tower, and the battle below, hunting. With their chains unbound, the darkness was ready to devour. There were be no mercy.

Because that was true darkness, the power to wield and destroy hope.

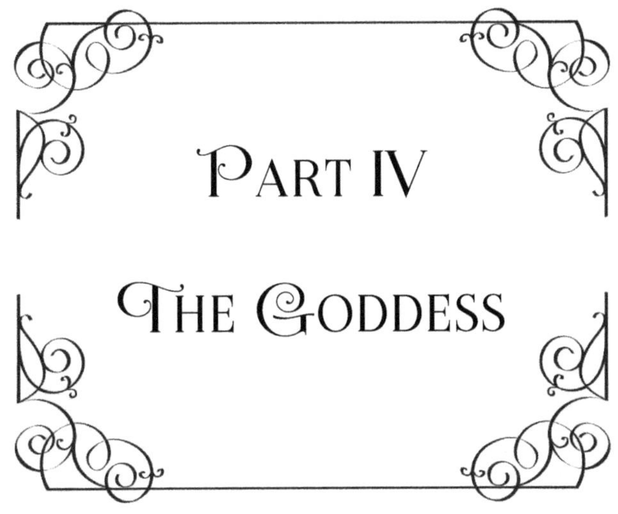

Part IV

The Goddess

CHAPTER 31

Just please be okay.

Madness did not mean his friends. He did not even mean Alfonso. All Madness thought of was that damned girl.

Saints and Soulless covered the estate. Madness watched fearless and skilful Water Saints fall helpless against Lightning and Light Saints. He wanted to help them, but Madness had no power. Not power he could wield and control, anyway.

"*Come on, Madness,*" The Pull called. "*We've worked long and hard the last month together for a moment like this. Let me out to play, even if it's for just a little.*"

Over the month, he and Samuel had trained relentlessly. The two traveled deep into the forest of the estate, away from lurking eyes. Samuel revealed he not only had the magical ability think, but he was once a healer and knew exactly how to tame Mephista. Samuel and his sister had not lived during the times of demons, but their families had, and the two had spent their mortal lives preparing for their possible return.

"You're the first I've met in two millennia," Samuel explained. "I thought they had all been terminated."

Madness and Samuel had formed a bond solely based on Madness' suffering. Samuel knew the darkest parts of him in ways Alfonso nor Aurora—anyone for that mattered—ever would.

"Make her submit!" he instructed. "Show her command her to know you are the master. You rule her.*"*

Madness had transformed more times than he cared to remember over the last month. Each time, his body ached with the fires of the Grounds Below, and Mephista took his body and soul. It was agony—never-ending agony. But each transformation became less messy and less bloodthirsty, and Madness felt himself gain power and will over the wretched curse within him.

Madness thought it better for his friends to think he was sulking rather than to know he was purposely inviting Mephista to play. They only saw an injured, hurt man whose ego was damaged by Aurora's lack of truth. It did bother him that she had not shared the details of the Soul Keepers sooner and that they were her objective all along. Madness admitted it was right of her to withhold the information, even if it pissed him off, but he would never forgive her for thinking she could save Nelabac alone.

A Soulless jumped before him, sword swinging. Madness bent back as a sword swung across his front. He rounded his body and slammed the sword, snapping the Soulless' spine. But it stood. The Soulless stared through its cat mask. It barreled its gaze like he was more than another piece of flesh to slash down, but a target to claim.

It terrified him.

Madness moved, knocking blows that would render the Soulless dead, but still, it rose. Both its legs were broken, so it lurched forward on its arms. Fear consumed him, so Madness swung his sword down across its neck. A head rolled across the dirt.

As the blood poured from the decapitated body, Madness felt The Pull. It tugged ever so slightly, wanting to join in the chaos and tear those around them apart.

No.

"When that happens, don't shove it down and ignore it." Samuel was clear in his instruction. "You bring that gods-damned demon face-to-face in its shackles and claim: I own you."

Like the feral creature it was, The Pull snarled at the memory. At his new-found restraint. Madness curled a grin and dove into the fury.

Onward Madness fought through the courtyard, searching high and low for his comrades and friends. He passed a few Water Saints he recognized. Some fought while others seeped into the earth. Madness would pray for their souls later.

Look at me, finding belief in something.

Water Saints covered the grounds in the ashes of their blood. The Light Knights and Lightning Saints were winning, and they were going to claim victory. They needed leaders, Aurora and Juvia.

Maybe they were fighting them on the opposite side of the estate. Maybe they were defeated—

I won't think that way.

Madness knew better by now than to underestimate immortals.

Lightning struck. The blast threw Madness back, tumbling over the dirt.

I guess these ear cuffs do work.

As he sat up, Madness faced a familiar attacker.

Helena.

It was the Lightning Saint he and Cerene fooled in Lightning Palace. She held a rod sparking with electricity, and her hands were bloody. Madness reached for his sword, but it had been thrown from reach in the blast.

"You!" She directed the rod at him. "You'll pay for what you've done!"

The Pull tore at his chest. It would have to be now—

"Get away from him!"

Helena's body folded as her ribs and bones crunched between the massive jaws. Pan shook the Lightning Saint side to side before tossing her across the grounds and stepping to defend Madness.

But Helena jumped the beast, sending electric shocks through her body. Pan went rigid. Madness gathered his feet and ran for the beast, but electric shocks paralyzed him. Helena stormed toward them with a grin of victory swooning across her face.

"Hey, you."

Championing from above, arrows fired, stabbing Helena in the back. The Lighting Saint pulled the arrow from her back.

"Hitting your opponent when their back is turned is pretty low." Helena spat, snapping the arrow in half. "But you are only a human."

"Exactly. I'm human." Cerene crouched like a rabid animal. "Which means I can become the lowest of the low if it's to protect my friends."

Using her bow and arrows, Cerene charged, and Madness watched her take on the form of revenge. The form of a warrior. Helena aimed her rod, but an arrow hit her forearm first. It shot clean through, throwing the rod right out of Helena's reach.

One arrow more.

And then two.

Helena snarled through her teeth. And so distracted in pain, she didn't see Cerene's punch. A punch with so much force a tooth flew across the field.

It was like they had been gifted a Goddess of War.

"Glad to see your hand is better." Helena staggered on her feet, unsteady, spitting blood.

"I should thank you, really." Cerene touched up her nails with the ends of the dagger-curved bow. "The scar is a nice reminder of what I'm fighting for."

Electricity pulsed, and Helena shot forward. Madness panicked, knowing Cerene wouldn't last long on her own, but another voice echoed. Bloom stood with her hands together and her mouth moving in the ancient language. The diamond on her forehead sparked to life, enchanting Cerene with great speed and strength, who took one good kick at Helena and sent her flying through the trees. The archer rose like a crowned queen.

"Did you get her?" Cerene ran over and embraced Madness. "Did you reach Aurora in time?"

"She ran to check on Elaina and Tobias and Bloom—wait, Bloom, why aren't you in the tower?"

"Elaina insisted we leave and join the battle." Bloom gave Pan a quick pat. "She said she'd be fine on her own."

Madness wanted to rush and see if all was okay in the Second Tower. He knew Aurora would move the stars and realign the darkness to keep Elaina safe. But there was no time.

"Where is everyone else?"

"Baer is on the opposite side of the castle, near the shores. I think Tobias went with him," Pan explained. "I don't know where Alexen ran off to, but Alfonso is further in the woods. I saw him rush in with Samuel and Katerina."

"Right, I'm going." Madness knew Samuel and Katerina were at the heart of the danger.

"Not without us," Cerene challenged.

"I'll go after Alfonso. You two find Aurora." Madness grabbed his sword. "Help keep her powers in check. She is too eager to protect us. She might break."

Cerene grinned. "Look who's grown a soft spot for all things dark."

Of course she would say such a thing as we're in the middle of an immortal battle.

A shock fired at their backs. Saints crowded from all sides. Madness grabbed his sword on the ground. Bloom sent spells of illusions, and Pan attacked full force. Cerene fired an arrow, each landing through their targets.

"Hurry!" Bloom's diamond was a bright, brilliant light. "We've got your back."

And then water flooded the plain. It gripped the Soulless and Light Saints in bubbles of water. The water filled their bodies and—

They popped like balloons.

In her Alter Realm, The Goddess of Water's eyes glowed blues and purple. Her body seemingly became water itself. Liquid wiped around Juvia like ancient beasts of the sea. She was a sight to behold, one never to forget.

"Go," she called, "now!"

Madness had no clue where he was racing toward. Madness only went off Bloom's hunch that Alfonso was deeper in the woods. With his brother at his side, Madness knew they could stand the rest of this battle together, no matter how messy it became.

In the thickness of the woods, water, lightning, and snow and the cries of a familiar, booming voice. Madness halted and dove into the bushes. He swore he felt Aurora's presence but realized it was the ear cuff. It was a piece of her attached to him and to his brother. As he thought, through the tree line, Madness made out his brother's shape, and he was not alone.

His opponents were Bolt and another woman with pin-straight blonde hair that stopped above her shoulders dressed in white and gold.

Sabelle.

From what Aurora and Tobias had described, Sabelle was not like the other advisors. Grounds Below, she wasn't like other saints. Other than her god, Sabelle possessed more power and twisted plans than any immortal put together.

Aurora claimed Mako was the only other saint to match her in power.

Katerina and Samuel stood in front of Alfonso, protecting him. Madness felt The Pull retreat altogether at the sight of the Water Saint. Madness knew Katerina and Samuel were stronger together, but against Sabelle, anyone was at a disadvantage.

"Why Bolt?" Katerina inquired. "What good can come from siding with them?"

"Blesk believed in Luna's plans long before they came to pass. Long before the Soul Keepers were ever discovered. Blesk has wanted the mortals of this land destroyed since the day he became a god." Bolt spat with hatred. But Madness sensed it was not at Katerina. "I do as he commands, and if Blesk wants to destroy this world at Luna's side and rebuild it from the ashes, then so be it."

"We don't have what you seek!" Samuel shouted. "Take your troops and retreat."

"Bolty, you're making yourself look like a fool before the enemy." Sabelle casually placed her hand against Bolt's chest. "Hush!"

It was strange to watch the Lightning Advisor struck with fear. Madness would have enjoyed it under different circumstances.

Sabelle stalked toward Katerina, Samuel, and Alfonso, spreading snow with each step. The Water Saints' tightened their position, ready for whatever onslaught she plotted.

But it happened—unseen. Unpredicted.

Crystals flew from the earth—

But Samuel caught them. Water pulled in around the Water Saint as he pushed his sister and Alfonso aside. Samuel gasped, reaching for air as blood spewed out his side.

"I came here for a Soul Keeper." Sabelle's eyes narrowed as her lips curled in a wicked rage. "And I'm *not* leaving without it!"

Madness had to Samuel—he had to save him. His teacher—his friend lay impaled. Blood dripped down the crystals as Samuel struggled to hold his body upright.

"Samuel!" Katerina reached for her brother.

Sabelle cackled, and menacing bloodlust spewed across the battle. Her silver hair remained untouched. Bolt stood by her side, his face twisting in confusion and rage.

"Samuel?" Madness touched Samuel's chest. His glasses were broken and blood dripped everywhere.

"Mad—" Blood splattered over Madness' shirt. "You're—here—"

How did I get here?

"Let me heal you." Madness' focused when he knew it was pointless. "Katerina needs you—*I* still need you."

"Shut up and listen." Samuel's hand gripped Madness' arm. "Now more than—"

"Stop being so stubborn, and let me try!"

"There is a rumor—in the north—"

So much blood.

"Someone like *you.*" Samuel's eyes were on the sky. "Rose—they're called. Promise—you'll find them—you are the key—"

Someone like me . . . Rose.

The light faded from Samuel and his fear filled Madness. Neither was ready.

"I'll find them." Madness gripped Samuel's hand. "I promise."

"I'm—I'm not ready, but—" Samuel squeezed his hand back. "It was a good life—and I've left Nelabac in the best of hands . . . that's all I ever wanted. Was to protect it—"

Madness only healed, even with nothing left, he tried. Through Madness' tears, he found solace in his brother's hand. In his soft, violet gaze.

"You ass." Madness bent his head.

"Sabelle!" Bolt's looked from the mangled body to the Light Advisor. "This was not the mission."

"Mad," Alfonso yelled to his brother, "we need to get out of here."

"He's right," Katerina was at their side. The Water Advisor was suffering unexplainable grief, yet still she fought. "You two are not safe. Retreat."

"Retreat? Oh, no, no, no!" Sabelle twirled her hair. "The three of you as dead as the man at your feet and the girl in that tower."

That tower?

The Pull—he called to her.

Sabelle had not only taken something dear to him—but the precious thing to Aurora. His god.

And that was unforgivable.

"We can get her, Madness," The Pull begged. *"Attack while she least expects it."*

"We are here to retrieve the Soul Keeper and Aurora." Lightning and Light continued their quarrel. "We were not instructed to go on a killing spree."

"Oh, hush, lightning boy. Luna told me to have some fun while I was here." Sabelle tapped his shoulder. "Water Saints have kept themselves from the battlefield for so long that they've forgotten how to fight. This sends the perfect message."

"*Sabelle.*" Katerina whirled in the water at her feet and pulled it to her palms. "There is no Soul Keeper here."

"Oh, but there is." Sabelle's voice practically sang in victory. "Explain, Bolty."

Bolt's eyes held contemplation as he looked at Samuel. Madness realized the two were once allies. For hundreds of years, they had known one another and even fought side-by-side at one point. Bolt felt remorse, but for saints, duty came before anything else.

"We found evidence that a Soul Keeper was harbored by a wizard who was residing in the Fourth Realm. He helped Aurora and her mortals escape over a month ago," Bolt explained. "Through our interrogation, we found the wizard's master had been part of the forging of the Soul Keepers. He had sacrificed his life in the process. Then the wizard became responsible for keeping it safe."

Madness fumbled in his pant pocket. Gods, he had forgotten completely.

"We learned he had passed it on to a new carrier. When he told us, we knew he had given it to Aurora."

Do not forget this either, young Madness: Even a boastful sun is penetrable.

Chapter 32

Never had Madness thought for a second he held one of the seven deadly items the gods were slaughtering one another over in his pocket.

I guess I owe Aurora an apology for all the secrets stuff.

Madness held the firestone above his head. "*This* is one of those things that could kill a god?"

"Put that away, boy!" Katerina called.

"Yeah, Mad," Alfonso reached for the stone. "What in the Grounds Below are you doing?"

"Oh, I simply love humans!" Sabelle licked her lips. "I wonder if Luna and Blesk would mind if we tested it out while we're here."

"Our orders are strict." Bolt stepped between Sabelle and the stone. "No stones will be tested until we have all six Soul Keepers and Aurora in our custody."

Sabelle grabbed the collar of his shirt. Her foot slid across the ground, blinding him by light brightening off her chest. "Lightning always was the dullest of the elements."

Katerina charged. "Sabelle!"

But Katerina did not see the giant, white crystal rise through the air. The Water Advisor tried to catch herself, but it was too late as she flung into the woods.

"Luna has grand plans with those stones," Sabelle marched, "and I'm not going to let you get in the way!"

"If she kills all the humans, elves, dwarves, or whatever Magicals still exist in Nelabac, there will be no world to rule over." Madness challenged the Light Advisor. He had to keep her busy until Katerina returned, or Juvia or Aurora arrived. "What would be the point? To rule an empty wasteland?"

"My boy, don't worry. You'll be there to see what happens." Sabelle took a step closer to him, and Madness felt a heat through his body that not even The Pull had given rise to. "I have no use for you right now, so in the meantime, your help was greatly appreciated."

The Light Advisor jumped in the air, but water crashed into her side. Katerina moved as water and crystal met with the same resistance and strength.

"We can't," Madness said. "We can't help her here."

"I know," Alfonso reached for his Weapons of Ore, "but I wish we could."

"Let's get out of here."

Lightning traveled across the ground and up Alfonso's body. Madness stared, helpless, as his brother writhed in pain.

"Al!" Madness reached for his brother.

"I don't think so, mortals." Bolt's scarred face twisted as it could. "I'm your opponent."

It was time, Madness realized. He didn't want to unleash it here, to show the world what he had become, but fate had left him with no other choice.

"Al," Madness felt Mephista's horns scrap against his skull, "whatever you do, don't stop me."

Alfonso steadied his feet. "Don't do anything I wouldn't do."

Madness grinned. "Without a doubt."

Mephista's taunts for control and submission echoed in his ears. All those days, writhing in pain at that wretched transformation.

"You can wield it as a weapon or let it destroy everything you love."

I'm about to test my resolve, Samuel. You better have my back, you damned saint.

Madness walked with the intent to destroy everything that lay in his path, to protect those he loved, and to remain. Blood filled his eyes, and malice filled his soul.

"Pretty love of you to take on a mortal," Madness taunted.

"I'm more human than you, demon." Bolt tried to get under Madness' skin, but it had no effect. All Madness noticed was that Bolt had no interest in Alfonso, and he planned to keep it that way.

"Listen here, static freak." Madness grumbled as Mephista lurched forward, forcing their voices to blend. "You want to be pissy about the state we left the Caris, then fine. But you have no right to harbor on the past."

Bolt bit his lip. "Excuse me?"

"Aurora made a bad call, but so did the other gods by agreeing with her." Their souls resonated. "Then, when the gods left, saints in every realm made a mistake in turning to war. In *not* trusting one another. In not working as one to stop the Light Knights. You all stood by and did nothing."

"Don't come at me, mortal!" Bolt charged. "I did all I could while Blesk was gone—and now that's back, I must follow his lead! I have no choice but to trust him!"

"Do the citizens of Caris know what Blesk wants to do? That, when the world dies, they die with it?" Madness swung his sword to Bolt. The power of Mephista shot around him—ran down and up his arms. Under the bandage, Madness felt the demon seal burn with her blue and black flames. The darkness of Aurora's powers shielded his body. Madness felt invincible. "Turning your back and slaughtering the innocent won't save anyone."

"She promises not to kill them," Bolt snapped. "She promises to spare our mortals."

Madness widened his stance. "Then you and Blesk are the bigger fools."

Lightning moved through pockets of air toward Madness, but he reached out his arm—his left arm. The bandage burst with black flames. The ancient language came to life as Madness and Mephista's desires molded into one. As they became one soul.

And Madness felt the lines blur. He felt the spaces where their minds were one, fine unit.

Madness could have sworn fear rippled in Bolt's pupils.

So this is what true power can do.

Bolt aimed again and again, but Madness dodged faster than even Alfonso.

"I've lived four thousand years." Electricity sparked through the air. "I refuse to allow a measly *mortal* think they know what is right and wrong in this world."

Then, Madness sensed more bodies. Behind, Lighting and Light Saints, followed by Soulless, crowded around Alfonso.

"That's right, Bolt smirked. "You left him completely open."

"Al!"

Alfonso's hammer and ax bled. His magic neared its end. Madness was so caught up in his battle—in his lust for more Mephista and power—that he had forgotten his brother. Forgotten what he was fighting to protect. Alfonso was stuck with mortal abilities, while his immortal opponents drew in energy from electricity buzzing in the air, the materials of the earth, and from the soul of their god determined to end the world. Madness knew the only reason his brother still stood was thanks to the shield provided in the ear cuff.

Behind, Sabelle flung Katerina into the trees.

"Humans are lowly creatures." Her eyes found Alfonso. "Luna was right: eliminating you one by one would put an end to this entire war."

Madness felt the break in the balance before the crystals spike his brothers' abdomen.

Just this once. Madness whispered to Mephista. *You can take control, and I'll let you out to play more often.*

"Promise?"

I promise.

"You evil, evil boy."

Mephista's soul bounced off his own. Madness' arms grew to black, unrecognizable claws. They extended to the ground and half the length of his body. The horns spiraled from his skull and his hair grew long and red. The transformation was agony while conscious.

Mephista rubbed against his spine, pressed just against his mind. She wanted him to undo the chains that bound her, but instead, they shared them. Madness shackled himself to her as they controlled his body.

This was freedom unlike any other. He had controlled Mephista, and the one to thank was dead.

It was infuriating.

Four Soulless bodies fell to his feet. Ten more lay behind him. Another's corpse was held in each of his demon hands.

Madness felt himself slipping—like maybe not even Alfonso could be his salvation.

Then shadows filled the space.

And Aurora appeared.

PAN

Chapter 33

The mangled bodies in his hands meant nothing as Madness tipped his head side to side. His ears buzzed with heat. His head was heavy with horns and scales. He tried to piece together how he got here. He felt Mephista sinking him deeper and deeper, the chains shifting from his body to hers—

A soft hand met his back, and a blue light resonated.

"You did well." Though Alfonso was not bringing Madness back to his senses, but letting him know it was okay. Madness gripped his lizard-like hand. He had control, and for the first time in his life, Madness held control over Mephista.

Samuel had truly taught him to use her to *his* advantage.

The undoing of the demon was not by her command and power over their souls, Madness realized, but it had been his own will. His decision.

"There you are."

It became a moonless evening as a veil of shadows emerged. Pitch-black shadows raced from Aurora like an ocean on a windy day. They lifted the Goddess of Dark, their deity, to the sky. Her torso became one with the darkness, absorbing moonlight. The darkest parts of Nelabac bent at Aurora's will as glorious wings took to their master.

Madness' soul soared at the sight of her, but he sensed something wrong. There was a halo darkening Aurora. It was a darkness that she didn't command, but one found in the pits of the Grounds Below.

She knows. She knows Elaina is dead.

The shadows' murky depths wrapped around Lightning and Light Saints' bodies and swallowed them whole. The few remaining stared at where their fellow soldiers had stood. Aurora made no motion or signal. She didn't even speak as her powers devoured.

"Bolty!" Sabelle called the Lightning Advisor. "I need some help here."

Bolt turned, but a shadow slithered across the ground and flicked him across the woods. He was a pest to the Goddess of Dark, for her target dwelled in the light.

"Rory's different." Alfonso's eyes held fear. "What's wrong with her?"

"She's wounded," Madness said. "More wounded than we've ever seen her."

Madness and Alfonso watched as straggling Light Saints and Soulless scrambled to flee, but like a game of cat and mouse, Aurora was not ready to let them go.

"Now, now, you can leave just yet." Her wings positioned her right above them. "The fun has just begun."

With a snap of her fingers, icicles dotted the air, pointing right at the Lightning and Light Saints. Madness glanced at Sabelle, who had lost some of her alien-like composure.

She's frightened.

"We retreated!" Bolt emerged from the woods. "With Aurora in this state, not even you can take her."

"No." Aurora extended her hand. "You will stay here. You'll *fall* here."

Bolt and the enemies in the clearing were swept into the Void. Madness and Alfonso watched as the shaded holes sucked them in, muffling their screams. Silence filled the battlefield.

Only Sabelle was left standing.

"You're one tough bitch, Goddess of Dark."

"Silence, Sabelle." Aurora's voice was not her own. It was not of the Alter Realm either. It was a being Madness had never heard, one not of this world or the one below.

"This whole time—" Sabelle licked her lips. "I waited long and patiently for Luna's return so she could tell me exactly what to do with her."

Elaina.

She provoked the Goddess of Dark, and Madness knew it. Aurora's eyes flickered, straining to withhold the power held behind those onyx spheres.

"What do we do?" Alfonso gripped the Weapons of Ore. "I meant, what *can* we do?"

They knew how to calm their Magical friends and stop a demon, but how did they stop a god?

Sabelle crystalized the ground in white ash with each step. The shadows swelled, consuming the land in a black haze.

"You two need to get back!" Katerina taped their backs. "They're going to tear this area apart!"

Sabelle continued circling Aurora, taunting and running her fingers through her hair. "Luna ordered before I did anything else in this battle, she wanted me to, oh, how did she put it—that's right: send Elaina off with the rest of them!"

Katerina took Madness' and Alfonso's hands and ran. They jumped over bodies and navigated the broken land. Madness didn't want to leave Aurora behind.

"But Aurora's powers—"

"Don't you see?" Katerina said. "Since Elaina was killed, Aurora has been restored!"

Light and dark clashed. Night became day and the lines of good and evil blurred. The veil unraveled, and the shadows' screams reached across the forest, reaching anyone who would hear them.

"*Sabelle. Sabelle. Sabelle*!"

Alfonso covered his ears as they ducked down. "It's so loud!"

"The Sisters of Balance." Katerina struggled against the noise. "Their powers are not restricted to only this world, are not drawn solely from our soils. They do not only absorb the magic of this world but of *every* world."

"What?" Madness guarded his neck as rubble flew. "You mean—"

"I mean, they are of *every* world." Katerina locked onto the battle. "Wherever darkness slumbers, and wherever light beams, the Goddesses of Balance call upon their graces. They are deities of deities—the beings of all beings."

The shadows around Aurora were alive. They were borrowed of other worlds, other spaces of darkness and night. Aurora was truly the embodiment of Darkness, and Sabelle was a pawn of the embodiment of Light.

Madness sat back. "She's incredible."

The two were on a level no one within the Seventh Realm could touch.

Now I see why Aurora was frightened all this time. She went from someone able to conjure the darkness of other worlds to someone who had to learn to walk again.

The clashing of the battle paused.

"Poor little *Elaina.*" Sabelle cackled. "She cried for you in the end."

Aurora snarled her teeth. "Don't you *dare* speak her name!"

Noise ruffled in the trees behind.

"Light Saints!" Katerina whirled the waters to her side. "You've got to run!"

Alfonso took his brother's hand. "Go!"

Powers flew past in every direction. Gods and saints. Immortals and Soulless. It was a battle Madness had never anticipated, had never dreamed of facing, let alone take part in. The brothers struggled across the landscape. Ice and crystals and puddles of darkness and splatters of light lay everywhere they ran. The enemy drew in closer.

"Shit!" Alfonso heaved.

They were surrounded on both sides. They pushed back as the enemy encircled them. Madness met his brother's gaze. There was no fear, only strength.

Above, Aurora raged against Sabelle. Her eyes were an endless abyss, and her body folded in and out of the shadows. Her screams were sorrow, a melody of heartbreak and anguish. Their god was here, but their friend was lost. She was consumed in the darkness and madness of her life.

She really is just like me.

Lightning struck from above and then beside them. Suddenly, surrounded on all sides, the enemy joined for one attack.

"Mad!" Alfonso reached for his brother.

"Al!"

Madness pushed his brother and braced himself. He knew his body would not survive the attack, that the ear cuff would not stop his body as it burned. He knew it was too late to summon Mephista.

Looks like I won't be able to keep that promise, Samuel.

He thought of his dearest friends. Cerene and Tobias. Of the loyal beast, Baer. He thought of his new friends, Bloom, Pan, and Alexen.

He thought of that damned girl, and smiled over at his brother.

In the end, Madness was happy Mephista never claimed him and that he would die protecting the ones he loved most.

"Enough!"

Water bubbled, and the lightning clashed above. The lightning pushed back the waters that blocked its target. The water rippled with the strength of a forming storm on the open sea, but it held as it protected Madness and Alfonso.

Madness was enwrapped in the Goddess of Water's waves. To his left, Alfonso lay unconscious but alive. When the dust settled over where the lightning had struck, all he could hear were wails and a sad, sad sister.

"This is done!" Juvia's resolve was strong, unwavering. She set Madness and Alfonso beside Katerina as she turned to the gathered Light Saints. "You're through."

Pulled from the air and trees and ground below, waters rushed the enemy and sent them far away from the scene.

"Don't worry, mortals. This is over now." Juvia rotated toward where darkness and light clashed.

Above, the Goddess of Dark and Advisor of Light paused. The darkness roared around Aurora, only growing and gaining in strength in its hold over their master.

"Are you not going to help her?" Madness asked the Goddess of Warer.

"This is a debt Aurora shall settle alone." Juvia closed her palms and the waters.

Sabelle glanced down, taking note of Juvia's arrival. Her face was bloody, but the Light Advisor remained steady.

"Nice to see you, Juvia," Sabelle crooned. "You're looking fresh as ever."

"Go back to your master, Sabelle. Tell her you lost," Juvia called. "We're done with her game of chess for today."

Madness watched Aurora as she flicked her hands. He watched the ice that laced her fingers shatter. She shook her head and pressed her temples.

"Get out of my head!" Aurora pressed against her temples, forcing Sabelle out. Madness remembered the advisor was a Think like Samuel, but Sabelle tortured her victims, carved their thoughts and memories into nothing.

But the darkness heeded one last call. "I am no puppet!"

Mortals. Magicals. The Second and Third Realm. Samuel. Elaina—Sabelle saw them as puppets, controlled by the master puppeteer, Luna, but Aurora was the one to cut the strings.

Madness knew it. His friends knew it, and it was about time Aurora recognized it.

She was Aurora, Goddess of Dark and Ruler of the Second Realm.

Time to fight or shatter, Goddess of Dark.

Darkness crawled down her body like spiders to a web and weaved their way across the ground and surrounded Sabelle. There was nowhere the Light Advisor could run. Wrapping up her body like fungus to a tree, Sabelle attacked with crystals, but the shadows grabbed her, constricting Sabelle entirely. Aurora moved close to the Light Advisor and screamed.

No matter what Sabelle tried now, her light and crystals were nothing against oblivion.

But in the end, a carved ice dagger hovered at the crease of her neck.

"Do it, Aurora." Sabelle only laughed. She held no fear, only true mania. "I have turned the Second Realm into nothing and took great joy in doing so! But nothing will compare to the pleasure I took in ending that scrawny little Elaina—"

Aurora's eyes held no spark. No light. They were darker than before, but not just their color. Despite her entire soul being intact, Aurora showed no trace of humanity. The healer in Madness knew what storm brewed in Aurora, but his fear for her had to wait.

"You think taunts and foul words will bring me deeper into your twisted game?" Darkness tightened on Sabelle. Madness heard the cracking of bones. Aurora's wings of light and dark and earth and ice and sky spread like those of the ancient dragons. Sabelle even flinched at the might of the power. "You are below me. *All* here are below me. Luna is my only equal—I suggest you get that through your thick, twisted skulls."

A shadow then wrapped around Sabelle and threw her to the earth.

Don't do it, Aurora. It's what she wants. She wants you to become more like her.

"Get the remains of your troops and crawl back to my sister." Aurora lowered to the earth. Her wings released, and her eyes became her own again. "But the next time I see you, I won't be so kind."

"She won't stop, you know," Sabelle smirked through pain. "She'll keep coming after you, the mortals, the other Gods and saints, until everyone that opposes her is dead under the dirt she walks on. They're going to get you killed."

"Emotions are not a weakness." The sun rose, dawning a new age. "And you tell my sister that I'm waiting for her—you tell her I'm going to win this war."

Chapter 34

Sabelle and the remaining forces faded into the dapples of the morning light. Sabelle's grimace was the last they saw of the Light Saints.

"Mad?" Alfonso came to. His head bled slightly, but Madness sensed no damage. "Is it over?"

"Yes, and she won."

The two stood and faced Aurora.

Her wings faded with the rising sun. Neither of the brothers said a word, though Madness knew she was breaking. Elaina was dead, Aurora was the last of the Second Realm, and a new darkness had settled in her soul. He wanted to go to her side, but Aurora was his god, and he was her subject. Madness knew to wait for her call.

Around the castle grounds, Water Saints moved, tending to the wounded or grieving the dead. Water Saints and Soulless lay scattered. The Light Saints did not bother taking the Soulless with them when they departed. Instead, Sabelle and the Light Saints had left their enslaved subjects to face death.

Juvia and Katerina were by their sides. Katerina held Samuel's body. Madness wanted to reach for his teacher and friend. He looked so small, so brittle.

"Samuel was an amazing teacher." Madness looked to Katerina.

"He died protecting what he cared for." Katerina gripped her brother's body tighter. "He died for those he believed would save the future."

"Samuel was most loyal of saints and deserves to be remembered as such, but we must grieve the dead at a later time." Juvia was graceful as ever. Her gown bared a few holes and stains. She stepped forward, each evaporating the stained blood into thin air. "Katerina, take his body somewhere safe and then round up any abled Water Saints and destroy the Soulless."

Katerina hesitated, then asked, "All of them, My Lady?"

Juvia leaned into Katerina's ear. Whatever the Goddess of Water said caught the advisor by surprise, but Katerina nodded.

"Of course, Lady Juvia." Katerina bowed and departed through a nearby puddle.

"You kept a secret." Juvia lowered her eyes and glared right at Madness. "From everyone."

"Controlling the demon was a new thing and—"

"Not that, boy." She pointed to his pocket. "I can feel the weakening of my bones. The water around me shifting from my grasp."

Madness gripped the firestone. "I wasn't exactly told what it was when it was given to me."

"And just what were you told?" Juvia challenged.

"I'll let my god decide what you should know you."

Juvia seemed angered by this response, but then, let out a *hmm*, and walked toward the castle. "It seems Aurora had some sense when picking you mortals for this journey."

Alfonso gave his brother a thumbs up, and Madness simply rolled his eyes.

"Show me this stone." Alfonso pulled at his brother's arm.

"Not until we see Aurora."

"Oh, Juvia's far enough away now. I can believe you didn't even tell *me* about it!"

"It really did slip my mind." Madness fumbled through his pocket.

Alfonso flipped the stone over and over, looking at the designs. "This is what all the fuss it over?"

Madness nodded.

"I'm going to hold on to it." Alfonso held it to the light. "Just in case they don't want it, I'll make it into a ring."

Madness chuckled. "You're impossible."

"Ah, but what would you do without me?" Alfonso patted his brother's shoulder and smiled. "I'm going to find the others. You good?"

Madness glanced at his left arm. It was vulnerable. The marks of a demon encircled by the seal were visible for everyone to see. He hated what he was, but after today, he hated himself just a little less.

For the first time in only the gods' know how long, Madness smiled, just a little. "Yeah, I think I'll be okay."

Madness felt time slow as his brother pulled him to his chest. Madness didn't know what to do with his arms, but when he felt his voice catch his throat, he wrapped them tightly around Alfonso.

"I'm proud of you, Mad."

And just that once, Madness let it all out before his brother.

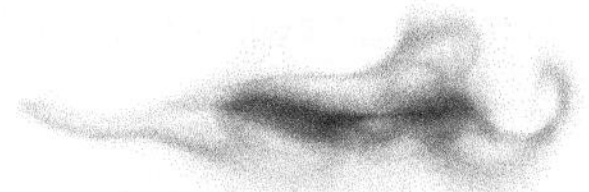

The marble floors ran liquid red. Water Saints wailed, clinging to their injuries as their bodies healed. Madness reached for some, but most insisted they would heal alone, but there were a few that accepted his offer with delight. Madness learned immortal bodies were denser, their blood clotted quicker, and their wounds healed at twice the speed of a human or Magical.

"Care for some healing?" Madness approached a Water Saint pressing against his leg. It was broken at the femur, but Madness knew it would be a quick heal with his help.

"I don't need your help," a Water Saint said. "I already feel my bones healing."

Apparently, being stubborn comes with the territory of being immortal.

"Nonsense." Madness lowered. "Just let me make it a little less painful, okay?"

The Water Saints rolled his eyes but relaxed. Madness moved his hands over the leg, feeling for the delicate breaks. This kind of break would force a human to use a crutch or cane for the rest of their life, but not an immortal.

Yet, somehow, I'm alive and many of them are dead.

"I lost a friend today." Madness was used to those he healed opening up about the traumas or details of their fight or battle. "You and your mortal friends knew him well."

"If you're referring to Samuel, then—"

"*Samuel* is dead?" The Water Saint grabbed Madness' arm. Madness realized information did not travel that fast in battle. Something he would need to remember for future ones. "Oh, gods no."

Madness placed his hand over the Water Saint's. "He was important to me, too."

"In my years of battle and war, I've never thought it could happen until today." The Water Saint shook his head. "Every immortal is vulnerable."

Over the next hour, Madness continued to move around the grounds. His hands shook, but his mind told him to keep helping—keep healing. He stood in a courtyard, unsure of where to go next.

A rock hit the back of his head. Madness bent down to pick it up.

"Al, is now really the time—"

It was a black ice cube.

Aurora's red blouse and trousers were torn and covered in mud and blood. Her hair flew wildly in the wind and her eyes were made new, but still, it was Aurora.

"Saints don't take kindly to their immortality seeming inadequate," Aurora gawked.

Madness beamed at her. "You're not as funny as you think."

All the duties and concerns of gods, saints, and the world drifted away. None were as important as holding her—feeling her against him. In knowing she was alive.

"You got kind of scary back there." He rubbed away some dirt on her cheek. "You okay?"

"Please, that was nothing." Aurora waved him off. "Your hair, it's so long."

"Oh, yeah, I guess so." Madness felt his hair brush against his shoulders. Since he fully transformed, his hair had grown.

"I like it," Aurora reached for it. "It suits you."

"Where are Blesk and the other Lightning Saints?" Madness asked.

"I sent them back to the Fourth Realm." Aurora twisted her mouth. "There is something off about the Lightning Saints. I don't think they truly want to be fighting this war."

He pushed back her hair. "You're too kind, Aurora."

Her fingers twirled against his shirt, and her glow disappeared. "But Elaina is dead."

"I know."

"Grayson, too."

Madness widened his eyes. "What?"

"Alexen was with me when we found . . . Elaina. We raced down to find the rest of you. On the way, Alexen got caught by a Lightning Saint, then Grayson showed up . . . I told him to protect Alexen with his life—and he did." Her eyes darkened. "Madness, so many of our people died."

"I know." He placed his forehead along hers. "I know."

A throat cleared from behind them. "Lady Aurora."

Madness and Aurora stepped back, pretending that Katerina had not been there for that moment. Katerina, too, was still in her bloody uniform, though a new cape covered most of it, but it did nothing to hide her grief. "Lady Juvia is waiting for you in God's Keep."

"The mortals and I will be there shortly."

Madness followed as Aurora led the way to their friends waiting by the fountains. All were bruised, but all were alive. Bloom and Pan turned from Alfonso and ran to embrace him first. Then, Cerene came rushing in.

"Madness, I was so worried." She threw her arms around his neck. Baer rested on her shoulder and gave a flick of his tail in agreeance.

"Gods," he returned the gesture, "I'm glad you're both safe."

Behind, he saw Tobias, who was also fine—safe. He wanted to rush to his dear friend, to tell him about Samuel. The Water Saint had asked Madness to keep his past a secret from the Shifter. Juvia had forbidden him from discussing the First Great Saint War or his time as the commander of the Soldiers of Night, but now Samuel was gone, and Madness wanted to tell his friend that the Water Saint had remembered him.

"The Shifter was so young then," Samuel said over lunch. "He ran through the camps, delivering food or messages. He trained alongside other shifters, perfecting his moves. In the thickness of the battle, he found me and I sent him off. I refused to let him die." He bit into an apple. "And now he's before me again, fighting for the Goddess of Dark and alongside you. This world . . . "

Madness made for his friend but Tobias held a hand. Alexen was curled in his lap, mourning. Alexen, in particular, had grown close to Grayson and Elaina over the past weeks. He was with Aurora when they found Elaina's body, and Grayson had died protecting him.

It can wait.

"I'm glad we are all safe." Aurora clicked her heels. "Come, as we have places to be."

One by one, they fell in line behind the Goddess of Dark. Baer and Pan flanked the far back, in their full beast form, with Alexen and Bloom at their fronts. Tobias traveled in front of Alexen on all four, and Cerene waltzed to Tobias' right, her marvelous silver bow gleaming across her back. Madness and Alfonso fell in closest to Aurora, shielding her left and right.

Through the castle, Water Saints bowed. They recognized not only the Goddess of Dark but her wings of mortals. They had fought in a battle of immortals for the Goddess of Dark and the Second Realm, finding honor and respect in the world of immortals.

Up they marched the massive silver-glossed stairs of the Seventh Tower. Aurora led them to the top room in the shape of a heptagon. Seven thrones gathered in the middle, facing one another. Below, a map of Nelabac was painted over the floor. Behind the thrones were rows of marble pews. Madness assumed they were for the saints of that realm.

Madness and the others watched Aurora make her way to the obsidian and onyx stone throne. He almost laughed as the throne was far from Aurora's taste. The wall behind her throne was darted in black marble and glistened in shades of silver and gold in the sunlight. An engraved crescent moon made of black diamonds was at the center. Around the room, all the symbols of the gods hovered on the walls behind their pews and thrones. Madness noted Aurora avoided the symbol of the sun.

Madness and his friends moved to the pews behind Aurora's throne.

"Cerene, you're on my toes."

"Al, I can't help you're sitting *literally* on me."

"Can you two go more than ten seconds without fussing?"

"I find that impossible to believe."

"Agreed."

A look from Aurora stirred silence. "Could you lot sit for *five* minutes and not argue about something?"

They all opened their mouths to protest but thought against it.

The doors swung open. Juvia hurried her way down the stairs and to her throne seated across from Aurora. She, too, still wore her battle gown.

"Well?" Aurora crossed her legs. "What are we waiting for?"

"We are waiting on some more arrivals." Juvia interlaced her fingers.

Aurora slammed her foot against the marble floors, scattering ice everywhere. "You didn't."

"You know as well as I do that everyone needs to be here for what we are about to discuss," Juvia said. "This is beyond just the two of us and what remains of our realms, Aurora."

"Rory?" Cerene asked. "What is she talking about?"

"All of them will be here before we know it." Aurora sighed. "Juvia has called a summons of the gods."

Chapter 35

"This is unbelievable," Aurora pinched her brow. "I've just come from an immortal battle of the bodies. I'm not ready for one of the mind!"

Aurora had given them lessons on the gods over the past month, explaining their personalities and tendencies, as well as histories, both personal histories and histories with one another. Madness and everyone were ready for whomever they were to encounter, but their god felt differently.

"Please, *A*." Cocky voice floated from above. "You really think we would attack you at a summons?"

Aurora turned away from the sound. "How'd you get here so fast?"

A man floated into his seat from the air above and winked. "Word travels fast on the wind."

"Mortals, this is Lust, God of Air and Ruler of the First Realm." Aurora kept her gaze on the newcomer. "He's much like his element: doing as he pleases *when* he pleases."

He dressed in attire exactly as Aurora had described of the First Realm: cloud-gray slacks and a tattered shirt, no shoes. His light gray hair was long, pulled into a sleek ponytail. Beside Lust stood Aster, the Air Advisor.

She took to her spot, standing beside the gray-pebbled throne made of refined stones.

"So, A." Lust propped his feet on one of the armrests and leaned back. "How goes it?"

"*Madness, your jealousy is showing.*" The Pull teased.

Piss off.

"Blow off, Lust." Aurora snorted at him.

Madness grinned.

"You haven't changed a bit." A smirk crept from the corner of his lips. "Still not interested, even though all those endless years of slumber?"

"Never," Aurora responded. "Not to mention you're what, eighteen?"

"You remember I'm, like, way older than you, right?"

"You're just *so* petite in stature, it's hard to remember." In a second, she was before him, patting the top of his head. Madness hadn't even seen her move.

"I see your powers have returned." Lust chuckled through a stressing look. "That's great."

Aurora extended a hand to the Air Advisor. "How are you holding up, Aster?"

"Oh you," she winked, "same attitude, different century."

"I've always liked you, Aster." Aurora walked back to her throne. "You've never been afraid to put air boy in his place."

A rush of heat blasted into the room, consuming them in little beads of sweat.

"I see you two still like to quarrel." A booming voice called. "I think the shorty has grown a bit over the last century. Anyone wanna bet on it?"

"You're as foul-mouthed as I remembered." Aurora countered. "I'm surprised you were even invited."

Madness did not need Aurora or anyone else in the room to tell him the arrival was Oberon, God of Fire and Ruler of the Fifth Realm. It was said the sun had kissed and blessed Oberon, not only as the master of fire but as the wielder of its strength. His tan, freckled skin complimented his red hair. As Oberon moved about the room, he pulled at his silky clothing. Madness noticed brutal and twisted scars covered the gods entire body.

The scars struck Madness as burns and ragged stab wounds. Aurora had mentioned Oberon was the only god who did not remember his life as a human. Madness assumed those scars were tied to those memories and were blocked from Oberon's mind for a reason.

Before taking to his throne, Oberon paused before Juvia, and everyone in the room held their breath.

"Lady Juvia." Oberon extended his scarred hand to hers, but his fiery gaze never left her gaze that begged to snuff out his flames.

"Off with you, pyro." Steam rolled off Oberon's cheeks from the water.

The two played this game, Aurora had explained. The God of Fire dotted and flirted with the Goddess of Water, who remained unimpressed. Well, rather, disgusted. The two were the same age in human and god years but had never gotten along. Juvia hated Oberon, but the Goddess of Water had never explained why.

"That's not very nice." Oberon backed way to his orange and red, ruby-stoned throne. "I'm glad to see you haven't changed, either, Goddess of Water."

"The fact she blew *him* off?" Cerene whispered to Bloom.

"What is wrong with her?" Bloom responded. "I'd take that man in a heartbeat."

Tobias, Alexen, Madness, and Alfonso each rolled their eyes.

"Now, now, Oberon." Draken, the God of Fire's advisor, came to his side. "Let's not get so hasty right off the bat."

Draken reined in his tough and wild demeanor god. Oberon had eyes like a flaming sunset, and his black hair was styled in a long-braided mohawk.

"Oh," Cerene swooned, leaning in close to Bloom. "He and Oberon *are* all Aurora said they would be."

Bloom giggled, "And *more*."

The Fure God and his advisor were the same in height and sculpted like warriors but were rather different in personality. It was as if they took on different forms of the same element: Oberon was the chaotic and wild side of fire, while Draken was the calm and warmth it could bring.

"We are sitting right here," Alfonso whispered. "In front of immortal beings, at that."

"You're one to talk." Cerene poked her finger at him. "You've been all googly-eyed over Katerina the past month!"

Aurora snapped her neck and raised a brow. Madness and Tobias only glanced at one another and snickered.

"Are we waiting on anyone else?" Oberon squatted in his throne.

"Terra," Lust said. "He, more than any of us, deserves to hear what we are about to discuss."

"If anyone would know of his location, it would be you." Oberon pointed out.

"We haven't spoken much since the Sixth Realm—"

"Became a wasteland?" A voice echoed through the tall columns. "Thanks for reminding me of the troubles *you all* tore me away from for a stupid meeting."

Terra, God of Earth and Ruler of the Sixth Realm skipped down the stairs. His skin was dark brown and his eyes were the brightest of forest greens. He dressed in clothes made from the giant tree leaves from the Sixth Realm, and his hat was woven from twisted roots.

Madness watched the God of Earth closely, fascinated. Five-thousand years ago, he was made the first God of Nelabac at the age of eighteen. He had fought and destroyed the demons. Those who had created the Demon Seal spell. Allowed Alfonso's and his bloodlines to fade with time. Terra knew more about Madness and Alfonso and their family than they ever would.

Behind, the Earth Advisor followed god. Eden, the full-blood elf, resembled Bloom but walked with even more grace and balance, her ears were more defined at the point, and her diamond reflected a multitude of colors. Madness noted her hair was tucked in a neat coronet, and she dressed in a similar fashion to Terra, but the clothes were thicker and built with underlying reinforced armor. Madness glanced at Bloom, who seemed eager to speak with someone of her kind.

Looks like we both long to unlock the secrets locked in immortals of the Sixth Realm.

Aurora had explained over the campfire that a thousand years after Terra was made, Lust followed, and the two of them bonded, as it was nine hundred years before Juvia and Oberon were created. Now, though, the two gods refused to look at one another.

Juvia walked through the room. "Light and Lightning formed a strategic attack on us today—"

"Lady Juvia, as much I enjoy you, I don't know how this concerns us?" Oberon asked. "I am the one in the midst of war from all sides."

"We need to focus on the attacks at hand," Aurora strummed her fingers. "The war has spread beyond a few places now. It's all of Nelabac now."

"None of this would have happened if we could have ended your sister then," Lust sneered.

"*Or* harbor a Soul Keeper—as I've been informed you did." Oberon jumped in to stir the pot.

"I did not even know I had a Soul Keeper in my possession," Aurora growled. "Besides, does that give *either* of you any good reason to attack me *or* my saints?"

"Ha! Saints?" Lust nearly fell from his chair in a fit of laughter. "Aurora, they're—they're mortals—two are simple humans!"

The gods continued their fussing and disagreements and insults of blame.

"They really like to harp on that term 'human' don't they, Cerene." Alexen sank into the pew.

"Yeah," Cerene pinched. "Really point that out whenever they get the chance."

"They act more like us than they'll ever care to acknowledge," Bloom mumbled.

"Speak for yourself," Alfonso added. "I like to think I'm a little more civilized than that hot mess."

Madness had never imagined the Gods of Old, had never believed in them until Aurora. Now, he believed in them, not because he could see, but because he felt the truth in Aurora's heart to change Nelabac.

Seeing them now, it's no wonder Nelabac fell apart.

Roots sprouted from the bottom of Terra's chair. The young god released his Altered Realm. His eyes glowed with the depths of the Everforest in the Sixth Realm and with the strength of the world toppling underneath him. One snap of his fingers—and the world would be gone.

"Half of the Sixth Realm is gone, and my mortals with it! The Second and Third Realm have nothing—and before long, *all* the realms will look the same as the East if this keeps on!" Vines and roots threatened the room. "I've seen the world fall to pieces before, and I'm not about to see it happen again! The beings of this world are fearing for their lives while we sit in a castle bickering over what's most inconvenient for *us*?"

Cerene leaned over. "Oh, I like him the most."

Juvia moved to the center of the room. "We don't have time for our petty disagreements. More than ever, Nelabac is in a state of live or die." The long sleeves of her sparkling blue gown spread over the marble floors like bird feathers. Oberon followed her like a panther with each movement. "Not only is Luna still determined to end Nelabac and us, but she is after the very things that started this whole mess, the Soul Keepers."

Madness watched the gods, even Aurora, pinch their brows in confusion.

Juvia turned to the God of Earth. "Terra."

"Eden," the God of Earth signaled, "present the paper to Katerina."

"Days after we disappeared, Water and Earth Saints united to find and retrieve the Soul Keepers," Juvia spoke as Eden handed a piece of parchment to Katerina. "Unfortunately, they didn't find a single one, but they did find this, the parchment of spells used to create the Soul Keepers."

Katerina handed Juvia the parchment. Madness watched Aurora cross her legs and flick her hair to the other shoulder.

Juvia didn't tell her?

"Thanks to Eden's generosity, we were able to learn more about the inner workings of the spells." Juvia explained. Eden, Advisor to the God of Earth and Ruler of the Sixth Realm, was the eldest of all the saints and all the gods. She lived when all races had survived and fought against demons. Elves like Eden possessed powers no being in Nelabac could phantom. "As predicted, the Soul Keepers were created by blood magic and self-sacrifice. The mortals and humans that made the keepers wanted to ensure their purpose would never die. The spell bounds the keepers to our souls, much the same as how saints are bound to us."

"Then why did not the saints not go out and look for them?" Aurora directed at the water and air advisors. "You are a piece of us, yes?"

Madness heard the hurt in her voice. Aurora had trusted Juvia as a friend, and she had kept crucial information from her about how to save Nelabac, and even her sister.

It seems secret keeping runs thick in immortal blood.

"Even though we saints are a piece of the gods, we are not the purpose the Soul Keepers were created for," Katerina explained. "We have no physical connection or reaction to them. Only gods can sense and feel out the keepers when in their presence. Only gods can heed their call."

"Any god to any keeper?" Lust asked.

"Yes," Eden confirmed.

"That's great and all, but what if it's *our* keeper?" Oberon asked. "No offense, but I could care less about finding someone else's."

"If it belongs to you, you'll be unable to move, paralyzed by unimaginable pain and fear. And if you touch it"—Juvia's fingers snapped—"lights out. Trapped, staring out at an infinite void forever."

One hundred years ago the gods had made decisions on the possibility of the Soul Keepers existing. With confirmation that the Soul Keepers were, indeed, real, Madness feared what rash decisions the gods would make now to stay alive.

"Did you attempt to break the spell?" Lust moved, unnerved in his chair. "Spells can be undone, yes? Changed? We know Blesk tampered with ours from one hundred years ago. What makes this one different?"

"Blesk made modifications prior to the spell's activation." Eden motioned. "But, even so, the casters used blood magic, sacrificing their lives. The only way we can change the spell is if all the Soul Keepers are united."

"Then we can make the spell whatever we choose?" Oberon inquired. "We can undo it?"

"Within the terms of the original spell," Eden said. "As long as we stick to the original intent, we can bend the rules in our favor."

The gods looked at one another. Madness looked to his companions, and even they knew what this meant. They knew the Soul Keepers were the key to ending the war but at a cost.

"So in other words, we would change the Soul Keepers' spell to seal Luna."

Aurora said it so calmly that Madness almost thought she had known this would happen all along. He wanted to wrap her in his arms, give what comfort he could for a fate so cruel.

Sisters destined to battle it to the death.

"Do we think this is Luna and Blesk's plan?" Terra asked. "To find the keepers and seal us within them?"

"No matter what Blesk believes," Aurora spoke, "Luna will rule this world as a single conqueror. She will seal us all. "

A world ruled by ice and blood, by death and chains. Luna would take them all down to see her world reborn with nothing less than the ashes of her enemies. Now, everyone in that room had to somehow work together to beat her.

"So," Lust fluttered, "if Lightning and Light attacked the Seventh Realm for a Soul Keeper, where is it?"

Aurora stood from her throne and turned to her companions.

She held out her hand. "Bring it forward."

Alfonso pulled it from his pocket but hesitated to place it in Aurora's palm. "Are you sure you want to—"

"Is he serious right now?" Cerene muttered.

"Gods before me—" Alexen rolled his eyes, grabbed the stone, and dropped it in Aurora's hand.

But Madness understood Alfonso's hesitation. "No, wait!"

Chapter 36

Madness leapt on Aurora, pulling her away before the firestone made contact with her hand. He would not lose her—not when he had finally found her. Not when they were so close to really changing the world.

The stone clanged against the fine marble floors. It echoed off the walls before settling in the middle of God's Keep before five of the gods of Nelabac.

The gods were the immortal, untouchable—but, as the stone slid across the room, true horror pulsed through the room so strongly that even The Pull lunged away.

One touch—one small moment of contact could seal their fate. Forever.

Advisors protected their gods as the stone absorbed power. It gleamed brighter and hotter, surging, growing stronger with each passing second it was in the presence of its vessel.

"Get it out of here!" Draken shouted. "It belongs to Oberon!"

Steam poured off the God of Fire's body. He screamed as the fire burning within betrayed and burned Oberon from the inside out.

Even a boastful sun is penetrable.

Bloom hurdled over the marble railing for the firestone, chanting ancient words. A purple barrier formed around it but broke immediately.

"It's immune to magic?" Bloom held the stone in her hands.

"You stupid, untrained half-blood!" Eden shouted. "Get it out of here!"

"Bloom!" Alexen rushed to the door, and immediately Bloom threw it his way. Once in hand, Alexen hastily exited.

"Rory?" Madness leaned over Aurora, rubbing her cheek. "Are you all right? Did you touch it?"

"I'm fine." She sat up. "What of Oberon?"

The deep tan of his skin returned, and steam no longer poured from his body. No god moved, all too terrified—too unsure of what would happen if they so much as said, s*aint.*

"I almost touched it." She was scared. "I knew what it was, but my mind stopped. It-it *made* me reach for it."

"It's okay." He softly stroked her long hair. "You're fine. Everyone is fine."

She blinked quickly and motioned for her seat. No matter how much he wanted to hold on, he let go.

Behind, he watched Draken checking over the God of Fire. Juvia had thrown herself back against her throne when the stone was tossed across the room. Katerina still stood guarding her. The God of Earth and Eden peeled back the vines used to shield them. Lust and Aster remained in the air above. Aurora was the only one who seemed to have recovered from the ordeal.

"Do we have a plan in place?" Oberon was the first to speak. "How are we going to defeat Luna?"

"We gather the Soul Keepers, reword their spell"—Juvia paused—"and then seal Luna within the Soul Keeper of Balance."

"And, how do we go about this, hm?" Lust lowered to his throne. "We can't pick up and leave our realms when war is about to rage across them."

"I think your realm will be fine, Lust," Terra vexed. The God of Air didn't rebuttal.

"We need to train our saints, prepare our people," Oberon added. "All the realms need to know war is coming."

"All the realms but one."

It was not only Madness who felt his heart tighten at Aurora's statement. Alfonso squeezed his hand. Cerene gripped the color of her torn tunic. The Second Realm was gone. Dandfol remained with the Resistance, but for how long, Madness hadn't a clue.

"I can find the keeps and bring them here." Shadows rippled, and ice took to the black throne. "We can find the Soul Keepers and seal my sister."

Their homeland did not survive to see the new world, but it would be reborn from its ashes It broke Madness' heart.

"Why should we trust just you for this task?" Lust questioned. "You're the reason we're in this predicament, to begin with."

"I've lost everything. My saints, my realm, my sister. The only way to stop this world from falling into the darkness is to find the Soul Keepers to end this mess." Aurora faced them with her head held high as she owned everything she was, who she was now, and who she was meant to be. "I'm the only one that can do this because I'm the only one with nothing left to lose."

"And the mortals?" Oberon added. "There is no way they would survive this mission. It's far too dangerous."

"Yes, let them live here with Juvia while you go out." Lust agreed. "They are far safer."

"They kept themselves alive, not you or me, these last one hundred years." Shadows danced. "My mortals are far more capable than you or any of the gods give them credit for."

"Do not say we did nothing when so many of our own were lost." Embers sparked under Oberon's boots as he made his way to Aurora. "Not just Fire Saints, but Earth, Water, and even Lightning Saints, *died* in battles for your people. This would never have happened to begin with if it wasn't for you."

"My people were innocent. Were we not created to protect *all* mortals?" Madness watched the gods tremble as darkness became the room. "I sacrificed and lost just as much as everyone else, yet my people remained vulnerable. Why were your saints not ordered to protect those outside their realm? Were we not created to protect Nelabac as a whole?"

The Oberon, Lust, Terra, and even Juvia, looked around the room at one another and at their advisors. Madness saw the murky darkness seeping from Aurora like smoke leaking from a closed, burning room.

When it seemed no god had a response, Aurora snapped.

"There is no excuse! My people suffered endlessly!"

"Because of *your* blunders." Lust rose with the winds. "You left them with nothing the moment you chose to save that wretched sister over them."

Madness searched for the shadows to spew out and grab hold of Lust, but they did not. Aurora just stood, the misty presents of dark lingering around her air and skin. Aurora's dark eyes turned to Madness. They pleaded for safety, but he could not offer it. None of them could offer Aurora sanctity in the presence of the gods.

"I made a mistake." Aurora's eyes cast down like a beaten dog. "I made a mistake and paid the ultimate price. I am fighting to fix what I broke, but that does not mean what happened to the Second Realm is just!"

Oberon played with fire on his fingertips while Terra eyed Eden for an answer. Lust glared at Aurora with hate in his eyes. Even Juvia seemed to not waver at expressing her anger. Aurora had scorned the gods one hundred years ago, and they were not easily ready to forgive or forget. They desired forgiveness from her and she from them, but Madness did not believe the gods were capable of such a human motion.

"She is not Blesk." Juvia rose. "Aurora acknowledges her mistakes, and I believe we should acknowledge ours, as well."

Lust snapped his neck in her direction. "Juvia—"

"The mortals in this room forgave not just Aurora, but it seems us, as well. They have suffered greater than any of our realms combined." Juvia faced Madness and his friends. "I am sorry for not protecting the Second Realm, and I will do what I can to protect what remains."

Madness and the others didn't know how to accept an apology from a *god*. They had become familiar with the Goddess of Water over the past month, and she was not one to admit defeat. She either truly needed Aurora and them to find the Soul Keepers or she was truly sorry.

"If Aurora and the Honorary Saints are going to save this world, they will need our support"—she glared at the other gods—"*all* of our support."

Juvia has a way with words—I'll give her that.

No one would survive Luna's war without cooperation.

"It is true the people of the realms have suffered greater than any immortal." Oberon directed toward Aurora. "The people of the Fifth Realm do not trust me . . . do not believe I am capable of protecting them. I attacked you and the mortals in the Mulga Woods out of selfish intent. I, too, apologize for my actions."

Aurora approached Oberon, and Madness half expected her to slap the fire god.

But she extended a hand. "All is forgiven."

"No matter what we did then, war was going to be the outcome." Lust stepped beside Aurora and Oberon. "You have my full support in the war to come."

"Together," Juvia joined in the alliance, "we can defeat them."

"No—we can *not* beat her."

Terra remained in his seat. "After witnessing what she did in the Sixth Realm . . . After learning just what Soulless are . . . I have little hope we can defeat such a monster."

Half of the Third Realm was gone. Luna's powers had split the realm in two. Terra was the God of Earth, yet even he could not stop his land from escaping him.

"What do we know about the Soulless, exactly?" Lust moved back to his throne. "We need to decide how to proceed when it comes to battles."

Alfonso whispered, "They mean if they should kill them or not?"

Madness nodded.

"Mortals. Like us." Cerene clenched her hands. "We've killed them, mortals trapped as those things."

Alfonso held her hand.

"In times of war," Tobias did not waver, "we do what we must to stay alive."

They pulled in a little closer to one another.

"As we know, Soulless are humans and Magicals capable to use Luna's powers and fight like any other Light Saint," Juvia said. "Only, their souls have been stripped of their bodies. They're unable to feel anything, think for themselves, or they cannot act without commands given by Luna, Sabelle, or any of the Light Saints in the Inner Circle."

Madness glanced at the God of Earth, who kept his eyes shielded under the rim of hat.

All these gods have tempers and vices large enough to destroy the world.

"Yes, that was all in the report your Water Saints delivered last week." Lust flapped his hand back and forth, "But why? Why is Luna claiming souls?"

"Luna is claiming the souls of mortals to feed her power and build an army as mindless followers who have been forced to fight and kill without the ability to resist," Aurora said. "And, I theorize . . . "

She was hesitant. For Aurora to speak out against her sister—to accuse her of vial crimes to those she had once defended her in front of.

You can say it, Aurora. It's okay.

Aurora regained her composure. "I theorize Luna started this process long before the spell. It's why the Third Realm was gone before we were sealed. It's why her powers remained in this world while she was sealed and why she's so strong now."

The other gods shifted in their thrones, sharing in fury. Sharing in sorrow. Feeling for those lost to the Third Realm. For those who remained in Nelabac.

"For the first time since this meeting began," Alfonso said. "I finally believe they're going save this world."

"Aurora," Terra said what everyone in God's Keep was thinking, "do whatever it takes to destroy her."

Madness noted the lack of kind words and exchanges between the gods before their departure from God's Keep. The gods and Aurora agreed to congregate once a month to share information gathered on the Soul Keepers, Luna's strategies, and the state of the realms. All but Lust had agreed to allow Aurora and the mortals safe passage through their realms to hunt the Soul Keepers. Lust threatened to attack if they approached the First Realm. Not even mercy to the mortals would be shown, but Aurora shut him down quickly. She claimed such actions would imply siding, of which the God of Air held his tongue and departed.

Soon after, the gods left as suddenly as they had appeared. Aurora, Juvia, Katerina, and the mortals lingered in God's Keep for some time after. Aurora positioned herself half in the throne and half on the floor.

"I forgot how grueling those could be." She sank lower into the floor. Madness chuckled.

"We still have one more issue to discuss." Juvia headed for the door. "Aurora, Honorary Saints, there's something you must see."

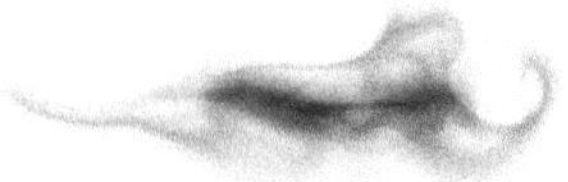

Juvia led them to the dungeons. Water flooded the floors by at least three feet. The iron cells held a bed and toilet above the water, confiding the prisoners to either shivering in their beds or pruning in the water.

Cerene and Bloom complained about their soaking, wet boots, while Pan and Baer shivered on their shoulders, avoiding the water at all costs.

Tobias even looked uncomfortable at the waters. Madness caught him reach for Alexen's hand, and the swordsman returned the gesture.

"I thought it was best to keep it at the back." Juvia proclaimed.

"Aurora inquired. "It?"

In the last cell, a prisoner lurched forward, chained to the back wall. It was a Soulless.

Chapter 37

"When in God's Realm did you do this?" Aurora was livid. "*Why* did you do this?"

The Soulless was a woman who appeared in her mid-to-late fifties. She fought relentlessly against the restraints. The waters around froze, and her skin fractured like broken glass. The white clothes she wore were stained in blood from the battle. Her eyes were like clouds, floaty and hollow. That body—that soulless body could be any one of them snarling and chomping at the bit.

Everything that woman was is gone.

"Research." Juvia faced them. "I believe by studying them, we can learn more about them."

"That's not possible." Shadows oozed into the water.

"We don't know that."

The water trembled and shadows crept. Madness reached for Aurora's hand, but she pulled away.

"These are people, Juvia!" Aurora shouted. "And you're using her as an experiment! It's wrong!"

"Aurora, she's not even a person anymore! Look at her!" Juvia reached her hand through the gate. "Feel the giant hole in her chest where a soul use to be."

The Soulless' head flipped around. No sense of direction or being. It was as if it were trying to find someone to give it direction. To give an order.

It's looking for its master. The one who left it here to die.

Aurora pressed her back into the iron gates. "What do you hope to accomplish?"

"I hope they can still speak or retain knowledge," Juvia said. "We won't know anything until we try."

Madness felt Mephista. She *reached* for the Soulless. He pulled on his arm, flexing the fresh bandages. When Madness looked, its edges were burning.

Alfonso cocked his head down. "You okay?"

"Yeah, yeah." Madness inclined. "My arm is acting up."

Can you shut it?

"*Oh, Madness,*" The Pull crooned. "*We share the same interest in this . . . soulless creature. Nothing wrong with a little curiosity?*"

There is when curiosity comes from you.

The pain subsided, and Madness stood straight again.

Aurora walked away from the cell and clicked her tongue. "Juvia, do you trust the gods?"

"Which ones?"

"All of them—rather, *any* of them."

"Not a second chance in the Grounds Below."

"Good." Darkness receded. "Me neither."

They had been awake for nearly two days, but they had to keep moving. Aurora had Madness and the others work alongside the Water Saints to clean the stained castle and gather the dead. Just lost five hundred

Water Saints in the battle. She released their bodies into the sea. Madness knew the Goddess of Water was on the verge of collapse, but she remained steady.

"And now, my lost ones," Juvia transfigured their bodies to water and let them become one with the glittering Rula Ocean. "Be at peace in the Land of the Deserving."

The Rula Ocean lapped heavily along the shore, grateful for new mighty and sturdy currents and tides. Madness watched Samuel's body until it was one with the ocean.

I'll carry on your will, Samuel. I'll do what I can to save this world.

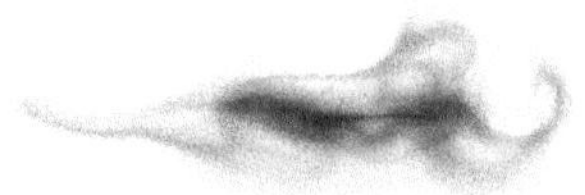

In the Second Tower, Madness found his friends mourning over Elaina's body. Sabelle had done more than just kill the girl. It churned his insides. She had brutally mutilated her. Tucked under the covers, Elaina appeared sleeping. Alexen was the only one not to weep or break at the sight of the girl they had accepted into their little family.

That's right, Alexen was here when Aurora discovered her body. He kept her moving in her darkest of moments.

Aurora changed the soaked, bloody dress for a long one of onyx and silk.

"Oh, Elaina . . ."

She carried Elaina like a parent cradled to carry their child back to their bedroom after falling asleep elsewhere. She led them through the suite and onto the balcony. There, Aurora tapped her foot, and an ice stairwell formed, leading way to the beach's sandy shores.

"I remember building sand castles, swimming with the waves, and enjoying pastries, cakes, and conversation," Aurora spoke delicately with each step. "These past weeks, Elaina . . . they've given me so much joy. They brought me back to when it was just us and Mako—when we thought those days would last forever. They were supposed to, weren't they?"

Aurora set Elaina in the sand and traced her finger around her body and then waved her hands, sprouting forth a coffin made of the blackest ice. Shadows and gray ice in the shape of so many flowers filled the space, their reflection sparkled and glistened in the moonlight. It was cruel to call it beautiful.

"You loved the ocean more than the flowers and your dresses." Aurora's hands folded to her lap. "It only seems fitting to say goodbye here."

"I'm sorry for leaving you alone all those years, Elaina." With each push and pull of the waves as the tide rose, Elaina moved into the calm waters. "I'm so sorry I did not save you. That you did not see our realm return."

And with a wave of her hand, Elaina shattered. All her pieces to the sea or back home to the Dark Manor. It was Elaina's choice.

Wherever she wanted to go, Elaina was free.

Instead of taking Aurora in his arms, he placed his hand on her shoulder. Everyone joined along the shoreline. Some of them stood, others sank into the sand, but all their eyes were on the distant moon high in the sky as it illuminated the ocean.

Madness gazed to her—his guiding light. He would do anything to protect her. Become whatever she needed to see this world reborn from its darkness.

"I believe in what's to come. In all of the mortals." She placed his hand in her own. "I believe in you."

But something stilled the air.

It was impossible to miss the tall, lean, and enwrapping figure gliding across the waters. Madness had seen her before, his friends, too. And Aurora, Aurora knew her all too well.

They stared, rippling in blinding, deadly light as the wind delivered her message.

"I see you."

Epilogue

Before Luna took half of the Sixth Realm, it sparked with life. The people of the Sixth Realm were lovers of nature, and they lived off the land and threw delicious feasts. Most were vegetarians.

They were all those things before Luna turned them to Soulless. Before she forced them to fight one another, feast off the animals, and kill the weak.

With them gone, the trees stopped growing. The animals have fled. The rivers are dry. The only thing I find beautiful is the snow-covered ground.

I can't complain too much, as I've contributed to this for nearly twenty years. When the Light Knights invaded my village, I chose to join their ranks and wait for the day their god could become my own. Escaping the Second Realm with the enemy was the only way to live a safe life. The people were suffocating, dying on my left and right. It was all because of the Goddess of Dark.

I scratch my nails across my hands.

Ice crunches under my white boots. I'm clothed in a white uniform with a red hood. Even though I'm human, Luna trusts me. The red shows I am a piece of her Inner Circle. That I am their equal. That I possess knowledge and abilities that they can only dream of. Only I can give Luna the support she needs.

No one but me.

I approach the crystal castle. It's square and dull. It reminds me more of a prison rather than a place for a god to call home. Light Saints salute as I pass by. A group of Soulless guard the next gate. Their faces are covered by white masks. A mouse and a dog.

I scratch at my hands again.

No snow means Luna is in a good mood. Light snow means she is brewing a blizzard, and the last few weeks have been nothing but blizzard after blizzard. To see a clouded sky without a single flake means the mission was a success.

A Light Saint approaches and hands me a letter.

"Good." I grin.

The castle is as cold inside as it is outside. The rooms are small, and the only way in or out is through the front gate. I weave through the tight snow halls and up a set of rounding stairs. The top floor opens to Luna's quarters. The room is bare, not even a bed.

The entire Inner Circle is there. Even Sabelle, who was away on the mission.

Klaus, the Second Commander of the Light Army, pats the back of a chair with his barrel-like arms. The man appears in his mid-forties but is one of Luna's oldest Light Saints. Scars cover his freckled face.

"Saved you a seat, mortal." It's a way to make fun of my humanity.

"How kind of you." I take the chair with care. "The snow makes walking rather tiresome."

I have learned it's better to play along. To let them think of me as weak-bodied and inferior, because even if they loathed my human status, they need me.

"Glad to see you made it." Sabelle throws her feet up on a stool. It is a child, a Soulless child. Luna did not kill the children when she calmed the land. Instead, she uses them as slaves around the castle.

"Let's just get to business."

The howling snow dances in the light. When the flakes meet, they make her. They make Luna.

Her blonde hair is so light it could easily be mistaken for white. Two small braids graced her front, but the rest flowed down her back, pin straight and an inch from the ground. The platinum-white cape she wore moves with her shining white tunic like a dress. As she walks, her long legs stretch like a stalking cat.

"Now." Luna sits in the chair beside me. I snicker at Klaus. "Sabelle, I guess since you're alive, everything went as planned?"

Sabelle tortures prisoners for the fun of it. They have nothing to offer us, but she does anyway. Even the children were her toys. Besides Luna, Sabelle is the only being in Nelabac to fear.

"Oh, yes, Aurora is much the same." Sabelle grins.

Our plan was to cause an upset among the gods, get them together, and set Aurora out on her own. We are sure it worked.

"Good." The crystal jewels on Luna's head chime. Her white eyes narrow, brewing with excitement. "I'm sure my little sister will take it upon herself to gather the rest."

"The humans she's been traveling with will surely be with her. She won't dare leave them behind since you killed the last of her vermin." Klaus leans his massive body against the wall. "Right, Sabelle?"

"Hearing her scream for Aurora only made the kill more satisfying." Sabelle's face lights up. "I'm glad that one is finally gone."

"My sister has never been one for planning. Capturing the mortals will be easy." Luna stands and walks to the window. Snow falls, a sign of her emotions ablaze. "They all possess such unique talents. Their souls will make for quite the meal, and their magics will be of good use for my army. Though, that one, in particular, I can't wait to get my hands on."

"He was something else." Sabelle taps her foot. "I've never seen anything like it."

"Demons have a crazy amount of power," Klaus says. "If the kid can learn to control it … he would be a powerful weapon."

"Yeah, but he's too loyal to that kid and Aurora." Sabelle throws her hands behind her head. "Getting him to switch sides is going to be a real problem."

"Loyalties can be broken." Luna cut her eyes back to us. "Just like people . . . we can shape him into what we want once we chip away the pieces we don't need."

"That's where you'll finally be some use to us, human." Sabelle licks her lips, and the other members of the Inner Circle snicker.

A smile spreads across my face. I've longed for this day. For the day we get him in our grasp, and I finally wrap my hands around him once more.

Before I realize it, my hands are bleeding. "I can't wait."

Acknowledgments

This book found me in 2015 while working on the kitting floor of my family's sock factory. As I slid across the greasy floors, I saw two sisters battling it out to the end: one passionate and good and the other devoted and evil. I saw two boys fighting by their side, trying to save a world from peril. Aurora and Luna, Alfonso and Madness, those four saved me when I needed saving—they found in me amongst the darkness.

The ear cuff is a last-minute addition to this story. I wear one that I bought while on a trip with my dear friends in Salem, Massachusetts, in 2022. I feel naked without it! I needed a way to connect Aurora and the mortals, and when I reached to my nightstand to put my cuff on, I just knew that was the solution. (Not that this has anything to do with thanks, but I wanted to share that little fun fact!)

The entire cast (known and unknown!) is important to me in ways other characters in other stories I've written never will be, but Aurora and Luna, specifically, are as much a part of me as my flesh and blood. In ways, I see pieces of my own soul in each of them. I'll forever be indebted to their bond, their sisterhood, and their determination to save each other.

I wrote and rewrote their novel more times than I can count. I went back to school to earn my degree in creative writing to learn the necessary skills to tell this story. I think part of me feels *A God of Dark and Sorrow*, the first in *The Realms of Nelabac* series, will never feel complete. It will always feel like something is missing, but that's not true. It's really just the place that holds what I've learned on my writing journey. And for that, I am grateful.

Now: To the thanks! This part is hard. People come and go over the course of eight years. It's difficult to include those that made a difference in not just the story, but those who made a difference in me—both for the better or the worse.

Thank you to the wonderful creatives I worked with! Beck, Alice, and Vincent—you brought the pages and characters to life. THANK YOU!

To the University of North Carolina Wilmington Creative Writing staff and program.

To my friends, far and wide. To the Vineyard staff, circa 2017 and 2018. Melissa and Sabrina, thank you for hearing all my love, personal, and writing woes and for cheering on my success. Thank you, Loganne for reading. To Melissa, for being my first and most loyal reader! To Taylor, for without our texts on personalities and plotting, this story would not be what it is (or what it will be!). To Ireland—my dear writing friend and great supporter; I will always cherish our friendship.

To the person who taught me when to love and when to let go.

To my family for housing me and encouraging me every step of the way. My siblings, Hiatt, Samuel, and Stella Blue. To my sweet, sweet Sally girl, my most loyal companion. To Link's sweet devotion.

To the vast amount of creative media. There are so many out there: books, manga, graphic novels, webtoons, T.V., etc. If something sparks your heart, something moves you in ways you never knew you could move, hold onto it! Being who you are, loving what you love, and embracing what makes you happy is the best way to live. It's the only way to enjoy what life has to offer and learn more about yourself and what you're capable of.

Lastly, I thank you, dear reader. I published this story because I feel the characters are relatable, funny, and comforting. Thank you for giving them a voice.

GLOSSARY

Damonist/Damonism: The cult that existed five thousand years ago that believed demons were the rightful rulers of Nelabac.

Grounds Below: A swear. It references the ancient world of the demons that once roamed Nelabac.

God's Code: Unwritten guidelines the gods follow to keep their realms and Nelabac orderly.

God's Keep: Where the gods gather for meetings. It is located at the top of Juvia's castle in the Seventh Realm.

Godly Order: The structure of the gods.

Landing of the Deserving: The believed afterlife.

Lower Demons: Demons that were defeated and sent back to the Grounds Below by Terra, God of Earth and Ruler of the Sixth Realm, five thousand years prior to the events of *A Goddess of Dark and Sorrow.*

Ruling Demons: Demons with greater power than Lower demons. Ruling demons are still found in Nelabac, sealed away within a demon seal.

Soul Keepers: Magic devices created by the mortals to seal away the gods.

Soulbeat: A play off "heartbeat."

Weapons of Ore: Weapons crafted by the dwarves during the first war. These weapons were gifted to mortals and can only be used by those who possess the bloodline they were created for.